A Sinful Temptation

BOOK 3: THE SINS & SCANDALS SERIES

KELLY BOYCE

To my second grade teacher at West Side Elementary School, Mrs. Phyllis Matheson, wherever you are – thank you for starting this journey with your little box of plots. I guess all that daydreaming paid off in the end.

Chapter One

A pox on the man's fickle heart.

It was the worst kind of luck to discover your intended's affections had drifted elsewhere.

Or rather your *intended* intended's. Lord Selward hadn't actually proposed as yet and, at the rate they were going, would not any time soon if drastic measures were not implemented. But what kind of drastic measures? Unfortunately subterfuge and machinations were not her strong suit.

Lady Rebecca Sheridan huffed out a breath and let her shoulders roll forward for only a moment before reinstating her posture. It would not do to be seen slumped over like a hunchback.

A proper lady comports herself in a dignified manner. Mrs. Dunbar's voice echoed in her mind even though her comportment instructor had passed on over two years ago. Likely she busied herself instructing the angels now, taking them to task for not holding their wings *just so*.

Not that anything Mrs. Dunbar taught her had proved useful this day. Did Lord Selward think she attended Lady Perth's annual tea to partake in the gossip about Rosalind

Caldwell's latest social gaffe—the third this week for those keeping count—or to nibble on overly sugared biscuits and sip tepid tea? No, she had come for the specific purpose of garnering his attention. Attention, he apparently preferred to lavish upon his gaggle of cronies rather than on her.

For Heaven's sake, must she jump onto her chair and wave her arms in the air to recapture his notice? If nothing else, it would give the gossips something new to titter about so they might leave poor Miss Caldwell alone, though Rebecca did not particularly care to take up the reins in that regard. Nor did she care to have her name mentioned in the scandal sheets.

Poor Father would roll over in his grave.

Rebecca pressed her gloved hands against the skirt of her new jade colored afternoon dress then kicked her feet out to stare at the pretty row of pink rosebuds embroidered into the hem. She'd had it made especially for this event, certain it would do the trick and catch Lord Selward's eye. The soft green made her silvery eyes stand out and gave her ivory skin a warm tone. Nancy had even styled her hair into a whimsical, yet intricate design—no easy feat given the length and thickness of her locks. Many of the other ladies had begun to shorten their hair, but Rebecca had often been told her inky black waves were her crowning glory and it seemed a little silly to rid herself of it for something as fleeting as fashion. Besides, Lord Selward had once complimented her on her hair and well...well.

She sighed again.

Hope. Such an irritating emotion. She had coasted on it for far too long.

At one and twenty, with her third Season on the verge of ending, the time to make good on Father's last wishes ran frighteningly short. Her next birthday loomed only a few months away. If Lord Selward didn't make good on his earlier attentions and propose, all would be lost.

Not that he had necessarily indicated he planned to make an offer, but a proposal had appeared promising based on his behavior, and surely that could be construed as almost the same thing. Could it not?

She had thought so, once upon a time.

Of course, once upon a time she had thought herself in love with him. Father's promotion of the pairing had been the icing on the cake. Perhaps that had something to do with the dictates of his will, though at the time she'd had no clue as to the late Lord Blackbourne's intentions. Father did not discuss such matters with her. It wasn't until after his death she'd become aware of his intentions as to whom she should marry. Father had always possessed a rather closed mind when it came to women and their capacity for understanding important matters. It had irritated her to no end, but she'd held her tongue in that regard. There had been enough strife in her family without adding more to the heap.

Regardless, because of the stipulations of Father's will, here she sat wishing for all the world that a man she no longer held an affection for would hurry up and propose. That she did not particularly want to marry him hardly mattered. The fact was, she *needed* to. Quickly.

"My dear, if you continue to sigh in such a manner, I am going to question whether or not you've sprung a leak."

Rebecca glanced up at her mother. "I simply don't understand why he will not come over. He has done nothing more than say hello since we arrived. Do you think he has truly passed me over for Lady Susan?"

The thought sickened her. After all, the only possible attribute Lady Susan possessed that one could consider even remotely positive was that her father was the Duke of Franklyn. Rumor had it, his coffers were richer than the King's. An exaggeration perhaps, though given that both Lady Susan and her mother, Lady Franklyn, were known to spend enough on fripperies alone to bankrupt Croesus, not much of one.

Mother reached over and patted Rebecca's clenched hands. "My dear, there is no reason we cannot take a turn about the garden and perhaps speak to some other gentlemen. There is any number waiting for you to show them some attention."

Rebecca gave her mother a sharp look. "I do not have time to encourage another gentleman, Mother. The Season is over in a few weeks!" She had not put all this work into capturing Lord Selward's attentions to simply give up now and start over with someone new. It was Lord Selward or...poverty.

"It is not as bad as all that," her mother said.

Rebecca gave her a dubious look. It was her mother who sighed this time. It *was* that bad, no matter how hard they tried to deny it.

The stipulations in Father's will were clear. She must marry a titled lord, or the first son of a titled lord, before her twenty-second birthday. If not, the entirety of their family's unentailed properties and income would transfer to a woman none of them had even known existed until Father's solicitor read the will to them following his death.

Mother glanced in the direction of Lord Selward and his group of friends. "But why this particular gentleman, dear? There are so many others to choose from and I cannot say I am pleased with Lord Selward's reticence at courting you properly."

"Lord Selward could hardly court me while we were in mourning. It would not have been proper. And Nicholas's scandalous behavior did not help matters, either. Lord Selward dislikes scandal of any kind."

"Your brother is now married and a respectable member of society." Mother's voice took on a defensive tone, as it often did when Nicholas's name was mentioned. Not that Rebecca blamed her. For the longest time, Mother had been her brother's sole champion. Heaven knew, Father had never been in his corner. "Is your affection for him so strong? I want you to be happy above all else."

Rebecca twisted her fingers around each other. She disliked lying. But neither did she care to have Mother worry about her daughter's future happiness. But how could she be happy knowing her failure to marry properly cast them both in the role of impoverished relative? Oh, Nicholas and Abigail would never see it that way. They would embrace them with all the love and kindness her brother and sister-in-law had always shown them. But *she* would see it that way. And Mother would as well. Neither cared to be a burden.

"Of course my affection for him is strong." She crossed her fingers. Not necessarily a lie. After all, she did harbor an affection. The only issue being said affection was not for Lord Selward, but another.

Not that it mattered. Not now. Not when they stood on the precipice of losing everything. Clearer heads must prevail and matters of the heart must be set aside. It was just the way of it.

A butterfly flitted next to her and landed gently on the flowering petals of a bright pink peony. Its wings batted slowly as it rested there for a moment before flying off again. Oh, to have that kind of freedom. How many times in the past year had she wished she could do just that? But reality kept her feet planted firmly on the earth, facing forward, the imminent future staring back at her in all its uninspiring glory.

Oh dear Heaven. Did she just sigh again? She attempted to focus on the positive in the hopes of convincing her mother. And herself.

"Lord Selward is a handsome man." Truth. He was, in fact, more handsome than many other gentlemen of his age and status. Was that not what first attracted her, after all? That her initial attraction had been nothing more than a fleeting infatuation of a young girl in her first Season did not bear mentioning, as it served no purpose now.

Mother took a sip of her tea and made a face, glaring at the lukewarm liquid as if it had greatly offended her. "A handsome face is well enough, but it will not sustain a marriage."

Rebecca hesitated. Mother held the foolish notion that one should marry for love. A wonderful thought. Warm and lovely and exactly what Rebecca had hoped for when her first Season began. But that had been three years ago. Perhaps, if luck prevailed, affection would grow between them over time.

Her gaze fell upon a wilted marigold, wizened by the sun and chewed upon by insects until what remained of its petals were pockmarked and browning. Was this what her heart would look like over time? She quickly looked away. Such thoughts were better not dwelled upon.

"He is a perfectly respectable gentleman." Rebecca forced enthusiasm into her words. "He is polite and handsome and well-dressed." All true, but sadly, not very interesting and none of which made her heart go pitter-pat. Or even just pitter, for that matter. As it turned out, she found Lord Selward somewhat dull for her liking. She had lost count of how many conversations they'd had about the weather.

Mother pursed her lips and turned her gaze back to Rebecca. "The cut of his jacket is all well and good, but all it signifies is his ability to pick a proper tailor. You will need more than that to build a good life together."

"Is that how you chose Father? By his character?" She winced. Curse her fool tongue! She should not have said that. She had loved her father, but she was not blind to his faults, and he'd had many. Most of all his inability to love his wife and son the way he had his daughter. It made for a rather lop-sided household, where not everyone loved the other and yet everyone loved her.

"Your father was selected for me and I will not insult your intelligence by telling you it was a happy union. You know well it was not. It's why I wish you to determine who you will marry without my interference, but a bad choice of husband can be made regardless of who does the picking. I would counsel you to choose wisely, for once you do, you are committed for life."

A lifetime with Lord Selward. A lifetime of conversations revolving around the blueness of the sky and whether or not they might see some rain.

She forced a smile. "I can think of no one I would rather spend my life with." Yet even as the words were said, another face tormented her mind. Her memory. She pushed it away and focused her attention back where it belonged. "I just don't know why he seems so entranced with Lady Susan of late. She is not fair to look upon and her personality is even less pleasing. How can he even consider her?" A man of Lord Selward's temperate disposition would be eaten alive by Lady Susan's caustic nature. Had the man on sense of self-preservation?

Mother set her teacup aside on a small table Lady Perth has set out for guests and opened her fan, waving it lightly beneath her chin. The motion caught the tendrils of her blonde hair where it framed her pretty face. "I expect it is her dowry and family connections he is entranced with, not whether she is fair of face. One can do much with the first two and only need blow out the candles to live with the last."

"Mother!" Truly, ever since Father died her mother had taken to making the most audacious statements.

Mother gave her a wicked smile and it struck Rebecca how young she appeared, as if she had come into a second bloom now that Father no longer held dominance over her.

Rebecca shook her head. "How am I to compete with the daughter of a duke?"

"You are a beautiful and accomplished lady, my dear. Do not forget that. Any man would be lucky to have you."

Accomplishments. She refrained from rolling her eyes. What accomplishments did she have that a gentleman would be interested in? Her aptitude at needlepoint? Her lifelike sketches? Hardly earth shattering. She enjoyed reading on any number of subjects and discussing opinions on philosophy and politics and poetry, but she could count on one hand the number of gentlemen who indulged her interest in such things, or believed a woman should possess it. Most men of her station wanted a wife with a pleasing face, a significant dowry and the ability to breed. Nothing more.

"Oh! He's coming over!" She tapped her mother's arm with her fan before snapping it open and waving it beneath her chin. "Smile, Mother!"

Rebecca sat up straighter and adopted a serene expression, glancing far enough away from Lord Selward to give the appearance she had not been sitting there waiting for his attention. It would not do to appear desperate. Even men as uninspiring as Lord Selward liked a bit of a chase.

Lord Selward arrived in front of them and executed a perfect bow. "Lady Blackbourne, Lady Rebecca, I hope you are enjoying the lovely weather. I am certain Lady Perth has made a pact with the Devil himself, as she always seems to have the best day for her tea."

Mother inclined her head politely, though she could have put a little more warmth into it, in Rebecca's estimation. Their future depended on it, after all. "The weather is most enjoyable, Lord Selward."

"And Lady Rebecca, you are even more beautiful than the weather."

Even in complimenting her, the man managed to reference the weather. Sweet Heaven. Could he not have compared her to the lovely flowers in the garden or perhaps referenced her quick wit, which her brother claimed she possessed? Though, in Lord Selward's defense, he had never actually witnessed said wit. How did one make an amusing anecdote about the clouds in the sky, after all? "Thank you, Lord Selward. I am having the most wonderful time. And you?"

She lowered her fan slightly and smiled. She had been told on several occasions she possessed a radiant smile. Maybe if she used it more often she could entice him to forget all about Lady Susan and her ridiculously large dowry and family connections.

He blinked, then smiled back. A good sign. "I am enjoying myself very much, yes."

"And your mother? I hope the Countess is enjoying herself as well?" His mother rarely spent much time in society. Her husband, the Earl of Walkerton, lived abroad, rarely returning to London. In fact, Rebecca could not remember a time when she had even met the man. His implied rejection of his family decades ago left many curious, but no explanation had ever been forthcoming, though most, it seemed, were happy to see him absent.

Thankfully, his eldest son did not share any of his father's disagreeable traits. He doted on his mother and busied himself with running his father's estates as one day they would be his own. He steered clear of scandal, did not attach himself to unsavory dealings or shenanigans, nor caused any type of uproar in the House of Lords. When she looked at it like that, she could almost convince herself she could eventually feel *something* for him.

Almost.

"Lady Walkerton is well and indicated she found the fare provided quite hearty."

Rebecca had visited the Countess on several occasions with Mother and could not claim to have found her very pleasing. She possessed an angry disposition and spent more time eating biscuits than partaking in conversation with her guests. Perhaps her husband's defection had made her bitter.

"I am happy to hear she enjoys herself. Will you both be attending Lady Berringsford's fete tomorrow evening? Mother and I were just talking about—"

"Oh! I daresay, is that Lady Susan?"

"Is that—" Rebecca's eyes widened at his sudden interruption. "I beg your pardon?"

"No, it is I who beg yours. Lady Blackbourne, Lady Rebecca, would you excuse me? I really should give my regards."

Rebecca sputtered a response as Lord Selward cut a swift bow, gifted her with a smile—a rather bland one that held little promise he would return any time soon—and then left. Poof. Like he'd never been there at all.

"Do not say it," she muttered under her breath when Mother's gaze slowly slid her way. "Not a word."

Mother fixed her with a stern look. "Rebecca, dear, if that is the man you want then you are going to have to come up with a better plan than asking after his mother's welfare to entice him into a proposal."

Rebecca gritted her teeth then stopped. Mrs. Dunbar had always taught her anger put lines on a lady's face and she could not afford that at this point. "What are you suggesting, Mother?"

Mother tilted her chin toward the group of gentlemen gathered near the tulip bed. They had been standing there for the better part of a half hour stealing glances her way. Their existence had not gone unnoticed, she simply hadn't given it much thought. Amongst them, those that bore a title numbered only three—Lord Cranbrook (no, thank you), Lord Llewellyn (given to drink), and Viscount Pepperidge (rumored to have predilections best not spoken of in polite society). Truly, as far as choices went, they made Lord Selward appear positively stellar. He may not be the most interesting of men, but at least he was handsome, polite, and had a full head of hair. Surely those attributes would be enough to overlook his strange obsession with the weather.

"My point being, if Lord Selward had a little competition he may stop dragging his feet and make this proposal you so eagerly seek."

"You mean...make him jealous?" She tried to picture Lord Selward writhing in a jealous rage, but the image would not come.

"Sometimes," Mother said. "A lady must do what a lady needs to in order to find the happiness she wants."

Happiness. This was not about happiness. If she wanted happiness, she would have pursued—

Well. It hardly mattered. In the end, she would be happy enough if she could keep them from becoming poor relations. Marriage to Lord Selward would save her and Mother from such a fate. If she succeeded, she would consider herself lucky, and try not to be too disappointed that she had missed out on a grand love affair.

But to make Lord Selward jealous? Would the prospect of potentially losing her truly push him to issue an offer? Perhaps. If nothing else, she must at least try. Time grew unbearably short. But what gentleman could she trust to help her with this charade?

Her brain worked furiously, streamlining the necessary attributes she would need in such an individual. Someone believable. Someone smart enough to see the viability of her plan and be willing to help her achieve its end. Someone who could be trusted. Lord Huntsleigh would have been ideal. Spencer was always up for such things, but now that he was happily married, it simply would not do.

Only one other man came to mind, but enlisting his help would create a different set of problems. Still, desperate times called for desperate measures. And with each day bringing her closer to losing everything, she had never been more desperate.

Marcus Bowen stared at the papers laid out in an orderly fashion across his desk. They competed with the efficient organization of his writing implements for supremacy. His quill sat sharpened and waiting in its holder. Next to it, a full bottle of ink, and beside that, a rather ornate letter opener—a birthday gift from his employer, the Marquess of Ellesmere.

Everything was as it should be.

Except that it wasn't.

He let out a long sigh. His fifth such sigh since the clock struck half past six less than thirty minutes ago. To be truthful, he grew weary of the wispy sound and the feeling that caused it, but try as he might he could rid himself of neither.

Restlessness was a strange beast and not one he was familiar with. At least not until recently.

Against the wall, a large, ornate clock sat atop the mantle and mocked him with its diligent pendulum swinging back and forth in a steady rhythm. Tick-tocking away the seconds of his life, a reminder of how quickly they passed. Of how easily they could stop forever. As if the clock knew better than to believe he would do anything drastic to change. That he would take a risk and throw his carefully constructed life into chaos. The clock did not believe he had the courage to grab life by the throat and give it a good shake.

Not him. Not the steady, dependable, Marcus Bowen.

He gritted his teeth and glared at the clock and everything it represented.

The light from the afternoon sun filtered in through the window of his office on the ground floor of the London home owned by Lord Ellesmere and tempted him with its warm rays. He'd opened the window earlier to allow the slight breeze to waft through the room in the hopes the fresh air would rid him of the strange melancholy that refused to leave.

The attempt failed.

Instead the melancholy and restlessness took hold, settled in and made themselves quite at home.

Surprising, really. One would think after spending the past two months recovering from an all too close brush with death he would be thankful to return to his normal life of ledgers and transactions and business opportunities. And while he was most pleased to be alive and well, sitting behind his desk—sitting anywhere for that matter—after being stabbed by a band of thieves while saving the Duchess of Franklyn, he could not say he was happy.

And it made him wonder—had he been unhappy before meeting the pointy end of the brigand's knife? Or was this a new state that had come upon him while Lord and Lady Ellesmere hovered at his sickbed clucking and worrying that each breath he drew would be his last? Not that they had been the only ones. Spence and his new wife, Caelie, also checked in on him regularly. Even Nicholas and Abigail, ensconced in their country estate awaiting their firstborn and possible future heir to the Blackbourne title, sent regular letters and demanded daily progress reports on his health.

He shook his head and puzzled over it, his fingers tapping a steady rhythm on the smooth surface of his mahogany desk. He should be pleased to find himself once again in his office, back at work, embracing the quiet and solitude his position as Lord Ellesmere's man of business offered.

Yet he didn't. In truth, he felt no peace at all.

The brouhaha over his injuries filled him with discomfort. Though raised as a ward of Lord and Lady Ellesmere since the age of eight, the fuss had been unnecessary.

He was not, after all, family.

He was an employee. A trusted employee, but still, just an employee.

Nothing more. Nothing less.

Despite his close friendships with Lord Ellesmere's grandson and heir, as well as Nicholas Sheridan, Earl of Blackbourne, Marcus himself held no title, no property, no standing in society. A fact he had not anticipated would change.

And yet.

His gaze drifted to the documents lying just beyond the estate account books. The Duke of Franklyn's solicitor had delivered the packet earlier that morning. The contents had been nothing short of ridiculous. An offer of Northill Hall—a small, but lucrative property—as recompense for saving the man's wife. A wife who had been attempting to run off with her former lover when Marcus saved her.

Hardly the thing to reward a man for. Not that it mattered. He could not accept such a generous gift. Could he?

He certainly had the ability and wherewithal to run such an estate. He'd been overseeing Lord Ellesmere's numerous estates for years, but something about accepting such a generous gift rubbed him the wrong way. As if it were...charity. He'd spent his childhood constantly reminded by others outside of the Kingsley family, that he was nothing short of a charity case. He had no desire to continue feeling that way.

Besides, if he wanted an estate, he would buy one. He may lack a title, but he possessed a sound business sense and he had used it to his best advantage, amassing a sizeable fortune that would be the envy of many of the lords he associated with. If they only knew.

But he had never been one to flaunt what he had. He knew how quickly it could disappear.

"There you are."

Marcus turned toward the door at the sound of the familiar voice and held up a hand. "Before you ask, I am fine."

Spencer Kingsley, Earl of Huntsleigh and future Marquess of Ellesmere stopped and made a face. "You could at least do me the courtesy of waiting until I ask the question, Bowen." His friend often referred to Marcus by his last name. As boys, Spence and Nick had decided Bowen sounded much more *dangerous*. And given his rather serious nature, they had determined Marcus needed all the help he could get in creating a more exciting persona. Their efforts had failed, but the name had stuck.

Marcus lowered his hand. "Fine. Ask."

"How are you feeling this fine day, my good man?" Spence asked in what Marcus assumed his friend thought was his best physician's voice. "Are you experiencing any delirium or discomfort? Any desires to throw yourself in front of another knife-wielding maniac?"

"None at all."

"Hm." Spence twisted his mouth to one side as he drew closer and leaned in as if to verify this claim.

"I assure you, I am fully recovered."

"As you say." Spence straightened. "Are you certain you won't come with us to the Abbey to rest? I'm sure Grandfather would not object."

"Quite certain. I do not need to convalesce and you need not continue feeling guilty. It doesn't become you."

Granted, had Spence not absconded with Lord Ellesmere's ship in an effort to avoid his former mistress and his grandfather's marital plans—the very ship Marcus was meant to be on—perhaps he would not have been left on the dock to save Spence's former mistress from knife-wielding thieves.

"Really? I thought I looked quite fetching in it."

Marcus shook his head. "I have work to do, Spence. Your future estates are not going to run themselves, you know."

"Then as your future employer, I demand you take a holiday."

"I took a long enough holiday while convalescing."

"I would hardly consider knocking at Death's door a holiday." But Spence let the matter drop and shoved a small package toward him. "Here. This came for you last week, but in all the hubbub I forgot to give it to you."

Marcus took the plainly wrapped package and turned it over in his hand. It was the size of a large tome, yet not quite heavy enough to be such. He looked at the postmark. Cornwall. An unwelcomed tingling edged the walls of his belly, close to where the knife had slid into him. He shook the sensation off and returned his attention to Spence's words.

"What hubbub was that?"

"It appears I am to join the ranks of fatherhood with Nick."

Marcus forgot about the package. His head shot up and he stared at his friend. If ever there had been a man opposed to marriage it had been the one standing in front of him. Now he was happily immersed in it and about to take the next step. Several months after the wedding, Marcus had yet to fully wrap his mind around the change.

"A baby?"

"Yes," Spence said. "I believe that is what one needs in order to be considered a father."

"And you are...?"

Spence lifted his arms then let them fall to slap against his thighs. "Happy. Thrilled. Terrified. I'm likely to make a complete mash of the whole thing."

Marcus shook his head and laughed. "I'm certain you will take to it like a dog to water."

"Not all dogs like water."

"You will be fine. Lady Huntsleigh will ensure you do not falter."

"Lady Huntsleigh insists you call her Caelie. You are family, after all."

Marcus's smile diminished slightly. Spence's view of family stretched beyond bloodlines, but his view did not change reality, a fact Marcus never lost sight of.

Spence pointed to the package. "Are you going to open it? I can't imagine what it is. Did you have family left there?"

"No." At least none he cared to associate with. He had left the MacCumbers behind when Lady Ellesmere whisked him away as a young boy. Why any of them would be contacting him now, he couldn't imagine. Nor did he care. He set the package down on the desk. "Likely it is business regarding your grandfather's estate. I will look at it later." He changed the subject. "Is that what brought you by?"

Spence shook his head. "Lady Berringsford's fete is tonight. As per Nick's instructions, we are to provide his mother and sister with an escort to the event."

Marcus nudged the package out of his way and reached for a ledger, flipping open the thick cover. "I can think of nothing I would like less."

He did not care for parties and even less for being thrust into a society where he did not belong. Nor did he care to play escort to Nick's sister, Lady Rebecca.

Liar.

Spence flopped down into one of the chairs opposite the ornate desk with its neatly arranged ledgers. "Oh, come now. The ton is practically salivating to see you. You are being lauded as a great hero. A veritable knight in shining armor. No doubt all the ladies will swoon the moment you arrive at Covent Garden."

"More reason to stay away." He was not a hero. He had been in the wrong place at the right time. He had acted without forethought or planning and paid the price. There had been nothing heroic about it.

"Fine then, do it because Nick has requested it of you. I have picked up the slack while you were laid up, but as you've indicated, you are well now and therefore can once again assist me in protecting the lovely Lady Rebecca from any lords who think to circle around her like a dog to a juicy bone."

Marcus scowled. "Hardly a thrilling prospect. I'm certain you don't need my assistance. Besides, Lady Rebecca has made it clear the only gentleman she has an interest in is Lord Selward, though why, I cannot imagine."

"You don't like him?"

"My opinion is irrelevant." Not that he didn't have one. The fact was, Selward had spent the better part of two Seasons dangling his interest in Lady Rebecca like a carrot in front of a horse, and now he did the same with Lord Franklyn's daughter, Lady Susan. It was unconscionable, and for the life of him, Marcus did not know why someone of Lady Rebecca's caliber put up with it. She could have her pick of suitors. Not that it was any of his business.

Because it wasn't. Nor did he plan on making it so.

Spence picked up the rock paperweight he had given Marcus as a gift when they were children and tossed it lightly in his hand. "The heart wants what the heart wants, I suppose."

"Then the heart is a foolish organ that is not to be trusted."

"Tut, tut. Such disparaging words from the one man I know who believes marriage is a union one should strive to achieve."

He could not deny he had once thought marriage an advantageous union, but while he was not opposed to it, he understood the ladies of his acquaintance did not marry the son of servants.

He turned the conversation away from him and back onto his friend. "Do you still believe it is not?"

Spence grinned and despite the turmoil that had hounded his past, it did Marcus's heart good to see his friend settled and happy, his demons put to rest. "I have seen the error of my ways. But you—here you are, still a bachelor. Have you considered that while fending off Lady Rebecca's suitors you could also be trading on your newfound popularity to find yourself a suitable bride?"

Marcus scowled. "I hardly think the ladies of the ton would set their caps for a man with no title or property." His gaze once again drifted to the documents lying next to the ledgers.

"All the more reason to capitalize on your hero status before people come to their senses and realize you are far too good for them. Besides, if you don't come with me, you will have to stay behind and entertain Grandmamma and her friends."

Marcus froze. "Not the ladies?"

Spence leaned back in his chair and smirked. "None other."

Marcus wanted to smack the triumphant expression from Spence's face, but he was too busy reliving the last time he had been forced to spend an evening with the elderly ladies who played whist as if their very lives depended on the outcome of the next card. He'd been forced to play the fourth. He had been to gaming hells with less chance of bloodshed than when Lady Ellesmere and her comrades broke out the cards and claret.

"Fine. I will attend the party with you."

"I thought you would see it my way. Now, I need to be off. My lovely wife has requested I bring her some of Mrs. Faraday's ginger biscuits. She claims they settle her stomach." He stood and set the rock down on top of the documents Marcus had gazed at only a moment before, then moved the rock aside and shot him a questioning look. "What is this?"

Marcus gave a non-committal response. "Nothing of import."

Spence picked up the papers, ignoring Marcus's protests. His eyes widened and he whistled. "He did it then. Franklyn gifted you Northill Hall. Why, you'll be within a stone's throw of Sheridan Park and Lakefield Abbey. It's perfect!"

"No, it isn't. I cannot accept." Disappointment sizzled in his belly.

Spence looked at him as if he'd sprouted a second head out of his ear. "Don't be a fool. Northill is not a large manor by Lakefield Abbey standards, but it is a good size and the lands are extensive enough, not to mention self-sustaining. I'm surprised Franklyn would divest himself of it."

"I believe it is in retaliation."

Spence glanced up from the documents. "Retaliation?"

"Northill came to the duke through his wife's dowry. The estate has been in her family for generations and was meant to become part of Lady Susan's dowry upon her marriage. Given the reason Lady Franklyn was on the docks to begin with," he gave Spence a knowing look, "I believe Lord Franklyn has decided to teach her a lesson by offering her family's estate to me for the hefty sum of one pound."

Spence cleared his throat and put the papers back on the desk. "Lord Franklyn always did have an interesting sense of justice about him. Either way, you should accept it."

"It is inappropriate."

"It is nothing of the sort. You nearly died saving his wife. It is the least he can do. Grandfather will understand."

"Perhaps." Though Marcus had his doubts. Lord Ellesmere had raised and educated him and given him a lucrative salary and position of importance when he grew into manhood. For Marcus to turn his back on everything the marquess had done for him would be the height of disloyalty. Wouldn't it?

"I will return the papers to Lord Franklyn tomorrow and tell him I cannot accept his generous offer."

"Very well then," Spence sighed. "Have it your way. But I think it idiotic to refuse. Now, if you will excuse me, I promised my wife ginger biscuits. I will see you tonight for the party?"

"If you insist."

"I do." Spence waved a hand in the air as he passed through the door but his voice drifted up the hallway and found Marcus's ears. "All work and no play makes for a very dull life, Bowen."

Perhaps so. But work was all he had.

Chapter Two

Spence's comment about all work making for a very dull life had stuck with Marcus long after his friend left his office. Watching Spence and his new wife, Caelie, over dinner that night had only served to drive the point home. The two were crazy in love and had a maddening way of interacting without using words, but rather through looks and touches and smiles; as if they had discovered a secret language only those graced by love could speak.

Marcus did not fool himself into thinking such a fate awaited him. True love did not bloom in every garden, certainly not in his. At least not where it counted. But perhaps —and only perhaps—the time had come to consider finding a bride. He had made a small fortune through his investments. It only made sense he should have someone to leave it to. An heir, as it were.

Which would require a wife to achieve.

Spence had the right of it. All work did make for a dull life.

Restlessness continued to plague him. He'd thought it would wear off in time, but it hadn't. Something was missing. Perhaps it had always been missing, but now, with the knowledge of how fleeting life could be, Marcus could not shake the need to do something about it. To loosen the tightly held control he had on every aspect of his regimented life and do the unthinkable.

Take a risk.

A ripple of unease settled over him. He did not take risk lightly. Unlike Spence and Nick who flung themselves into things with little forethought or planning, Marcus did not have that luxury. Circumstances changed without notice. One minute you had love and security and the next—

Well, the next you stared into the dark abyss of what Fate could do.

Marcus toyed with the idea of marriage and children and considered what it would take to achieve such an end as the carriage conveyed them to the Sheridans' home. His thoughts sustained him through the chatter created as Lady Rebecca and her mother conversed with Spence over the goings on at Lady Perth's tea the day before. He held his tongue, as he often did when he had nothing of value to contribute to the conversation.

To be certain, he should be able to provide said wife with a comfortable home, perhaps a small townhouse within the city during the Season in the event she wished to partake in any parties and events as ladies often did, and a country estate during the rest of the year.

Such as Northill.

He shook his head. No. He would not accept the duke's charity or assist the man in retaliation for his wife's transgressions.

Still...it was a lovely property. One he was fairly familiar with given its proximity to Lakefield Abbey, where he had spent many a summer growing up. Estates such as Northill did not grow on trees. He supposed he could let such a property, but the idea held no appeal. He craved ownership.

Permanence. Something of his own that could not be taken away.

"You have been very quiet, Marcus."

Lady Rebecca's clear voice cut across the space separating them as the carriage stopped at the entrance to the Pavilion inside of Covent Garden. She had referred to him by his given name for as far back as he could remember; save for when her father had been present, when she reverted to the more formal use of Mr. Bowen.

He preferred the former, though the latter was safer. Less likely to blur the line between them. A line he should never have crossed. Wouldn't again.

He glanced at her, her stark beauty striking him as it often did. No wonder Nick wanted both he and Spence to watch over her. He could well imagine any number of suitors dogged her well-shod heels at every step. Whether she noticed them or not, he preferred not to think on.

"Forgive me," he answered, though offered nothing more and avoided looking directly at her. The pure silver of her eyes had the power to mesmerize, and one did foolish things when under such a spell.

"You are forgiven." Her voice held a sweetness to it and he took a deep breath, as if he could breath it in, hold it within him. "It is nice to find a gentleman who does not feel the need to pollute the air with nonsense."

"Is it?" Spence said. "I find it annoying, myself. Leaves the rest of us to pick up the slack. Frightfully rude, I think."

Lady Blackbourne laughed. "Huntsleigh, I doubt you require any assistance in holding up your end of the conversation. Besides, I suspect Mr. Bowen needs to brace himself before stepping into the fray."

Marcus swallowed. "The fray?"

Lady Blackbourne smiled, a motion that lit eyes a shade darker than her daughter's. "The ton has been abuzz with your heroics," she told him. "Your absence in society has only served to stir their curiosity even more. I expect your return tonight will be quite the thing."

"Oh dear," Lady Rebecca leaned forward, exposing the gentle swell of her breasts where they pushed above the bodice of her gown. "Think of it, Marcus. You shall be mentioned in the scandal sheets for certain. How exciting!"

Her teasing was duly noted, as was his body's unwanted reaction to her breasts. He quickly looked away. Spence's muffled laughter mocked him. "I'm so happy to be able to provide you both with endless amusement."

"Somebody has to, my good man," Spence laughed as the carriage door opened and a liveried footman set a step down in front of it.

Marcus escaped the confines of their conveyance, though at the prospect of being the center of attention, he considered diving back in and instructing the driver to return him to Ellesmere House with all due haste. He did not care for such public accolades or attention. He had spent the past twenty-two years of his life keeping a low profile, not making waves, going unnoticed. It was better that way. If no one noticed you, they were less likely to try to disturb your life.

Unless, of course, they were Lady Rebecca. But the fault for that could not be laid entirely at her feet, could it? He pushed the thought away.

Spence jumped down behind him, but Marcus stayed in place to assist the ladies from the carriage. First Lady Blackbourne, then her daughter. As Lady Rebecca's gloved hand slid into his, she gripped him harder than necessary and leaned in, bringing her lips shockingly close to his ear. Her heady scent overpowered his senses. Not the sweet scent of flowers as one might expect, but something wilder. Spicy. Elemental.

And in that moment, time peeled away and returned him

to Sheridan Park, where he stood in the moonlight, holding her in his arms as she cried silent tears into his shoulder.

"Marcus," she whispered, her voice silk. Just as she had then. He braced himself against the warmth her closeness spread through him as her breath brushed his skin. "I must speak with you."

"Now?"

"No." She leaned away and gave him a plaintive, imploring look. Warning bells went off somewhere in the recesses of his mind and while he heard them, he paid them little heed. Her gaze held him captive. "Later. It is of utmost importance, however."

He fought against the pull she had over him.

"I can come by the house tomorrow, if that is convenient?"

She shook her head. A thick, inky black curl bounced against the delicate curve of her cheekbone. "No, it must be this evening. After the first dance, come and find me. Claim I appear overheated and should get some air. We can step out onto the terrace where we will have some privacy."

Privacy? He did not like the sound of that. There was no reason in the world Lady Rebecca should require a private audience with him and no grounds for him to grant it. The last time they met in private, regardless how inadvertent it had been, it had resulted in a kiss. A kiss that nearly one year later he could not forget. A kiss that had affected him so deeply, he could close his eyes and recollect every second of it—the taste, feel, sensation. The longing it created. The need.

If he had been a less than honorable man he'd have—

He shook his head. It mattered not. He was an honorable man, though not enough of one that he'd told her brother what had transpired. Honorable did not equate to stupid.

And yet, as she requested a private audience with him this

night, he did not refuse her. Could not. Curiosity stalked him like a dangerous animal after its prey.

"Come, you two," Lady Blackbourne called over her shoulder as she took Spence's arm and led the way. Lady Rebecca looped her arm through his.

"Thank you," she whispered, though he did not recall having answered her out loud. Any hope he'd had of avoiding her this night drifted away on the light breeze that followed them into the Pavilion.

The crush of lords and ladies attending Lord Berringsford's fiftieth birthday celebrations reminded Marcus of a stampede of swine rushing to the trough. It would not be difficult to convince anyone Lady Rebecca appeared overheated, as already warmth rose up from his starched collar and he longed to escape to the gardens if only to relieve himself of the cacophony of voices that reverberated throughout the room.

The wait proved interminable. Lord Rankin had claimed the first dance with Lady Rebecca while Spence took a turn with Lady Blackbourne, leaving Marcus to stand near a potted plant by the wall, sipping a sickly sweet drink that set his teeth on edge. Or perhaps it was Lady Rebecca's request that had done that.

His mind conjured up any number of topics that required such subterfuge on her part but rejected each one in short order. By the time he spied Lord Selward winding his way through the crowd, he was no closer to a conclusion than when he started.

The object of Lady Rebecca's affections stopped briefly to speak to a few of the older ladies sitting in chairs lining the edge of the dance floor before he moved on. Marcus continued to watch him. The man did nothing out of the ordinary, nothing irksome or inappropriate. As always, the young lord comported himself much as any gentleman would. He chatted with a few lords, paid attention to several ladies, though within the bounds of what was considered proper, and continued on his way around the room.

Marcus lost sight of him until Selward reappeared around the other side of the room. He had picked up company along the way. Lady Susan had attached herself to his arm. The duke's daughter strutted past the dancers, paying more attention to being seen than whom she was with, though if Lord Selward noticed, Marcus could not tell. The couple slowed when they reached the foursome that included Lady Rebecca. Lady Susan lifted her upturned nose a little higher and her mouth pulled into a smirk of satisfaction. Not a flattering look for her.

Marcus's attention left the couple to see if Lady Rebecca had noticed. Based on the desperation written across her lovely face, she had. He scowled in Selward's direction though the man paid him no more attention than the potted plant he stood next to.

Lady Rebecca's feelings for the future earl left him unsettled and he cursed Nick for impregnating his wife and remaining at Sheridan Park for the Season. He did not appreciate being cast in the role of Lady Rebecca's protector.

Who was to protect her from him?

He bit down on the thought as the music ended. With a flick of his wrist, he dumped the contents of his glass into the potted plant, tossed it onto a nearby table and hurried to claim Lady Rebecca before any of the other gentlemen hovering near the edges could intercept.

Rebecca clung to Marcus's arm to hurry him along. Her nerves zipped around inside of her like a loose bolt of lightning. Every second wasted was a second stolen from implementing her plan. A plan that must be put into place immediately. Lady Susan had made her intentions clear when she pranced around the outskirts of the dance floor on Lord Selward's arm.

Oh, the frustration of it all—to work so hard for a proposal her heart dreaded!

She led Marcus out onto the terrace. It allowed a lovely view of the lit gardens below. Not that she particularly cared what the gardens looked like at the moment. The only thing she cared about was convincing Marcus to assist her in her endeavor. Somewhat of a Herculean task, given he was not the type to partake in such tomfooleries and, it seemed, had made an acute study of avoiding her company whenever possible. Truthfully, she did not wish to involve him. The idea he would help her capture the attentions of another man smacked of hypocrisy, but whom else could she trust in such a matter? No one.

Her brother had entrusted Marcus with the role of protector in his absence. Nick trusted him beyond a doubt and being the type of man Marcus was, he did not shirk his responsibilities. She hoped to call upon this sense of honor now. After all, he had saved her life once before. Surely she could convince him to do it again.

She smiled at the memory. As a young girl, Marcus's stoic demeanor played upon her imagination until she had conjured up any number of daydreams about his past. She had made him a pirate king, then a knight fallen upon hard times, and once, even the long lost heir to a duchy.

Such silly nonsense. Marcus was, in truth, the son of servants, caretakers to Braemore Manor, one of Lord Ellesmere's Cornwall properties. A fact her father had made abundantly clear when she had revealed to him her childish fantasies. Father's tirade had lasted for a full hour, during which he had harped about her duty to choose a proper husband, one befitting her station and her family's good name. Had that been the impetus for the constraints he'd placed in his will, ensuring she marry a titled gentleman such as Lord Selward or risk losing everything?

It hardly mattered now, and as it turned out, Marcus was not a pirate king. Nor a downtrodden knight or lost duke. He was just a man. A man who had given her the first and only kiss she'd ever received, behind the marble statue of Athena in the gardens of Sheridan Park.

He'd been mortified by his behavior afterward, despite her insistence she was equally to blame. She had been despondent over Father's death, guilty that Nicholas had been given only the entailed properties attached to the title and stunned to learn her father had kept a lover for the past ten years. She feared what her future held and she had sought comfort in the solitude of the garden, only to realize the empty moonlit night offered her no comfort at all.

But Marcus had. He'd wrapped her in the safety of his arms when he found her crying and whispered that everything would be fine. And she had believed him. Reveled in the safety of his embrace. Let his strength console her. When he pressed his cheek to her temple, it had seemed the most natural thing in the world to lift her gaze, to touch her lips to his. To kiss him.

Her blood heated at the remembrance of that moment. Of being swept away.

The crash back to earth when Marcus had come to his senses had been most unwelcome.

She set the memory aside. The past was the past. She could not relive it, recapture it, or change it. She simply had to soldier on with the cards now dealt her. Cards she needed Marcus's help to turn into a winning hand. She clasped her hands together in front of her bodice. "Promise me you will hear me out before you give me your answer."

What she asked bordered on the edge of impropriety and, in all likelihood, went against every sensible bone in Marcus's body. She would have her work cut out for her to convince him to help.

"Very well. I will hear you out." He held his hands behind his back and stood unmoving in front of her. The stance showed off the breadth of his shoulders and chest and for a moment, it took her away from her intended speech. He was a study in lean, hard angles, his stillness reminiscent of the marble statues populating Sheridan Park's gardens where they had shared their kiss.

A slight breeze drifted past them and ruffled his dark hair, turning him into the pirate king of daydreams past. Despite his buttoned-up demeanor, he possessed a certain wildness. Nothing obvious, one had to look beneath the surface to see it. He kept it tightly battened down, but it was there, in a glance or a movement. In his kiss. What would happen if he gave it free reign once more? She quickly shook off the thought away, reminding herself of what happened to the cat when it attempted to sate its curiosity. Better she not meet the same fate.

"As you may know, Lord Selward and I have been courting."

Marcus raised one eyebrow. "You have?"

He truly had the loveliest eyes. The color of dark chocolate. Warm and trustworthy, yet with a hint of mystery lingering in their depths. Unfathomable eyes that rested their gaze upon her without flinching. A fluttering teased her stomach. She shifted her weight from one foot to the other.

"Yes. Well, somewhat."

"I see." He straightened to his full height that came close to matching her brother's six feet. Tall enough for her to tuck comfortably beneath his chin.

"The thing is, while I was in mourning after Father's passing, Lady Susan used my absence in society to worm her way into Lord Selward's affections, leaving him torn."

"Torn?"

"Between the two of us."

"I see," he repeated. In those two words she heard the ones he did not speak. That Lord Selward lacked the passion to be torn between anything, let alone two women. An observation she could not refute, but that was neither here nor there. "And you believe it is affection he feels for Lady Susan?"

"Perhaps affection is too strong a word. I can't imagine someone feeling more affection for her than they would a scorpion about to strike. But the fact remains, she is the daughter of a duke—"

"A very wealthy and connected duke."

"Yes. Thank you for the reminder. Very helpful." Not that her dowry did not come with a hefty fortune attached, but nothing like that of Lord Franklyn. In fact, the only peer likely to be wealthier than the duke was Lord Ellesmere, and much of that could be attributed to Marcus's smart business handling, if Huntsleigh was to be believed.

"I suspect it would be a most advantageous match for him."

"I'm sure." Though he need not argue the point so succinctly.

"And what do you wish to offer him that Lady Susan cannot?"

"Offer him?"

"Yes. I would think you would need to bring something to the table to balance what Lady Susan offers. What shall it be?"

Leave it to Marcus to request specifics. Always the businessman. She cleared her throat. "I can offer him...affection. Friendship and pleasing companionship. Do you think he can get these from Lady Susan?"

Marcus remained silent for the span of several maddening heartbeats, then, "No. I doubt she is capable of such."

"Surely you cannot put a price on such things, can you?"

He stared at her for a full minute without responding. His silence did not bother her. He often thought first and spoke second—unlike her brother or Huntsleigh, who preferred to let the first thought in their heads fly out of their mouths. But this time, something about his silence was different. Tension crackled in the air, though she could not discern its origins.

Marcus's gaze pierced deep inside of her and traveled from the top of her head down through every hidden pathway in her body, until she tingled with—with what? *Expectation?*

"Marcus?" She prodded, needing to break the silence and interrupt her foolish thoughts. The only thing she expected from Marcus was his assistance in acquiring a proposal from Lord Selward. Anything else would be improper. Unfair.

He looked away, out toward the gardens. "No, I don't believe you can put a price on genuine affection or companionship."

She clasped her hands beneath her chin and breathed a sigh of relief. "Then will you help me?"

His gaze swung back to her with sharp focus. "Help you?"

"Recapture Lord Selward's full affections."

Marcus blinked. My, but he had the thickest lashes. Dark crescents that brushed against his skin. They looked soft to the touch.

"How is it I am to help you do this exactly?"

She dug for her courage and blurted the words out. "By courting me." He opened his mouth—to protest, no doubt— but she hurried on before he could. Before she lost her nerve. "If Lord Selward sees he has another rival for my affections, he will be forced to act or risk losing me to another. I do not believe he wants to lose me—he was most attentive before Father died. He just needs a little prompting to remind him of this fact."

Marcus's dark eyebrows hiked skyward. Oh dear. She had shocked him. She offered him an encouraging smile, but that only appeared to anger him, based on the harsh breath that shot out of him as he swept an arm toward the French doors that led back to the dancing.

"You have any number of rivals for your affections. I could not swing a cat by the tail without hitting several gentlemen more than willing to play the part of your suitor."

"I can't imagine why you would want to swing a cat by the tail, Marcus. That seems rather—"

"I don't!"

She winced. Truly, she had not thought he'd become quite so riled by her suggestion. "You need not shout."

He glared at her, but lowered his voice. "My point is —why me?"

"Oh. That."

"Yes, *that*."

Poor man. He had no inkling of how his popularity amongst the ladies had risen since he'd nearly died saving one of their own. She'd caught several of them looking his way when they entered the Pavilion, a mixture of longing and lust in their hungry eyes. A look she understood only too well.

"I chose you because I need someone I can trust. You are an honorable man and I know my reputation will be safe with you." She smiled and then added the one thing that would leave him no option but to comply, though she did not care for being so underhanded. "I suppose I could choose one of the other gentlemen you claim is out there—" She waved toward the French doors. "But who is to say whether they will behave in a respectful manner?"

"And you are certain I will?"

She gave a small smile. "I believe you already have. I could not be in safer hands than if I enlisted Huntsleigh."

"Huntsleigh is married."

"Which is why he is wholly unsuited to assist me in this endeavor."

"Unfortunate," Marcus said, the hardness in his tone surprising her. "Because such a farcical scheme would be right up his alley."

"It is not farcical! It makes perfect sense. I'm sure if you think about it—"

"I do not need to think about it. The very idea is ludicrous. If Selward refuses to offer for you, then clearly he is not worth your time and effort. You should forget him and move on—"

"But I can't!" She clamped her mouth shut before she said more.

Silence echoed around them.

"Do you love him then?" The question came quietly yet the look he gave her stopped her heart. She tried to grasp it, read it and understand, but he looked away before she could and whatever expression she saw in his dark eyes disappeared, leaving her none the wiser to its origins.

"I—I—that is, he is—"

He held out a hand and she stopped, thankful for the interruption. She did not want to tell Marcus her motives. She had made Nicholas promise not to reveal the contents of Father's will to anyone. It embarrassed her and she did not want to contend with fortune hunters who were more interested in the size of her dowry than in her.

When he spoke, Marcus's tone came measured and quiet. "Is a proposal from Lord Selward truly that important to you?"

She thought of Mother, of what the future held for them if she failed in her quest.

"Yes."

"How exactly do you intend for this ruse to work?"

She sighed with relief. He would help her after all.

"It is simple. You will appear to court me. Pay me visits, perhaps a carriage ride in the park. I will let you know what parties Mother and I will be attending and you will go as well and dance with me just enough to get tongues wagging, but not enough to be deemed improper. This will send the message to Lord Selward that you are serious in your intentions toward me."

Marcus walked to the low stone wall that ran the edge of the terrace and gazed out into the night. His shoulders were rigid, allowing little compromise in his posture.

"I believe you are forgetting one small detail."

"Such as?"

"Why would Lord Selward, or anyone for that matter, believe you would ever accept a proposal from a man with no title or property to his name?"

"Oh, that." She dismissed his question with a wave of her hand and stood next to him. "Given your current status as hero and the fact my mother adores you and Nicholas thinks of you as a brother, it makes an odd kind of sense."

He kept his gaze fixed straight ahead. "Does it?"

She shrugged. In a perfect world, it would have. "We can say that your heroic actions and near death made me realize my feelings for you had gone beyond friendship."

"Except that it didn't."

"Well, no." She had realized her affection for him well before he saved Lady Franklyn, but she had set those feelings aside. She'd had little choice in the matter. A shame, really. It would have been lovely to be married to someone who could make her toes curl with just a look.

"So…will you assist me in my endeavor, or shall I ask someone else?"

Marcus let out a sound somewhere between a growl and a groan. He tilted his head up to the night sky and stared at the stars where they twinkled above. She studied his sharp profile; the way the light of the moon bathed his face and enhanced the marked angles of his cheekbones. And her toes curled.

Under different circumstances—

But these weren't different circumstances. These were the ones Father had dealt her. These were the ones she must contend with.

"Please," she implored when he had yet to answer.

He glanced down at her and his gaze roved over her face until an unexpected tingle made gooseflesh skitter across her skin. She leaned closer to Marcus, pulled by the sensation, but he quickly looked away, taking the strange awareness with him.

"Very well then."

Chapter Three

Marcus waited until Rebecca returned to the ballroom before he let his legs fold and sat with a heavy thud upon the low stone wall.

What had he just agreed to?

He should have said no. This was far too dangerous a scheme and Lady Rebecca far too tempting a woman. The ruse she suggested smacked of naiveté on her part. Did she honestly think society would look favorably upon the idea of him courting her? She was the daughter of an earl. A member of the ton. And he...well, he was none of those things, was he?

His current popularity would fade as quickly as it arrived and when it did, society would claim he used his friendship with Nick and his relationship as Lord Ellesmere's former ward and current man of business to jump above his station and affect airs he had no right to.

To court a lady well beyond his reach.

And what of Nick? What would he think about this debacle? He'd entrusted his sister's safety and reputation to Marcus. Instead, what did he do? He'd agreed to help her perpetrate a foolish ruse that could have them all mired in scandal before the Season ended. And for what? To snag a proposal from Lord Selward—a man who'd shown a severe lack of reliability or good sense. Instead of proposing to Lady Rebecca, as he should have long before now, his attentions had strayed to another the moment she'd had to remove herself from society to properly mourn her father.

What in the name of all that was sensible did she see in the man anyway? What Selward had in title and property, he clearly lacked in substance and depth. Did she not want a man who could match her wit and intelligence? Her warmth and good heart? Someone who would appreciate the hidden aspects of her character and see the good in them?

Lord Selward failed in all these respects. Yet Lady Rebecca claimed she needed the future earl. There was something he was not seeing. There had to be.

Either way, he'd committed to it now.

Marcus hung his head. The rough stone bit into his palms where he gripped the edge of the wall. He'd sent Lady Rebecca back into the ballroom with the promise he would follow shortly to begin their ruse.

To act besotted with her.

What special kind of hell had he agreed to?

"Do not think you can hide out here all night while I fight off the wives and widows."

Marcus looked up. Spence stood in front of him holding two brandies. "Where did you get those?"

Spence smirked. "Never you mind. Here." He handed one to Marcus, who took it gratefully. He tossed the drink back and winced as it burned his throat. The warmth spread through his chest.

Spence gave him a dubious look. "That was meant to be sipped."

"Sorry." Marcus took the second brandy from Spence's hand despite a sputtering protest and downed it as quickly as the first.

"Bowen! Sweet Judas, man. What the hell is going on?"

It took him a moment before he could speak. He did not often imbibe and when he did, he did not shoot drinks down his throat like a man dying of thirst. When he managed to speak, his words came out strangled. "I may have done something foolish."

Spence snorted and sat next to him. "You? I doubt that."

Though meant as a compliment, Marcus could not escape how frighteningly dull it made him sound and for a fleeting moment he wondered if he was every bit as bland as Lord Selward. The idea did not sit well. "I agreed to court Lady Rebecca."

"You did—" Spence's mouth moved, but it took a minute for him to finish his sentence. "What?"

Marcus cleared his throat. "It's a ruse meant to draw Selward's attentions. Lady Rebecca's idea."

"She means to use you to make Selward jealous?"

Marcus nodded. He rubbed at his chest. Lord, how long before the brandy stopped burning? Perhaps the sensation wasn't from the drink, but rather his body's response to his own abject stupidity. He was not one given to rash action. He preferred to think on things. Ruminate a bit and then base his decision on cold, hard facts. But Lady Rebecca had not given him such opportunity. She'd asked and he'd acquiesced. He did not know how to say no to her, nor bear the thought she might make the request to some lack wit who then tried to make good on his chance to weasel his way into the Sheridan family.

He could not risk her being hurt. No matter the cost to him.

"Well," Spence tilted his head to one side as if considering the matter. "I can't say the idea doesn't have merit. I employed a similar strategy to find Caelie a husband and was quite successful."

"You failed miserably. You meant to find her a suitable husband other than yourself."

"Yes, but then I determined I was the most suitable husband, to which she agreed."

"If memory serves, she turned you down. Repeatedly."

Spence gave him a withering look. "She agreed *eventually*. I think it is the final outcome that is the point here. My plan worked. I suppose there's no reason Lady Rebecca's won't as well. Although, I can't imagine what Nick will think about it. You know how protective he is over the women in his family."

"Yes, I recall. I was the one that kept him from tearing your limbs off and beating you to death with them after he learned you'd compromised his cousin-in-law."

"Yes. Well. Then consider me the voice of experience. Are you certain this is the best course of action? Could you not dissuade her from this?"

Marcus shook his head. "She is quite determined."

"She is usually much more sensible," Spence muttered. "It's been ages since she's gotten up to such mischief. Not since the incident at the lake, I would think."

As a child, Rebecca had tried to keep up with the Nick, Spence and himself, to capture their attention and not be left behind. An attempt that led her to jump into a lake, despite her inability to swim. Over time, however, she had put such behavior aside and grown into a proper young lady who never gave her family any concern or worry.

Perhaps the family dynamic left her little choice. Nick had commented often that Lady Rebecca played the part of peacemaker in an attempt to buffer the contempt between himself, their mother and the late Lord Blackbourne.

Her father had been adamant she not cause the family any

scandal as her brother had done his fair share to damage the family name, a dictate she had taken to heart and strove to achieve. Until tonight.

Now she dove into the lake once again, and in the process put them both in a rather untenable position.

Spence let out a slow breath. "I suppose if she is determined, she will be far safer with you playing the courting fool than some young fop who may take advantage or press his own agenda."

"My thoughts as well," Marcus said. Though it wasn't Rebecca's safety he was concerned with at the moment, but rather his own sanity. A sanity that had ebbed significantly upon his agreeing to her foolish scheme.

Spence flashed his usual grin, the one that made most of the ladies of the ton swoon, not that the man paid any heed to the effect he had on them. Since meeting his wife, it was as if all other women ceased to exist. "Well, enough of Lady Rebecca. My point in finding you was to impart some good news."

"Oh?" He could use some good news.

"I have found the perfect woman for you."

Marcus groaned and wished he had another brandy. Ever since Spence had done a complete turnaround on the subject of marriage, he'd made it his new mission in life to ensure his friend met with the same blissful fate as he had.

"And who is this perfect woman?"

"Miss Rosalind Caldwell."

"Miss—" He looked at Spence incredulously. "You can't be serious? What would Nick have to say about that?"

"What is there to say?" Spence shrugged. "It was her older sister that tried to trap Nick into marriage, and I have it on good authority that Rosalind is not the ruthless type. In fact, she imparted to me this very evening that she wishes to speak to you. Something about some charity with soldiers or what not. It sounds like a rather noble cause."

"How does that make her the best choice for me?"

"Well, she's rather bookish."

"So we are suited because we both read?"

Spence ignored his question. "She is opinionated, I hear, but I shouldn't think that would put you off. And Baron Caldwell is desperate to see his daughters wed before he meets his Maker—"

"Baron Caldwell is hale and hearty. I doubt he will be passing any time soon."

"Either way. Rosalind is one and twenty and this is her third Season with nary a hint of a proposal. I'm certain Caldwell would be thrilled to promote the match. And if you find Rosalind isn't to your liking, there is the youngest, Audrey, though I don't think she would suit. A bit flighty and flirty, that one."

Marcus dropped his head into his hands and rubbed at his face. When had this evening gotten so far away from him?

"I'm beginning to think cards with Lady Ellesmere and her cohorts would have been the better way to go tonight."

Spence laughed and smacked him on the back. "Come now. Give it some thought. You can't stay locked up in your office until the end of your days. In the meantime, you'd best return to the ballroom. I believe you have a ruse to perpetrate with our dear Lady Rebecca."

Rebecca smiled as Lord Selward went to fetch a glass of punch. Her idea sparkled with brilliance, if she did say so herself. After two dances with Marcus, Lord Selward had made a beeline toward her to claim the next, leaving Lady Susan to circle the dance floor like a vulture. To his credit, Marcus proved to be quite charming in his own serious way, though one would never consider him chatty. Not that it mattered. She found a great comfort in his quiet presence.

"My, my, but you have created quite the stir with your new gentleman." The vulture had stopped circling and swooped in, interrupting Rebecca's mental musings.

She straightened her spine and imagined herself to be made of the strongest iron. It was a trick Marcus had taught her when she was younger and Nicholas teased her.

"Close your eyes. Take a deep breath. Imagine your outsides are made of iron and nothing can penetrate it."

Funny how she had forgotten that until now, when Lady Susan's claws attempted to dig deep into her flesh. Funnier still how effective such mental imagery could be. She should thank him for it later, though she doubted he even remembered giving her such advice. It had been so long ago.

"Lord Selward is hardly new," she said. "Why, he has been paying me attention for over two Seasons."

Lady Susan clucked and Rebecca imagined her to be a chicken bobbing about the yard. Not such a vulture after all. "Two Seasons and yet no proposal? Well, I wouldn't fret. Every man needs a diversion or two, does he not?" Lady Susan wrinkled her upturned nose until her face appeared both pinched and scrunched. "Either way, it was not Lord Selward I referred to, but Mr. Bowen. An odd choice, is he not?"

Rebecca opened her fan with a practiced flick and slowly waved it beneath her chin to ward off the flash of anger that coursed through her at the way Lady Susan said Marcus's name. With distaste. As if he was unworthy. A surge of loyalty raged to the forefront. Marcus's worth far outweighed Lady Susan's. She considered him family and she would not allow her family to be disparaged.

"Odd in what way?"

Lady Susan opened her own fan and peered over its edge at the lords and ladies mingling around them. "Mr. Bowen may be the talk of the ton at the moment for the good turn he did Mother—"

"Good turn?" Rebecca glared at Lady Susan. "Is that what we call saving someone's life at their own peril?" She had been beside herself when she'd heard the news of Marcus's injury and had hovered on the precipice of fear and hope until word came that he had come through the worst of it and would survive. She'd cried herself to sleep that night, relief sweeping through her and releasing the pent up emotions she'd held in, too afraid to feel or give voice to.

Lady Susan made an unpleasant face. Or perhaps that was her actual face. It was difficult to tell at times. "My point is others will find it unseemly for you to allow him to pay such attentions. He is after all—" She waved a hand. "No one of any consequence, is he?"

The caustic remark scraped along Rebecca's last nerve. She snapped her fan shut and turned on Lady Susan, anger bubbling over. "Mr. Bowen is a good and honorable man. He is smarter than most and commands the respect of all. He may not be in possession of a title, but he is more of a gentleman than most men I know!"

The truth of it hit home as the words shot out of her mouth. Marcus *was* a good man despite all his silences and dark looks. He had always treated her with the utmost respect, even when she had heedlessly turned to him for comfort, kissed him, wished for more. Had it not been for his honor, who knew how far things might have gone that night. His kiss had set off a firestorm inside of her that made her crave more, though what all that *more* entailed she could not say. It did not come with a name, only a sense that filled her and tormented her even after all this time.

An acidic smile stretched across Lady Susan's face. "My, my. Have your affections turned so quickly? I will be sure to inform Lord Selward he no longer curries your favor."

Rebecca took a deep breath but made no attempt to dissuade Lady Susan from her course. If she wanted to unknowingly help her convince Lord Selward he had a rival, Rebecca would not stand in her way. That was the point of the exercise after all, was it not?

"I have not settled on one gentleman or the other as yet, but you must do what you feel is right."

"Lady Susan, Lady Rebecca." As if drawn by their conversation, Lord Selward reappeared, his gaze bouncing from one of them to the other. The glass of punch he had fetched Rebecca wavered in his hand as if he was unsure of what to do with it now that two ladies stood before him.

"Lord Selward." Lady Susan's voice softened until it oozed out of her, so filled with false affection it made Rebecca want to retch. "I understand Lady Berringsford has arranged for the last dance to be a waltz. How very exciting, don't you think?"

"Indeed," he said, though in Rebecca's estimation, excited was the last thing he looked. Uncomfortable would be a more apt description. "A waltz...yes...very...yes."

"I do so love the waltz," Lady Susan continued. "Don't you, Lord Selward?"

"Oh. I suppose...of course, that is to say..."

Rebecca bit the inside of her cheek. Heavens, was it truly so difficult to stop gulping air and stuttering to make a choice? Marcus never hemmed and hawed. He asked the pertinent questions, made a decision then stuck by it. Why Lord Selward could not do the same, went beyond her understanding. Either you loved the waltz or you didn't. It wasn't as if they had asked him to give a dissertation on Plato's opinion of the intellectual consequences of denial.

Lady Susan continued to press the advantage. "Have you promised someone the last dance, my lord?"

Lord Selward's handsome face took on a reddish cast. "Ah...no...no...I...yes, well..." He took a sip of the punch he had brought for Rebecca then cleared his throat again. And smiled. At least Rebecca thought that's what it was meant to be. Either that or a grimace. She couldn't blame him. She had tasted the punch. It was dreadful.

"Ah, Lady Rebecca. There you are."

She started. With her attentions focused on Lord Selward, she had missed Marcus's approach. She gifted him with a smile, his presence creating an ease within her. "Mr. Bowen. We were just talking about the last dance. It is to be a waltz."

"As I have heard."

"Yes," Lord Selward said, finally over his verbal lollygagging, at least for the time being. "I thought I might...that is... would you permit me the last dance, Lady Rebecca?"

Lady Susan hissed behind her fan. Rebecca smiled and opened her mouth to accept when Marcus interrupted.

"I'm afraid you are too late, my good man. She has already promised me the last dance."

Rebecca looked at Marcus in surprise. She had not promised him any such thing. In fact, she had purposely left the dance free in the hope Lord Selward would ask and thereby publically solidify his interest in her. She made to negate Marcus's claim, but before she could find the words, a sly grin spread across his face. She had never seen such an expression on him before. It altered everything about him, bringing his solemn features to life in a way that quite robbed her of breath.

She closed her mouth and held her tongue, unable to look away.

Next to her, Lord Selward stammered. "B-but you have already danced with her twice."

"And this will make a third." Marcus shrugged and grinned wider. He had very straight teeth. He really should smile more often. "When one has the opportunity to dance with a beautiful woman, Selward, he does not worry over the math."

"But how will it look?"

"I suspect," Marcus said, as he held out his hand to Rebecca. "It will look as if I am dancing with the most beautiful woman in the room and therefore must be the luckiest of men."

Rebecca swallowed and blinked, stunned by the dashing stranger standing before her. This wasn't the Marcus Bowen she knew. This was the pirate king she had once dreamed of.

She slid her hand into his and allowed him to tuck it through his arm as he led her onto the dance floor. She did not recall if she said good-bye to Lord Selward. She had never seen Marcus behave in such a bold manner. The errant knight claiming his princess.

"Why did you do that?" She whispered, once her wits returned. Marcus turned to face her and stepped closer, resting a hand on her waist. It didn't take long for warmth to spread through the layers of silk and linen and into her skin until every inch blazed with heat.

She loved the waltz. It possessed a secret decadence that could not be denied. For several moments you stood closer to a man than would normally be permissible and his hands rested in places that, under any other circumstances, would send tongues wagging.

Though tongues were sure to be wagging regardless. Three dances would definitely be noticed.

"I claimed the last dance," Marcus said as the strains of the waltz threaded around them and they began to move. "Because you wanted to make Lord Selward jealous. Did you not?"

"Yes, but I believe we have accomplished that with the other two dances. He made note of it to me. He wanted to waltz with me. Mission accomplished."

Marcus shook his head and she had the sudden urge to sink her fingers through the dark waves of his hair to see if it was as soft as it looked. During his convalescence, it had grown a bit longer than fashion dictated, but it suited him. It gave his otherwise buttoned down exterior a hint of unruliness that contradicted the other parts. But such unruliness had never translated into action until now.

He leaned in and she smelled the hint of brandy. Had he been drinking? She breathed it in. Breathed him in. Brandy and sandalwood. Intoxicating.

"Our mission has only just begun."

"It has?"

She had not been this close to him since their ill-fated kiss. The potency of which rushed back to her now and made her long to return to the gardens, to hide behind the statue of Athena with Marcus and without the prying eyes of the ton. A foolish wish. That moment had come and gone and would not return. Their fates traveled divergent paths.

"Indeed. It is not a dance you seek, but a proposal. Lord Selward is now aware he has a rival for your affections. If you give in now, he will not believe a true threat exists and therefore will have no reason to act. We must make him believe the risk of losing you is very real."

What he said made perfect sense, but patience had never been a virtue Rebecca embraced with any sense of familiarity. Nor could she deny the risk spending too much time in Marcus's company created. She gobbled up her time with him like a greedy thief stealing things that did not belong to her. That she was not meant to have. Too much time with Marcus and likely she would not even remember Lord Selward's name.

A dangerous proposition, but not one she had the inner fortitude to change.

"How long do you think it will take?"

Marcus shrugged, no mean feat as they swirled about. She had danced with him before on the rare occasions Nicholas or Huntsleigh convinced him to come out into society, but never the waltz. His agility on the dance floor surprised her, as did the strength in his arms as he held her.

"It could take several weeks."

"But the Season is almost over!" She must have a proposal before her next birthday; otherwise all of this had been for naught.

"I assume Lord Selward will be in attendance at the annual party at Sheridan Park?"

"Of course, but that's a month away." A month of Marcus. Dear heavens. A thrill shot through her, one that had nothing to do with ensuring her and Mother's future security.

Marcus offered her a small smile. "The time will pass regardless. Have faith. If the man has any sense at all, he will make an offer with all due haste."

She hoped he was right—almost as much as she wished he could be wrong.

The music swirled around them and Rebecca set aside her pressing problems and followed Marcus's lead around the dance floor, losing herself in the sensation of being in his arms once again. The power of it had not lessened, nor it seemed, had her need to stay there for as long as possible; to revel in the strength and sense of safety and belonging.

How she wished Father had not been so biased in his beliefs that a man must be a lord to be worthy of her. How different her life would be.

The last strains of the music faded far too quickly. Marcus took a small step away and bowed low over her hand, bringing her knuckles to his lips. Despite the barrier of her silk gloves, the heat from his mouth seeped into her veins and ran up her arm, warming her throughout. Had it not robbed her of breath, she would have gasped from the surprise of such a shocking gesture. Had he not claimed they must never kiss again?

Marcus straightened, but continued to hold her hand as he stared into her eyes. He stood close. Too close. She could feel the curious glances of those around them, but she was too lost in the dark depth of his gaze to care. His eyes were a deep, soulful brown. They reminded her of warm chocolate on a cold day where the first decadent sip made you close your eyes and sigh with pleasure. She wanted to fall into them and never land.

"I should not have done that," he said, his voice barely above a whisper, but his words lacked conviction and for a fleeting moment hope—that most irritating of all emotions—soared within her.

"I suspect it should give Lord Selward proper notice he has a rival."

Marcus smiled and her heart stuttered for a brief second. It wasn't a full smile, not the kind you receive when someone is happy to see you after a long absence. No, this was a smile one gave a lover—or so she imagined. Sinful and tempting, full of dark mystery and secret promises. Oh, how she longed to discover all of those things. Likely he would be the most wonderful of teachers.

Did Marcus have a lover? The notion hit her from behind without warning. She had not considered it when she proposed her plan. Nor did she particularly like the thought coming to her now.

"Shall I return you to your mother?"

She nodded. Words failed her at the moment as her brain tried to digest all the new facts and suppositions she had discovered this night about a man she'd thought she knew backward and forward. Strange sensations curled inside her belly creating a lightness that made it feel as if her toes did not even touch the floor. She glanced down just to be sure.

Her feet remained firmly on the ground. Her heart, however—well, that was another matter entirely.

Chapter Four

Marcus headed to his study. Despite the late hour, the events of the night had him too wound up to sleep and the three brandies he'd ingested did not help. His nerves sang and his mind whirled and other parts of him protested against needs not met. Needs unduly disturbed by a certain lady and her foolish requests.

He should never have kissed her. Not the first time, and not tonight, regardless of how chaste the second had been. The moment his lips had touched her gloved hand, long hidden desire rushed to the forefront until it took every last ounce of his will not to drag her back into his arms and kiss that damnable mouth of hers until she begged for air. Or something else.

Shit.

He let out a harsh breath and glanced down at his desk. Everything remained where he'd left it, patiently awaiting his inevitable return. Any other night, he would have dove in once again without a second thought. But tonight, work held no interest for him. His thoughts refused to settle.

His gaze rested on the package Spence had delivered

earlier. He'd purposely ignored it. Any dealings with respect to Braemore Manor usually went through Lord Ellesmere first. His employer thought it might be too painful for Marcus to deal directly with the steward who watched over the property. The man who had taken over after his father's sudden passing.

Yet this package was not addressed to Lord Ellesmere. Marcus's name graced the package, written in a bold, curling script. Doubtful it came from his family. The MacCumbers lacked the ability to print his name, let alone possess the wherewithal to determine his current location. Nor could they afford the postage to send such a package. Even if they could, they would not spend it on him. They had not cared for him during the brief time he'd lived under their roof and he could imagine no circumstance where that would have changed that.

But who else could it be?

"You could open it and find out," he muttered to himself, the sound whispering through the quiet room. His fingers tapped a rhythm on the package, solid beneath his touch. Wood, perhaps? He curled his hand around it and drew it closer. The fire in the hearth snapped and popped, goading him for his cowardice.

"It is not cowardice," he said, glaring at the fire. "It is—" He searched for the proper word, but in the end *cowardice* was the only one that remained. Foolish. It was just a package, after all.

Besides, what did he have to fear? The MacCumbers could not hurt him now.

Anger rushed through him. Anger that he had allowed the old memories to filter back in and seep into him like acid.

Marcus had spent eight months with his aunt and uncle being treated as more of a servant than a son. Beaten and starved whenever the whim took them. He'd often thought of running away, but to where? And to whom? He was alone in the world; the only people who'd ever loved him, dead and buried. He pushed the memories back, then grabbed the package. The tie broke with a snap and he ripped the paper away to reveal a plain wooden box.

Resting on top was a piece of folded vellum. Marcus lifted it and flicked it open. It was addressed to him on printed stationery from Wickwire & Hellum, Barristers and Solicitors. He furrowed his brow and leaned forward to turn up the wick on the lamp at the corner of his desk. Light spilled across the feathery writing.

Dear Mr. Bowen,

Please forgive the tardiness with respect to receipt of this package. My father, Alistair Wickwire, Solicitor, recently passed away and the contents were found amongst his belongings. Unfortunately, my father's ailing health over the past decade allowed several matters to fall to the wayside, this being one of them.

The items contained within this package were given to my father by Mrs. Mary Bowen shortly before her death. She requested it be held in safekeeping until such time as you reached the age of majority, at which time it was to be passed onto you. After a few inquiries to the local magistrate in office at the time of your mother's passing, I was able to locate you, and in doing so, fulfill your mother's request.

Again, my most humble of apologies for the lateness in receiving this package. I hope it finds you well.

Sincerely, Miss Evelyn Wickwire.

Marcus read the letter a second time. Why would his mother have held onto the contents of the box for so long? Why not instruct the solicitor to give it to Lord and Lady Ellesmere upon her death? Then again, his mother had no way of knowing he would end up with her employers. She had arranged for him to stay with her brother and his family upon her death, unaware of what awaited him there.

It wasn't until Lord and Lady Ellesmere had arrived to check on the estate that he was taken from the squalor and abuse. He had never seen the grand lord and lady before that day. They had never ventured to Cornwall but ran the estate instead through correspondence with his parents. His father had run the lands as steward until his unexpected death. One of the workers had found him face down in the field one afternoon. His heart, the doctor claimed.

Marcus remembered his mother's sadness, though more as a sensory thing than a firm memory. The pervasiveness of it had tainted everything grey. Shortly after Father's burial, Mother had taken ill. Sadness turned to fear for Marcus. He recalled arguments between his mother and his uncle during her illness and the message had been clear.

Floyd MacCumber did not want him.

Yet when Mother died, that was where he'd ended up. He did his best to be quiet and unobtrusive. To be helpful and work hard, hoping it would make his aunt and uncle and their brood of children warm up to him, or at least not resent him as strongly as they did.

He lost that battle. After a few weeks, his aunt and uncle's anger had turned physical and threats turned to promises of orphanages and workhouses. His fear grew to terror.

Then Lady Ellesmere came to visit. He'd stood in a corner near the cook stove after bringing in the wood; wide-eyed and amazed at the lady dressed in such finery. Her presence brought a bright light to the dark and dreary room. He couldn't pull his gaze away. Heat from the stove pressed against him until rivulets of sweat trickled down his back and dampened his shirt and still, he continued to stare. He pulled himself farther into the corner to avoid discovery.

Mrs. MacCumber had not been pleased the grand lady had descended upon her household. Marcus could tell by her sharp movements and the way the dishes hit the hard surfaces beneath them and rattled. She prepared tea and scraped up some biscuits, though the lady had insisted it wasn't necessary.

She wasn't there for tea and biscuits. She'd come for only one thing. He remembered the words as clearly as if she'd spoken them only yesterday.

I've come for young Marcus.

To claim Lord and Lady Ellesmere had changed the course of his life did not do service to their generosity. They had given him every advantage. A roof over his head, food in his belly, an education befitting any lord of the ton. They had given him the life he now had and they had asked nothing in return. They showered him with love and treated him as if he were a member of the family.

But he had known better. For the longest while, he held tight to his loyalty to his parents and the fear that at any moment he would be sent back to the MacCumbers. That his time with the Kingsleys was only a brief reprieve. Eventually, the fear ebbed and the memories of his parents softened around the edges. But he continued to avoid the sense of belonging that tempted him. He did not trust it. He'd belonged somewhere once and it had been torn away.

He would not be so complacent a second time.

Marcus set the letter down and reached inside the box where a cloth had been wrapped around the contents. He peeled it back to reveal a gold pocket watch. A crest had been engraved on the outside, but time had worn down the fine lines making it unrecognizable to him.

How had his mother come into possession of such an expensive piece?

He opened the watch. It no longer kept time. The hands read half-past ten and the glass had a small crack beginning in the center and stretching to wrap around the number eleven. The inside lid bore more engraving. Was it an *M* perhaps?

He closed it and set it aside to pull out the final item—a leather-bound journal. The well-worn bindings opened easily and inside the penmanship etched across the page, small and neat. A woman's handwriting, clearly, though too refined to be his mother's.

His gaze ingested the words at the top of the page.

It is difficult to say what will happen. Each day passes into the next and my worry grows. I know what Mother wishes, but I fear my own wants will make it impossible to honor hers.

A strange sense passed through him, as if in those two sentences he could feel the writer's desperation. Her fear. Who was she? And what was his mother doing with her journal? More curious, why had she passed it onto him years after her death?

He flipped to the first page but instead of finding a name, he found yet another letter. It slipped out and landed on the desk in front of him. He set the journal down and picked up the folded vellum sheet.

My dearest boy,

Mother. She had always called him that. He could still hear her voice, though it had faded over the years to little more than a whisper.

I have arranged for you to receive these items well after my passing and hopefully at a time when you will be closer to understanding. And forgiving.

Marcus furrowed his brow.

I loved you as my own, but the truth of it was you were not our true-born son. You may not have come from our bodies, but please know it mattered not. You lived in our hearts.

His own heart pounded in his chest. There had been

rumors, of course. Hardly an uncommon thing when a ranking peer took in an unknown lad, but Marcus had shaken them off. He had known his parents, known where he was from. He'd ignored the obvious signs—his parents were older, the lack of likeness between he and them. He once recalled his uncle telling him he wasn't true family. He had not understood at the time, but he understood perfectly now as his mother's words sunk in and turned his insides hollow. The thin thread of belonging he had clung to over the years stripped away until the edges of his life dangled loosely, attached to nothing.

I swore to never reveal your mother's true identity and I have kept my vow in this regard. But I also made a promise to pass these things onto you when I deemed it appropriate. The time has come, and the items enclosed are now yours. I am sorry I cannot give you more than this, but it is the only way I know to keep my promise to one, without breaking it to another.

Please know you were loved, my dearest boy. With all our hearts we wished you were truly ours. We hope we made you feel no different.

All my love, Mary.

Mary. Not Mother. Perhaps in telling the truth she no longer believed she owned the title, but instead had only borrowed it for a short time and now must give it back. But to whom?

Something welled up inside of him. Something he couldn't define. Anger? Betrayal? Disbelief? Perhaps all of these things mashed together so tightly he could not tell one apart from the other.

He fumbled for the journal again flipped through it, letting the pages fall one on top of the other, the same neat penmanship followed throughout, ending halfway through. He found no indication of ownership on the front or the back.

He set it down again, not ready to read the words. To accept the revelations his mother passed on from beyond the grave. How could it be true? His heart rejected her words at the same time his mind opened to them and let them in.

If the Bowens were not his parents, who was? And who owned the journal—the woman who had given birth to him? And what of her? Had she abandoned him? Left him with the Bowens? If so, why?

Questions tumbled through his brain with no corresponding answers save for one. The Bowens were not his true parents. He did not belong to them.

He did not belong to anyone.

His jaw clenched and he closed his eyes against the sense of loss rushing at him. His eyes burned beneath their lids. He'd been up since daybreak and another dawn fast approached. Part of him wanted to dive into the journal and devour its words, looking for answers. The other part of him shied away, reeling from the impact of the truth.

He needed time to absorb it. To believe it. He returned the journal to the box it arrived in and set the watch on top of it before closing the lid firmly, as if he could lock away the truth it had revealed, but he could not. It echoed in the quiet of the room, soaked into the walls and the furniture. It tainted everything around him and left nothing untouched. Everything he'd once believed crashed around him like broken glass.

In the aftermath, one question demanded an answer.

If the Bowens were not his true parents, then who?

The question was as simple—and as difficult—as that.

Chapter Five

June 22nd

Mother has determined we will travel away from London. She fears what will happen if we stay. I will miss Father horribly, though I have shamed him and likely he wishes me gone so he is not faced with my disgrace should it be discovered. I know he wants to ask me why I allowed this to happen, but I have no answers for him. It simply did and I cannot change it, nor do I care to think about it, though try as I might, I cannot forget it. I was such a fool to trust as I did and for that folly I paid a horrible price.

"Marcus?"

Rebecca stood in the open doorway of Marcus's office. He stood on the far side of the room, his silhouette framed by the large bay window that overlooked the street beyond. At the sound of his name, he set something on the table next to him—a small book, but did not immediately turn around.

Her gaze traveled over him, past the breadth of his shoulders and down the long, lean lines of his back, buttocks and legs. He still wore his clothes from the night before, though his jacket had been tossed on a nearby chair and his cravat, once wound around his neck with crisp efficiency, lay atop it. His waistcoat and shirtsleeves remained, though the latter had been rolled up, leaving his corded forearms bare.

"What are you doing here?"

Weariness invaded his tone. Had he not been to bed at all? Had he returned from Lord Berringsford's birthday party only to take up his work when he arrived home?

It was moments like this when the difference in their stations hit her and how escorting her to parties that ran late into the wee hours of the morning might affect him. Though he never gave a word of complaint, his less than hospitable greeting indicated the lack of sleep wore on him. It was unlike him to be so brusque.

She tried to cajole him out of his ill humor. "I would have gone for something a bit different. Perhaps, *'Good afternoon, Lady Rebecca. You look lovely this day. Would you like to come in?'* But I suppose, *'What are you doing here?'* has its own special charm."

His shoulders slumped, though he did not offer an apology or amend his original greeting. Marcus could generally be counted on to be the epitome of politeness, regardless of the situation. She found it odd to see him less so now. Did he regret agreeing to help her last night, or the three dances that had the gossips whispering? Mother had read the scandal sheet delivered this morning intimating a certain lady of good reputation had spent an inordinate amount of time on the dance floor with a gentleman of no consequence.

Of no consequence.

The untrue reference made her want to roll the sheet up

and beat the writer over the head with it until he retracted it for the piece of drivel it was.

Marcus Bowen was a man of great consequence.

"Are you well?" She could think of no other question to ask him.

He turned to face her and something in his expression caught her, but she could not see into the depth of it, as if his wary gaze held her at arm's length and obscured her view.

"Why do you ask?"

She smiled, wishing he would do the same. He did not. "Because the last time I saw you in such a state, you had just finished fishing me out of a lake."

"Ah." But he said no more and a strange silence created a barrier between them she struggled to breach.

"I had been testing my theory that day," she blurted out, then wished she hadn't as it meant explaining said theory and surely that would make her appear quite the fool.

"Which theory was that?"

Heat burned her cheeks but she forced herself to continue. "My belief that you were a pirate king and therefore, if my hypothesis was correct, would be able to swim like a fish."

"A pirate king?"

Why hadn't she kept her mouth shut? Marcus did not need to be informed of her silly girlhood fantasies. "Your past allowed for such imaginings, I suppose."

"You must have been quite disappointed to discover I could not swim." A small flicker of a smile pulled at the corner of his mouth but quickly disappeared.

"Not at all." Nothing Marcus did disappointed her, save for ending their first and only kiss. "Surprised, perhaps. You pulled me to shore safely regardless."

In truth, she had been unsure what to make of his dislike of water, and in the end decided that if he did not care for water, he could not possibly be a pirate king. And, as she had already determined his parents were steward and housekeeper for Lord Ellesmere's property in Cornwall, he therefore, must be just as he presented himself. An ordinary man.

Yet looking at him now—his gaze dark and penetrating, the rush of sensations his behavior of last night had conjured within her—she wondered if she didn't have it wrong after all, as in that moment, he seemed anything but ordinary.

He looked away, breaking the tension coiling around them. "To answer your earlier question, I am perfectly well. I wish people would stop inquiring after my health as if I were about to drop dead at their feet at any given moment."

The irritation in his tone made her lift one eyebrow skyward. "Then I retract my question and replace it with a statement. You look awful. Well, perhaps not *awful*—" She wasn't sure a man as handsome as Marcus could ever manage that. "But you do look tired and while I doubt you are about to drop dead at my feet, I would not be surprised if you did fall onto the rug and into a fitful slumber. Better?"

Marcus rubbed at his eyes then let his hand drop away. His expression eased but a hint of whatever had him in such a bear of a mood remained kindled in his eyes.

"Do you not have tea and biscuits to return to, my lady?"

"*My lady*." She made a face at him. She loathed his insistence on the use of her proper title and address. A practice he'd renewed with a vengeance after their kiss. "How perfectly formal of you, *Mr. Bowen*. And yes, I do. But I thought I might pay you a visit while I was here and return your book to you." She held out the volume of Voltaire he'd lent her last month. It provided nothing more than a reason to see him. "And I wanted to thank you for last night. I'm sure there were a hundred things you would have preferred to do."

"You would be correct." He made no move to take the book from her.

Her own irritation peaked. It had been him, after all, who

stole the last waltz, but she held her tongue and tried to maintain a sunny disposition with the failing hope she may still lighten his.

"You should be happy to hear that our ruse has met with success. I received a lovely bouquet of flowers from Lord Selward today with a note indicating he looks forward to seeing me at Lady Blyton's garden party tomorrow." She tried her best to infuse her delivery with a modicum of enthusiasm. She could not attest to the results, however.

"I am beyond thrilled," he said in a tone that indicated he was clearly not.

"Good heavens, Marcus. You're like an angry bear today. Can I say nothing that pleases you?" She walked further into the room and didn't stop until she was a few feet from him. The whites of his eyes were bloodshot and weariness clung to his rumpled appearance. Neither of which made him any less appealing. If anything, it somehow made him more so, as if he had just tumbled out of bed. "Are you certain you're feeling well?"

"I am fine. I simply wish to be left alone so I might go about my business in peace and quiet."

She ignored his plea. In her opinion, he looked as if he could use a respite from business, or whatever had put him in such a surly mood, and given the good turn he had done for her, it was the least she could do for him. She set the volume of Voltaire on the table. Its edge hit upon an object hidden within the shadow his body had cast across the table. She reached for it.

"What is this?"

Marcus moved to snatch it away but she tucked it close to her breast and his hand dropped before reaching her, as if scalded.

"It is a watch."

Rebecca turned it over in her hand and laughed. The

chuckle bounced off the walls around them as if they were unfamiliar to the sound. "You're quite adept at stating the obvious."

He gifted her with a withering glare.

She ignored it and moved closer to the window to lift the watch up to the light to better reveal the detail carved into its top cover. Standing this close to Marcus, who had not budged an inch, made concentrating difficult at best. She corralled the turmoil roiling within her at being only inches away from him as best she could and focused on the watch. It took her a moment to realize what she saw, and then another moment to convince herself she was not mistaken

What she saw made no sense.

"Is that the Walkerton crest etched into it?"

Marcus didn't move. "I beg your pardon?"

She turned to face him and looked over the edge of the watch. "Finally, a hint of politeness. Well done."

His lips pulled into a grim line. "You are not nearly as amusing as you seem to think."

"Of course I am." She held the watch up again and closed one eye, but before she could confirm her suspicions he plucked it out of her hand. His fingers brushed against hers, startling her, making it easy for him to wrest it away.

"It is not the Walkerton crest," he stated with flat finality. "What would I be doing with such a thing?"

Her mind swirled from the unexpected heat of his touch.

"How should I know? You're the one with the watch."

"It is not the Walkerton crest," he repeated. "It is nothing. Is there a reason you're still here?"

"Heavens, Marcus! Have I done something to displease you?"

He closed his eyes and let his head fall back, exposing the length of his throat and giving Rebecca a clear view of the small V where his shirt opened and revealed a portion of his chest. It rose and fell and she had the urgent need to slip her hand beneath the linen and place it over his heart to feel the steady motion of his breath. She curled her fingers into her palm, the memory of him holding her in his arms still ripe. The emotions his embrace had evoked stirred close to the surface. How easily her girlhood fantasies had resurrected, as if they had been waiting for the perfect moment to do so. But this was not the perfect moment. This was, in fact, a most inconvenient moment.

Marcus opened his eyes. "Forgive me, my lady—"

"Rebecca," she interrupted.

He ignored her. "I promise to improve my mood immediately. Now—is there anything else I can do for you or shall I escort you back to Ladies Ellesmere and Blackbourne?"

"Given your state of undress, perhaps it best I make my own way back. I just thought I would extend an invitation for you to join us at the garden party tomorrow. Will you come?"

She'd had no intention of asking him when she'd entered the room, but something about seeing him standing there, angry and desolate over some subject she could not pinpoint had made her want to...what? Rescue him? Such silliness. If anyone was in less need of rescue, it was Marcus Bowen.

"I will think about it."

"Good." She smiled and though there seemed nothing else to be said, she found herself reluctant to leave him. Reluctant to move away, to put a proper distance between them.

His expression softened and for a brief moment neither of them said anything. Something passed between them. A memory of what had been? A wish for what could be if only things were different? Whatever it was, it moved swift and silent. Rebecca tried to grasp it, to hold onto it long enough to absorb what it meant, but it eluded her, then disappeared.

"You should go," he said quietly.

"Very well." Though she preferred to stay. "Promise you will think about joining us tomorrow?"

He continued to look at her and for a moment she wondered if he had heard her, but then he nodded.

"I promise."

She could hope for nothing more.

Chapter Six

July 29th

The staff has been most courteous. Mrs. Bowen, the housekeeper, has been especially attentive, seeing to my comfort and bringing me mint tea when my stomach upset makes it difficult to even consider anything more. Several times, she has sat at my bedside and read to me. How fortunate I am for her company, as I am certain she has many duties to see to in running the household now that Mother and I have come to stay.

It is difficult to say what will happen. Each day passes into the next and my worry grows. I know what Mother wishes, but I fear my own wants will make this impossible.

Mrs. Bowen has offered such comfort in listening to my woes without judging. What a godsend to find such acceptance during this trying time. I can't imagine how I could ever repay her kindness.

"I hope you do not mind my inviting Miss Caldwell to join us," Lady Rebecca whispered as she leaned against Marcus's arm. They had taken a stroll along the stone pathway that wound through the extensive gardens of Blyton House. Behind them, Caelie and Miss Rosalind Caldwell trailed at a slower pace.

"Not at all." Though he did question his own sanity at accepting the invitation she'd issued the day before. For a smart man, he could be a complete fool in some regards. This one in particular.

It had taken him the better part of the afternoon to restore his concentration after she had left him standing in his study, the gold watch in his hand and the effect of the gaze they had shared sliding through his body like liquid fire. Her words echoed in her absence.

Walkerton.

The name landed with a dull thud in his mind.

Lord Selward's father, the current Lord Walkerton, had been absent from London for several years now. Selward had taken on the running of the estates, to respectable results, Marcus admitted grudgingly. But, provided Lady Rebecca's suggestion proved correct, what business did his mother have holding it in her possession? Mary Bowen had never worked for the Earl of Walkerton, nor, to the best of his knowledge, had even known the man. She lived her life in Cornwall and never ventured far from the town where she had been born. None of the Walkerton estates were anywhere near there.

He could make neither heads nor tails of it.

Nor could he make sense of why he now strolled down the pathway of Lady Blyton's gardens with Lady Rebecca on his arm when he had told himself countless times after her departure he would not take her up on her invitation. Yet here he was, looking down at her, drinking up her beauty as the sun dappled through the leaves of the spindly trees lining the pathway. The warm rays slipped past her bonnet and suffused her skin as she smiled up at him, her appearance almost angelic. The effect on him much less so.

If anything, it more closely resembled his own private hell.

Her hand squeezed his forearm, her touch arresting his wayward thoughts.

"Miss Caldwell is most anxious to speak to you about her charity and I thought it a good opportunity that would cause the least amount of concern. Apparently she has been dropping by homes uninvited and it has caused some talk."

"Do you feel it a worthwhile cause to give my attention?"

"I do, and she is quite passionate about it. I thought you might be able to assist her."

"I will do what I can."

She smiled and returned her gaze to the path in front of them, though for a brief heartbeat her head rested against his upper arm, a small intimacy borne out of familiarity, and though he understood it meant nothing, he held his breath just the same and waited for the connection to end. Longed for it not to.

"I knew I could count on you. You are a good man, Marcus."

Except he was anything but. At least in this moment, leading her along a pathway to the grotto that waited at its end, wishing for all he was worth that he could pull her off the trail and hold her in his arms as he had only two days prior. That he could lose himself in the sensation and forget everything else that had happened since, as if it would provide him some small amount of salvation.

He really should not have come. Sleep had eluded him once again and exhaustion made it impossible to mask his own needs, or to push them back into the dark recesses of his mind along with all the other things he had no business thinking about.

He needed sleep. Sleep would shore up his reserves, give him the strength to tamp his recalcitrant desires down, box them back up and shove them in a corner where he'd put them a year ago to collect dust. To be forgotten.

Nothing could come of them. She was destined to marry another and he—

Marcus bowed his head. He had no idea what his destiny held. He had started to read the journal, but after only a few entries set it aside. The revelations about his parentage raised too many questions. The lack of answers as to who the author was and what it all meant, tormented him and he had to set the journal aside or risk letting the unknown drive him mad.

Much as the scent of Lady Rebecca's perfume did now, reaching up to tease his senses.

He changed the subject. "Have you heard from your brother? Has he been delivered of an heir as yet? He promised me the role of godfather and I am anxious to begin."

She laughed and the sound washed over him like a cool breeze, calming and taunting all at once. "Godfather, is it? Well, I cannot think of a better role model, but alas, the newest Sheridan has yet to make an appearance, though Abigail's last letter indicated it should be any day. Ah, here is the grotto. Shall we sit?"

Marcus stepped aside and let her pass. Lady Huntsleigh and Miss Caldwell had lagged behind. Likely Miss Caldwell had set a more sedate pace out of consideration for her companion's condition, though Lady Huntsleigh showed no signs of needing it.

He ducked his head to keep it from brushing the low lattice and joined Lady Rebecca. She had taken a seat on one of the stone benches, but when he moved to take the one opposite, she stopped him.

"Sit beside me," she said, patting the spot next to her. He hesitated, a fact she noted and a smile sparked in her silvery eyes. "Come now, Marcus. I promise not to do anything untoward. No stolen kisses and such."

Her jest surprised him. Before her father's death, she would never have dared make such a comment. She'd kept her wit carefully under wraps, but in the past year, bit by bit, the teasing nature of her youth returned. It added a lightness to her that had been missing in recent years.

Marcus refrained from answering her jest, however. Better not to dwell on things that could not be changed, nor revisited, though the expression on his face must have indicated his discomfort as she saw fit not to follow his lead.

"Don't look so shocked," she smiled. "I have it on good authority that a little teasing does a body good."

"Who told you that?" He sat next to her, ensuring a proper separation.

"You did."

"I did?" He could not recall an instance when he would have issued such a proclamation.

"Indeed. I was complaining that Nicholas was teasing me endlessly about the freckles on my nose and you, very seriously, said a body needed to learn to withstand a little teasing so it might learn to laugh at itself."

"I said that, did I?" He vaguely recollected the conversation. She had been ten at the time and he, Spence and Nicholas had returned from Eton for the holidays. He had found her hiding beneath a desk in the library; teary-eyed that her brother had said something so unkind when she had awaited his return with great anticipation. He had sat next to her on the floor and issued his sage advice. How odd to think a dozen years later his words had stayed with her.

"You did. Which I find most amusing; given your penchant toward seriousness. It's a shame really."

"Being serious?"

She shrugged. "Oh, I suppose being serious isn't such a bad thing. But you mustn't overdo it. You should laugh a little more. You have a lovely smile, you know. I should like to see it more often."

Marcus stared at the empty bench across from them, her words soaking into him with less than pleasant results. "You paint a rather dull picture of me."

"I do not think you dull at all." Rebecca reached over and touched his arm. Another unconscious gesture. The muscles beneath his jacket shifted in response.

"What *do* you think of me?" The question left him before he could wish it back.

"I believe you are quite an accomplished dancer."

Hardly anything to hang his hat on. "Perhaps if Lord Ellesmere decides he is no longer in need of my services I can make my way as a dance instructor to young ladies."

She smiled and it filled him, that one little movement, nothing more than a curl of her lips. It made her eyes sparkle and his heart beat a little faster. Perhaps she was right. A smile held great power. Hers did, at least.

"You are also a wonderful kisser, though I don't suggest you hire yourself out on that account."

"Rebecca!"

Laughter erupted from her and she threw her head back in abandon at his reaction. "Oh, forgive me, Marcus. That was improper, was it not? Mother would be scandalized."

"As well she should be."

He gritted his teeth. Hell and damnation. Would she find the matter so amusing if she could see the mental images her teasing conjured? Or if she discovered how much he longed to kiss her again, properly this time, with forethought and intention. He would bury his hands in the mass of her thick, inky waves until they tumbled down her back and the pins scattered on the ground around them. He would capture her mouth in his and slowly ravage it until she gave in to the pleasure and allowed him to coax her lips apart. He would taste the sweetness of her tongue and hear the whimper of desire that erupted deep within her telling him she wanted so much more than a kiss. That she wished him to—

He cleared his throat and promptly looked away before she realized the nature of his thoughts. He blinked until reality resettled around him, its colors far more muted than the mosaic his mind had painted only seconds before.

"Good heavens, I have scandalized you, haven't I? Forgive me? I promise to behave from here on in." She smiled at him once again and the power and beauty of it soothed and tormented and, despite the anguish of being drawn into something he could never have, his anger failed him.

"I do not mean to tell you how to conduct yourself, it is just that—"

"That everyone wishes me to be the proper young miss, perfect in every way." Her gaze dropped to her gloved hands where they rested primly in her lap.

"Lady Rebecca—"

She glanced up and shook her head before he could finish. "No. I understand. It is the way of things. But, oh, how I wish I could simply marry and retire to the country, far away from society. Wouldn't that be grand? I could relieve myself of all the false pretenses and never again worry about being proper and perfect. Doesn't that sound like a wonderful way to live?"

He did not know what to say. She seemed earnest in her conviction and he found he could not refute the lovely scenario she suggested. In a scenario like that, away from the dictates and expectations of society, perhaps they would have stood a chance. Perhaps when she had kissed him, he would have given in as he longed to, and not ended it so quickly. In a perfect world, she could say to him whatever she wished and he could tell her everything that had lived in his heart for longer than he cared to admit.

Only they did not live in a perfect world, and as much as she wished to escape to the country, when she did, it would not be with him, but in all likelihood with Selward.

But his chance to tell her any of that disappeared with the arrival of Lady Huntsleigh and Miss Caldwell. Marcus stood as the two ladies entered the grotto and took a seat opposite them.

He shoved his thoughts aside. No place existed for them in his world, or hers.

In their world, she would marry a man he considered unworthy of her, yet the rest of society would look upon as the perfect match. And he would go on with his life, much as it was now, dying a little inside with each passing day. Maybe he would marry too, find a lady who would fit the description of what he needed, even though she would never be the one he wanted.

In moments like this, he wondered if he should have simply succumbed to the fever that ravaged his body after being stabbed while saving Lady Franklyn.

Surely, it would have been a less painful fate.

"Ah, shade!" Lady Huntsleigh waved her fan. The fiery curls around her face moved against the breeze.

Marcus turned away from Lady Rebecca, from dreams that were never meant to come true and futures they could not alter. He rested his gaze on Miss Caldwell and tried to find a reprieve from the restlessness Rebecca's words had disturbed within him.

"Miss Caldwell, I understand from Lady Rebecca you are spearheading a charity you wished to speak to me about."

Miss Caldwell straightened in her seat as Marcus retook his. Her eyes held a lively glimmer. "Indeed, Mr. Bowen. I find myself most concerned with the soldiers who have returned from the wars."

"The soldiers?" The war had been over for years now.

"Yes. You see, after their service to this country, many came home to find their situations much more dire than when they left. The jobs they held before their service have been given to others and often they have incurred injuries that make it difficult for them to find new employment. And yet nothing has been done about it. And why? Is it because we have no further need of them? Because their value has been used up?"

As she spoke, Miss Caldwell's expression turned from rather ordinary to something else entirely. Her eyes burned with a fire that seemed lit from the inside and color painted her cheeks. Her hands moved as she spoke, punctuating her words. Here was a woman who did not give in to convention. Though, to hear Lady Rebecca tell it, her reputation had not come out of this endeavor unscathed. Was that the future Lady Rebecca feared would befall her if she stopped playing the part of the proper lady?

Marcus shook the thought away. "And what are you doing to combat this way of thinking?"

"The Ladies of Charity and I have recently begun to assist these soldiers. We hope to enlist men such as yourself who are in a position to provide them with a livelihood. It is slow going, I grant you. Many are unwilling to overlook what they deem to be an infirmity, but I have seen what these soldiers can do when given the opportunity and I will not stop fighting for them. It seems unfair, given all they have done for us, do you not agree?"

"I do," Marcus answered.

"Do you think you can help them?" Lady Rebecca asked.

"What did you have in mind?"

"I know of a gentleman, Mr. Grantham Cosgrove. He is a former steward and quite qualified, but he lost his position after his return from Waterloo and has fallen on hard times. He is a good man and I had hoped you might be able to find a position for him on one of Lord Ellesmere's estates."

Lady Huntsleigh nodded her encouragement. "I'm quite certain Lord Ellesmere would have no objection if you were to meet with Mr. Cosgrove and ascertain his skills."

"I would be pleased to meet with the man." Lord and Lady Ellesmere were great proponents of charity. Was Marcus not the perfect example of their generosity? It would be the height of hypocrisy to refuse someone what he himself had benefited from.

"Good afternoon. I hope I am not intruding."

Marcus glanced up to see Lord Selward standing beneath the arbor. He had almost forgotten the man had indicated his desire to see Lady Rebecca at this event. In the time he'd spent with her, he'd been able to conveniently set aside the future earl's interest. She had not mentioned Selward's name once since their arrival at the garden party.

Lady Rebecca smiled. "Of course not, Lord Selward. Would you care to join us?"

Selward stepped further into the grotto and issued a greeting to the others before returning his attention to Lady Rebecca. "I can only stay a moment, but I wished to find you. I thought I might convince you to take a ride with me tomorrow in the park."

"Oh." She did not sound enthused. Obviously, Lord Selward did not know of Lady Rebecca's dislike of riding. Marcus could count on one hand how many times he had seen her atop a horse and none of those instances lasted longer than a minute before she requested someone assist her in setting both her feet on solid ground.

"I have a new mare. Quite a beauty. I'd love to show her off to you."

The edges of her smile stiffened. "Indeed, I think that would be most agreeable."

Lord Selward bowed and shot Marcus a look of triumph. Then he straightened and transferred his attention to Miss Caldwell, though when he spoke, his voice did not hold the same soft tone it had when conversing with Lady Rebecca. "Did I hear you mention a Mr. Cosgrove?"

"I'm sorry, but no," Miss Caldwell said with a warm smile. "You must have been mistaken."

Marcus glanced at Miss Caldwell. She spoke the lie with such conviction, Marcus had to question if he had heard the name correctly in the first place.

"Ah. Well then." Lord Selward's attention skimmed around the small group and an awkward silence descended, as if they searched for something to say to overcome the lie that had been told and came up empty.

"Mr. Bowen, you should show Lord Selward your watch."

Marcus clenched his teeth and shot Lady Rebecca a silencing glare, but it was too late.

"Watch?" Lord Selward let out a short laugh. "I can't imagine I would be interested in such an item in Mr. Bowen's possession."

The haughty response delivered its message clearly. Marcus was beneath his station and therefore beneath his interest. The man's rudeness irritated, but it was hardly the first time he'd received it from a titled lord. Despite his connection to the Kingsley family, most considered him to be well outside the social stratosphere they travelled.

Lady Rebecca straightened in her seat, a sure sign her back was up. He wanted to tell her to leave it alone, but she spoke up before he could stop her. "On the contrary, this watch bears the Walkerton crest, I believe. Though Marcus claims otherwise. Perhaps you could clear it up and tell us who has the right of it?"

Selward took a step toward their bench, his earlier claim at not being interested quickly forgotten. "What would you be doing with a watch bearing the Walkerton crest?"

Marcus maintained a relaxed posture, something he had become adept at doing from his experience dealing with business matters and brokering deals. "As Lady Rebecca has indicated, I do not believe it is the Walkerton crest. In fact, I am quite certain it is not."

"It is growing quite warm, is it not?" Lady Huntsleigh waved her fan beneath her chin with a little more fervor. "Perhaps it is time to return to the house."

Miss Caldwell stood, bringing Marcus to his feet as well. "Indeed," she agreed. "Shall we?"

"I would be most happy to escort you ladies," Lord Selward said offering both Lady Huntsleigh and Lady Rebecca an arm. As Miss Caldwell and Marcus were of lower station, they were left to take up the rear together.

After they stepped back onto the pathway, Miss Caldwell pulled on Marcus's arm, slowing his pace while the other three continued on. "Forgive me for the lie, Mr. Bowen. I understand it put everyone in a rather awkward position."

"Quite, though I suspect there was a reason behind it?" Miss Caldwell did not seem the flighty type to tell falsehoods simply for the sake of having something to say.

She nodded and slowed their pace a little more. "I did not want to say so in front of Lady Rebecca, given her affiliation and hopes with respect to Lord Selward, but Mr. Cosgrove was once in the employ of Lord Selward's father, the Earl of Walkerton, and I'm afraid it did not end amicably. So much so that Lord Walkerton refused him a reference."

The news did not bode well for Mr. Cosgrove or his future employment on the Ellesmere estates. "Did he have grounds to do so?"

"No, he did not. But I should allow Mr. Cosgrove to

answer your questions in this regard so you may decide for yourself. Will you still agree to meet with him?"

While he had no interest in becoming entangled in anything to do with either Selward or his father, Marcus could not deny the opportunity such a meeting presented.

"Of course, Miss Caldwell. I would be delighted to meet the man."

Perhaps Cosgrove could shed light on the watch's true origins and refute Lady Rebecca's disturbing claims.

Chapter Seven

August 10th

I had trusted where I shouldn't have. Believed myself safe. Had I not always been?

Such innocence is precious in children, but I am no longer a child, and now I would have one of my own because I allowed my own innocence to override the sense that this man was not to be trusted. This man, this father of my child that would never know the destruction his actions wrought. Nor likely care.

I will take care that my own child, when he or she comes, is well versed in the vagaries of life once beyond the innocence of childhood. I will ensure they trust their instincts and are true to themselves. I will do what I must so their life is never tainted by my own mistakes.

"I thought you disliked horses?"

Rebecca glanced over at Caelie who had agreed to accompany her as chaperone, claiming the fresh air—or at least as fresh as one could get during June in London—

would do her good. She insisted stretching her legs and viewing the flowers budding in the park was just what the doctor ordered.

"It isn't so much that I dislike them," Rebecca said. "They are gorgeous creatures and when I am on the ground I feel very safe around them. It is just when I sit atop them and look down and realize how high up I am and at the mercy of a beast that does not speak my language—then, perhaps, I get a little nervous."

Caelie laughed and the light sound filled the air around them as they walked the path that led to Rotten Row. Lord Selward had offered to escort her himself, but she had declined, taking Marcus's advice to not seem overly eager and have Lord Selward thinking he had won her over entirely. The harder he had to fight for something, the more he would want it. Marcus claimed it was inherent in men to want what they could not have.

She refrained from telling him the same could be said for women. Herself in particular.

"Well, I'm sure you'll do fine. Surely, Lord Selward would not do anything that might cause you harm."

"I'm certain you are right." Though Caelie's claim did little to quell the nervousness roiling in her belly.

"I visited with Marcus before I left. I had hoped to convince him to join us, but he indicated he had too much work to do." Caelie sighed and looped her arm through Rebecca's. The closeness calmed her. For most of her life, those of the male persuasion had surrounded her, save for her mother. It wasn't until Abigail and Caelie Laytham entered her life a year ago that she finally had a sense of what it might have been like to have sisters.

"Poor Marcus," Rebecca said. "I fear he will work himself to death and never look up long enough to realize life is passing him by."

"I had hoped to spark an interest between him and Miss Caldwell, but neither seems interested. Miss Caldwell is too wrapped up in her charity to notice any man beyond what service he can provide her cause, and Marcus, well he's—" Caelie waved a hand in the air. "He's Marcus. Who knows what thoughts go on inside that head of his?"

Rebecca's heart plummeted at the idea of Marcus and Miss Caldwell being matched, which was of course completely unfair as she made her way to meet with a man she hoped to coerce a proposal from. What did she expect? That the kiss they had shared would cause Marcus to pine for her? Such foolishness. He had not even been the one to initiate it. Though, granted, he had not stopped it, not at first. Likely she had taken him quite by surprise. He had offered her comfort, and yet, the most comfort she found had not been in the words he offered, but in the solid safety of his arms and the enticing promise of his kiss.

A promise quickly broken when he ended the kiss and informed her it had been a mistake not to be repeated.

How unkind of her that she could not wish him good fortune in finding a lady to spend his life with. Her failure in this regard shamed her. He deserved better from her.

They reached the south side of Hyde Park and Rotten Row where it seemed half of London's elite had gathered this day to see and be seen as they rode up and down the Row on their horses. Rebecca sought out the meeting place as indicated on a note sent by Lord Selward earlier that day and was somewhat dismayed to find he had a rather large collection of lords and ladies surrounding him. One lady in particular stuck out more than the others, likely due to the hideous bonnet she wore.

Frustration curdled any enthusiasm she had tried to summon. Had Lord Selward invited Lady Susan to join him as well? She had been certain the invitation had been meant for her alone. To discover she must yet again share his attention with Lady Susan soured whatever hope she'd had for the afternoon. How much longer did he expect her to compete for his affections like some dancing monkey to a vendor's music box?

"Would you rather we not join them?" Caelie asked, slowing her pace and forcing Rebecca to do the same.

Rebecca shook her head. She had come this far and she did not have the luxury of time. The Season would end in a matter of weeks; her birthday loomed in the near future. She did not have time to choose another titled lord and try to curry enough of his favor to elicit a proposal. "No. No, of course not. I have put up with Lady Susan's presence this long. Surely I can endure one more afternoon."

They made their way toward the group of individuals standing around Lord Selward's beloved mare. It was a beautiful animal, a deep chestnut brown with sooty black socks that matched its mane and tail. It snorted and pawed the ground with its hoof before giving a quick shake of its head.

Rebecca swallowed.

Caelie squeezed her arm. "You do not have to—"

But she did. Lady Susan was an expert horsewoman, after all, and it would not do for her to appear less so, given Lord Selward's love of all things equestrian. If she did not go through with setting herself upon that horse, her rival would, and likely with far more aplomb than Rebecca could ever manage. For the sake of her plan, she must persevere.

"No. It is fine. I will be fine." Perhaps if she repeated those words enough, it would calm the pounding of her heart and the shaking of her hands.

"Lady Rebecca!" The shrill tone of Lady Susan cut through the air. Truly, how could anyone wish to be married to that, day in and day out? "It is so lovely of you to join us."

Us. As if their coupledom was already a foregone conclusion, and Rebecca relegated to nothing more than a guest who had come to call. Lord Selward stepped forward to greet her.

"Lady Huntsleigh. Lady Rebecca." He took her hand and bowed over it, continuing to hold it as he stared into her eyes, much as Marcus had done after their waltz, though the results today were far less...well, far less.

Her insides did not warm, and her skin did not tingle despite the glove's protective covering. Lord Selward's eyes were a bluish-green, and while a lovely color, she had to admit they lacked the depth of Marcus's brown eyes. "I am so happy to see you could make it. Lady Susan indicated you feared horses and I worried you might have changed your mind."

"Don't be silly. I have no idea what Lady Susan referred to. Why, I positively love horses. Such majestic creatures, are they not?" She forced a smile and wished a pox would befall Lady Susan before the day was out.

"Shall I settle you upon Belle, then? I can lead you down the Row and you can tell me how you like her."

Rebecca fixed the forced smile to her face and used her last scrap of will not to glare in Lady Susan's direction or run in the other to avoid her fate. "That would be splendid." Her stomach disagreed and somersaulted several times over.

Lady Susan stepped forward. "But I thought I might like to try Belle first, Lord Selward. I am the better horsewoman, after all. Everyone knows that." The duke's daughter lowered her fan and gave a coquettish smile that held all the sickly sweetness of an over-sugared butter tart.

Lord Selward hesitated, as he always did when faced with any type of confrontation, especially those that placed him solely in the middle. An increasingly irritating trait, in Rebecca's estimation.

"Then all the more reason I should be first, Lady Susan, as obviously I need the practice." Rebecca gave Lord Selward her sweetest smile and ignored his companion as best she could, though it was difficult given Lady Susan's beady eyes bored into her like a pair of sharpened daggers. Lord Selward, who appeared quite thankful someone had made the decision for him, moved quickly to offer her his hand.

"Let me assist you up."

Rebecca stepped onto the box at her feet and allowed him to lift her into the sidesaddle he had thoughtfully provided. She positioned herself properly, arranging her skirts and wishing vanity hadn't dictated she wear her favorite afternoon dress instead of the more serviceable riding habit. She had debated, but as she had no plans of actually riding the horse, only sitting upon it, she had opted for the dress. A decision she now regretted as she struggled to keep her ankles covered while still maintaining her seat.

She glanced down at Caelie—who looked very far away at the moment—only to see her dear friend looking as apprehensive as Rebecca felt.

The horse shifted beneath her and she quickly forgot Caelie as she grabbed for the pommel. Nearby, Lady Susan snickered. Rebecca gritted her teeth and forced herself not to look down again. It didn't help. She could sense how far from the ground she was and her insides quaked. The horse snorted. Could it smell her fear? Or was that dogs? Her palms turned sweaty inside her dainty gloves. What fool wears such attire when atop a horse?

"Are you quite comfortable, Lady Rebecca?"

She kept her gaze fixed at a point in the distance, afraid to look down at Lord Selward in case the fear rolling through her had stamped itself across her face. "Oh, yes. Yes, of course."

"You don't look so well," Lady Susan offered, in her nasally, saccharine tone. "Are you feeling ill?"

Ill would be an understatement as the light lunch she'd eaten two hours previous threatened to make an unwanted reappearance, but she refused to give Lady Susan the satisfaction. "I am perfectly fine, thank you."

The horse snorted and shifted again. Sweat beaded Rebecca's forehead and she gritted her teeth.

"Would you like down," Lord Selward asked, stepping closer, the reins held lightly in his hand. "It is quite all right if you do."

Except it wasn't all right. Lord Selward loved horses. If she had any hope of capturing a proposal it would serve her well to share this passion. Heavens knew they were unlikely to share passion in any other areas. Besides, her pride would not allow her to admit public defeat in front of Lady Susan who would use it against her and—

"She truly is a superior piece of horseflesh," Lady Susan said.

From the corner of her eye, Rebecca saw a flash but it wasn't until the horse lurched forward that she made the connection. Lady Susan's hand slapped against the animal's hindquarters. Too late, Rebecca screamed as the horse took off, the reins torn from Lord Selward's grip. She forgot screaming and quickly turned to pleading for God and anyone else who would listen to save her from the equine hell-beast. But apparently God had more important things to attend to, as the hell-beast in question raced down Rotten Row as if the Devil nipped at its hooves, leaving Rebecca little choice but to hang on for dear life.

A life she suspected wavered on the edge of ending.

Everything on either side of her blurred and the air filled with shouts and screams, not all of them hers, which did not bode well for a good outcome. The horse stumbled slightly and her heart lodged in her throat. The mare quickly recovered, but the motion had loosened Rebecca's seat until only sheer force of will kept her atop the horse.

Something dark flashed in front of her—her life perhaps?

If so, she was too busy to pay it much notice. Then, without warning, the horse stopped and she vaulted through the air, weightless. The ground rushed up to meet her and she squeezed her eyes shut, waiting for the end. It came with a splash and bone-jarring jolt that left her gasping for air. When she dared to reopen her eyes, she blinked up at the sky. Puffy white clouds drifted above her as if nothing untoward had just occurred.

"Rebecca!" A pair of booted legs skidded to a stop in front of her, spraying muck onto her exposed stockings. She watched as Marcus dropped to his knees on the ground next to her, his features tightened with fear and worry.

She breathed a sigh of relief and closed her eyes. Not dead. Oh, how wonderful. For surely if she were dead, Marcus would not be with her. Unless he'd tried to avert another band of knife-wielding thieves. Oh dear, had he?

Her eyes snapped open. "Are you dead?"

"No." His hand touched her face then moved to squeeze her arms and legs. Despite his highly inappropriate behavior, she could not recall ever being so happy to see someone.

"Then I am not dead?"

"You are alive and well. Are you injured?"

"I don't think so." Unless feeling the fool quantified as injury, in which case her wounds were quite fatal. "It feels cold."

Marcus let out a harsh breath and yanked her skirts down until they almost reached her ankles. "You landed in a puddle of water and muck. It likely cushioned your fall."

She looked down and wondered that she hadn't noticed that earlier. Her nose wrinkled. It smelled horrid. It tasted even worse.

Marcus turned away from her and returned to manhandling her knee with strict efficiency as if she were a filly he considered for purchase. Which brought to mind the beast that had thrown her. She pushed herself up on her elbows and glanced around. Belle—such a sweet name for such a mercurial beast--nibbled at a thin patch of grass near the edge of Rotten Row, not a care in the world.

She should be so lucky.

"I could have died." The reality of what had happened sunk in, as did the reality of where she was, sitting in a puddle, her muddied skirts plastered against her legs while Marcus ran his hands over her body.

He shot her a dark look and applied pressure to her ankle. "Does this hurt?"

"No. What are you doing?"

"Looking for broken bones."

"Oh."

"And this?" The other ankle. His touch sent a rush of heat up her leg but she doubted that was the sensation he asked about.

She shook her head. "You're here." The oddity of his sudden appearance dawned as the fog lifted from her mind. "Why are you here?"

"Lady Huntsleigh invited me."

"Oh." But Caelie had said he'd declined. "I'm very glad to see you."

The dark look vanished and for the briefest moment, his expression softened and relief swept across his handsome features. She wanted to reach out and touch him, run her fingers over his face as if she could capture that look and hold it forever. But all too quickly it left, replaced by something else. Anger. Frustration.

"You could have been killed."

He didn't give her time to respond as he moved to her shoulder and tore off his gloves. His fingers slid through her hair, loosening what pins were left from the fall. My goodness what a glorious feeling. If her brain didn't feel so scrambled at that moment she'd have closed her eyes again and given over to the abandon of it. But as her eyes were open, and Marcus's handsome face hovered sinfully close to her own, it was hard to know what to do. Or where to look.

He pulled his hands away and looked at them. Aside from being covered in muck—oh sweet Heaven, was that in her hair?—he seemed pleased with what he found. At least as pleased as someone with a scowl stamped across his face could look.

"Can you stand?"

"Usually."

"Now?"

"Oh. Yes, I think so." She moved her legs, testing them. "Perhaps you could assist me?" The crowd converged upon them in the distance and she had no desire to be found with her skirts hiked above her ankles, sitting in a puddle of muck. It was embarrassing enough to have Marcus find her in such a state. Though, she had to admit, seeing her legs exposed in such a manner had appeared to have no effect on him, as if he hadn't even noticed. Then again, he had been rather occupied determining her state of health, so she supposed she could forgive the oversight.

He lifted her to her feet without saying a word. She grasped the lapels of his jacket. While uninjured, her legs wobbled from the stress of her ordeal. Thankfully, Marcus made no move to pull away. Had he, likely she would have toppled back into the muck. Now that the shock of what had happened receded, her body shook and her mind whirled with scenarios of what might have been. None presented a very pretty picture.

She looked up and found Marcus glaring down at her. His jaw tensed and the deadly look still burned in his eyes. He pulled her away from his body, a fact she deeply regretted, and grabbed her by both shoulders to give her a small shake.

"What in bloody hell were you doing? You had no business being on such a spirited animal!"

"I was only trying to—"

His grip on her tightened and anger seethed out of him until it warmed her flesh beneath. "You could have been killed!"

"Yes, I believe we have established that fact. But I am fine."

He was right, of course, but she did not appreciate how his words made her feel like an errant child. She spied Caelie hurrying down the Row, a hand at the bottom of the small curve of her belly. Lord Selward was ahead of her and Lady Susan behind with her parasol twirling in the breeze, no doubt gloating with each step she took.

"I am fine," she called out to them and noted her declaration was enough to cause Lord Selward to slow his pace, though concern marred his face. Likely he would blame himself, but it hadn't been his fault. Lady Susan had set the horse in motion. There was little he could have done.

A crowd quickly gathered around her and Marcus, lords and ladies who had witnessed her folly and its disastrous results. Muck and dung and who knew what else covered her. The dress that she had taken such care to choose was ruined beyond repair and now stuck to her body in a rather inappropriate manner everywhere the water had soaked through. Humiliation scalded her from the inside out.

She must look a dreadful sight! How would she ever live this down?

Lord Selward stopped several feet from her as if the muck had taken hold of his boots and prevented him from moving closer. "Lady Rebecca. Forgive me. I—I do not know what could have happened."

Before she could absolve him of responsibility, however, Marcus's voice cut through the din from the crowd. "What happened is that you put a young lady upon your godforsaken horse and did not take the proper care to ensure her safety."

Marcus's angry condemnation silenced Lord Selward for a moment, then his spine straightened and his chin lifted at a haughty angle. "I beg your pardon, Mr. Bowen, but I don't think—"

"That much was obvious."

Rebecca blinked. She had never heard Marcus speak to so harshly to anyone, let alone a man above him in rank. Worry cut through her own humiliation. Though Lord Selward possessed a mild manner, men often acted irrationally when their egos became involved. Would he take issue at the dressing down he'd just received?

And what of Marcus? Calm and collected, as steady and solid as stone, and yet here she stood, pressed into his chest, his arm wrapped around her. The muscles beneath his jacket flexed and shifted with barely controlled anger. Would he strike Lord Selward? She could not risk it.

"Mr. Bowen, would you take me home, please? I—I wish to go home." And then, for added measure. "I'm feeling a bit faint."

Marcus glanced down at her and a war waged inside of him until his eyes turned the color of obsidian.

"Please," she whispered, placing a hand against his chest, heedless of propriety which she had abandoned at some point between her arc through the air and landing in the mud with her skirts hiked. "I want to go home."

His heart beat furiously against her palm.

With one last cold glare aimed at Lord Selward, Marcus stepped away from her and undid the buttons of his jacket. He pulled his arms out of the sleeves then swung the garment over her shoulders. It swallowed her up and Marcus's masculine scent swirled around her and calmed her rattled nerves. If only it had the same effect on the mortification growing inside of her as the other lords and ladies whispered behind their gloves and fans. No doubt her escapade would figure prominently in tomorrow morning's scandal sheet.

Without notice, Marcus swung her up into his arms.

"Marcus," she hissed. Had she not suffered enough? "This is unnecessary. I am uninjured."

He paid her no heed, a reminder his anger extended beyond Lord Selward and rested with her in equal measures. But what had she done? She had only sat upon a horse. It was Lady Susan who had swatted the animal's behind and sent it off at a dead run.

"We shall let a doctor determine that."

"Mr. Bowen is right," Caelie said, having pushed her way through the growing crowd to reach them. Guilt swamped Rebecca at the thought of causing her cousin any undue concern given her state, but if Caelie was any the worse for wear, it did not show through her calm, sensible manner. "It is the prudent thing to do."

Rebecca's embarrassment grew worse as the curious gazes of the crowd followed her to an awaiting hackney someone had hailed. Their notice sliced into her like razors against her skin. Over Marcus's shoulder, she could see Lord Selward. He made no attempt to follow and her hope for the afternoon fizzled in her chest.

How could she ever face him again? What would she say? What was there to say? She had pretended to possess a skill she did not own, perpetrated a fraud and paid the price, embarrassing herself beyond repair. By tomorrow morning, all of the ton would be aware of her foolishness and whisper and gossip about it for weeks to come, tittering behind hands and fans whenever she passed by. The Season would be over before she could show her face again and who knew how deeply Lady Susan would have dug her claws into Lord Selward by then? Her chances of receiving a proposal dimmed significantly. Her hopes of saving her family's unentailed estates grew more dismal.

Tears pricked her eyes and she huddled deeper into Marcus's side, wishing for all the world she could crawl inside his coat, pull it over her head and stay there for an eternity. What hope was there now? She could not start all over again. There was no time! How would she face Mother, knowing her foolish actions had ruined their last chance?

She bit her lower lip and held in a sob as everything she had struggled to hang onto slithered from her grasp.

Chapter Eight

Marcus paced back and forth. His anger rose a notch as each step echoed against the hardwood of the Sheridan receiving room. What had she been thinking? What if he had not reached her when he had? What if he had let his better sense rule and stayed behind his desk instead of leaving his ledgers and making his way over to Hyde Park because he could not abide the thought of her being alone with Selward, who had no inkling of her fear of horses?

Not that he had actually been working. Since he'd roused himself from bed early that morning the knowledge Rebecca would be spending part of the day with Selward and his prize mare gnawed at him. Her excitement at the prospect, despite her fear, did nothing to improve his mood or his concentration.

Her fear of horses had been fed by the late Lord Blackbourne, who had constantly enforced the idea in the hopes of keeping her away from the large beasts. Her father had treated Rebecca as if she were a fragile doll that could break at the slightest thing.

Perhaps the old bastard had been onto something given today's outcome.

Regardless, knowing her plans for the day had worn on him and by late afternoon he escaped Ellesmere House to stretch his legs and clear his head. Before he knew it, he was at the park and then onto Rotten Row. His arrival coincided with Rebecca's mare jolting and taking off in his direction. There had been no time to think or plan. Instinct surged through him and he pulled some poor gentleman from his mount and vaulted into the saddle to ride straight toward Rebecca. His heart exploded in his chest when the horse stumbled on a loose rein, then caught itself. The stumble slowed the horse's speed but by then Rebecca had lost her seat and slipped in the saddle.

He'd spurred his horse on, then spun it in a wide arc in time to block the runaway horse. The mare stopped short, but Rebecca flew over its shoulder, her skirts flapping around her before she landed in a heap in a large puddle left behind by last night's rain. He'd jumped from his own horse and rushed to her side.

If she was hurt or worse—

But she hadn't been. Stunned and shaken, yes, and likely with a few more bruises than she began the day with, but otherwise uninjured. A fact that did nothing to quell the violence he wanted to visit upon Selward for putting her in such danger in the first place.

He turned on his heel now to face her. They had returned to her home as it was closer to the park than Ellesmere House, but Lady Blackbourne had stepped out. She'd had an appointment with her modiste. Caelie volunteered to retrieve her and send for the doctor as a precaution, leaving Marcus and his anger alone with Rebecca. Her maid, Nancy, had joined them, sitting just outside the room.

"I am sorry," Rebecca whispered. "I did not mean to create such a commotion. I only wanted to—"

"Capture Selward's attention. Yes, I am aware. Well done." The words spit out of him in harsh bites.

She flinched at his caustic tone, but his anger chased off a fleeting remorse before it could take hold. How easily he could have brought home her lifeless body instead.

His stomach dipped. He could have lost her. Not that he'd ever really had her in the first place. He had no claim on her. She was not his. And yet...

And yet she was. In his heart. From the moment he'd allowed that one kiss, a kiss he'd thought of, hoped for, dreamed about for longer than she would ever know. Like a fool, his stupid, ridiculous, ignorant heart refused to believe in a world where she could not be his. Where fate would dangle her in front of him like a promise and then renege.

And she had wanted him, too. That was the worst of it. She had kissed him from a place of desolation and need, but desire had sparked, as if it had been lingering beneath the surface the entire time, waiting for him. Only him. He felt it in the way her mouth opened to him and her hands clung to the lapels of his jacket with a desperation borne of need. Of want. He'd seen it in her eyes when he broke the kiss and held her from him, telling her it could not happen again, because where his heart had failed in knowing the way things were, his head had not.

She was the daughter of an earl. He was the son of servants.

Perhaps not even that, now.

But whatever had begun with that kiss, still smoldered beneath the surface, its reminder seen in lingering glances, quiet smiles, teasing words, innocent touches.

And in one fleeting moment, he could have lost it all. The anger and wrongness of that spread through him like a wildfire that burned his insides and refused to be extinguished.

"You needn't look so bleak," Rebecca said. "This is not your fault."

"I am well aware."

She made a face, apparently less than pleased with his answer.

He stalked to the doorway to where her maid sat. "Nancy, see about arranging a bath for Lady Rebecca and inform us once it is ready."

Nancy stood and hesitated, glancing at Rebecca but her lady was too busy worrying her gloved hands to give her acquiescence and after a moment, Nancy left to carry out Marcus's request, leaving the door open for propriety's sake.

He turned back to Rebecca. "What were you thinking?"

Her head shot up and for a brief moment a fire blazed in the silvery depth of her eyes. "I only intended to sit upon the animal, to show Lord Selward I could share in his love of horses. Lady Susan is an avid horsewoman and I—"

"You cannot ride and therefore had no business on the back of such a spirited horse."

Again, the fire in her eyes blazed hot. How far could he push her before it boiled over? And what would happen if it did?

"Lady Susan swatted the horse's flank and startled it! Otherwise I would have been perfectly—"

"Selward should have had better control of it!" As much as Rebecca's decision had been reckless, Selward's inability to protect her did him no credit. It had taken every ounce of Marcus's control not to punch the young lord in the throat.

"Why do you dislike him so? He is not as bad as you make him out to be."

Why indeed? But he knew. So deep in his bones the truth whispered through him with each breath he took. Because

Selward would take her away from him and there wasn't a damn thing he could do to prevent it. Because his lordship was too stupid to even realize what a prize he held in his hands. A fact made obvious by how little care he had given in keeping her safe.

Anger seared his veins as the memory of her catapulting through the air flashed through his mind for the hundredth time. He rubbed at his eyes as if he could erase the image. He could not.

"His invitation explicitly put your safety in his hands, a task which he failed at miserably."

"Regardless, I am fine. A little bruised, perhaps, but otherwise unscathed," Rebecca said, waving off his claim as if it meant nothing. "It appears Lady Susan will get her wish. I am humiliated. I will not be able to show my face in public for what remains of the Season. I am done and she will end up marrying Lord Selward while I end up with nothing."

"The two deserve each other," he muttered.

"And what do I deserve, Marcus?"

He wanted to tell her she deserved him, but that would have been nothing more than wishful thinking on his part. What did he have to offer anyway? His name? He didn't even know what that was anymore.

"You deserve better than a man who values you so little he has yet to make an offer long past due."

"And now he never will. I have ruined everything. All I wanted was to—" She stopped and bit her bottom lip as it trembled. Fat tears bled through her bottom lashes and streaked down her mud-stained cheeks. His heart softened. It did not help matters that she stood in the middle of the drawing room swallowed up by his coat, a blatant reminder of how easily he could have lost her.

"I should never have let you go without my—"

Her head snapped up. "Your what? Protection? You are

not my protector, Marcus, nor do you have a wish to be. You made yourself clear on that point a year ago, if I recall."

"*Please,*" she'd said to him, when he'd broken the kiss. A single, quiet plea that he allow what had happened to stand. Continue. Grow.

"*I cannot.*"

And that had been that. How he wished to go back to that moment, to give her another answer. But to what end? The outcome would have been the same.

"You deserve a better life than the one I can give you," he said.

She shook her head. Her hair had come undone and now blanketed her shoulders in clumps and curls. It did nothing to detract from the beauty that came alive with her anger. Often her beauty had the quality of glass, now it rivaled fire and burned every bit as brightly.

"What do you know of the life I deserve? The life I want?" She shook her head. "I would have taken the chance if you'd only asked."

But he hadn't. He hadn't risked it.

"You never act rashly," she said, as if reading his mind. "Everything you do gets mulled over and thought out, all the pros and cons weighed and considered. I don't mean it as a criticism. This is an admirable quality under most circumstances, but the heart does not know of pros and cons. It knows what it wants and understands that sometimes you need to take a risk!" She pressed a fisted hand against her breast.

How dull she must think him. How cowardly. Yet he could not refute her claim. He *did* think first and act second. He could not help it. Such thinking had been his mainstay since he'd had to fend for himself in the volatile household of the MacCumbers. Any rash nature he'd once possessed had been carefully tucked away, every step he made thereafter planned and executed out of necessity and survival.

It was this careful control that kept him from declaring his feelings for her. Such rashness would only result in ruination for one or both of them. Especially now. Yet, here she stood, taking him to task for it.

But what did she know of such things? He did not expect her to understand the control he needed to hold things together. To keep from giving into his feelings and taking what he wanted, heedless of the outcome, caring little for the hurt it would cause in the long term.

"It is you who do not understand." He took a step toward her. Just one. No more.

She swiped at the tears and smeared mud across her cheek. "What don't I understand, Marcus? That you prefer to live in the safe little world you've created for yourself, thinking and mulling and refusing any risk that might upset your carefully constructed apple cart. You didn't care enough for me to even try. I thought you might have, but your abhorrence of risk far outweighed any feelings you had for me."

Another step. "That's not the way it was."

The memory of it, every breath, every touch, every second had burned itself into his memory and refused to leave no matter how often he tried to banish it. He hadn't set her aside because he feared the risk. He had set her aside to protect her from the consequences. Society would never countenance a match between the two of them. She would be whispered about, maligned, shunned by the only world she knew. He could not do that to her.

Another step.

"Then tell me," she said. "Tell me the way of it."

But he didn't. He couldn't.

"And what of you? You take me to task for my decisions, but what of yours, chasing after Lord Selward with a desperation that does not become you." She gasped and he should have stopped but he didn't. "Do you love him so much that you are willing to risk your own safety—your life—to gain his attentions? And for what?"

"For—" She stopped. Hesitated. Why? What was she holding back? There had to be something. Something that explained why someone as vibrant and alive as Rebecca would trade her future happiness for the title of Countess and marriage to a man who did not possess one iota of the passion he'd discovered when she kissed him.

"What is it? Tell me."

"He is a means to an end!"

Whatever he had expected, it wasn't that. "A what?"

She shook her head. "It is Father's will. There are stipulations in it that I must adhere to or Mother and I lose everything."

The air stilled around him. The daily noises outside on the street beyond went silent and blood thrummed in his veins.

"Then...you don't love him?"

She glanced down at the tip of her shoes where mud caked at the toes. "No. I thought I did, in the beginning. But then I got to know him and..." Her voice trailed off and she shrugged.

"Then why marry him?"

"Father's will states that I must marry a titled lord, or his first son. If I do not, all of his unentailed property, which was to be part of my dowry, will go to his mistress." She said the last word with a twist of her lips. Nick had told him of the late Earl's mistress, though not the specific details of the will that could leave the woman with such a boon should Rebecca not capitulate to her father's wishes. The late Lord Blackbourne had always been a bastard determined to control everyone around him, but attaching such conditions to his will, forcing his daughter into a life she did not want, went beyond cruel.

Worse still that Marcus could do nothing to save her from it. He did not possess the necessary title. Lord Selward did. Knots twisted in his stomach and a sense of abject helplessness invaded his veins.

He stepped closer to offer comfort. It was all he had.

"But why Selward? Can you not find a gentleman more suited to you?"

"I did," she told him, glancing up so he saw the sheen of tears in her eyes and his heart squeezed, caught in the talons of fate as it mocked him without mercy. "But he did not want me."

Except that he had. Did still. He wanted her with every ounce of his being and then some. He wanted her in a way that went beyond the physical and settled in the deepest recesses of his heart. He wanted her body, mind and soul. But he could not have her. Not then and especially not now.

"Either way," she said. "I do not have the luxury of time. Father's will states I must marry before my next birthday."

"But that's only three months away."

She nodded. Likely she had it down to the day, the hour. "I do not have time to begin a courtship anew. I need to convince Lord Selward—"

"But your brother will take care of you—" He would take care of her, though perhaps not in the grand style she was accustomed to, but she shook her head before he finished speaking.

"Neither Mother nor I wish to be a burden, a poor relation, dependent on Nicholas for every crumb we eat and every new dress we buy. I know he would do it without hesitation and nary a blink and I love him all the more for it, but it's more than that. Much of the unentailed property came to Father through Mother's dowry. She gave up much to marry Father and now, with her family gone, this is all that's left of her history, her memories. I cannot stand by and watch her lose it—especially to this *mistress*. Not if it is in my power to prevent it."

Determination blazed in the silver of her eyes as she spoke each word with conviction and purpose. Marcus had never admired her courage more. Or hated it in equal measure. But surely Lady Blackbourne would not expect this of her only daughter.

He closed the gap between them, hoping to make her see sense, to understand there had to be another way that didn't involve her bartering her future for brick and mortar, or someone else's memories.

He lifted a hand and brushed at the trail of tears that had begun to dry on her cheek. "Would your mother consign you to a life with Selward in order to hang onto these memories?"

"No. She would never ask such a thing. But I am not doing it because she asked, I am doing it because she deserves better than what she had. Because I cannot live with the guilt knowing my failure took it away from her. That is why I requested your assistance in procuring a proposal from Lord Selward. I would not have involved you otherwise, but I needed someone I trusted."

He hated to see her like this, planning her future out with clear, calculated logic as if life was meant to be lived in a step-by-step fashion; things falling into place simply because one had planned it.

Though wasn't he guilty of that too? Hadn't he done the same thing before a knife had sliced into his gut and taught him that all the plans in the world, all the careful, calculated logic meant nothing? That fate had its own plan and cared little for the desires of mere mortals.

Marcus wanted to say more, to somehow convince her she was in the wrong; that there was another way, but there wasn't. Even as his mind sped through and cast out scenario after implausible scenario, the truth of it could not be refuted.

She had set her course and he could offer nothing to remove her from it.

His thumb caressed her cheekbone. "If I were a lord, I would—"

She took his hand and brought it to her lips, pressing her mouth against the backs of his fingers. A sad smile pulled at the corners of her mouth but not enough to stop the slight tremble in her lower lip. "I know. If you were, I would let you."

And that was all that was said. No declarations, no irrefutable statements. Just a deep understanding that what had started with a kiss a year ago—perhaps even before—had quietly built into an unbreakable bond. Piece by piece, day by day. But in the end, even that could not save them. Save her. Fate, it seemed, would not be denied.

Hang fate.

Marcus slipped his hand from hers and tilted her chin to capture her mouth. Memories paled in comparison to the reality of her lips on his, moving, searching. She gasped but did not pull away, then her body leaned into him and he wrapped her in his arms wishing he could protect her from the future that awaited her. He kissed her with a desperation that burned through every vein in his body and pulsed with every beat of his heart.

His hand buried in her hair and held her there, heedless of the mud and muck that clung to her dress and stained his own clothing. He teased her, tasted her and she responded in kind, quick to learn, to let her own passionate nature free of its constraints until they were both locked in an embrace he had dreamed of for the past year. Heat raged through his body like a river after the rain, washing everything else away—the room, the mud, the past, the future. All of it evaporated until there was only this moment, this kiss. This woman.

"Rebecca!"

Lady Blackbourne's voice carried down the long hallway and reached Marcus from far away, breaking through the fever ravaging his brain and body. He pulled away, resting his forehead against hers as their breaths came in gulps. She grabbed his wrist where his hand cupped her face and clung to him with a significance he understood. He wanted to save her. She wished he could.

Marry me.

He wanted to say the words, but stayed his tongue. She could not. *Would* not.

For several long heartbeats they stood as they were, staring at each other. Sadness and the remnants of passion imprinted across her lovely features.

"I am sorry," she whispered. She moved slightly and pressed her lips against his cheek, then quickly stepped away. He shivered from her absence as if he'd been tossed into the cool water of the Thames. She hurried from the room, toward the mother she meant to save, regardless of the expense to herself.

He let her go, unable to offer anything that would stop her.

Chapter Nine

September 20th

How appreciative I am for the wind the sea brings in each day as the last of the summer heat beats down without compromise. The unholy illness that gripped me early on has abated for the most part, though I find myself so very tired most days. The swelling has begun to show and I have had to let out my dresses. Mother has said little, but I catch her watching me when she thinks I do not see. Sometimes with sadness, other times with regret. I despise the worry and upset I have caused her. I wish I could make it go away. If only she knew how much. How it haunts me every time I shut my eyes. But I cannot speak to her of it. And I cannot undo what was done. Oh, how I wish I could.

The diary entry struck close to home. Marcus's own despair mirrored that of the young woman's and he understood only too well the price of folly, the understanding that once it was done there was no going back.

He should not have kissed Rebecca, but if he expected regret to wash over him, he'd be waiting a long time. What if he hadn't stopped? What if her mother had not called from down the hall and interrupted them? Would he have come to his senses, stopped the madness that had engulfed them in that moment?

No.

He closed the journal.

What had he been thinking?

He hadn't. Thought had never entered into it. Anger, relief, fear—those were the emotions running riot through him when he'd taken her into his arms and lowered his mouth to hers.

And need.

Yes, need. He'd needed her. Needed to touch her. Needed to convince her to not throw her life away on Selward.

But to what end? He was not a lord and there was not a damn thing he could do to change that one, simple fact. No matter the money in his bank accounts or the land offered him by Lord Franklyn. No matter that he had the loyal friendship of her brother and Spence. No matter that her mother and Lord and Lady Ellesmere considered him a part of their family.

He was not a lord.

He pushed the journal away until it butted up against the deed to Northill Hall that still rested on the table. He had yet to return it. Yet to refuse Lord Franklyn's offer of the property for the paltry sum of one pound. Pride had kept him from signing the documents, though now pride seemed cold comfort. He had accused Rebecca of not taking a true risk, yet neither had he. Not really. He railed at the restlessness that had plagued him these past few months and yet balked at the solution only a mere signature away.

He made excuses. He owed his loyalty to Lord Ellesmere

for all he'd been given. He had responsibilities. He loved his work. The list went on and on. But the truth of it was, he was afraid. He had fallen into the unknown before and the memories of it plagued him to this day.

Sometimes you need to take a risk.

Did he dare?

His fingers toyed with the edge of the documents before he pushed them away with an angry breath. What was the point? He had nothing to risk for. Tomorrow he would return the papers to Lord Franklyn with his regrets.

Tomorrow for certain.

"Sir?"

Marcus glanced up to where Fenton, the Ellesmere butler, hovered at the door. The man moved with the silence of a wraith. "Yes, Fenton?"

"A Mr. Cosgrove is here to see you? He came through the servants' entrance." Fenton said the words as if they meant nothing, but the one raised eyebrow spoke volumes with respect to his curiosity over the matter of why Lord Ellesmere's man of business would be entertaining a servant in the middle of the day. Or any time of the day for that matter, given the hiring of household servants was left to the providence of Fenton and Mrs. Faraday.

"Please show him in and have tea and refreshments brought." He hadn't eaten since breakfast and his stomach gnawed at him with distinct displeasure.

Fenton's eyebrows slowly lowered and he nodded once before retreating down the hallway. Or, at least Marcus assumed he had, as no footsteps were actually heard. Did the man wrap his shoes in cotton cloth?

Mr. Cosgrove arrived a moment later, his hat clenched tightly in one hand—his only hand. The space where his other arm should have been remained empty, the sleeve of his suit neatly folded and pinned.

Marcus blinked, unsure if he should withdraw his own where he'd held it out to shake with Mr. Cosgrove, but before he could, the former Walkerton steward tucked the hat beneath his existing arm in a deft movement and extended his hand. He possessed a strong grip. There was nothing frail about the older man, save for a slight frame and the hint of gauntness that showed under the arc of his cheekbones before being swallowed up by a well-trimmed, snow-white beard. It appeared he had made an attempt to tame the thick waves of hair that drifted around his head like a cloud, but they were less willing to comply.

"I shall assume by the surprise on your face that Miss Caldwell did not forewarn you I lacked an appendage."

The man's voice sounded as if it scratched over sand on its way out of his throat and a rumble waited just beyond. Though his tone carried a deep sense of wisdom within it, humor lingered behind his blue eyes.

"She did not," Marcus admitted. He waved to the table near the window. "Please, have a seat."

His mind worked quickly, discerning whether the lack of an arm would be of much concern, but as he had not yet determined whether or not he planned on hiring the man, he let the matter drop. It wasn't just the man's ability to work that interested him, but his former employer as well.

Mr. Cosgrove settled himself into one of the chairs at the table by the window and Marcus took the one across from him. Upon closer inspection, the telltale signs of wear and tear were evident on the man's suit. The cuff of his jacket hand worn thin and signs of darning showed in other areas, though the work had been expertly done and barely noticeable until one was up close. Regardless of the state of his clothing, which belied the hard times he'd fallen upon, Cosgrove carried himself with pride, unbroken by his circumstances. It spoke volumes to the man's character in Marcus's estimation and he took an instant liking to him.

"Can I assume the lack of appendage is the reason Lord Walkerton chose not to reinstate you upon your return from service to our country?"

"That is the reason he gave." His answer left the impression there was more to the story that went unsaid.

"How did you lose it?"

"During a skirmish, my unit was ambushed. We managed to prevail but we lost many a good man, and I my arm, after being shot. Infection had set in and I was given the choice to lose my arm or my life. I had a young daughter at the time. I did not think she'd take kindly to me dying, so I told them to take my arm."

"And it cost you your livelihood."

Cosgrove neither confirmed nor denied the claim. "I've managed to pick up work here and there, but most people see the missing limb and assume I am unable to perform a job. I have managed to scrape by, though it has been tough at times, I won't lie. My daughter has been forced to find employment instead of a proper husband so that we can keep food in our bellies and a roof over our heads."

"And your wife?"

"Gone. Madalene, my daughter, stayed with her aunt until my return from the war, but the aunt has since passed on as well. It is just the two of us now."

"And you are hoping to find steady work?"

"As any honorable man should. Madalene's a good girl. She deserves a better life than living hand to mouth. There have been times, I'm ashamed to say, that I have resorted to begging on the streets to put food on the table when decent work could not be found. But I am determined to find a permanent position. Maddie is but twenty and pretty as a summer's day. I won't see her life go to waste if it is in my power to prevent it"

The older man's voice filled with love and fierce determination when he spoke of his daughter and somewhere deep inside the curious question arose, would Marcus's mother have done the same for him? Not Mary Bowen, but the author of the journal. If she had not abandoned him to others, would she speak his name with the same parental love as Cosgrove did his daughter? Or would she speak of him with shame and regret? Was that why she'd abandoned him? Because she could not endure the constant reminder of her fall from grace? Or did she believe he would have a better life than what she was able to provide?

Marcus cleared his mind of the thought, though it lingered in the air around him like a half-remembered dream.

"Your determination is very commendable. Tell me, when you were with Lord Walkerton, what were your duties?"

"I was steward to his country seat, Westcombe Court, as my father was before me and his before him. The Cosgroves have given three generations of stewardship to the lordships of Walkerton."

"And how was it you left the position to enlist in the war?"

"His lordship decided to enlist as an officer in the British Army. He insisted I enlist as well as his soldier-servant."

"And you agreed?"

"I was not given much in the way of choice. He promised to keep Mrs. Cosgrove and Maddie in a small home on the estate and ensure they were cared for until we returned."

"I see. And did he?"

"He did."

"How long were you away for?"

"It was '04 when we enlisted. We came and went over the years. Lord Walkerton received several furloughs. As heir, he should not have enlisted at all, but he often looked for ways to shirk his duties, I'm sad to say. I believe he was more interested in playing the dashing hero than in running the estates. He did not think any true harm would come to him. He had a rather romanticized idea of what war was. When his ideas proved false, he preferred to cower rather than put himself in harm's way."

"Though he did not have any difficulty if you did?"

Cosgrove lifted the shoulder of the missing limb. "Maddie saw me sporadically, as did her mother. She spent her early years knowing little of me save for the letters I sent. When we returned in 1814 for another furlough, Lord Walkerton feigned illness and when it came time to return, he sent me in his stead."

"Could he do that?" Marcus had little knowledge of how the military worked, having been only a boy during the Napoleonic Wars.

Again, Cosgrove shrugged. Sun shone in through the window and lit the older man's white hair, revealing hints of the blonde it had once been. Though thin lines marked his face, Marcus realized he was not as old as he'd originally perceived. Perhaps fifty-five, maybe a little more.

"No one questioned it and where my future employment depended upon my compliance, I went. It was during the Battle of Waterloo that I sustained my injury and when I was well enough, I returned home. Upon my arrival, I was dismissed."

"Why?"

Cosgrove's gaze left Marcus and he glanced out the window for a moment, the first hint of discomfort given, as if he wanted to choose his words carefully before he spoke them. "We had a disagreement over his treatment of one of the maids. It became heated and when I refused to back down in my opinions, he dismissed me without reference."

"But without a reference—"

"I had no hope of obtaining another similar position. The lack of an arm did not help my circumstances."

"And so here you are."

"And so here I am."

The man's story shook Marcus, reminding him of how quickly a man's fortunes could turn when he did not have an inheritance or title to fall back on. He could just as easily be Cosgrove if a bastard as cowardly as Walkerton had employed him.

"What were the circumstances regarding the other employee?"

Again, Cosgrove hesitated before he spoke. "There was a young maid—Alma, her name was. A sweet girl. I often believed Walkerton took advantage of her, but she was too timid to speak against him. While I was away, she finally worked up the courage to refuse his advances. In return, he accused her of stealing from him and dismissed her."

"Was there any evidence to support the claim of theft?"

Cosgrove shook his head. "The housekeeper searched her room but nothing was found. When I discovered this, I raised my objections. But Lord Walkerton was adamant and refused to change his decision."

"What was it she was accused of stealing?"

"A watch."

Marcus stilled and his heart banged against his ribs until each beat became more painful than the last. "May I show you something?"

The older man's brow dipped slightly. "You may."

Marcus rose and walked back to his desk, opening the top drawer. He stared down at the watch and hesitated. A part of him rejected the idea that the watch his mother had sent could be the same one Cosgrove spoke of, yet Rebecca had been adamant it was the Walkerton crest engraved on the outside.

Was she right?

He picked up the watch and returned to the table, setting it in front of the former steward.

"Do you recognize this?"

Cosgrove lifted the timepiece in his hand and turned it over. His mouth pulled into a grim line and his sharp gaze lifted to meet Marcus's. "Yes."

He answered with a question of his own. "Is that the Walkerton crest?"

"It is."

"Is this the item the maid was accused of stealing?"

His calloused thumb rubbed against the worn engravings. "It is. How did you come by it?"

"It was left to me by someone who, near as I can fathom, had no reason to have it in their possession. Do you know what happened to Alma?" Was this maid his mother? It didn't make sense. The journal read as if written by a lady of quality. Someone educated and refined. Had he assumed wrongly? Could it have been the maid, after all? And if so, how had she ended up at Braemore and, if so, where was she now?

Cosgrove stared at the cracked glass for a moment. "Alma fell upon hard times as you can imagine. A charge of theft, regardless of how unfounded, made it impossible for her to find respectable work and so she turned to less reputable ways to survive."

The former steward set the watch onto the table and pushed it toward Marcus with his fingertips as if it was tainted. "I wanted to help, but I could barely afford to put food on my own table and I had Maddie to consider. I lost track of Alma after a bit, but I heard from others she had not lasted long in that life." He shook his head and sadness invaded his blue eyes. "She had far too gentle a nature for such work."

"Then you're certain she is dead?"

He nodded. "They buried her in a pauper's grave."

The idea soured Marcus's gut. Walkerton seemed to have

no compunction about tossing people out like they held no more value than last week's news. It sickened him.

"And you're certain this is the watch in question?"

Cosgrove nodded. "It had been commissioned by the second Lord Walkerton and he passed it down to his son, who then passed it onto his, until it came into the possession of the current Lord Walkerton."

Confusion pulled at Marcus's brow. Based on Cosgrove's information, it was obvious Alma had not stolen the watch, nor authored the journal. How, then, had Mary Bowen come to have it in her possession? Had the woman who gave birth to him had an association with Walkerton? An illicit dalliance, perhaps, that had landed her in such a state? But why would she take the watch? Or if Walkerton gifted it to her, why did he then claim the maid had stolen it?

He shook his head. The entire matter remained a mystery he could not solve. Though one piece of the puzzle had become clear.

Lord Walkerton could possibly be the man who'd fathered him.

His stomach churned at such a prospect.

He picked the watch up and slid it into his jacket pocket. "Thank you, Mr. Cosgrove. I appreciate your honesty and what information you have been able to give. Can I trust you to keep this conversation between us?"

Mr. Cosgrove stood. "You may, sir. I hope you find the answers you seek. Now, if I might beg your leave, there is still daylight left and I need to continue my search for work if I am to put food on the table this evening."

Marcus quickly rose to his feet. "Forgive me. I should have said something sooner. I wish to offer you employment, Mr. Cosgrove. I cannot say at this moment what the position will be. I need to look at the estates and see where your skills will best suit. Until then, I will pay you a retainer. A good faith gesture."

"Your word is enough, sir."

Marcus shook his head, compelled to right a wrong he had no part in. "Which you have along with the retainer to hold you over until I can find the proper placement."

Mr. Cosgrove's shoulders drooped, then lifted again as if his body had heaved a sigh of much needed relief. "I accept then, sir. Most heartily and with much gratitude."

Marcus smiled and shook Mr. Cosgrove's hand then went to his desk and wrote the man a bank note. "I will be in touch, very soon."

As the older man walked out onto the street, his step appeared much spryer than when he had walked in. It did Marcus's heart good to know he had helped. It was clear Cosgrove was a good man through and through. Yet beneath his good feelings, questions lingered. Marcus touched his pocket where the watch resided.

How had the watch fallen into his mother's possession?

And was he the bastard son of the Earl of Walkerton?

Chapter Ten

Rebecca tried not to fidget during the recitation given by Lady Prudence, but the entire piece left her ears pleading for mercy. How could the girl take daily lessons on her violin and *still* sound as if she were massacring each note? It went beyond all comprehension. Regardless, the unmitigated relief experienced once the impromptu concert ended left Rebecca seeking the solace of the small garden as even the din of conversation coming from the drawing room proved too much for her tender ears.

Lady Martindale, mother of the aforementioned butcher of all things musical, had a small but pretty garden that bloomed in all different colors of the rainbow. Its bounty filled the June afternoon with a pleasantly sweet scent that blocked out the stench of coal and smog that sometimes drifted in from the city beyond. If Rebecca closed her eyes and tilted her head back to feel the warmth of the sun on her skin, she could almost imagine she was at Sheridan Park once more.

In another garden, behind a certain statue, kissing a certain man.

Her eyes snapped open.

No. She would not think of that.

A lofty goal, though not one she had succeeded at since the last kiss. It had been even more potent than the first. It resurrected every feeling she had tried to squash, every attempt to convince herself the kiss had resulted from nothing more than the grief she had experienced over Father's death. But it was a lie. She'd known in her heart her feelings for Marcus were true, yet somehow it had become easier to pretend otherwise. Easier to block out the disappointment. The regret. The fact that it could never be.

But Marcus's latest kiss had robbed her of that. Now, there was no going back. No pretending her heart didn't demand its due.

Perhaps if she escaped to the countryside—but no. Marcus had been such a mainstay in their lives, there was not a room on the large estate where his presence had not been imprinted, save her own bedchamber—the one room she wished to see him in most of all.

The idea shocked her, coming unbidden. Though it wasn't the first time. Marcus stirred her desires, fuelled her daydreams, and made her long for things she could not name.

How did a kiss, a touching of the lips, a melding of bodies, fire her blood until it boiled, until the heat of it flowed from the roots of her hair to the tips of her toes? She could not get close enough to him and the press of his body against hers made her long shamefully for the layers of their clothing to be stripped away so she might feel his skin against hers. The emotions he evoked frightened her because they were everything she wanted. Everything she had ever dreamed of.

And the one thing she could not have.

"I am of the strong opinion that there are some instances in which no amount of practice will improve a situation."

Rebecca turned toward the intruding voice and shielded her eyes against the sunlight as Miss Eugenie Caldwell took a seat on the bench next to her. Rebecca had seen Miss Caldwell within the group attending the performance—for lack of a better word—but they had not spoken. In truth, they had barely said a word to each other since the engagement debacle with her brother a year earlier.

Rebecca had not thought too much of it, to be truthful. They had never been bosom bows after all, but she had attempted to cultivate a friendship with the woman her brother had been set to marry. It had proven a bit of a Herculean task. Eugenie Caldwell did not necessarily exude warmth, though as she got to know her, Rebecca had the sense it was not so much that Eugenie was a cold person, but more that she was so tightly wound no one could break through the barrier to see what hid beneath. At least, Rebecca had never been able to.

After the broken engagement with Nicholas, however, she and Eugenie had little to do with one another. Though Eugenie had sent a nice note to her upon the death of Father and she had responded with a proper thank you, awkwardness had invaded their acquaintance and it became easier to simply avoid one another rather than try to breach it.

Which is why it took her by surprise to find Eugenie seeking her out now. "Yes, indeed. I think perhaps Lady Prudence should attempt a different instrument. The wood blocks, perhaps."

Eugenie smiled—at least as much as Eugenie ever smiled—but a small bit of it warmed her brown eyes if only briefly.

"I understand you had a bit of a scare at the Park the other day."

Heat rushed to Rebecca's cheeks. "Yes, it was rather frightening." Not to mention mortifying. Embarrassing. Humiliating.

"I am also told Lord Selward was beside himself over the

notion you could have been grievously injured and is determined to make it up to you."

Rebecca had been equally determined to hide away for the rest of the Season, certain any hope she had in regards to Lord Selward had ended. Had Mother not suggested hiding away in her room was not the best way to capture a proposal, she might still be there. But the suggestion reminded Rebecca of why a proposal from the future earl was so important. For Mother. For her memories and her heritage.

As it turned out, Lord Selward came by the house to ensure her good health and reiterate his own wish that she not keep herself locked away. He took full responsibility and ensured everyone was made aware of it. He should have taken better care of her, as Mr. Bowen intimated, and he was overcome with guilt that he had not.

Guilt plagued her as well, for completely different reasons. For as solicitous as Lord Selward behaved, and despite how desperate she was for his proposal, she could not look at him without wishing for all the world it was another man sitting there. Another man whose attention she commanded.

It had been an odd thing to speak to the man she planned to marry while the taste of another man still teased the tip of her tongue.

Rebecca cleared her throat and shoved the memory away. She would not deal with this now. Mostly because she did not know *how* to deal with it. How did one go into a marriage with one man when another held her heart?

Perhaps she could ask Mother for advice, but she would only counsel her to follow her heart above all else. That ignoring one's heart brought only strife. But so would losing everything her mother held dear.

Putting Rebecca in the proverbial middle between a rock and a hard place.

She refocused her attention back on Eugenie. "It was most

kind of Lord Selward to say so and he has been most attentive."

Eugenie folded her hands in her lap, her back ramrod straight as if it took no effort at all. Rebecca, on the other hand, despite years of comportment training, wished to slouch, even just a little.

"I also understand my sister, Rosalind, has spoken to Mr. Bowen in her endeavor to find employment for those who have fallen on hard times." Disapproval edged Eugenie's voice.

"Yes. It's a very good cause, I think. You must be proud of her generous nature. The good work she does is an inspiration to the rest of us."

"Indeed, though such behavior does not come without a price."

"A price?"

Eugenie nodded. "Mother worries her ferocity toward helping the under-privileged and wrongly treated eclipses her wish to marry to such a degree the latter will never happen. My dear sister does nothing to thwart this notion and I fear eventually it will come back to haunt her."

"In what way?"

Eugenie glanced down at her gloves and rubbed her thumb along the finger on her opposite hand. "Am I wrong in assuming Lady Huntsleigh's introduction of Mr. Bowen to Rosalind was in the hopes of making a possible match?"

Rebecca didn't know quite how to answer. Caelie had mentioned to her that Huntsleigh had thought them well-suited, but in the end, it had been she who had asked Rosalind to join them. "I'm afraid the invitation was my doing. She had suggested to me Mr. Bowen might be able to help her with the charity. Although, I believe Lady Huntsleigh thought the two might strike up a friendship."

"Which did not happen, did it?"

"I'm sure they liked each other just fine." But when

Eugenie gave her a knowing look, Rebecca gave up the pretense of politeness. "But no, I do not think there was an attraction."

How odd to speak of Marcus in such a way, as if he were meant for someone else, when in her heart, he had already been claimed. A claim she had no right to make.

"That is my fear."

"That she and Mr. Bowen will not be attracted to one another?"

Eugenie waved a hand in the air. "Not Mr. Bowen in particular, but anyone. It is only a matter of time before her diligence toward her causes drives even the most lenient of gentleman away. Many in our circles have already begun to look at her dubiously. Soon, she will make herself a pariah and no one will pay much attention to her or her cause. I have tried to speak to about it, suggest she marry first. A married woman has much more leniency in these matters, does she not? But she will not listen to my counsel."

True concern laced Eugenie's voice. Surprising, given her carefully modulated tone rarely conveyed any emotion at all, regardless the subject.

"You think people will turn their back on her?"

"I do. You know how society is. Everything is to be done in such a manner as to avoid the appearance of anything scandalous. Those of us yet to marry must comport ourselves without even the smallest hint of scandal or impropriety if we wish to make a proper marriage."

Unlike Rebecca, who, in an effort to capture a proposal from a man she did not love, had flown from the saddle of a horse she did not want to be on, landed, skirts high, in a mud puddle then preceded to kiss her rescuer until her toes curled in her muddy slippers and her body wished to do so much more.

Good heavens! Was scandalous behavior an inheritable

trait? Was this what Father had meant to keep her from with his strict rules of conduct and comportment? Were Eugenie's words as much a warning to Rebecca as her younger sister?

"Is there anything I can do?"

"I doubt it." Eugenie sighed and Rebecca's eyes widened. When had Eugenie Caldwell ever *sighed*? The situation must be dire indeed!

"Because of what happened in the park?" Mother and Lord Selward had both tried to tell her it wasn't as bad as she imagined and so she had shrugged off the stares as she'd entered Lady Martindale's drawing room. But what if they were wrong? What if they were only placating her and Lord Selward's visit had been out of guilt and not because he had any intention of offering a proposal? "Have I have ruined my reputation completely?"

Eugenie glanced at her, her dark eyebrows furrowed. "You? No. I think you will come away from the incident at the park relatively unscathed. You have, after all, conducted yourself in a perfectly agreeable manner up until that point, and clearly the fault of the incident did not rest on your shoulders. But that is not what brought me here to speak with you."

"It isn't?"

Eugenie shook her head and the sunlight caught its glossy darkness and pulled out strands of mahogany. "I have heard a piece of news I thought you might be interested in."

Rebecca gasped then smiled. "Miss Caldwell, are you partaking in gossip!"

Eugenie pursed her lips and slid Rebecca a stern look. "It is not gossip. Gossip is for those with nothing better to do with their time. This is *news*."

"Of course. How foolish of me."

"I overheard—"

"If you overheard doesn't that make it gossip?"

Again, the pursed lips. "Do you wish to hear what I have to tell you, or not?"

Rebecca suppressed a laugh and primly folded her hands in her lap and straightened her posture. "By all means. Please, continue."

Eugenie cleared her throat lightly. "As I was saying, it has come to my attention that Lord Selward's father, Lord Walkerton, is returning to England. Lady Herringsby, who is the cousin to Lady Walkerton, indicated Lord Selward had received word his lordship is expected within the week. Lady Herringsby believes his return is due to his son's plans to offer for a wife by Season's end."

"Truly?"

"This is what I have heard. I cannot claim to know the amount of truth attached to it, as it is—"

"Gossip?"

Eugenie's shoulders dropped, though only slightly and only for a second. "Really, Lady Rebecca, must you be so difficult?"

"Really, Miss Caldwell, must you be so proper?"

But any humor in the statement was lost on Eugenie. "It is such propriety that will afford me a good marriage with a proper gentleman." She shot Rebecca a sideways glance. "We are not all in possession of a sizeable dowry."

Rebecca lost her grin. The Caldwell women were in rather desperate need of husbands as their father had no male heirs to care for them when he was gone. Given her own predicament, she could sympathize. Her sizable dowry would be a thing of the past should she not find her own proper husband to marry within the next few weeks. But even if she failed, she had Nicholas to fall back on. Eugenie and her sisters had no one.

She reached over and patted Eugenie's hand, ignoring the discomfort it caused the other woman. "Forgive me. And thank you for telling me. I wish you all the best, I hope you know that."

"You're quite welcome." Eugenie stood and looked across the garden avoiding Rebecca's gaze. "I hope you get what you wish for as well."

Rebecca nodded but said nothing. What she wished for and what she needed were two entirely different things.

Chapter Eleven

October 14*th*

How strange to think of this little human growing in my womb, that one day they will be on the outside, looking to me for guidance. For answers. And what shall I tell them? What can I tell them? Not the truth. Such innocence does not need to know the ugliness of the world.

Perhaps instead I should beg their forgiveness for thrusting them into a world not of their making. A world so harshly unforgiving. How can I force them to carry the scourge of events they had no part in?

I had hoped Braemore would give me the answers. That they would come to me on the salt wind and rustle through my hair. But while the wind has been forthcoming, no answers ride on its tail. I am no closer to a decision now than when I arrived. Mother continues to hover, to hope, but I have no news to give her.

Braemore.

The name of Marcus's home kept appearing, leaving no doubt that was where the authoress resided at the time of the writing and how his mother—Mary—had come to know her.

Marcus closed the journal and walked the floor of his study, unable to settle. His mind worked furiously, asking questions he had no answer to. Who was the authoress? What ugliness did she refer to? And where was she now, this woman? His mother.

The quest to find answers gave him no peace and he could not rid himself of a sense of disloyalty, as if searching for the truth betrayed every memory he had of Mary Bowen—of her kindness, her gentle nature, her loving arms. She had cared for him for as long as she was able and when illness came, she'd done her best to see he did not end up in an orphanage or workhouse. How could she have known what her brother intended?

In the end, it had been Mary Bowen who had sent him the tools to discover the truth.

If only she'd made it easier to unravel.

The woman who wrote the journal had been the one to give birth to him. Of that, he was certain. Yet, for whatever reason, she had abandoned him, left him behind at Braemore Manor to be raised by the Bowens.

And if it happened at Braemore Manor, then Lady Ellesmere must have known the woman's identity. Surely his mother would never have taken someone in without the express permission of her employer.

Which meant if Marcus wanted answers, he must speak with Lady Ellesmere. But was it worth it? Did he wish to rouse such skeletons from their resting place or was it best to leave them be?

As much as he searched for the truth of his past, to put the doubts and questions to rest, he feared it. The truth would change everything. How could it not? If the author of the journal was his mother, it was obvious she had been compromised and he born on the wrong side of the blanket. Had Walkerton been involved? Was that how he came by the watch? Had it been a token of his affection or a promise never upheld? Or a parting gift as she was shuttled out the door? At the time of Marcus's birth, Walkerton had already been married to Lord Selward's mother.

The truth of his impending birth had been kept secret, worthy of shame—a shame meant to stay buried beneath the subterfuge piled atop it.

But it had not. His mother had handed him a shovel and left the decision of whether to excavate it his hands.

He debated his choices, though in his mind only one existed.

He wanted the truth. To know his true identity and where he came from.

Who he came from.

He dismissed the idea of speaking to Lord Ellesmere on the matter. The man had a long held belief that scandal should be avoided at all costs. His own family had steeped themselves in it, all of his brothers coming to rather disreputable ends. His own son and daughter-in-law, Spence's parents, had died in a shocking accident when the late Lady Huntsleigh had taken Spence and tried to leave her husband for another man.

No, asking Lord Ellesmere to help him uncover a past others had put much effort into burying was not the way to go.

It would have to be Lady Ellesmere.

He let out a long sigh and stood in front of the window that faced out onto the street. His reflection stared back and he studied it. Dark hair, dark eyes, tall, though not overly so, with a lean, solid build. He looked nothing like his parents. Though they had greyed by the time most of his memories formed, he had some recollection of his father having blonde hair, his mother light brown. Each had possessed blue eyes. His mother had been short with a thick, sturdy build and round, pleasant face, while his father had been tall and reed thin, his features fine and narrow.

Marcus tilted his head to one side. His own face consisted of sharp angles and defined strokes with a full mouth that appeared to be neither smiling nor frowning, a serious brow and a straight nose. Not a bad face, he supposed. But not a face that resembled either Mother or Father.

With a deep breath, Marcus turned away from his reflection and went in search of the woman who had raised him for most of his life. He found her in the solar, reclined on the settee with a pair of knitting needles in her hands. They clicked and clacked in a steady rhythm, the only sound to penetrate the quiet of the room. Next to her on the chair, a small grey kitten swatted at the yarn stretching from the needles to the ball in her lap.

"Lady Ellesmere?" She'd requested from the beginning that he call her Grandmama as Spence did, but he'd resisted, afraid to grow too comfortable lest the winds of change blow him off course once again. He had not wanted to become too attached or to assume a position he had no right to. He was not their grandson. He was nothing to them. And they could turn him out as quickly as they'd brought him in. After awhile, Lady Ellesmere stopped making the request, though her actions remained as they had always been—warm and loving. It was for this reason alone he hesitated now, afraid of causing her upset.

"Marcus, my dear. Come in." She lowered the needles to her lap.

He took a fortifying breath and stepped into the room. "I see you have a new friend."

Lady Ellesmere often took in strays from the mews, much to Lord Ellesmere's dismay.

She smiled and stroked the kitten. "This is Bouncer. The poor thing was abandoned by his mother, and I just could not convince myself to leave him to his fate."

Such had been his own circumstances. Another stray Lady Ellesmere had rescued from fate. What would his life had been like had she not arrived that day and uttered those words to his aunt? Would he have survived childhood? It made the questions he must ask her now weigh heavy on his heart. He did not want her to think him ungrateful for all she and Lord Ellesmere had done.

"I wondered if I may speak with you about something."

"Of course, Marcus. Come and sit. You have been so busy of late; I have not had a minute to spend with you. You cannot push yourself so hard, my dear. You are still healing from your wounds."

She delivered the admonishment with equal doses of worry and warmth. Marcus's heart twisted. "I am fully healed, my lady. You need not worry after my health."

"You may as well ask the sun not to rise."

He smiled, but no joy filled his heart. Lady Ellesmere had been by his bedside night and day after the stabbing, seeing to his care with the ferocity of a mother bear. Asking her these questions now felt like a betrayal to everything she'd done for him. Yet how could he not ask them? How could he live each day knowing the truth was within his grasp and yet he did not reach for it?

He took the straight back chair closest to her, the hard wood construction pressing through the fine wool of his jacket. He hesitated a moment, trying to determine the best way to introduce the sensitive subject.

"From the grave expression on your face, may I assume this conversation is of a serious nature?" Lady Ellesmere was one of the few who seemed able to tell his serious expression from his regular one. Rebecca was the other, though he pushed that thought away. He had enough to contend with without bringing thoughts of her into the mix.

"It is."

"Are you here to tell me you have chosen a bride? I understand you've been introduced to one of the Caldwell girls. Can I have hope there?"

He laughed lightly. Since Spence's marriage to Caelie several months earlier, Lady Ellesmere had turned her matchmaking attentions to him. He hated to disappoint, for even if he had an interest in Miss Caldwell—which he did not—how could he marry anyone without knowing who he was, where he came from, and what was attached to it—good or bad.

"I'm afraid not."

"What am I to do with you, Marcus?" She sighed but her pale blue eyes sparkled. How he hated to take that away from her.

He gripped his hands together and leaned forward resting his forearms against his thighs. "I received a package from Cornwall last week." Had it really been only a week since his world had come crashing down? Since he'd discovered his past was a lie and the woman who tempted him above all else could never be his?

The knitting needles slowed but did not stop. "Cornwall?"

"Yes."

"Business regarding Braemore?"

He shook his head. "Not exactly. It came from a solicitor, a Mr. Wickwire. Or, his daughter, actually. It appears her father passed on and she found it while going through his things. The instructions were for it to be sent to me when I reached my majority, but—" He shrugged.

Lady Ellesmere stopped knitting completely, but did not meet his gaze. Instead, she ran a hand down the small head of Bouncer who continued to lay waste to the trailing string of yarn. A strange tension filled the quiet between them, pregnant with expectation and things not yet said. Outside, the sound of a carriage passing by on the cobbled street drifted up to the open window, then slowly dissipated.

Marcus swallowed. His throat had turned dry. "What can you tell me about my parents?"

"Your parents?" Her grip on the knitting needles tightened. Bouncer's tiny grey paw moved to rest upon Lady Ellesmere's hand as if the tiny animal could sense her growing distress. When she spoke again, her voice lowered. "What did you want to know?"

He shook his head. He wasn't sure how or where to start. "They were older, were they not?"

"Yes. I suppose they were."

"Too old for child-bearing when I came along."

Lady Ellesmere released her hold on the needles and became engrossed in winding the loose yarn around the ball. Bouncer tried to capture the strands but to no avail. "It isn't unheard of for a couple to have a child later in life."

"Not unheard of, but uncommon. Mother and Father had to have been close to fifty when I was born. I didn't realize it at the time; such things didn't mean anything to me as a child. But looking back, I see it differently."

"And why are you looking back now? Does it matter?"

The answer bled through him in swift response.

Yes.

It did matter. He wanted to know. *Needed* to.

"The Bowens were not my true parents, were they?"

"What a silly thing to say," Lady Ellesmere said, her tone colored with a hint of anger and much denial. She unwound the yarn she had just finished wrapping around the ball. "Mary and Edmore loved you very much, Marcus. They cared for you and…and they loved you. What else matters?"

"The truth." He said it plainly, for there was no other way to say it. "The truth matters."

A pinched look tightened the loose skin around Lady Ellesmere's face and she glanced away from the knitting in her lap to the window next to her, then down at Bouncer who had decided to launch a full-scale assault on the yarn.

"Now Bouncer, you leave that alone." The high pitch of her voice strangled the words with tension. She shooed the grey ball of fluff away, but instead of leaving, the kitten nudged at her hand. She scratched between its ears and it purred loud enough to be heard from where Marcus sat. He noted the gesture for what it was, a stall tactic.

"Lady Ellesmere?"

She pursed her lips as if to keep the truth he sought vaulted inside of her. He had been correct in his assumption. She did know something. When she spoke again, her words came as a whisper.

"They loved you as their own."

"Except that I wasn't."

She would not meet his gaze. The purring stopped and when Marcus glanced down he realized her hand had stilled. He pressed on.

"A lady came to stay with them. I suspect she had found herself in an untenable situation—unmarried and with child. Am I correct?"

Bouncer jumped off the settee and hopped from the room, revealing how he came by his name. Marcus watched him go and when his gaze returned to the marchioness, her complexion had paled against the warm sunlight.

"The Bowens loved you. *We* love you. That is the only thing that matters. You are family, Marcus."

"No," he whispered, hating the injury his words caused

her, but understanding the truth of them with a depth he had not before. "I am not."

Her lower lip trembled and guilt stabbed far deeper than the blade of any thief. She took a shuddering breath; pain etched into the lines of her face. Her gaze remained fixed on the window. "Have we done something? Have you been unhappy here?"

He shook his head emphatically. "No, of course not. You and Lord Ellesmere have given me opportunities a boy from my background could never have dreamed of, I will be forever grateful—"

"We do not want your gratitude, Marcus." Anger made her eyes flash. She turned to look at him and strength returned to her voice. "We did not do it for gratitude. We did it because we loved you. And regardless of how you may feel about the matter, you will always be family to us."

Her eyes glistened and she glanced away again as if she could not bear to look upon him and be hurt any further by his questions and opinions. His stomach turned. It was the worst kind of feeling, knowing you had hurt someone who had given you the world. The knife twisted deep until each beat of his heart made the wound bleed all the more. But he needed the truth. Without it, he remained stuck in an unwanted purgatory, the truth just beyond his reach.

Marcus pressed on. "If the lady stayed at Braemore, you must have known her identity. Who was she? Why did she give me to the Bowens?"

"Mary and Edmore were your parents, Marcus. They raised you until their deaths and they did a wonderful job. The fact Mary did not birth you on her own does not change that fact, nor should you say otherwise!"

"I am not saying that!" Marcus sprang to his feet, propelled by his own anger and frustration. Lady Ellesmere jolted at his sudden movement and guilt flooded him once again. He rubbed at his eyes and took a calming breath. "Forgive me. I did not mean to raise my voice. Nor do I mean to diminish what the Bowens did for me. They gave me their name and I wear it proudly. But it is not my true name and they are not my true blood. My entire history has been based on a lie and all I ask is that the truth finally be revealed to me. Who was the lady who stayed at Braemore Manor?" He placed a hand against his chest. "Who am I?"

"You are Marcus Bowen," Lady Ellesmere said, her words laced with urgency. "You are a part of our family. You have people that love you. People who wish you nothing but the best. You had parents who cherished you regardless of where you came from and that is all I have to say on the matter!"

Marcus's hands fisted at his sides. They chased each other in circles.

Lady Ellesmere set her knitting aside on the table next to her and stood. Her chin lifted as she stared up at him, her proud, imperial bearing coming through every pore.

"Nothing good can come of this, Marcus. The past should be left in the past. Digging it up will only taint the future and cause hurt for all involved. I beg you to leave this be."

Her words soaked deep into his core as she strode from the room without a single glance back.

He dropped back to his chair and hung his head, staring at the patterned rug beneath his feet. She may not have given him the identity of his mother, but one thing remained certain—whoever she was, his birth had come at a price, and if he pursued this course, payment would come due.

Chapter Twelve

November 5th

I had hoped for happiness as a young girl. I had hoped for it as I drew closer to my first Season. Romantic expectations of true love danced about my foolish head. How naive I was. How little I knew of the world and the ugliness it held. Oh, it was dressed in all the latest fashion and from a distance I thought it looked quite respectable. Handsome. But then it drew closer; close enough to suffocate. Then I saw the ugliness inside. I should have screamed until my screams sent it running. But fear stayed my tongue and shame robbed me of my voice.

How I hated my dreams after that. How I longed for my naiveté to return. But once it had been torn aside, the edges were far too frayed for it to do anything but fall away.

Rebecca hurried into the Kingsley's drawing room, excitement mixed with trepidation making her unable to sit as she waited for Lady Ellesmere and Caelie to arrive. The news she had to deliver filled her with excitement, but the thought of seeing Marcus again for the first time since they'd kissed tied her stomach into knots.

How would he receive her? How should she behave? Should she act as if nothing untoward had happened between them?

She twisted her hands over and over, her gloves left behind in her haste to share the news. Mother busied herself with penning a response to Nicholas and Abigail before heading over to pay a visit to Lord Glenmor, while Rebecca had hurried over to Ellesmere House to inform Caelie in the event the news had not reached her and Huntsleigh as yet.

And to tell Marcus, as he was, after all, to be little Lord Roxton's godfather.

"My lady."

Rebecca jumped at the deep baritone behind her and spun around to find the Ellesmere butler standing in the doorway. "Oh, Fenton! You surprised me. Is Lady Ellesmere and Lady Huntsleigh available?"

"I am afraid Lady Ellesmere is indisposed at the moment, my lady and Lady Huntsleigh is paying calls. I expect she will return shortly if you would care to wait. I can have Mrs. Faraday bring tea and biscuits."

"Mrs. Faraday's Ginger biscuits? One cannot have a proper celebration without them."

A ghost of a smile pulled at the corner of Fenton's dour expression before resettling. "Yes, ma'am. I will ensure I request the ginger biscuits."

"And...Mr. Bowen? Is he here?" She had hoped to have Caelie and Lady Ellesmere present when she informed him of

Nicholas and Abigail's new arrival, afraid of how to behave, or what seeing him would make her feel.

Though it couldn't have been any worse than how not seeing him made her feel. Each day dragged until it doubled in length. The nights were no better. She could not close her eyes without seeing his handsome face, imagining the taste of his kiss, the pressure of his hands on her body, even in places he had not touched. Places she longed for him to touch.

"I suspect Mr. Bowen is in his study as usual, my lady."

"Perhaps I might have the tea and biscuits delivered there, then," she suggested before her better judgment had time to inform her such an idea was a breach of propriety, not to mention good sense.

Being alone with Marcus served no purpose. Nothing could come of it. She must put this silly longing for something else—someone else—away. It could come to naught. Her path had been mapped. She must marry Lord Selward and she needed to put her feelings for Marcus aside. Lock them away as one does a bad memory.

Except the only thing bad about the memory of their kiss was that it could not happen again. And that she did not have more to remember than just a kiss. Not that it had been *just* a kiss, for there had been nothing ordinary about it. She had never imagined one could be taken to such heights from a mere meeting of mouths. And yet she had. Marcus's touch had left her seared, ruined for all other kisses to follow lest they be delivered by him.

"My lady?"

"Hm? Oh!" Heat burned her cheeks. "Forgive me, Fenton."

The butler inclined his head. "I indicated I would have the biscuits delivered and send your maid along with you."

"That is unnecessary, Fenton. Mr. Bowen and I are old friends and I'm certain Lady Huntsleigh will be along shortly.

I would hate to interrupt Nancy's visit with Mrs. Faraday. We keep her so busy, she rarely has time to visit her mother save when we come to call."

Fenton inclined his head once more, though the grim line of his mouth indicated he did not like being a party to such a breach of propriety. But his discomfort was not her concern. Perhaps it was better she did not have witnesses to whatever folly or foolishness came out of her mouth when she saw Marcus next.

She left the drawing room and went down the steps to the floor below and found him where Fenton had indicated. In his study, sitting at the round table by the window, his legs crossed and a small book resting in his lap. Whatever the book contained, it had so captivated his attention he had not noted her arrival. She opened her mouth to greet him but closed it just as quickly, drinking in the sight of him.

The sunlight silhouetted his strong, lean frame and touched upon his dark hair until it shone. With his head tilted forward, reading, she could see the straight sweep of his nose, the serious set of his lips. Awareness rushed through her at what those lips could do. She stood there a moment and let the sensation pull her under its spell and tried to imagine a world without Marcus in it.

She could not. And yet, if she married Selward that would be the world she lived in. It would hardly be appropriate for her to continue her friendship with a man who, had their circumstances been different, she would have chosen for her husband over the man she married.

Not that Marcus had ever proposed to her. Not properly. But the inference had been there in his words, lingering behind the things he hadn't said. It had burned in his kiss, in the glances he gave her, the way he never let her down. He didn't have to say the words. A man as controlled and contained as Marcus Bowen did not kiss a lady in such a way without it meaning something. Everything.

How wrong a world they lived in that they could not be together. If only she had not witnessed the look in Mother's eyes at the thought of losing everything to her husband's mistress. Maybe then she might have turned a blind eye, forged a new future built on what she wanted, instead of what her father had dictated must be.

But she *had* seen the look in Mother's eyes and in it, understood the breadth of everything she had given up upon a marriage she did not want, everything she had lost. Rebecca could not live with herself if she took away whatever Mother had left.

Which meant she must learn to live without Marcus.

Desperation clawed at her insides until her hand pressed against her belly as if she could hold it still.

It was then Marcus looked up. Had he sensed her sudden distress? His gaze traveled over her for a brief moment and he set the book aside and stood, his movements languid, as if in a dream.

"How long have you been standing there?"

She shook her head. She did not know. Seconds? Minutes? Longer?

He took a step toward her. "Is something wrong?"

"No." Yes. Everything. "I came to give you happy news."

He smiled, a small, quiet gesture that filled his eyes with warmth and her body with heat. How she loved his smiles. He had a hundred different ones and each of them provided a different type of delight, pulling at emotions she had not expected, wrapping around her until she became encompassed in them. In him.

"I would appreciate a little good news today."

"Nicholas and Abigail sent word. The baby has arrived. A boy. You have a godson." She smiled, but it came with a stab of pain at the idea of Marcus's own sons, all dark haired with serious expressions. Sons that would never belong to her.

He stepped forward and took her hands, an unconscious gesture that forced heat to shoot up her arms and into her heart.

"That is good news. Everyone is well then?"

"Yes. Healthy and hearty. Nicholas claims he has quite a set of lungs on him already."

She looked down at his strong hands where they encompassed hers. How small she looked in comparison. How easily he swallowed her up and made her feel safe. Would Lord Selward ever accomplish such a feat? No. The answer came quick as a flash. Lord Selward was a nice man, but he lacked Marcus's strength and conviction. He went along and did as was expected of him. He was a man who let life happen to him. Marcus was a man who tackled life, who came from little and made a life any man could be proud to call his own. He was good and honest and solid and kind.

"Have they decided on a name yet? I should like to know how to address the young man."

A small laugh escaped her and she pictured Marcus holding the babe in his arms, imparting all of his knowledge. The heir to the Blackbourne title would be in good hands with his counsel.

"They are, as Nicholas says, currently in negotiation over the names. For now, I am referring to his lordship as Little Lord Roxton."

"It shall do for now," Marcus said. He turned away from her but kept hold of one of her hands and led her into his study as if it were the most natural thing in the world to share such an intimacy. She was thankful she'd forgotten her gloves at home. She relished his touch and mourned a little when he let her go, to pull out a seat at the table where he'd been reading.

She took her seat and Marcus reclaimed his. With her news delivered, she did not know what else to say or do and a silence fell between them, punctuated by the memory of their last meeting, the kiss they had shared. The words they had spoken.

Marcus cleared his throat. "I met with Mr. Cosgrove. A fine man, as Miss Caldwell claimed. I have promised him a position once I determine where he will be best suited."

"Oh, how lovely. Rosalind will be so pleased. I spoke with her older sister the other day."

"Did you? And what did the elder Miss Caldwell have to say?"

Eugenie's delivery of the gossip she had heard burned in the pit of Rebecca's stomach. She had said nothing to anyone about it, not even Mother. She did not want to tell Marcus, but he deserved to know.

"She indicated she had heard Lord Walkerton is set to arrive in London any day now. It is believed his arrival precedes a betrothal announcement by Lord Selward."

Marcus stilled, his steady gaze never leaving her. "I see." And then, "You do not seem as pleased by this news as I would have expected."

She looked down at her hands and splayed her fingertips across her lap. She could still feel his touch lingering on her skin. "I suppose there is no guarantee the offer he makes will be for me."

"He'd be a fool to ask another."

It was meant as a compliment, but it angered her how easily he spoke of her potential marriage to another. Did it not tear him apart to think of her with another man the same way it broke her heart to know someday he would choose another woman for his wife?

"That is kind of you to say."

"Kindness has nothing to do with it," he said. "It is simply the truth."

She lifted her gaze to meet his and let herself fall into the dark depths of his eyes, to see the things he left unsaid, all the feelings roiling around in her own heart. The words they did not speak. The truth they did not tell. The secrets they would keep forever. This was wrong. So very, very wrong.

"I don't want to marry him." The words choked out of her on a sob she hadn't expected. Hadn't prepared for.

Marcus leaned forward in one swift moment and grasped her hand in his and she held on for all she was worth, because the moment the words left her mouth, her world spiraled out of control, a ship broken loose from its moorings. Marcus's hands anchored her in place.

"Then don't. Don't marry him."

But she had to. A fact she hated more than she had ever hated anything in her life, but she could not escape it. Once this moment passed, she would be faced once again with the idea of breaking Mother's heart, giving her memories and past away to another woman, in favor of her own selfish needs.

"I must," she whispered and the declaration fell between them like a silent guillotine, cutting through any hope the moment brought, and any possibility that the future held something different for them.

A brief knock at the door made them straighten, the connection between them broken. Rebecca took a deep breath and tried to restore the happiness news of her nephew's arrival had brought, but the emotion remained elusive.

A maid entered the room on Marcus's command with tea and biscuits. She set the tray on the table and quietly left the room with a brief curtsey.

"Mrs. Faraday sent her ginger biscuits, I see," he said, as if the tension between them needed words to smooth it over.

"I requested them." Though she suspected if she were to bite into one now it would turn to sand in her mouth and land like a lump in her throat when she tried to swallow.

Marcus poured the tea and set a cup and saucer in front of her, then did the same for himself before retaking his seat. Neither touched the biscuits. Rebecca glanced at the table and noted the book. It was the same one he had been reading before, when she came to return his volume of Voltaire after the Berringsford's fete.

"What is it you're reading?" She reached out a hand to feel the smooth leather surface of the book. Marcus's hand met her there and the tip of their fingers touched and stayed.

He did not answer immediately, but sat and stared at the book, at their hands. His brow furrowed and she waited.

"It is a journal."

"A journal? Your own?"

Another hesitation, then, "No. My mother's."

Marcus had not meant to tell her. When she asked the question, his mind shouted to retreat, to shrug it off as immaterial and move onto another subject before she could inquire further. But his heart held firm, concentrated on the smallest bit of skin on the tips of his fingers where they touched hers. Connected. Fused.

The truth he had tried to resolve over the past week had become a behemoth of perplexity. A labyrinth of secrets that provided more dead-ends than answers. Questions spun inside his head until he became dizzy from the effort of trying to make sense of them and still he was no further ahead.

"I did not know you had a journal from your mother," Rebecca said. "It must bring you comfort."

"No. I'm afraid not." It had done anything but.

Twin lines cropped up between her eyebrows as she glanced down at the journal then back up to meet his gaze. "Why ever not?"

He clenched his jaw until the muscles ached. He needed to

leave her out of it, keep her safe. But again, his heart and its selfish need to share his burden, to find comfort in her softness, overrode his good sense.

"It is not from Mary Bowen," he said.

The twin lines grew deeper. "I thought you said it was from your mother?"

"It is."

Rebecca didn't answer immediately and Marcus waited patiently, knowing when the gasp left her that she had put the puzzle together. He was a bastard.

"But how—" And then, "I thought—"

When she did not continue, he filled the void left by her unspoken words. "The journal arrived a week ago." He gave a brief summary of the delay in its arrival. The words came haltingly and he prayed she did not reject the truth as Lady Ellesmere had. Or worse—reject him.

"Who is she?"

"I do not know. There is no indication other than she stayed at Braemore during her confinement and left me with the Bowens upon my birth. I suspect my imminent arrival was neither planned nor happily anticipated."

"You mean to say you are—"

She stopped and he filled in the rest. "A bastard. It would seem so."

"Oh, Marcus." She turned her hand and curled her fingers into his. He relished the idea that despite what she had learned she still touched him, she hadn't turned away.

"I have told no one," he said. His conversation with Lady Ellesmere did not seem worth bringing up. It had yielded nothing but hurt feelings and tension.

She nodded. "I shall keep your confidence." An expression crossed her pretty features and he could see her mind working behind her silvery eyes. They widened as whatever she puzzled over bore fruit. She leaned back in her chair, her fingers sliding away, leaving him cold. He wanted to grab her, bring he back, but something about what he saw in her expression stayed his actions. "The watch."

He pursed his lips. Damnation.

"It arrived at the same time, didn't it? It was on the table the first time I saw you with the journal."

He nodded, but said nothing else. He had not anticipated her making the connection and now wished he had left the matter alone, that she would do the same. He should have known better.

"It bore the Walkerton crest."

"It did."

"But you insisted that it wasn't the Walkerton crest."

"I had hoped you were wrong."

He hadn't wanted to believe it. Shied away from the truth of it the same way he avoided reading the journal in one sitting. As if by prolonging truth's delivery, he could circumvent it somehow. Make it not true. He realized now he could not. He'd quickly skimmed through the journal to its end, looking for some hint of his mother's identity. None existed. Disappointed, he'd gone back and begun to read it through more thoroughly, hoping to find a small detail that would point him in the right direction.

"But I wasn't."

"No. Mr. Cosgrove confirmed it. He was a former employee of the Walkerton estate."

When she spoke next the words were barely a whisper. "Do you believe you may be Walkerton's—"

She stopped, but the word she'd left unspoken hung in the gaping silence.

Bastard.

"It's possible."

"But if that is true, that would make you and Lord Selward—"

"Blood." He would not deem to call the man brother. It took more than a common father to make such a claim. "Perhaps."

"I must go." She rose from the chair in one swift motion but Marcus joined her at a much slower pace, his body had aged a decade in the few moments since he'd revealed his truth to her. "It is improper for me to be here."

That she had just reached that conclusion spoke volumes. She had been fine sitting alone with him in his study when he was the son of Mary and Edmore Bowen. But now that he was a bastard, things were different.

The daughter of an earl did not maintain close associations with bastards.

He wasn't sure what he had expected when he told her, but the pain in his heart made it clear, it hadn't been this.

"Rebecca—"

She shook her head, cutting him off. "Will you give Caelie and Huntsleigh the news? I had planned to stay, but I forgot I must—" She backed out of the room, away from him, away from the truth as if it could be so easily avoided. He should have warned her it could not be, but it hardly mattered now. She would figure it out in time.

"Very well then." He did not follow her. His limbs declined to move and his pride refused to beg her to stay. It was better this way. She was not his to keep.

"We will speak later," she offered, but he would not hold her to it. She didn't mean it anyway.

He forced a smile and tried to ignore how his heart tore out of his chest and went with her when she left. It hardly mattered.

He wouldn't need it any time soon.

Chapter Thirteen

For a dinner meant to celebrate the happy occasion of the newest addition to the Sheridan and Laytham family, the affair held a distinctly subdued air about it. Despite the smiles and chatter amongst the guests, a thin line of tension wound around the table, threading its way around Marcus at one end of the table, until it found Rebecca at the other. He had not looked at her or acknowledged her in any way outside of a nod of greeting when she entered the drawing room before dinner was served.

If any of the other guests noticed, no one said as much. In truth, most of them appeared untouched by the unease. Mother and Caelie discussed names they thought might be appropriate for the new little lord, and the upcoming party Mother put on every year at Sheridan Park, while Lord Ellesmere and Huntsleigh spoke of estate business, with Marcus joining in occasionally if asked a direct question. Lady Ellesmere had been uncharacteristically quiet, but as she had been indisposed the other day when Rebecca stopped by with the news, she suspected the marchioness continued to feel a bit under the weather.

She had yet to speak to Marcus since he revealed the potential truth of his parentage to her. Over the past several days she had wanted to explain her hasty departure, but the words failed her. His news had taken her world and turned it upside down.

Walkerton's bastard son.

Was it even possible? And if so...

If so, she could not marry Selward.

How could she? The prospect had proved difficult enough knowing another had engaged her heart, but to discover that person might well be Lord Selward's own brother?

She shook her head. No. She could not marry one man knowing in her heart it was his brother she wanted. She could not endure Lord Selward's touch or his kiss, when it was the touch and kiss of his brother she longed for. Dreamed of.

The torment would be too great. The remorse suffocating.

She could not marry Lord Selward. And if she could not marry him then all was lost. She and Mother would lose everything.

Rebecca glanced across the table where Mother's pretty face sparkled as she discussed the impending visit with her first grandson. How happy she looked. How long she had waited to be so. How much she had suffered and lost to reach this point.

Rebecca bit down against the guilt that rushed up her throat and lodged there, a solid lump of unshed tears. If Marcus was Lord Selward's brother, all of the effort she had put into currying his favor had been for naught.

Then what? With no significant dowry to bring to the marriage mart, where would that leave her? Would she grow old alone? Nothing more than a spinster aunt with no family of her own? Or worse, be forced to marry whatever lord would accept the paltry dowry she offered?

Neither prospect painted a very rosy future.

She needed to speak with Marcus. Perhaps he was wrong. Perhaps he was mistaken in his association with Lord Walkerton. Maybe the watch had come into his mother's possession in a much different way than they assumed. And if not, she at least needed to apologize and explain why she had left so quickly.

If only she could find the words.

She pursed her lips. No, she had found the words, but the reasons for why she'd left opened a Pandora's Box that they had so far managed to dance around. If she were to admit the reasons for her hasty departure aloud—to reveal that her feelings for him had grown to such a degree they overshadowed everything else—meant to give voice to her heart.

She had requested help in fully captivating Lord Selward's attentions because she trusted him. She should have known better. For as trustworthy as Marcus was, such a trait proved no competition for her own feelings.

Feelings rekindled over the past week until they raged like a wildfire out of control. The more she tried to douse them, the brighter they burned. The touch of his lips upon her own set off a lightning bolt of sensation shooting through her until she could barely remember her own name. In the span of a week, sensible, stable Marcus Bowen had become something else entirely. He had turned into the pirate king of her childhood dreams and whisked her so far out onto rocky seas she could not naviagate her way back.

And now, because of that, her carefully laid plans to marry Lord Selward—a plan painstakingly devised and implemented—lay in ruins at her feet.

She could not marry Marcus's brother.

Perhaps he realized this too. Perhaps that was why he had yet to speak to her, or look her way despite the numerous times she'd attempted to catch his gaze through dinner and convey, with a look, her regret at leaving so abruptly when he'd delivered the news.

What she had wanted to do was the complete opposite. She had wanted to take him into her arms, to offer him the comfort he had so obviously needed. To hold him as he had held her when Father's passing and the reading of the will left her overwhelmed with grief. She wanted to kiss him. Touch him. Convey with her body what words failed to express.

Rebecca quickly shoved a forkful of roasted chicken covered in egg sauce into her mouth to distract her thoughts. This wouldn't do. Perhaps Father was correct, and passion was nothing more than a road to ruin. Had it not wrecked havoc upon Mother and Father? And Nicholas? Had giving into her passion for Marcus not destroyed all her hopes for saving her and Mother from becoming nothing more but impoverished relatives?

She could not give into temptation. If she and Marcus married, she would lose everything. *Mother* would lose everything. Marcus was a man of business and successful in his own right, but surely he would expect to marry to improve his position and if she lost everything, she would have nothing to offer him. No dowry, no land holdings, no estates. All of it would go to Father's mistress.

Why, even if he married one of the Caldwell girls he would receive more than she could bring to a marriage. Even with the dowry Nicholas would provide, there would be no property, nothing to last after the initial sum was run through. He inherited only the entailed properties, and those would eventually pass to his new son. She stabbed another piece of chicken and left it to hover on her fork. Was it right to rob Marcus of such an opportunity to better himself? To have all that he deserved?

No. Her shoulders drooped.

She would apologize to him and offer to help him get to

the bottom of the mystery involving his parentage. Perhaps they may discover he was not Lord Selward's brother after all, and all this worry will have been for naught. She could marry Lord Selward, secure her and Mother's future and put away any thoughts the sinful temptation Marcus's heady kisses elicited.

Yes. A very sound plan. She would seek Marcus out, make amends for her behavior and offer him whatever assistance she could to help him get to the truth.

No more wayward daydreams.

No more desiring what she could not have.

No more kisses.

Her frown deepened.

"Is the roast chicken not to your liking, or are you having an argument inside of your head that you're on the losing side of?"

Rebecca turned to her right where Benedict Laytham, Abigail's older brother and the new Earl of Glenmor sat looking down at her, an amused grin on his face. He'd kept his voice low and for her ears only. A fact she was more than grateful for since his perception hit the mark with deadly accuracy. A blush burst forth and burned her cheeks.

"Ah, the latter then," he said and smiled until the corners of his slate blue eyes crinkled in amusement.

"Forgive me," she said. "I haven't been the best dinner companion, have I?"

"You have been splendid company. You've allowed me to eat my meal in peace without having to attempt banal conversation about the weather or listen to a long dissertation on the hat Lady Engraine wore to the park."

"Did she wear a hat worthy of a long dissertation?"

"I cannot say. You have been quite silent on the matter, so I am left in the dark."

Rebecca laughed, thankful for Glenmor's diversion. Her

thoughts had become dangerously tangled and rather dismal. He'd diverted them with expert ease. Abigail's older brother was a fine addition to their family circle. He possessed the steady nature of Marcus, yet the charm and quick wit of Huntsleigh.

If not for the crushing debt and hideous scandal left in the wake of his uncle's death, she suspected he would have every marriage-minded mama in society hot on his heels in the hopes he would pay their daughters attention and offer a proposal. Not that it would matter if they were. According to Abigail, her brother was far too busy restoring the family finances to pay much attention to courting anyone.

She had considered him after Father's will had been read, but it went no farther than a thought. Though handsome and engaging, she thought of him as a brother and it seemed rather mercenary to marry him knowing she only did so to save herself and Mother. She would not do that to a man she held in such high regard. He deserved better.

"Are you excited about being an uncle, Glenmor?"

"Indeed, I am," he said. "It does my heart good to see both Abigail and Caelie settled and happy. I have grand plans to spoil the new lad to an embarrassing degree."

Rebecca laughed and for the first time that evening, Marcus's gaze slid in her direction, though it rested only briefly on her before returning to the food on his plate.

"Ah, well you may have to wait in line behind me, as those are my plans as well."

"He shall not lack for attention then. Now tell me, despite this happy occasion, have you noticed anything odd about the dinner tonight?"

Rebecca stared down at her plate. "Odd?"

"Indeed. It seems to me certain individuals who can usually be counted on to contribute to the conversation are unusually quiet."

"Individuals?" Her gaze skimmed over Marcus and fell upon Lady Ellesmere, who kept her head bowed over her plate, her usually warm expression pulled tight.

"Strange, wouldn't you agree?" Benedict asked, inclining his head in Lady Ellesmere's direction.

"Indeed, it is." Her gaze bounced from Marcus to Lady Ellesmere and back. Both shared the same insular demeanor on what should have been a most happy occasion. The marchioness had barely spoken at all and when she had, her manner lacked the usually boisterous nature one expected from her. Was she feeling ill, or was it something else?

"I think between the two of them," Benedict said, "You could fit the number of words they have spoken this evening in your pocket and still have room for more."

Rebecca nodded in agreement. Was it possible Marcus's behavior had nothing to do with how they had left things?

"I heard Mr. Bowen plans on rejecting Lord Franklyn's offer. Perhaps Lady Ellesmere disagrees with this decision," Glenmor said, reaching for the wine in front of his plate.

"Lord Franklyn's offer?"

Glenmor's brows snapped together. "You do not know?"

She shook her head. What possible offer could Lord Franklyn have made to Marcus?

"Ah. Well, it seems Lord Franklyn has offered our Mr. Bowen Northill Hall in reward for having saved Lady Franklyn's life, but Huntsleigh indicates he plans to refuse it."

Her mind whirled with the news and what it meant for Marcus. He would be a landowner in his own right. "Northill Hall is a prime piece of land. Why would he refuse?"

Glenmor shrugged. "Bowen is a proud man used to making his own way. Perhaps he feels accepting such a gift too much."

"And you don't agree?"

"I do not. He more than earned it with what he went

through. But he did not ask my counsel on the matter and it is not my place to give it otherwise."

"Should I speak to him?" Rebecca whispered, more to herself than to Glenmor, though he answered regardless, not knowing the difference.

"Do you think you could sway him to sound reasoning?"

She chose not to answer given when they were together neither of them displayed anything resembling sound reasoning. Heat returned to her cheeks.

"You're blushing again," Glenmor said as he bent his head to take a bite of the braised carrots.

"Oh, hush!" She nudged the new earl with her foot beneath the table, but her thoughts had returned to his question. *Should* she speak to Marcus on the matter? Giving up such a boon as Northill Hall, well, it was nothing short of ludicrous.

She needed to speak with him. To clear the air and set things right between them, and now, to also convince him to accept Northill Hall, to not let pride stand in the way of getting what he deserved.

It was well after dinner finished and the men and women separated then gathered together again before she was able to steal away. Marcus had not returned with the rest of the gentlemen. She went to his study first, but he was not there. After a few minutes, she found him on the small balcony off the library.

"Marcus?"

He turned slightly, his brow furrowed as if she had caught him in the middle of an unpleasant thought. "You shouldn't be out here."

She didn't answer right away. Mostly because she had the sense he was right. Being this close to him altered things. Made it difficult to think clearly. She wished it didn't, but she could not ignore the memory of being held in his arms. The strength, the sense of safety found there. She could still taste him; feel his length pressed against her. As much as she tried to set her desires aside, they refused to be ignored. Being near him made her head swim and put her emotions in turmoil.

She wrapped her shawl more tightly around her shoulders, as if it could block out the confusion his closeness created.

"I wanted to apologize. For leaving so abruptly the other day."

His attention left her and he stared at the flowers in the planter in front of him. She followed his gaze. There was not much to see. The blossoms had curled into themselves, protection against the night. A shame people were not afforded the same skill. She should like to use it right about now.

"I believe you made your feelings on the matter quite clear."

She hung her head at the curtness in his tone. She had hurt him. The realization cut through her.

"I am sorry for the way I behaved. I should not have left. It is just that your news surprised me and—"

"You do not need to explain."

"But I think I do." She wished he'd look at her. "I've hurt you, that is clear, and it was not my intent. It is just that, if what you suggested is true, then...then it means you are Lord Selward's brother. And if you are, then—"

"It is of no consequence."

She stopped. *Of no consequence?* She would hardly call it *of no consequence*. It was very much filled with all kinds of consequence. Deep, meaningful, disturbing consequence that left her stomach tied up in knots, sent her mind into a whirling turmoil and made her heart ache for all the things she wanted and could not have.

"You don't understand," she told him. Because if he understood there was no way he could make such a claim.

"On the contrary. I understand perfectly. I am a bastard. If not Walkerton's then someone else's. And you...well, you are a daughter of an earl and must marry someone of equal social standing. Of which I am not. You were right to leave as you did. We have allowed whatever it is between us to lead us into temptation, but that temptation is best avoided now that we know who I am. What I am. Nothing can ever come of it."

His words punched into her and left her stunned. Is that what he believed she thought? That he was nothing but a bastard?

"What you are, is the best of men." *Please look at me!* But he continued to gaze at some point in the darkness, as if she had said nothing at all.

"If anything," he continued, "I should seek your forgiveness. I had no right to take such liberties. I allowed my— well, it matters not why, only that I should not have allowed it."

But she did not want him to apologize for the liberties he took. He had not been the only one. She'd accepted his kisses and given back with equal measure. She'd reveled in his touch, basked in the heat of her desire, and lost herself to the passion. None of which she regretted.

"Perhaps," he said. "We should simply chalk both incidences up to the heightened emotions of the moment and leave it at that. We shall not speak of it again. It will be as if it never happened."

Except that it had happened.

And, God help her, she wanted it to happen again.

She wanted to know the feel of his body against hers, his mouth devouring hers. She wanted to once again experience such passion that burned through her like a fire set upon dry brush, burning hot and fast until it consumed everything in its path.

"Is that what you want?" *Please say no.*

"I think it best. We are wholly unsuited after all. You must marry a lord and I am but a bastard."

"Stop saying that!"

He shrugged. "It is the truth. I need to accept it, as do you."

He glanced down at her then and smiled, but it was void of emotion, the kind one gave when they made polite conversation with a stranger and discussed nothing of more import than the weather.

"Have you made any more progress other than Mr. Cosgrove's confirmation?"

He shook his head. "I tried to speak with Lady Ellesmere, but she would have nothing of it. She indicated I should leave the matter alone, that there was nothing good that could come of my digging into the past."

"Then she must know something. Perhaps if you give her time, she will—"

"No. She made it clear she wants no part of this. She's barely spoken to me since the matter was brought up. Whatever she knows, she will take it to the grave."

Rebecca stared up at him. Weak moonlight filtered through the thin cloud cover and bathed his dark hair until it matched the midnight sky. A breeze teased its ends giving him a wild, almost elemental appearance. She tried to imagine what it would be like to discover your past was a lie and that people you loved knew the truth yet refused to share it with you. She could not. That he must suffer through such a thing made her heart give a painful twist.

For a long moment they stayed that way, each looking at the other until she wanted to scream. To beat against his chest and make him understand he was so much more than the circumstances of his birth. That if her own circumstances were different, she would choose him in a heartbeat. With every heartbeat. But she could not. And, as it turned out, he did not want her to.

"We shall be friends then," he suggested. "That is not such a bad thing."

She nodded. "Of course." But the words scraped across her throat, barbed with regret. It was better than losing him forever, yet the idea left her bereft.

They turned back to the garden and stood side by side in silence. Rebecca wanted to say more—so much more, to set things back on an even footing. She grasped the only thing she could think of, the first thing that came to mind.

"Glenmor told me Lord Franklyn offered you Northill Hall."

"He did."

"And that you are refusing to take it."

"I am."

"You shouldn't, you know—give it up. You should accept it. It's a wonderful property." And close enough to Sheridan Park he would not be so very far away from her. Then again, after she married Lord Selward her time at Sheridan Park would be minimized as the Walkerton seat was in the next county over.

"What does it matter to you?" Though the words were not spoken harshly, they stung nonetheless.

"I only wish to see you happy."

"And you think Northill Hall is what will make me happy?" He turned to face her and this time he truly looked at her. No. Not at her—*into her*. Deep inside to where all the things he'd stirred in her heart were laid bare. It frightened her, the things he would see, the truth of her feelings. The depth of them.

She struggled to find a distraction, to cover up the sudden vulnerability this knowledge created. "Yes."

When had he stepped closer? No. He had not moved. She had.

His hand reached up and touched her cheek. His warmth

seeped through her, invaded her blood and rushed through her veins to spread heat throughout her body. She turned into his touch with a sigh, closed her eyes and basked in it. His lips pressed against her forehead and she held her breath as wondrous sensations rolled and tumbled through her so quickly she could not make sense of any of them save for one. Hope. Hope that he would kiss her as he had before. And need. The need to be lost in that moment one last time.

"Then you know nothing of happiness," he whispered.

She opened her mouth to protest, but his lips halted whatever she had meant to say as he dropped an all too brief kiss upon them. It held nothing of the passion of previous kisses, but bestowed instead something else. Loss. Regret. Farewell.

"Good-bye, Lady Rebecca."

And then he was gone and the cool night air rushed in to herald his absence, but it was his words that left her cold.

You know nothing of happiness.

The chaste kiss burned against her lips and fear wrapped around her like a cloak as the insidious truth soaked into her pores.

In her heart, she recognized the truth. He was right. She did not know happiness. And now she never would.

Chapter Fourteen

November 18th

My belly protrudes and I feel somewhat awkward with the changes. They are so horribly obvious and when I pass by the servants in the hall, there is no longer any hope of disguising my situation. Still, their kindness and understanding remains and Mrs. Bowen, who has remained steadfast in her kindness and her loyalties, visits regularly, though I am certain it takes her away from more important duties.

Mother has said little since our argument of two days ago. She brought up the subject of what would happen at the end of this journey, as she calls it. I can think of no other option than the one Mother has suggested and yet I balk. How can I? It would be as if my own heart were ripped out of my chest and cast aside. Have I not suffered enough? Must this be taken from me as well?

"I've heard if you stare at it long enough, the big hand will move."

Marcus snapped the watch shut and set it onto the desk as Spence walked into the room. "Is that right?"

Spence dropped his lean frame into one of the chairs facing Marcus's desk. One leg dangled over the arm. "It is a true and established fact. Tell me, did you finally buy yourself a proper watch? Have you actually made a purchase? Loosened your purse strings, allowed a few pence to fall through and showered yourself with a gift?" Spence reached out and picked up the watch. Marcus leaned across the desk and snatched it back, startling his friend.

"It is none of your business. Good heavens, you're like a small child looking for entertainment. Do you not have anything better to do?"

Spence shrugged. "I do not. Caelie has decided to retire early this evening. Apparently carrying another human inside of you can leave one quite exhausted. I shall be sure to scold the little scamp for it when he arrives."

"That he could be a she."

"Bite your tongue." A look of abject horror crossed Spence's face. "Good lord."

Marcus took pity on his friend. "I would not worry about it. Who better to save her from men like you than, well, you."

"That's hardly encouraging." Spence bounded out of his chair. "What say we take my mind off this and go find ourselves some entertainment?"

"I cannot. I have an appointment."

Spence glanced at the clock over Marcus's shoulder. "At this hour? Surely Grandfather does not have you working this late."

"It is a personal matter."

Spence's eyes widened and Marcus suddenly wished he'd

kept his mouth shut. "Why Bowen, do you have an assignation this evening?"

"It is nothing of the sort."

"Pity. When exactly was the last time you had carnal knowledge of a woman?"

Marcus choked on his next breath. "I beg your pardon?"

"Carnal knowledge. Of a woman. Last time. When?"

An unwanted image conjured in his mind of a certain raven-haired beauty laid back against lily-white sheets, her porcelain skin begging to be touched. Marcus rubbed the bridge of his nose in an effort to remove the image.

"Honestly, Spence. Do you have no sense of decency? Just because you and Nick preferred to live out your bachelorhood in the scandal sheets with everyone knowing your business, doesn't mean I choose to. It is none of your business."

Not that the scandal sheets would have much interest in what Lord Ellesmere's man of business did. Although they might, had they been aware that on two occasions of late he'd found himself kissing a certain lady. A lady whose brother would likely murder him where he stood if he had any idea his trusted friend had wished to do far more than just kiss said lady. Still wished it.

Spence nodded. "A long time, then. That's what I thought."

Too long. "Shut up."

"You know," Spence said, twirling a finger in Marcus's direction. "They say that if you don't use it, it will rot and fall off."

"Who, pray tell, is *they*?"

Spence gave a sly smile. "I shall never reveal my sources, but you should heed my warning just in case. Find yourself a mistress or get yourself a wife. I highly recommend the latter."

"I am in need of neither," he bit out.

"Suit yourself, but if you are not off to an assignation then you are in a fine position to keep me entertained, which my darling wife has indicated she wishes you to do this evening."

"Did she now?" Somehow Marcus doubted that.

"Something to that effect. I believe her exact words were more like, *'Spencer, your incessant chatter is interrupting my attempts at sleep. Please leave.'* Though she said it with such a sweet smile I find it hard to know if she was serious or not."

"Likely she was. You can be quite annoying."

"Can I?"

"Completely. Many people have said so. Take now for instance."

"Nobody says so. I am the soul of charm."

"I say so."

"Yes, but you have been a positive bear this past week so I take that with a grain of salt. Now, where are you off to if not a secret rendezvous with a lady of ill repute?"

"Would it matter if I told you it was none of your business?"

"Doubtful. Likely I'd just follow you for the fun of it and find out that way."

Marcus let out a slow breath knowing full well that is exactly what Spence would do. "Fine. If you must know, I am going to White's. I have requested a meeting with Lord Selward and he has accepted."

"Selward? Why the devil do you want to speak with him? Sweet Judas, Bowen, do you mean to read him the riot act over the park incident in the middle of White's?"

"I believe I have already made my feelings on that matter very clear to him. This is of a more personal nature." His attempt at discovering information less overtly had come to naught. The time had come to take the questions to the Walkerton clan itself.

"Well, I shall tag along either way."

"I do not require a chaperone." He did not want Spence

involved in this. He had spoken of his secret to Rebecca and her reaction left him rattled. To watch Spence, whom he thought of as a brother, share the same reaction, look at him differently...he could not do it. Not yet.

"Do not think of me as a chaperone. Think of me as a comrade in arms. After all, if you do decide to kill the young lord for his shoddy treatment of Lady Rebecca, then you will require my assistance in disposing of the body."

"No one is going to die. You will have to find other amusements this evening."

Spence shook his head. "Afraid not, old chap. I have made up my mind."

"Have I ever mentioned what a colossal pain in my ass you can be?"

"Yes, but I'm certain it was said with much affection and therefore I did not take it to heart. Shall we go?"

Marcus sighed. The man was like a bulldog with a juicy bone. There would be no dissuading him. That much was clear.

"Very well. But I would request you not butt into the conversation nor hound me with questions afterward over anything you may hear."

Spence's eyebrows rose and he leaned forward in his chair. "Indeed? Well, now I am intrigued. Come, let's be off!"

Allowing Spence to join him would narrow the line of questioning he had planned, but perhaps having him come would help prevent any disaster should Marcus's anger get the best of him. Not that it usually did. He'd always kept a tight rein on his emotions. Until recently.

They arrived at the club and took a seat near the fireplace, then ordered a drink while they waited for young Selward to arrive.

"How do I become a good father?" Spence asked as their drinks arrived.

Marcus shook his head. "How should I know? In case you haven't noticed, I do not have children, nor have I spent any time around them. My memory of my own parents—" He stuttered slightly over the word, the knowledge he'd come into leaving him unsure how to refer to Mary and Edmore Bowen. "—is limited."

"I thought you knew everything."

"I'm flattered, but I'm afraid on this matter you are on your own. Perhaps you can interrogate Nick, now that his firstborn has arrived."

"Good idea. Perhaps he would allow me to borrow the lad for a bit so I might practice."

"Highly unlikely. Even if Nick was willing, Abigail might think it less than a good idea."

"Bollocks." Spence slumped in his chair and swirled the brandy in his glass. "By the way, you never did tell me what was in the package from Cornwall?"

Marcus hesitated. Once Selward arrived, the truth would be out. Perhaps he should give Spence a heads up now. Not the whole truth, but enough to keep him from interrupting once Marcus began questioning the young lord.

"The package contained old papers from a solicitor my parents had hired years before. And a watch."

"The watch you grabbed out of my hand? I knew there was something up with that. And you say I'm not observant." Spence grinned and leaned forward and held out his hand. "Come, come. Let me see it. I know you have it with you. You dropped it in your pocket after you rudely snatched it away from me."

Marcus sighed. Refusal would only result in Spence hounding him relentlessly until he gave in and handed over the watch. Better to save himself the aggravation. He reached into his pocket and retrieved it.

Spence's eyebrows lifted as he took it from him and turned

the watch over in his hands a few times before flipping the top of it open. "It's broken."

"Yes. I know."

"Is it a family heirloom then?"

"I do not know." But before he could elaborate, they were interrupted.

"Good day, gentlemen."

"Selward," Marcus waved to the empty chair between him and Spence, without getting up, as would be proper.

Selward gave a nervous smile and took the offered seat, glancing first at Spence, then at Marcus. His chin tilted at a haughty angle and his back stiffened. "And what is the meaning of this meeting, Mr. Bowen?"

"We thought you would be up for a night of debauchery before you chose your bride. You do intend on choosing a bride this Season, do you not?" Spence maintained his smile, but his words held an edge to them.

Selward's stiff posture weakened somewhat. "Uh, yes. T-to the bride, not the night of debauchery."

"How unfortunate." Spence twirled the watch on the table, setting it to spin. "To the debauchery, not the bride."

Marcus watched the watch twirl. "Ignore him. He is drunk."

"I am at least four drinks away from being drunk, I'll have you know. Should we begin to remedy that situation? What say you, Selward?"

Selward's gaze bounced between the two of them as if he wasn't sure what to say or do. Not an uncommon condition for him, from what Marcus had seen thus far. "I—no, that is —I came here only to speak with Mr. Bowen." He turned to Marcus. "You indicated it was in regards to a personal matter. As it turns out, I too, wish to have words with you."

Spence left the watch alone and leaned back in his chair.

"Ah, well then, carry on. Don't mind me. I'll just sit here, quietly, and enjoy my drink."

Marcus doubted that would last long. "What is it you wished to speak to me about?"

Lord Selward shifted in his seat, his dislike of confrontations visible in every move he made. Still, the young man pressed on and, Marcus supposed he ought to respect him for that. Ought to, but didn't.

"I wish to ask you to step aside."

"But he's sitting," Spence pointed out.

Ten seconds, Marcus noted with a slight shake of his head. Such remarkable restraint.

"I mean—that is to say, step aside with respect to Lady Rebecca."

"Had he stepped on her?" Spence looked at Marcus. "Bowen, have you stepped on the lady in question?"

Perhaps he should have tied Spence to a chair in his study. "I have not, to the best of my knowledge, stepped on Lady Rebecca."

"Good to hear. Height of rudeness that would be. Nick would not be pleased."

Selward cleared his throat, his frustration evident. "Metaphorically speaking."

"Ah. I see." Spence nodded. "Thank you for that clarification. What were we speaking about again?"

"I believe the young man wishes me to step aside, *metaphorically*, where Lady Rebecca is concerned to better allow him to have her full attention."

"Is that so? And why is that, Selward?" Spence asked. "I mean, unless my addition is incorrect—and Bowen, please correct me if need be as you are the mathematical wizard, not I—but have you not already had Lady Rebecca's full attention for the better part of two Seasons now?

"I—yes—but—"

"And yet you have done nothing about it," Marcus added. "Why is that?"

To his credit, Selward had the good sense not to attempt any denial of the charge. Instead, he stared down at his hands where they rested on the table. Marcus's stomach churned. The idea of Lady Rebecca marrying him, of those hands having providence over her body, sickened him.

"You do not deserve her." The words were out before Lord Selward could answer and he looked over at him, shocked. Even Spence's brow lifted and amusement lit his features.

"It was never my intention to lead Lady Rebecca on, or to create the impression my interest in her had waned. I care about her, truly I do."

The lord's claims raised Marcus's ire. He had only begun to show her a true interest once the prospect of losing her attentions to Marcus became evident. "I find that hard to believe. If you cared about her, you would have offered for her well before now. That is how it is done."

Selward pursed his lips and glared at Marcus, obviously not caring to be dressed down—yet again—by someone beneath his social standing, but Marcus cared even less for Selward's thoughts or feelings. The man deserved it for what he'd put Rebecca through.

"It is not as simple as that, I'm afraid."

"It never is," Spence drawled. "But I doubt such an explanation will satisfy Blackbourne. If you have no intention of offering for Lady Rebecca might I suggest you stop leading her on and raising her expectations. Blackbourne will not hesitate to retaliate if you injure her tender heart. Nor will Bowen for that matter. Have you ever seen Bowen angry?" Spence leaned forward, amplified horror stamped across his features. "Frightening, my dear man. Frightening."

"I have every intention of offering for her. That is why I

am asking you to step aside, to not muddy the waters. We both know I am better suited to her and that you are—" He stopped and it occurred to Marcus then that if he was indeed the bastard son of Walkerton, Selward may well be cognizant of that fact. Would know of his illegitimacy and how it left him lacking.

Selward could use the knowledge to publically ruin him. There would be no more hiding from the truth. Lady Ellesmere's words of warning rolled over in his head and his stomach coiled into knots.

He reached for the watch that had stopped spinning, leaving Selward's request unanswered. "Do you recognize this?"

Selward reached for the watch but Marcus moved it from his reach.

"Where did you get this?"

"It was handed down to me through my family."

"But it is not yours."

Marcus's heartbeat accelerated. "It is in my possession and therefore it is mine."

"I beg to differ. It bears the Walkerton crest."

At this proclamation, Spence straightened in his seat and leaned forward. Marcus's fingers turned icy where they clenched around the gold timepiece, but he forced his voice to remain calm and forceful. "Then perhaps you would care to tell me how my parents came into possession of it."

"How should I know? The watch was stolen years ago. Before I was born."

"If that is the case, how do you know it is even the same watch?" Spence said, cutting into the conversation.

"I know because it is the only watch of its kind. My great-great grandfather had it made and it was passed down through each generation until it reached my father. It was stolen while he was serving his country, fighting the French."

Hiding like a coward. "Who stole it?"

"A—a maid, I believe. I cannot say for sure." But his voice lacked conviction. What did he know? "I demand you return it to me at once."

Marcus pulled the watch back and safely pocketed it. "The watch was passed on to me and shall remain in my possession until I determine why that was so."

A silent war waged between them. Marcus stood on a precarious edge. If Selward pressed the issue, he could make his life difficult to say the least, but member of the peerage or not, Marcus had come this far, risked this much. He would not turn back now.

Spence stood, and when he addressed Selward the threat of danger slid around his words and carried the promise of violence should they not be heeded. "I believe you have outstayed your welcome, Selward. This conversation is at an end. I would ask that you leave. Quietly and without incidence."

Selward looked from Spence to Marcus, his cheeks burning with heat and his eyes blazing with anger and uncertainty. Confrontation was not his forte; a fact Marcus hoped would work in his favor. It did, but only for the moment.

Selward stood. "This is not the end of it, Mr. Bowen."

Marcus didn't answer. He knew the truth of it far better than the young lord standing in front of him with clenched fists and an air of uncertainty about him, as if unsure where to take the matter from here.

But one thing Selward could be sure of. This was, indeed, not the end.

If anything, it was only the beginning.

Rebecca had enjoyed the past few days immensely. Well, perhaps not immensely. Perhaps *somewhat* would have been a better term. Although in truth, *not much at all* would be far more accurate. Despite the attention Lord Selward had paid her since the incident at the park, she could not shake the wrongness that took hold whenever she spent time with him.

She found herself staring at him, trying to find some resemblance between him and Marcus. Could it be true? They both had brown hair, though Marcus's held a much darker, richer hue. And where Marcus's eyes were the shade of dark chocolate, Lord Selward's bore a greenish-blue cast. They were of a similar build—lean and athletic, but each moved differently than the other and shared no related mannerisms she could discern.

And yet...

Marcus possessed the bearing of someone of noble birth. She had always assumed that came from his years spent amongst the aristocracy, an assumed nature absorbed from being surrounded by others who were, in fact, born to it.

But what if she was wrong? What if he came by his bearing honestly? What if—

Lord Selward's barouche hit a small rut in the road and interrupted her thoughts. He had brought her out for a ride in the park. It was a beautiful day, warm and lovely with the summer flowers blooming and more buds waiting in the wings to burst forth once the existing ones died away. Above her, the birds sang in the trees and on the ground squirrels scampered about, zigzagging their way between bushes and trees as they foraged for nuts and seeds. The scene could not be more bucolic if painted by a master.

And yet she could not enjoy it.

She squirmed in her seat.

"Are you uncomfortable, Lady Rebecca? Would you prefer to stop and walk for a bit?"

Rebecca glanced over at Lord Selward and his open, eager expression. "Oh no, I'm fine. I'm just—" Just what? Could not stop thinking of another man. A man who could be your brother? She bit back the words and swallowed them whole. "I am fine, my lord."

Lord Selward nodded and did not inquire further. Marcus would have. Marcus would have seen through the lie and inquired upon her upset, listening quietly as she spewed out her problem. Then he would offer her a word or two of advice, comfort.

The only difficulty with that scenario was that Marcus *was* the problem.

I am a bastard.

No matter how far she pushed his claim from her mind, it continued to find its way back, unwelcomed footprints that echoed in her heart like a sullen whisper. She wished she could prove them wrong. Protect him from the hurt they caused.

But he did not want her comfort. He did not want her involved in his life at all. He had shut her out of it, but not before stirring within her needs and wants and desires that now had nowhere to go.

"I feel as if I should inform you of something," Lord Selward said, breaking through her thoughts once again. It likely did not bode well for their future that she kept forgetting he was there.

"Oh?"

He cleared his throat and appeared nervous, which made her nervous. She took a quick glance back at Nancy who sat behind them. Her lady's maid gave a small shrug and half smile which did nothing to dissipate the sudden unease that cropped up at Lord Selward's proclamation.

"I have received word that my father is set to arrive back in London any day."

She swallowed. Did he mean to propose? Here? Now?

"Oh, how lovely." Although she had no idea whether it was lovely or not. She had never met Lord Walkerton. Lord Selward rarely mentioned him and when he did, his words were brief and contained little in the way of warmth. Not an encouraging sign. "You will be glad to see him then? I understand he has been away for quite some time."

"Indeed, he has," Lord Selward said, his gaze fixed on the pathway in front of them. Rebecca studied his profile, the stiff set of his jaw, the tension in his shoulders and noted that while he replied to the question of his father being away, he did not respond to the other and, given his demeanor, she could only surmise that he was not happy in the least to see his father.

"Will he be staying long?" Lord Walkerton rarely spent time in London, or England for that matter. Rumors abounded as to why, though many of those rumors were kept from the ears of proper young ladies, which could only mean the rumors were of a scandalous nature. Perhaps that explained why Lord Selward kept clear of anything that held the hint of scandal.

"I have been given no indication of the length of his stay." The tone of his voice gave the impression he hoped it would be short.

"Will I meet him, your father?"

Lord Selward skirted around the subject as if she had not spoken. "I understand the Doddington masquerade is to be quite the thing. Do you plan to attend?"

"Yes, though I have yet to decide what to wear. I thought perhaps the goddess Athena."

He smiled at her. "The goddess of love?"

She made a face. "No, that was Aphrodite. Athena was the goddess of wisdom and reason." *Marcus would have known that*. They had kissed behind her, after all. She chased the thought away as soon as it arrived.

"Oh." He furrowed his brow. "Perhaps I should have paid more attention during my Greek mythology lessons."

"What will you go as?"

"I do not know. I'm sure Wesley will think of something." He waved a hand as if the matter was not even worth his consideration.

Odd, that one would let their valet determine their costume. She thought of the costume as a reflection of who you were, or who you wished to be. She had chosen Athena *because* she was the goddess of wisdom and reason, both of which she found herself in short supply of. And for other reasons she tried not to think about.

"Will your father arrive in time to attend the masquerade?"

The tension in Lord Selward's jaw returned. "I cannot claim to know what my father will do or when." He fell silent and said no more on the matter, but a sudden awkwardness left her with the impression.

Lord Selward looked at her. "May I ask you something personal?"

She lifted her eyebrows. He had never asked her anything personal during their acquaintance, save for her feelings about the weather. "Yes, of course."

"How well do you know Mr. Bowen?"

"Mar—Mr. Bowen?" His question startled her.

Nor did she have a ready answer for it.

If he had asked her that question a few weeks ago, she would have said as well as the back of her hand. But now...now he had thrown her so many surprises, shown aspects of his personality she had been previously unaware of, that she had come to realize there were depths to Marcus that remained unknown to her. Depths she wished desperately to delve into.

But that was hardly the type of thing one admitted to the man she needed to marry, was it?

"I have known him my whole life. Why?"

Lord Selward squirmed in his seat and shifted the reins from one hand to the other. "It is just—and I do not mean to upset you—"

"Upset me? What about Mr. Bowen could possibly upset me?" What indeed. It seemed everything about Marcus upset her of late, but she doubted this is what Lord Selward referred to.

He let out a breath and twisted his mouth to one side, then the other. She wished he would spit it out, whatever it was.

"I discovered the other day he is in possession of a stolen piece of property that belongs to my family. A watch."

The watch. Unease rippled through her. How had Lord Selward learned of its existence? She moved her mouth, but no sound came from it, the words had bottlenecked themselves in her throat. She shook her head and waited until her thoughts settled.

"I see. And did he indicate how he came into possession of this watch?"

Lord Selward pulled on the reins and brought the barouche to a halt at the side of the path then turned toward her. "He claims it was passed to him from his parents. But either way, it does not belong to him. It belongs to my family, yet he refuses to return it which leaves him in possession of stolen property."

She had never seen Lord Selward so heated before. His eyes blazed with agitation. "You must calm yourself, my lord. It is not as if Mr. Bowen stole the watch himself, nor do I believe either of his parents guilty of such a crime. Lord and Lady Ellesmere held the Bowens in very high regard, so much so, they took in their only son and raised him as a member of their own family. I cannot believe they would do so if they thought either of them to be of less than respectable character."

And yet...somehow they held possession of the watch, and now, as a result, Marcus did. Her mind raced to make sense of what it all meant. How it would have happened.

"Father claimed a maid had stolen it. He had her sacked, but the watch was never recovered. It was believed she must have pawned it, but—"

"But now you think to suggest, what? That Mr. Bowen—who was born in Cornwall, I might add—crawled from his crib all the way to London, found the watch and held onto it all these years?"

"Of course not! I do not know how he came to have the watch, but the fact remains it belongs to *my* family and it must be returned."

My family. Would Lord Selward know if Marcus belonged to his family, albeit from the wrong side of the blanket? Or had he been kept in the dark much in the same manner Marcus had?

"Did he indicate why he refused to return it to you?" Though she could imagine. The watch and the journal were the only two pieces of evidence Marcus had connecting him to a past that remained shrouded in mystery. Knowing him, he would not release either until he got to the root of it, regardless of whether those roots were tangled around the Selward family tree in such a way that removing them would cause nothing but pain and ruin.

"He did not though, I must say, I found his demeanor at refusing my demand unsuitable given his station. I believe he has notions of being above himself."

"I beg your pardon, but I am quite certain Mr. Bowen thinks no such thing. He is a fine, respectable gentleman and a heroic one at that, if you'll recall. I cannot abide such slanderous words to be said against him! Your claims are most upsetting."

As if sensing her anger, the horse shifted and forced Lord Selward to draw his attention away from her outburst to settle the animal.

He took a breath and when he spoke again calmness had returned to his voice though it did not sound genuine. "Forgive me. It is not my intention to cause you upset. I had hoped you could shed light on the matter before I take further action."

Her heart stuttered.

"Further action? Do you honestly mean to call the authorities on him?" Her voice peaked and drew the attention of Lord Phillip and Mrs. Pettigrew as they rode by. They slowed somewhat and Lord Phillip tipped his hat, giving them a curious glance. Rebecca forced a pleasant smile, but it dropped immediately once the couple had passed.

"I have no intention of contacting the authorities if such can be avoided, but with my father's return, I cannot allow the matter to drop. I intend to pay a visit to Lord Ellesmere—"

"No!" Her arm shot out and grabbed Lord Selward's sleeve, heedless of the impropriety of it. If there was a man alive who detested scandal more than Lord Selward, it was Lord Ellesmere and, given Lady Ellesmere's rejection of Marcus's request for answers, involving them further would do no one any good. "I will speak with Mr. Bowen."

"You?"

She released his sleeve and straightened. Her hands tightened into fists where they rested in her lap. "Yes, who better? We are friends, as I have stated. Please allow me to try and convince him to release the watch to you before you escalate the matter. It would not be fair to jeopardize Mr. Bowen's position with Lord Ellesmere by suggesting he has done something disreputable."

"I cannot ask you to put yourself in such a position."

"You are not asking. Promise me you will do nothing until I speak with Mr. Bowen."

Lord Selward inclined his head. "Very well then."

"Could you see me home, please?" She had no desire to spend any more time in his company today. His threats against Marcus frightened her and she needed to get to the bottom of things before Marcus's search for his past ruined him beyond repair.

Chapter Fifteen

January 1st

How easily he had led me away—a lamb to the slaughter. And I, the consummate fool, traipsed along after him as if safety was my due and nothing bad could ever happen. Until it did. And even then, I was certain it could not be happening, as if part of my mind had separated from the act itself and went far away to debate the issue, to convince the rest of me the pain and horror was not real. Except that it was and all the debate and denial in the world could not change that. And in the end, all that was left was shame.

But shame will not claim me now. I feel you move about, anxious to make your debut and I will not allow shame to touch you, not while it is within my power to do so.

Rebecca waited anxiously for Nancy's mother, Mrs. Faraday, to arrive for her weekly visit. The visit lasted only long enough for mother and daughter to have tea before they both returned to their duties, and Rebecca loathed to rob them of their time together, but her discussion with Lord Selward the day before struck fear deep into her core. Marcus walked a very precarious line between what would be tolerated by the peerage and what would not. If Lord Selward, or his father, decided to make an issue over the matter of the watch and Marcus's refusal to return it, it could cause grievous problems, the worst of which would see him arrested.

But if Marcus had set his mind to discovering the truth of his birth, he would do what he must to achieve that end. For all his steadiness and respectability, he was not a man who backed down. Nicholas had once told her it was that strength of character more than any other that had made Marcus so successful.

Unfortunately, it may become the same thing that caused his ruin.

Perhaps if she learned something of import with respect to his parentage, she could convince him to give up the watch. He had met a dead end with Lady Ellesmere, but as Lord Selward had taken her home and assisted Nancy down from the carriage upon their arrival, it dawned on Rebecca that Mrs. Faraday had been in the Kingsley's employ for well on forty years. Perhaps she could shed some light on the mystery. The question remained, however, would Mrs. Faraday breach the confidence of Lord and Lady Ellesmere, even for the sake of Marcus's safety?

Rebecca wiped the palms of her hands against the deep navy of her dress and fixed a smile on her face as the door to their housekeeper's small office opened and Mrs. Faraday and Nancy stepped into the room.

Mrs. Faraday stopped short her eyebrows lifting high. "Oh, my lady! I'm sorry. Have we disturbed you?"

Rebecca stood and rushed forward, which only took two steps given the tiny dimensions of the room. Honestly, how did Mrs. Robinson spend any time in here? "No, not at all, Mrs. Faraday. In fact, I asked Nancy if she would mind if I stole you away for a few moments to assist me in a rather delicate matter. Would you mind?"

Mrs. Faraday's gaze shifted from Rebecca to her daughter, a confused look replacing her jolly expression. "Oh, well, yes, I suppose."

"I'll leave the two of you in privacy," Nancy said, dropping a quick kiss on her mother's cheek. "I'll be in the kitchens when you're done, mum."

Rebecca waited for Nancy's departure, the door closing firmly behind her, before she waved a hand toward the small table and it's two chairs. Mrs. Faraday waited for Rebecca to be seated before taking her own.

"I mus' confess, my lady, I'm quite curious as to what it is ye think I can 'elp you with."

Rebecca worried her hands. Where was the best place to start? She did not want to give Marcus's secrets away, but at the same time, it was not inconceivable Mrs. Faraday had knowledge of what had happened at Braemore. The servants always knew as much, if not more, than those who lived above stairs.

She took a deep breath and jumped in. "It involves Mr. Bowen."

Mrs. Faraday's eyebrows lifted once more until they disappeared beneath the frizzy red bangs poking out from beneath her cap, but she said nothing, her silence encouraging Rebecca to continue.

"You see, Mr. Bowen received information a fortnight ago that has proven rather distressing to him and in trying to uncover the truth behind it, he may have put himself in a bit of a pickle, as it were. My fear is if he continues along this path, he may find himself in a very precarious position. I had hoped, if I share with you what I know, you may be able to alleviate some of mystery surrounding the situation and help me prevent Mr. Bowen from landing himself in gaol."

Mrs. Faraday gasped and a hand flew to her neck. "Gaol?"

Rebecca nodded. "Yes. Would you mind terribly if I asked you some questions?"

The older woman shook her head, the fingers at her neck twitching in distress. The housekeeper had a large brood of children of her own, but she had never failed to treat Huntsleigh and Marcus as part of it, giving them the same love and attention she had doled out to her own children. But would this love be strong enough to loosen Mrs. Faraday's tongue?

"Before I begin, I must ask for your absolute discretion on what I am about to say, and please know anything you tell me will be treated with the same."

"Yes, yes, of course." Her hand dropped to her lap.

Rebecca took a deep breath. "Mr. Bowen received a package from Cornwall. Within the contents of this package was a letter from Mary Bowen indicating she was not the woman who had given birth to him." She stopped and watched for a change in Mrs. Faraday's expression at the news. There was none. "You knew."

Mrs. Faraday nodded but said nothing more.

Hope exploded in Rebecca's breast and she forged on. "This same package also contained an old watch and a journal."

Mrs. Faraday's gaze sharpened, but again, she remained silent.

"The watch has a crest etched on its outer cover. He has identified it as the Walkerton crest and a former steward, Mr. Cosgrove, has confirmed this and also indicated the watch was reportedly stolen from the current Lord Walkerton many years ago."

"Mr. Cosgrove?"

"Do you know him?"

"Oh yes, yes. Lovely man. Didn't deserve wha' 'appened to him, he didn't."

"Then you will be pleased to know Mr. Bowen agreed with you on that account and has offered Mr. Cosgrove employment."

Mrs. Faraday smiled. "Such a good boy, he is. Always such a good boy."

"Yes, he is. Which is why I hope you can help keep him from harm."

She shook her head. "I'm not certain what you wish me to do?"

Rebecca spread her fingers wide against her skirts and forged on. "Having discovered the Bowens were not his true parents, Mr. Bowen is determined to discover who is. He is quite adamant about this and refuses to be dissuaded. He spoke with Lord Selward about the watch at which point, Lord Selward demanded that he return the stolen watch or suffer the consequences. Mr. Bowen refused and Lord Selward has now indicated to me he plans to speak to Lord Ellesmere about the matter and if that does not result in the watch being returned, he will speak with the authorities."

Mrs. Faraday's hand flew to her throat once again and her ruddy skin paled considerably. "Dear 'eaven! He mustn't!"

Rebecca reached out a comforting hand to rest upon the one that remained in Mrs. Faraday's lap. "I have managed to convince Lord Selward not to take action until I speak with Mr. Bowen. But my fear is that he will not return the watch as he feels this is his only connection to discovering who his parents were. I thought, perhaps you could tell me—"

"I do not know." The words came out quickly and the hope Rebecca harbored in her heart died a sudden death.

"But—"

Mrs. Faraday held out a hand to stay Rebecca's tongue. "I knew Mary Bowen when she was still jus' Mary Filmore. She was a lovely lady, a 'ard worker and as good a person as the day was long. She 'ad a sickness when she was young though, made it so she couldn't 'ave babies. She 'ad come to London to work 'ere but dearly missed Cornwall an' when the time came an' Lady Ellesmere needed a new 'ousekeeper for Braemore, she sent Mary 'ome. When I 'eard Mary 'ad a baby..." Mrs. Faraday shrugged. "I knew it couldn't be 'er own."

Rebecca's heart banged against her ribs. "Do you know whose it was?"

"I 'ave a strong suspicion, but I will no' ruin a lady by sayin' so."

Rebecca gripped the housekeeper's hand tighter. "But Mrs. Faraday—"

She shook her head. "No. I cannot. There is much more at stake than what you know. I wish I could 'elp you more. But you can tell Mr. Bowen this—the watch belongs to the man whose seed fathered him—forgive my bluntness, my lady."

"Think nothing of it." She cared little about bluntness at the moment and more about the fact Marcus and Lord Selward shared the same blood. What did this mean for Marcus, if anything? And what did it mean for her and her plans for the future? She pursed her lips and forced back her fears. For now.

"You must convince 'im to return the watch. Lord Walkerton will not hesitate to ruin Mr. Bowen if that is wha' it comes to. Mark my word on that." She hesitated, then asked,

"The journal. Is there any indication as to who it belonged to?"

Rebecca released Mrs. Faraday's hand and leaned back in her chair. "No, though Mr. Bowen indicated it was written by the woman who gave birth to him."

Relief washed over Mrs. Faraday's expression, though whether it was from the knowledge Marcus knew the journal belonged to his mother or the fact he did not know the lady's identity, she could not say.

"I wish I could be more help. But it is a matter best left in the past, m'lady."

Rebecca stood, disappointed she had not learned more, but perhaps being able to confirm the identity of his father would appease Marcus to a large degree and allow him enough peace of mind to return the watch before calamity struck.

"Thank you, Mrs. Faraday. I appreciate your assistance, and your confidence in this regard. If you think of anything else that might be helpful, please send word."

"I will, m' lady."

Rebecca nodded. "May I request another favor?"

"Of course, m' lady."

Rebecca reached into the pocket of her dress and handed a note she had written prior to their meeting. "Would you see this delivered to Mr. Bowen?"

Mrs. Faraday glanced at the sealed letter then up at Rebecca.

"I know it is highly improper to send such a correspondence, but I must speak to him with all do haste."

The housekeeper reached out and took the letter, slipping it the pocket of her dress and nodding. "Very well, m' lady. I will see he gets it."

Rebecca stared at her reflection in the mirror. Nancy had outdone herself, wrangling Rebecca's thick locks high atop her head into an open silver netting that allowed the ebony waves to cascade over her shoulders. Her dress, rather than being the usual plain white silk most ladies wore when masquerading as one of the Grecian goddesses, had been threaded throughout with silver, and shimmered as if moonlight touched her wherever she went. The masque, which she had yet to don, sparkled with a darker grey hue that, when held against her face, made her eyes an almost translucent silver and her lips a deep rose.

"You are a vision, my dear," her mother said standing in the open doorway of Rebecca's bedchamber.

"Am I?" She tilted her head to one side, her fingers pulling at a lock of hair that curled over her breast. She supposed her mother was right. Rebecca had never been so blind as to not be aware of her beauty, but she still hesitated to give it the same level of importance others did. Though, even as the thought slipped through her mind, she thought her own mother's beauty would make Aphrodite herself weep with envy.

Mother came into the room and stood behind her, placing her hands on Rebecca's shoulders. "I have some news."

"News?" Rebecca turned to face her mother.

Mother ushered her over to her bed and motioned for her to sit next to her. "When Lord Selward heard Nicholas was set to arrive tomorrow to escort us to Sheridan Park, he sent word he would like to speak with him. That, coupled with the rumors Selward plans on making an offer this Season can only mean one thing—your efforts were successful."

Rebecca's stomach turned sour. "He wants to speak with Nicholas?"

Mother's clear gaze roamed over Rebecca's face. She tried

to force a smile, but instead her lips trembled with the effort and she pulled them in and held them in her teeth. This was wrong, it was all so terribly wrong, and yet...what choice did she have? In the day since speaking with Mrs. Faraday, the thought had struck her that, should Marcus refuse to return the watch, perhaps the only alternative she had to keep him safe from Lord Walkerton would be to marry his son and use her influence in that regard. But would it be enough?

"You are not happy? I thought this is what you wanted?"

Rebecca nodded, still holding her lips with her teeth until they hurt from the effort. She feared speaking, afraid nothing would come out of her but the wail that built in her breast. Everything she had worked for had come to fruition and brought with it the leaden realization of how very much she did not want it. And how very, *very* much she wanted something else—*someone* else. Her heart fully and completely belonged to another man. A man she could not have.

A man she would save no matter the cost.

Mother sat quietly for a moment then reached out, wrapping her fingers around Rebecca's fisted hand. "You do not love him, do you?" Rebecca didn't answer. She didn't have to. Somehow, Mother understood her heart, in that strange way mothers had.

"I—" It was all she managed before her voice cracked and her throat choked with unspent tears. She could not tell her mother the truth. It changed nothing. If she did not marry Lord Selward, she would lose everything. Mother would watch her late husband's mistress inherit her past, and Marcus...Marcus could lose his freedom.

Mother's hand squeezed tighter. "When I was about your age, I loved a man. Quite an unsuitable man according to my parents—well, according to everybody really, but I cared little. He was handsome and charming and when I was with him, it was as if the whole world had opened up to greet me. A world that, until I had met him, I didn't even know existed."

Rebecca had heard the arguments since early childhood, her Father's accusations of infidelity, and his resentment of her. Of Nicholas. Their house had tasted of bitterness for as long as she could remember and, for just as long, something in her mother's grey eyes spoke of sadness and regret.

The man Mother had loved was not Rebecca's father. "What happened to him?"

"My father had already entered into a marriage contract with your father. It was an extremely advantageous match, one your grandfather desperately needed to make. Our family fortunes had dwindled with each passing generation. He could no longer afford the upkeep of many of the properties. In the end, the only thing of value he had left was his daughter. He bartered me and most of the unentailed properties to the highest bidder, and that bidder happened to be your father."

"So you gave up the man you loved?"

"Not at first. In the beginning, I refused. I threatened to run off with him if they did not accept my choice. But I was young and naïve. When it came down to it, threats were made. I was told if I did not marry your father, the man I loved, and his family, would be forever ruined, and so what else could I do?"

Rebecca understood her mother's dilemma with a clarity that broke her heart. She did not need to ask who made the threats. Her father had been a powerful man from a powerful family. He did not brook disobedience or disloyalty. "Did you ever see him again, this man?"

"Briefly. But—" Mother stopped and looked away, past Rebecca to the window beyond, though she thought her gaze stretched even farther, seeing a past that was transposed over the one she had dreamed of. Would that be her fate as well?

"But by then it was too late. Afterward, he went away, and I never saw him again."

The tale did nothing to lift Rebecca's spirits, to make her believe maybe there was another way. "Why did you tell me this?"

Mother's gaze returned to her. "As a cautionary tale, I suppose. Choose with your heart, Rebecca. Not your head. I'm sure you have had a strategy this whole time, thinking you need to marry Lord Selward to keep the family properties from going to *that woman*. But I would never forgive myself if you consigned yourself to a marriage you did not want, a man you do not love, for the sake of brick and mortar, or land we rarely see. We will still have the original Blackbourne House and Sheridan Park. Nicholas will see that we do not go without. Do we really need more?"

Rebecca let her gaze drop to her lap. Despite the brave words, she did not believe her. It wasn't brick and mortar Mother held onto. It was memories. Memories her mother deserved to keep. The only thing she had left. If Rebecca did not marry Lord Selward, these would be gone. Given away as if they meant nothing. Her father's final retaliation against a woman who did not love him, who had been forced into a life she hadn't asked for or wanted. A life she chose in order to save the man she loved. Rebecca understood her mother's choice and hoped she could show as much grace and courage when the time came to make her own.

"It is not too late for you, my dear. Your destiny remains open. We will survive. If you do not love Lord Selward, do not marry him. He is a nice man, I grant you, but his family—" She stopped and shook her head.

Rebecca's head snapped up. "What of his family?"

Mother's pretty mouth pulled into a grim line. "Let's just say Lord Selward is the first heir to the Walkerton title who embodies the traits one wishes to see in a lord, but the rest of them..." She shook her head. "I would not regret for a moment if you were to disassociate yourself from his family."

"And if I did not?"

Mother fell silent for a moment, then, "I will support whatever decision you make. I know what it is like to have that choice taken away from you. I will not do to you what my parents did to me. But I beg you to think long and hard. I will counsel Nicholas to avoid meeting with Lord Selward while he is here, to put him off. It will allow you more time to make your final decision."

"Thank you," Rebecca whispered, but the reprieve did not help her heart. Even if her mother absolved her of saving the land and property rightly their own, she could not deny Lord Selward's proposal if it meant saving Marcus from persecution at Lord Walkerton's hands.

Her only hope in this regard would be to convince him to return the watch. If he did that he would be safe, and if he was safe, perhaps she could convince herself to let go of the dream of saving the properties that had once upon a time belonged to Mother's family. Maybe she could choose her future with an open heart and clear conscience.

Mother leaned in and pressed her lips against Rebecca's temple. "Now, come. We must go if we are to make the party at a respectable time."

Rebecca nodded her head in agreement, hoping Marcus adhered to her request and made an appearance. More importantly, she hoped he would agree to return the watch and save them both a future filled with misery and regret.

Rebecca had danced the quadrille and a reel, using each change and turn to sweep her gaze over the crowded ballroom in hopes of catching sight of Marcus. Her note had begged him to come, and stated that she had discovered information regarding his past. Would he heed her request? Would he give her the opportunity to change the course of their futures, to find the happiness they both deserved?

She hoped so, but hope had disappointed her too many times before for her to hold much stock in it.

The reel ended and she thanked her partner, Lord Mincer, who had done a miserable job of avoiding her toes throughout the dance. As she threaded her way through the crowd to retrieve her makeshift spear from where she had rested it near a potted plant, a hand reached out and wrapped around her arm.

"Come with me."

Chapter Sixteen

Rebecca spun on her slippered heel and came face to face with a pirate king. *Her* pirate king. The one who had filled her girlhood fantasies, with eyes so dark and deep, one glance and she was lost.

"Hurry," he said, bending to whisper the command against her ear. A shiver slithered through her. She did not hesitate to obey. Together, they skirted the edge of the crowd, avoided the dancers who were taking their places for the next set and hurried out onto the balcony that wrapped along the outer edge of Lord and Lady Doddington's stately home. They kept to the shadows, trying each door as they passed it, but all remained locked as if to keep the guests from disappearing for private assignations that might lead to scandal or ruination.

Rebecca cared little. She would risk both if it saved Marcus, though she suspected he might have a different opinion on the matter.

At the far end of the terrace they took a stairway that led down into the gardens beyond. Marcus's hand slid into hers, interlacing their fingers, and they hurried downward into the shadows and darkness. With a quick movement, he pulled her to his chest and pressed her back into an alcove created by the house's architecture and thick ivy where it crawled up the walls on either side of them. The small space left them cloaked in secrecy and, if discovered, scandal.

Moonlight sought them out and crept between the cracks and crevices of the ivy illuminating one side of Marcus's face.

"A very dramatic escape," she whispered, breathing in the scent of sandalwood and something else. Something indefinable she had come to associate with Marcus alone.

Marcus pushed his mask up, away from his face. "I believe the lady requested an audience. Have I satisfied your wishes?"

There was an edge to his voice she did not care for.

"You have."

"Good." Though he did not sound happy about his success. He released her from his arms and took a small step back. His hands came to rest on hips encased in black breeches. He wore no jacket, nor cravat, just his white shirt-sleeves and midnight colored waistcoat. It was a daring ensemble even for the masquerade and she found it hard to marry it to the Marcus who embodied the epitome of respectability. Then again, there were many aspects of his personality that had surprised her of late so likely she should take this one in her stride as well, though it was not easy. Her gaze kept drifting to the shirt ties at his throat and the narrow V that gave her a brief glimpse of his chest when he moved and the moonlight flickered over him.

"Are you angry with me?"

"Angry does not begin to touch upon it. What in the name of all that is holy were you doing poking around in my personal business? Did you give any thought to what might have happened should your note to me be intercepted? Why must you continue to put yourself in jeopardy with such foolish actions?"

She winced at his words. "When have I ever—"

"The debacle at the park."

She twisted her mouth to one side. "I can hardly be held accountable for the horse's—"

He cut her off. "Jumping in the lake."

"Fine. Two times, but—"

"Insisting I act as your besotted suitor or you would enlist some other gentleman and risk scandal should he decide to twist the situation to his own advantage."

She huffed out a breath. "None of these are neither here nor there. I needed to meet with you. Lord Selward is threatening to speak to Lord Ellesmere, possibly even the authorities, about the watch. So I decided to speak with Mrs. Faraday about your parents—"

"You did what?" The whispered words came fast and harsh. He rubbed at his forehead.

"Mrs. Faraday was in Lord and Lady Ellesmere's employ at the time you were born. I thought she might know something that could help you uncover who your parents were!"

"You had no right to involve her in this. You had no right to involve yourself!"

Rebecca took a step forward until she stood toe to toe with him. Heat radiated from his body and she wanted to envelope herself in it. Wrap her arms around him and hold him close. Protect him. Protect herself.

"You involved me, if you'll recall. You told me about the watch and the journal. And Lord Selward involved me when he indicated he meant to speak with Lord Ellesmere. I managed to hold him off with the promise I would try to convince you to return the watch to him—"

"I will not."

Oh, why must he be so stubborn!

She reached out a hand and placed it against his solid chest. Beneath her palm, his heart beat a steady rhythm. The sensation of it reverberated down her arm and calmed her at the same time it excited her.

"Is it worth your ruin not to? You do not need it. Mrs. Faraday confirmed that to the best of her knowledge Lord Walkerton is your father."

Marcus stilled and his muscles tensed. "How does she know this?"

Rebecca shook her head. "I'm uncertain. She would not say. Nor could she give a definitive answer on the identity of your mother, though she alluded to having her suspicions. But don't you see—now that you know the identity of your father—"

"Walkerton is not my father." The words cut into the space between them, sharp and dangerous.

"But, Mrs. Faraday said—"

"Edmore Bowen was my father. Walkerton is nothing to me but a man who laid with my mother and abandoned her."

Rebecca could think of nothing to say to refute his claim. Given what Mrs. Faraday insinuated with respect to Walkerton's character, she understood Marcus's need to distance himself from him.

A narrow slice of moonlight cut across his cheekbone and she reached a hand up to touch the lit skin. The hint of stubble scratched against her fingertips and a small muscle in his jaw twitched.

"You may well be right," she said. "But you know this now and so there is no reason to keep the watch. Be rid of it, and be rid of Walkerton if you so choose. Lord Selward indicated if it is not returned, his father will likely set the authorities upon you. You will be ruined, Marcus. Or worse. You do not have the protection of the House of Lords. You could be sent to gaol. I could not bear it!"

"Why? What would it matter?"

What would it matter? Did he think she didn't care? That she had no regard for him at all? Was he that blind?

"How can you ask such a thing?"

"You will continue on with your life, become Lady Selward, then Lady Walkerton, raise your children, and attend your parties. Whatever happens to me is immaterial to all of this."

He spoke the words so plainly and yet each one carved into her until the hand that touched his face fell away and her fingers curled into a fist to hit upon his chest. "Of course it is material! I do not care about parties or Lord Selward. I care about you!"

His hand came up to hold hers in place. "Do you?"

She bit down, the words that had rushed out so easily only seconds before now lodged like a lump in her throat.

"Yes." And there it was. All the emotions they had danced around. All of the feelings she had bottled up and tried to find a sensible place for. But there was no sense to this. It simply was what it was. She could no longer deny her feelings, or the sentiment behind them. "Very much."

He tilted his head to one side, studying her as if she were a new species just discovered. "Is that so?"

"Yes, it is very so." She peered up at him through her lashes. Starlight danced along the angles of his face. He returned her gaze, steady but unreadable. She took a deep breath and with that, forged ahead. "I don't want to pretend any more. Do you?"

The hint of a smile glimmered on his lips. His hand lifted and his fingers entwined in a lock of her hair, following it to where it curled over her breast. A deep ache pulled at her. "You'll be the death of me one of these days, Rebecca Sheridan, I swear it."

"I'm sorry." She wasn't sure if that was a good or bad thing, but since he did not seem overly distressed by it, she took it as good news. And, given their past, she could not fault his reasoning.

He gave a light shrug. "I suppose there are worse ways to go."

"I don't want you to go anywhere, especially not to gaol. Will you please return the watch?"

"And then what? Will you go on to marry your lord, protect your inheritance, live your life as you had planned?"

"No." She couldn't. Standing here with Marcus, his touch upon her, she could no longer deny what she had spent a fortnight—longer even—dancing around. She had tried to deny it, to do the right thing. She had failed. She could not marry Lord Selward, not when she loved another.

"You should."

His fingertips traced a line along her jaw, down her throat. The ache between her thighs increased. Deepened.

"I can't. I love—"

"Don't say it."

His words startled her. Did he not want to know? Did he not share her feelings?

"You don't feel the same?" She had been so certain. She could feel it, like this ethereal string that bound them together and refused to be broken.

He closed his eyes and tension furrowed his brow. "It does not matter what I feel. Nothing can come of this. I will not be responsible for you losing everything, nor allow you to be ruined by marrying the bastard son of some lord."

The bastard son of some lord. The words drove into her, demanded she pay attention, but to what? She did not care who Marcus's parents were; it did not change her heart.

"Would you prefer I marry a man I do not love? To be consigned to a future of unhappiness? Do you think me well-suited to Lord Selward?"

"He can give you what you deserve. I cannot."

"What do I deserve? You accused me of not knowing what happiness is, so tell me. Is this happiness?" She lifted onto her tiptoes and pressed her lips gently against the hollow beneath his cheekbone and felt the swift intake of his breath. She stayed but a heartbeat before lowering herself back down.

"Don't—"

She lifted again and this time teased the corner of his mouth. Just for a brief second, a little taste of heaven. A sinful temptation. His arm slipped around her waist and held her tight.

"Rebecca. I cannot—"

She kissed the other corner, not wanting it to feel left out. Heat pulsated through her, demanded she do more, go farther, but she held back, just a little. Just enough.

"Yes, you can. We can. Mother prefers I marry for love. I tried to deny it, but she is right. I cannot marry Lord Selward. I love you."

Something in those words, a strange bit of magic, wound around them, protected them from their past, their future, and allowed them the present, this moment. She kissed him fully this time, sealing her words and showing him everything that lived in her heart.

At first, he did not move. Tension threaded through his muscles and she sensed the inner war that waged beneath his skin. But in the end, even his good sense and his need to do the right thing could not conquer the truth.

"Rebecca." He whispered her name against her lips and she did not think anything had ever sounded so sweet or felt so complete until he kissed her, and she remembered that there was. There was this. And it was wonderful. Heady and exhilarating, it whisked away all her fear and worry. It erased their past and burned the obstacles to their future until they were nothing but cinder and ash.

His hands cradled her face and his body pushed her back,

farther into the alcove until cool stone met her back. Desire raged through her and she hated the barrier of silk and wool and linen that kept her from feeling him, all of him. She relished his kiss, but wanted so much more. She wanted all of him, and she wanted to give him all of her.

But all too soon it ended, the glorious dream of what could be. Too soon he pulled away and allowed reality to creep in and spoil the rosy glow his kiss had created.

Marcus's chest rose and fell with each breath and his forehead pressed against hers, his eyes shut tightly against the night.

"We cannot do this. I will not drag you into whatever it is I must face." He lifted his head away from her and Rebecca hated the distance even those few inches created. She wanted to go back, back to the kiss, back to the vision of their future it had built. "I will not have you tarnished by it. I am not a lord. I'm a bastard, for chrissakes!"

And then it hit her; even before she could refute his claim. The words in her father's will. How had she not seen it before?

She gripped the front of his shirt and fisted it in her hand. Excitement shot through her and victory seared her veins. "You are Walkerton's eldest son!"

He looked down at her, confusion mixed with the remnants of passion. "What of it?"

"Father's will stated I must marry a titled lord or *the eldest son of a titled lord*. Don't you see? We can be together and I will not lose anything!"

Marcus shook his head. "I am not his recognized son. I was born on the wrong side of the blanket."

"But the will says nothing about that, only that it be a titled lord's eldest son. You are several years old than Lord Selward, and therefore the eldest." Why was he not as excited about this as she? It was the answer to all their problems! She'd been a fool not to see it before.

He smiled at her, but the gesture held no mirth, none of the happiness or relief she'd experienced at the revelation.

"Walkerton has not recognized me as his son and therefore, neither will the law."

"But—"

Marcus shook his head. "It is a fine idea. But not one that will bear fruit, I'm afraid. I have lived amongst the ton for over twenty years, and at no point has he ever come forward to claim me. Even now, when I am in possession of this watch, there has been no overture to exchange acknowledgement for its return."

Hope—damnable hope!—crashed around her.

"Is there nothing we can do?" The plea whispered out of her, laced with desperation. She could not let him go. She could not stand here and watch him walk away, taking every hope and dream she had for the future with him.

His fingers touched her face, tipped her chin upward to meet his lips. He kissed her gently but when she tried to deepen it, he pulled away.

"I will not drag you into this."

And then he stepped away, robbing her of the heat from his body, his kiss.

"Marcus—"

"No." One word. One word to end the last shred of hope she had within her. "Go," he said, pointing toward the staircase that led up to the terrace. "Keep to the shadows then slip back inside. I will follow in a few moments."

She took a step toward him but he took two back. He would not allow her to touch him, to pull them back into the lie the hope had been.

It was over. Tears lumped in her throat, dense and painful. She stumbled from the alcove, unable to feel her legs, or anything else for that matter. When she reached the staircase, she turned.

"Tell me one thing," she whispered. "Do you love me too?"

He stood silent but something in her question had wounded him in such a way not even the dark and shadow could hide it. She thought he wouldn't answer, but then he did, and she'd almost wished he hadn't.

"More than my own life."

And yet it still wasn't enough.

Chapter Seventeen

"Will you not reconsider and join us at Lakefield Abbey? Surely you can carry on business from there, Bowen," Spence said, taking a sip of the aged brandy.

Marcus shook his head as he bent over the billiards table and lined up his shot. Nick and Spence had convinced him to join them at the Devil's Lair as the guest of the notorious Lord Hawksmoor who owned the controlling interest in the gaming hell. The man was an old friend of Nick's acquaintance and one of the few he'd kept from his life before he'd unburdened himself of his scandalous past and married Abigail. Marcus had not wanted to go. He had not wanted to do much of anything but stare out the window and brood.

If he hadn't recognized how damned pathetic he'd become, likely he would still be sitting there instead of being soundly trounced at billiards by the far more skilled Hawksmoor.

"I cannot leave London. I have business to attend to." That it had little to do with Lord Ellesmere's estates and everything to do with digging into his own past he did not bother to mention. "I promise I will arrive in time for the annual party at Sheridan Park."

He took his shot and watched as the ball teetered on the edge of the pocket, mocking him before it stilled and stayed. How closely it symbolized his luck of late. Just when he thought he was getting close to something, the truth eluded him and left him wavering on the edge.

"Why, thank you, Mr. Bowen," Hawksmoor said with a sly smile. "I almost wish we had bet money on the game. And I don't recall receiving an invite to the party, Blackbourne. I'm injured."

"What you are," Nick said. "—is an abominable liar. You know full well you received an invite. You simply ignored it because you have no more interest in spending two weeks in the country surrounded by lords and ladies you've stripped of large quantities of money than you do in marrying a proper young lady and squeezing out a few pups of your own."

Hawksmoor chuckled, the only answer he'd give on the matter, and bent over the table, his dark hair meshing with the shadows. He split two balls in opposite directions, knocking both—and the one Marcus left teetering on the edge—into the corner pockets. The viscount's skill at billiards was a thing to behold.

"Disgusting," Spence muttered in praise before turning back to Marcus. "What business is so pressing that you cannot conduct it from the Abbey?"

"I simply wish to tie up a few loose ends before I leave the city." Loose ends. As if his identity and origins could be summed up so easily. As if it would change anything and make it possible to put the matter to rest, marry Rebecca and live the life he'd always dreamed of.

But it wasn't that simple.

When he sent her back to the masquerade he had been determined that was the end of it. He should have known better. He'd spent the better part of the night tossing and turning, his mind working furiously to find a solution and his body reliving her touch, her kiss, her taste, until it became difficult to concentrate on anything else.

By the time morning dawned, he determined he must turn over every stone, look into every dark corner. He could not walk away from her. He could not consign them both to a life neither wanted, without at least trying.

"Then there is no reason for you not to come sooner rather than later," Nick said. "You need to see your godson, after all."

Marcus smiled and leaned a hip against the billiards table. "That I do."

"Why you chose him to be the boy's godfather is beyond me," Spence said. "It is obvious I am the better choice."

Nick turned to Spence and crossed his arms over his chest. "You are his uncle."

"How can I be his uncle? At best I am a second cousin through marriage or something of that sort. Glenmor is the child's only uncle."

"True enough," Nick allowed. "Either way, we shall make you an honorary uncle."

Spence appeared only somewhat mollified. "I suppose that will do."

Marcus didn't bother to suggest that should things turn out badly with his quest for his true parentage, Nick might want to rethink his godfather status. After all, what lord wanted a bastard for his heir's godfather? Or as his brother-in-law?

"I cannot believe what I'm hearing." Hawksmoor straightened as the last ball sunk into the pocket in the far corner of the table. "I invited the three of you here in the hopes of recapturing some semblance of our more youthful escapades and instead the three of you are nattering on about babies like old nannies. What has happened to the lot of you?"

"I believe it's called happiness, Hawksmoor," Nick said.

Hawksmoor scowled as he wracked the balls on the table once more. "A state of delusion is more like it. Mr. Bowen, shall we have another go? And have none of you considered that Mr. Bowen here may have a mistress of untold talent, and cannot bear to leave her side any sooner than necessary?" Hawksmoor broke and two balls slid into pockets on opposite sides of the table.

Nick turned with a wide-eyed expression. Marcus didn't know whether to be amused or insulted that the idea he had a mistress seemed so shocking. "Do you?"

"He doesn't," Spence informed them. "I have already asked."

Marcus leaned over the table and took his first shot. One ball, corner pocket. "Both of you need to learn to mind your own business."

"Why should we," Nick said, a lazy grin spreading across his face as he leaned a hip against the table. "Yours is proving far more interesting."

Spence grabbed at his chest. "Sweet Judas! Is this what we have come to, Nick? Have we become so tame that now Bowen is more interesting than either of us?"

Marcus toyed with the idea of running them both through with his billiards' cue but he didn't think Hawksmoor would appreciate the bloodletting on his expensive rug. He took another shot but missed.

The game went quickly, though Marcus did not fool himself into how it would end. That was the thing with games such as this. When one went up against a far more skilled player, the end was predictable and inevitable. The best you could do was try not to make a raging fool of yourself.

Hawksmoor knocked another ball into a side pocket. There were only two left. He would not get another chance. He turned his attention to Nick.

"I spoke with Lady Rebecca the other day. She mentioned to me the stipulations regarding your father's will."

Nick's dark eyebrows lifted. "Let me understand correctly, my darling little sister swore me to secrecy about the will and yet she told you?"

"Hardly surprising," Spence said, as Hawksmoor racked the balls on the table under the misguided thought someone would be foolish enough to damage their ego further by playing another game with him.

Nick turned to face Spence. "Why is it not surprising?"

Spence jerked his head in Marcus's direction. "She's always been rather fond of Bowen. She told me once she thought him a pirate king." He whispered the last part as if it were a secret. "Which I found infinitely amusing given his fear of water."

"I do not have a fear of water," Marcus said.

Nick grinned. "No? What would you call it?"

"A healthy distaste. And if you'll recall, I was the one who jumped into the water to save your darling sister when she decided to swim fully clothed in the lake. If memory serves, the two of you were too busy trying to charm your way beneath the skirts of a rather buxom dairy maid."

"Ah," Nick looked upward as if pulling the memory out of the air. "I do recall. Dear Maisie—"

"Marnie," Spence corrected. "I believe her name was Marnie."

Nick straightened. "Was it?"

"Quite certain. Regardless, the way that woman pulled on the teats of those cows with long, sure strokes..." Spence let out a long sigh. "It made my heart ache."

Marcus scowled. "I don't believe your heart was the organ affected. And regardless, that is not the point of my bringing the matter of Lady Rebecca's inheritance stipulations up."

"Right. The will. Of course. What is your point on that?" Nick turned to Spence and filled him in.

Hawksmoor let out a long whistle. "Bloody hell. For a dowry like that, I'd almost be inclined to marry her."

Nick pointed a finger at the disreputable viscount. "Stay away from my sister."

"He'd have to get past Bowen first," Spence said and Marcus considered skewering his friend once again.

"What is that supposed to mean? Have you and Rebecca... do you mean to tell me...Bowen!" The words sputtered out of Nick as he forgot Hawksmoor and turned on Marcus who held up both hands in a calming manner, never letting go of the pool cue, just in case. Nick did not always listen to reason when it came to the women in his family.

"Calm down. My point is, I have come to the understanding she may be marrying Selward for no other reason than to ensure the properties are not lost to your father's mistress. She feels a duty in that regard."

"Thank God," Nick said on a sharp exhale. "That makes much more sense than her actually loving that spineless fop."

"Oh, come now," Hawksmoor said, setting aside his billiards' cue when no one offered to be embarrassed by him yet again. "Selward is a tad spiritless, I will give you that, but would we call him a fop? The boy is yet young and, in truth, he's carried much on his shoulders during his father's repeated and lengthy absences. He can't be all bad."

"Would you marry him?" Nick asked.

"I'm afraid not. Much too hairy for my tastes and should I ever get around to taking a bride, I far prefer the parts that dangle be situated a bit higher than those of young Selward."

"Can we return to the matter at hand," Marcus suggested. Having a conversation with these three ranked on the same level as herding geese.

Nick turned his attention back to Marcus. "Why are you concerned about who Rebecca marries?"

Marcus opened his mouth but the words would not come. Mostly due to the fact he had not expected the question and therefore had not prepared an answer. He only meant to convince Nick to delay the situation as best he could until Marcus could find a way around it, or through it. Hell, he'd settle for over or under it. Anything that allowed Rebecca to keep the family properties intact without spending a lifetime with a man she did not love.

"He's smitten with her," Spence said, filling the empty space left by Marcus's own lack of explanation.

Marcus sorely regretted not partaking in the skewering.

Nick's eyes widened. "Is it true?"

"It's true," Spence answered. "He may try to deny it. I suspect he's been lying to himself about it for quite some time, but honestly, Bowen, is it not time to face facts?"

Forget skewering. He preferred a much slower, painful death for his least favorite friend. "My feelings are irrelevant—"

Nick took a step toward him and Marcus considered grabbing Spence and using him as a shield. It would serve the man right. "Then you *do* have feelings for her?"

Marcus cleared his throat. "My point is—" If these two idiots would ever let him get it out, "—is that if you allow me to look at the language of the document, I may be able to find a loophole that would allow Lady Rebecca a bit more freedom of choice in regards to her husband."

Another step. "So that she might choose you?"

Marcus did not answer. That was the problem, she had

already chosen him. She had claimed her love and he had admitted to the same. It mattered not that his head told him nothing could come of it, his heart refused to listen. Instead, it insisted there had to be a way. Surely Fate, even at its most cruel, would not dangle such a perfect future in front of him then yank it away just as he reached for it.

"Jesus, Bowen." Nick rubbed a hand over his forehead and stared at Marcus with disbelief. "How did I not see this?"

"Uh, I believe you have been a bit busy of late," Spence said. "What with scandals—"

"And Abigail," Marcus added.

"And babies and such." Hawksmoor pushed away from the billiards table and went to the sideboard to pour a drink that he handed to Spence. Who handed it to Marcus. Who then passed it to Nick.

Nick threw his head back as the dark liquid shot down his throat. He winced then returned his attention to the group.

"She could have made a worse choice," Spence suggested.

Nick's shoulders slumped and he shook his head. "She could not have made a better one."

Something in Marcus eased as Nick smiled at him. "Don't start calling me brother just yet. This story is far from over."

Nick's brows snapped together. "What do you mean?"

"Does this have something to do with that deuced watch?" Spence asked.

"Watch? What watch? Would someone tell me what the hell has been going on while I've been gone?" Nick threw his arms up in frustration but before Marcus could grant his request, the billiards room door slammed opened and bounced against the wall behind it.

"You, there!"

The group turned to face the man brave enough to breach the inner sanctum of The Devil's Lair and incur Hawksmoor's legendry wrath. The intruder was older; weathered more by excess than age based on his haggard appearance. One hand held a brandy and from the way the gentleman stumbled into the room, Marcus guessed it wasn't his first.

He could not claim an acquaintance, though the man's attention and accusing finger pointed directly at Marcus's chest.

Walkerton.

A chill ran up Marcus's spine and settled at the base of his neck. His gaze searched the man's face, trying to decipher a hint of resemblance. He found none.

Hawksmoor picked up his billiards cue and moved forward, the essence of danger in each silent step. "Walkerton. Returned to London for a brief sojourn, have we? I see you've made good use of your time thus far."

Walkerton took another step but Hawksmoor's cue shot out like a saber and hit the other man square in the chest, stopping him cold. His body swayed as if equilibrium was a foreign concept. After a few seconds, his glare found Marcus once again.

"You have my watch, you thieving bastard."

Bastard. The moniker cut into him.

Hawksmoor tilted his head to one side and pushed the cue farther into Walkerton's chest, eliciting a grunt from the man. "Are you honestly breaking into my private rooms to throw salacious accusations at my guests?"

"You've obviously had too much to drink," Nick said. "Bowen is neither a thief nor a bastard."

Marcus could attest to the veracity of the first, but not the latter. Still, he held his tongue. Let Walkerton reveal his cards first, then, once he understood what he dealt with, he would determine how best to act.

"Do you deny you have in your possession the watch stolen from my family thirty years ago?" Walkerton swiped an arm through the air and the drink sloshed over the rim and soaked into the wool sleeve of his coat.

"Sweet Judas, Bowen!" Spence asked, a hint of laughter in his voice. He turned to Marcus, his eyebrows arching upward. "Is this what you get up to in your spare time? Shame on you!"

Nick shook his head. "It's always the quiet ones, isn't it?"

Walkerton drank down the last of his drink in one toss and set the snifter on a table next to him, but his aim was off and the glass wobbled on the edge before falling to the floor. It hit the carpet and rolled on its curved edges to rest against the clawed foot of the table.

"It matters not how he came to it, but he has it now. My son demanded its return and he refused." *His son.* An intentional slight? If so, likely Walkerton would never acknowledge him as such. "The insipid idiot let it go at that, but I'm here now and you will return it to me or know my full wrath."

Nick started to step forward but Marcus held out a hand and stopped him. He did not want Nick or Spence involved in this mess. He approached Walkerton, resting a hand on the cue Hawksmoor jabbed into the man's chest and moving it out of his way. He stood toe-to-toe with Walkerton. The earl reeked of drink and the whites of his eyes were bloodshot, the rims edged in red. He searched his face, but aside from the brown eyes and lean build, he could see nothing that pinpointed a relation.

"I thought you had already discovered the thief, Walkerton. Had you not accused one of your maids of stealing it? Tossed her out into the streets without even the benefit of a reference, I was told."

"Why would I have offered the slut a reference?" The words seethed out of him.

"I suspect the reason for that has more to do with your own lack of character than any guilt the young lady bore."

"Lady," Walkerton spat. "She spread her legs like all the

rest and then expected payment for her willingness. When I didn't give it, she took it herself."

"You're a pig." That this man's blood ran through his veins sickened him.

"You'll give me back my watch or suffer—"

"What do you know of suffering?" Marcus had known this man all of two minutes and already despised him. The picture Cosgrove had painted of him had been far too kind. "From what I hear, you've brought nothing but grief to anyone unfortunate enough to cross your path."

"A fact you will discover for yourself if my watch is not returned."

A man, larger than any two of them put together, appeared in the open door. "Sorry, boss. He got by us somehow."

Hawksmoor's voice came from behind Marcus. "Remove him from the Lair, Tobias, and see that he does not grace us with his presence again."

"Yes, boss." Tobias reached for Walkerton, but the earl pulled his arm away. "Touch me and you will regret it, you son of a whore!"

"If he does not touch you, I will." Marcus issued his own threat, the words laced with menace and disgust. Whoever his mother was, she had done him a great service allowing him to claim Edmore Bowen as his father instead of this man. "And if you think to threaten me again, save your breath. The watch is mine."

"You'll regret that, you bastard. Mark my words."

"Mark mine."

Tobias dragged the drunken Walkerton from the room but it was a long while after before Marcus's muscles relaxed. And a long while after that before the man's threats stopped echoing inside his head.

"What the hell was that?" Nick asked.

"That," Marcus said, turning to face the man he had called friend for most of his life, "was my father."

The snifter of brandy slid from Nick's hand and hit the floor with a thud that echoed through the quiet room.

"As I said," Marcus continued. "The story is far from over."

Chapter Eighteen

"Rebecca!"

Rebecca started out of a sound sleep, the first one she'd had since the masquerade and one she'd fought hard to achieve with heavy helpings of warm milk and lavender, which Cook insisted would assist her in finding the escape she wished for. It had worked, and blessed oblivion was hers. At least until her brother arrived home and bellowed her name up the stairwell, heedless of the sleeping household.

She pushed aside the blankets and reached for her dressing gown at the end of the bed. By the time she'd shrugged into it her brother had reached her door and banged upon the other side until it rattled in its frame.

She crossed the room and yanked the door open, stopping her brother mid-pound. "Good heavens, Nicholas, do you mean to wake the dead?"

He straightened and pulled at the sleeves of his jacket, appearing only slightly chagrined. "No. Not the dead. Just you."

"Well you have failed in your endeavor then." Rebecca poked her gaze around her brother's large frame to follow the voice that had joined them. Mother strode down the hallway, her dressing gown billowing around her like a specter and a stern expression on her face. A thick blonde braid curled over her shoulder. "What is the meaning of this, Nicholas?"

"Oh. Mother. Sorry, I did not mean to wake you."

"It appears I was his intended target." Rebecca turned back to Nicholas. "Have you been drinking?"

"No! Well, I mean, yes, but not in excess and I really do not think you are in a position to question my behavior."

Her heart stuttered to a stop. "I beg your pardon?"

Mother let out an exasperated sigh, one she often used when Nicholas was behaving like a total boor. As he was now. "Nicholas, what are you about? You're talking nonsense."

Her brother pointed a finger in Rebecca's direction and straightened. "Do you know what she has been up to?"

Good heavens! What did he know? Had Marcus—? But no, Marcus would never have...would he? A sinking doubt entered her mind. If Marcus was determined they not be together, what better way than to confess all to her overprotective brother. A few passionate kisses would be enough to make Nicholas whisk her away to the country and that would be the end of it.

Mother folded her arms and cocked her head to one side. "And what has she been up to?"

"She and Marcus have—" The finger that had pointed at her now swirled in a small circle. "That is, they've—"

"Fallen in love?" Mother added.

Both Rebecca and Nicholas looked at her in shock. How did she know?

"How did you know?" Nicholas echoed.

"Oh, for heaven's sakes, I am not blind," Mother said. "Rebecca has harbored feelings for Marcus since she was a young girl."

"Mother!" Rebecca could not believe what she was hearing. Her own truth, the one she had tried to deny for so long, had been obvious to all the entire time!

Mother's expression softened. "Why do you think I have counseled you to put aside this notion you have of preserving your inheritance in favor of being with the man you love? The estates and the property, the income that comes with it is all well and good, but it won't keep you company into your old age. It won't fill your heart with joy. And you cannot put a price on joy, my dear."

But what joy could she feel if it came at the expense of her own mother's? "It isn't as easy as that."

Marcus had tried to tell her but she'd refused to listen. Yet over the past two days she'd been able to think of little else, wishing there was something more she could do, wracking her brain and exhausting her imagination, but every scenario she concocted had the ugly and unwanted stamp of improbability on it.

"She's right, Mother," Nicholas said.

Rebecca's head snapped up and she stared at her brother. *He knew.* "What did Marcus tell you?"

Nicholas let out a long breath and his gaze moved between Rebecca and their mother. "He told me the Bowens are not his true parents." Rebecca watched her mother closely, but instead of looking shocked she simply nodded.

"You knew?"

"I suspected."

Rebecca narrowed her gaze. "What else do you know?"

Mother shook her head. "Nothing that will be of any help, I'm afraid."

"Did you know Walkerton was the man who fathered him?" Nicholas asked.

Shock rippled across Mother's expression then settled into something deeper, as if on some level she had known something without realizing it. "No."

Nicholas turned his attention back to Rebecca. "I suppose that creates a bit of a conundrum for you."

"One might say." Choose one brother, save her inheritance and live a life of comfort and station. Choose the other and lose her inheritance, rob her mother of everything she'd once had and stand by while her father's lover reaped the reward.

"Unless we can get Walkerton to acknowledge he is, indeed, Bowen's father," Nicholas said.

Rebecca's shoulders slumped and she leaned against the doorframe for support. "Marcus said that wouldn't work. I already thought of it."

"Bowen looked at the language of the will," Nicholas said. "He said you were right. All that is required is that your husband be either a titled lord, or the eldest son of a titled lord. Where no specific stipulation of legitimacy being a requirement is made, it cannot be factored in. All we need is to verify Bowen is indeed the eldest son of Walkerton, and have Walkerton admit as much."

"When did Marcus see the will?"

"Just now. He's downstairs in my study." Rebecca pushed past her brother. "Rebecca! You cannot go down there like that."

"Let her be." Mother's words echoed behind her but she had already reached the steps and had no intention of stopping. Hang propriety. She needed to see him, to hear the words from his own mouth.

Her feet flew down the steps, barely touching them. She hung onto the banister when she reached the end and used it to propel her around the corner and down the hallway where she found him exactly where Nicholas said he would be. She stopped short.

Papers were strewn about the flat surface of Nicholas's desk where Marcus poured studiously over them. He'd divested himself of his jacket and cravat and his sleeves were rolled up, as if he meant to wrestle the words of the will into submission and not stop until he'd won.

He'd never looked more handsome to her than in that moment. This man, who even when the odds were stacked against them and they stood on the sharp edge of ruin or rescue, refused to give up. Her errant knight. Her pirate king.

The candle flame in front of him wavered and he glanced up. Surprise registered in his expression and then something else. Something deeper, something that drew her into the room. To him.

"Rebecca." He rose from the chair and looked past her as if expecting to see someone else.

"Nicholas is upstairs," she supplied. "Mother made him stay."

"Your mother?"

Rebecca smiled. "It is a long story. Suffice to say, she knows a thing or two about love."

She stepped farther into the room, her walk quickly turning to a run. She vaulted into his arms that opened to accept her and clung to him tightly, afraid to let go. Afraid if she did, she would wake up and discover it was nothing but a dream brought on by too much warm milk and lavender.

His lips pressed into her hair and his embrace tightened, as if he shared the same fear.

"It's a long shot," he whispered, the heat of his breath against her ear sending shivers down her spine.

"I don't care." She lifted her head and gazed up at him, seeing the resolve in his eyes. "We'll find a way."

He touched her face, brushing aside the stray tendrils that sleep had dislodged from her braid, letting them tangle around his fingers. "I told Spence and your brother."

"I know."

"About everything."

"Everything being...?"

"The kiss. Well, kisses actually."

"We do seem to have a habit of doing that, don't we?"

A smile tugged at his lips now and she desperately wanted to kiss him, but a smile from Marcus was such a precious thing she did not want to miss it.

"I would like to do it now," he whispered, as if reading her mind.

"I would like that too."

He needed to stop. They were in her brother's study, for God sakes, even if Rebecca's mother had instructed Nick to stay put. But he couldn't stop. Wouldn't. Rebecca's nearness did not allow him to consider consequences, to weigh out the pros and cons. When he held her in his arms, he could think only of her, of having her in his life, fully and completely. Forever.

He touched her face, letting his fingers trail over its delicate structure and gentle valleys. She was pure perfection. Even the barely discernible scar that edged her top lip was exactly as it should be. His thumb brushed over it and he leaned down to press a gentle kiss there, as if some long forgotten hurt remained.

That one small contact was not enough. He needed more. So much more. He kissed her slowly, an exploration of light kisses, nibbles and bites, teasing until the passion that had burned low for so long roared to life and raged hot, scorching everything in his path.

He'd lived his whole life being careful and his caution had served him well—to a point. But the point had now been reached where careful did not suffice. This was a moment of risk, a time to step beyond what was comfortable and safe. He could hide in the background no more. If he wanted her, boldness must prevail, no matter the danger involved.

One hand slid to her curved buttock and he pulled her fully against him until the softness of her body pushed against his cock through the thin fabric of her nightdress. A low moan echoed in his throat when she shifted her hips and pressed against him with more force. He grew hard in an instant.

His fingertips made a slow, torturous trail down the length of her throat and heat pulsated throughout his body, pooling in his groin, demanding more. He palmed her breast and his thumb brushed the nipple. Her hips pushed forward again as she gasped into his mouth.

Dear lord, how would he ever survive this?

He wouldn't. He understood that now. It would change him, forever. There would be no going back. Everything would have a different cast to it, a different meaning. Nothing would remain untouched.

And if he failed?

He closed his eyes, resisting the thought, the voice in his head that still counseled prudence, restraint. But the voice refused to quiet, refused to allow him this moment. Not now. Not yet. *Damn it!*

He lifted his head, his breath coming hard and fast. "We need to stop."

Rebecca shook her head and reached for his mouth again. "We have Nicholas's blessing. And Mother's."

Marcus let out a short laugh. "Not for this." For this, Nicholas would flog him in the middle of Hyde Park. Her tongue teased the crease of his lips. It would be worth every bloody strike. He took in a shuddering breath. "We need to wait."

"For what? Marriage?"

He nodded. Words eluded him as her nimble fingers unfastened the buttons of his waistcoat and shoved it off his shoulders. Sweet Jesus. His head fell back as her mouth pressed against his neck, and the buttons of his shirt met the same fate as his waistcoat. When her lips pressed against his hot skin he stumbled back against the edge of the desk, bringing her with him.

His cock strained against the front of his trousers and God help him, if she went any farther down with her exploration he'd embarrass himself like a green boy.

"Stop."

But she did not listen. He gripped her hands as they rested on his hips and hauled her up to face him, turning her swiftly until her soft little rump nestled between his legs and he learned the true meaning of exquisite torture. Learned it could kill a man for certain when she wiggled against him.

"Marcus, please! It aches."

He stilled. "What aches?"

"I—me. Deep inside. Please." She shifted against him, agitated, the fever raging through his veins invading hers as well. His forehead fell against her shoulder. He couldn't. It wasn't right. Then, "Make it stop."

He squeezed his eyes shut then felt her hand move and he reached for it as she pressed it against the juncture at her thighs. And he was lost. Lost in want and need and lust and love. Everything about her consumed him and he did not know how to make it stop. How to set it aside so he could think straight and do the right thing.

But what was the right thing?

His muddled mind could not find the answer and when it tried, his body simply ignored it and went on about its business of holding and caressing her and letting her move his hand to replace her own. Her heat seared his skin through the thin cotton and he wished for all the world they were not leaning against the desk in her brother's study, her family one floor above, and she still an innocent he had no right to. Not yet.

As if she sensed his hesitancy, she placed her hand over his to hold it in place. "If you make the ache stop and I won't ask for anything beyond that. Please, Marcus. I only want—" She shook her head. "I don't know what I want, but you know, don't you? You know what will make it stop?"

She pushed into his hand and he shut his eyes and nodded. He could not give her everything he wanted, everything she wanted. But he could give her this. "Lift your nightdress," he whispered.

She complied, inching the light material upward bit by bit, gathering it in her hands until it was bunched around her hips.

"Now what?"

"Spread your legs a little and lean your weight against me."

Again, she did as he bade, trusting him. He kissed her neck and tried to ignore the burgeoning erection as her backside pressed into him. An impossible task. He reached around her to the thin pair of cotton drawers. His fingertips slipped beneath the hem at her thigh and teased her skin. Her breath caught and she threw her head back against his shoulder. The candle on the desk wavered, its light licking her ivory skin. She was the most remarkable creature he had ever encountered. Equal parts beauty and intelligence, warmth and courage.

"That's making it worse."

He smiled, kissed the rim of her ear then teased her inner thigh until she squirmed against him and he risked losing himself if he she didn't stop. His fingers found her moist heat and slid slowly inside. Her body stiffened in shock.

"Oh!"

He waited. The seconds ticked by on the clock above the mantle, each one a slow torment until her body accepted his touch and relaxed once more. "Do you want me to keep going?"

"Oh, yes." The words came on a breath.

She was slick with wanting as he slid his fingers through the folds of her innocence. She arched her back and one hand released her skirts and reached for him, attempting to find purchase as his hand moved back and forth in a slow, torturous motion. He applied the pressure of his palm against the nub at the base of her womanhood with each stroke until she writhed against him, words coming from her, nonsensical and interrupted as she gasped for breath. She was close and it killed him that he could not share it with her. But this was enough. He would take care of himself later, alone, with the memories of this moment ripe in his mind.

He shifted her slightly, giving him more access and slipped a finger through the folds and let it be enveloped in her wet warmth. She gasped then pushed against him. He withdrew then did it again, mimicking the movements he wished another part of his anatomy made. She moved against him, lifting herself up and down just enough, thrusting her hips against his hand with increasing fervor, lost in the sensations that coursed through her body. She no longer made any sound, just breath and movement and he let her be, holding her tightly to him with one arm as he pleasured her.

Her movements became shorter and her body stiffened, the muscles pulling in on themselves as she convulsed around his fingers, her head thrown back against his chest so he could watch her expression of pleasure and surprise. As her climax came to an end, he withdrew his fingers and pressed his hand against her one last time, then let her nightdress fall down to cover her shapely legs.

Her breath came deeply as he held her.

"Are you all right, my love?" Did she regret what she asked of him?

"Oh, yes," she said, and he could hear the smile in her words. The relief was short-lived as worry and guilt charged in.

He should have waited. Put her off. There was much left to be settled and they may still fail at the task set out before them.

Rebecca turned in his arms and cupped her hands to his face. "You are a most astonishing man, Marcus Bowen. I had no idea you could do such things."

He thought to tell her that likely any man worth his weight in salt possessed the same knowledge as he in this regard, but he did not want her thinking about other men and what they could do and so he held his tongue.

"You should return upstairs before Nick decides your Mother is mad for allowing us to be together alone."

Her cheeks glowed from the pleasure she'd found at his hands. "I do not wish to leave you. I want to help."

He lifted an eyebrow and any number of images rushed through his mind as to what help she could give that would alleviate the pressure in his groin.

She laughed lightly as if sensing his thoughts. "I mean with getting Lord Walkerton to claim you are his son."

"No. I do not want you involved in this. There is no assurance this will turn out well and I will not have you adversely affected if things do not. Walkerton is unpredictable. Nick is taking you and your mother to Sheridan Park on the morrow and I am traveling to Cornwall."

She pushed at his chest until he reluctantly released her. "Cornwall? Why?"

"Because it is where I was born and there may be evidence yet to support my claim. If so, I need to uncover it. I won't be gone long. When I return, I will take up residence at Northill Hall."

"Northill? But I thought you—"

He shook his head. "Nick and Spence suggested my claim might be given more credence if I hold the status of landowner, successful in my own right and not someone simply trying to jump above their station. I signed the papers and dispatched them to Lord Franklyn this night and delivered a note to Mr. Cosgrove hiring him to care for the property. He and his daughter will leave tomorrow as well."

"His daughter?"

"Yes. Madalene."

A disgruntled look settled upon her lovely face. "Is there even a remote chance she is old and covered in warts?"

He smiled. He should not be so thrilled at this show of possessiveness but he could not help himself. "I'm afraid not. She's about your age. Quite pretty, actually." He had yet to actually meet the young lady in question and only had her father's word to go on, but he didn't bother mentioning that.

"I do not like the idea of you living with another woman."

He pulled her back into his arms and planted a quick kiss on her lips then tucked her beneath his chin. "If all goes as I wish it to, we will be together soon enough."

She lifted her head, refusing to be mollified. "And if all does not as you wish it?"

He held her gaze, wishing platitudes would hold her fears at bay. His fingers traced the line of her cheekbone, jaw, his thumb brushed over her plump bottom lip.

"Then I will let you go."

Her expression stilled, anger lighting her eyes. "I find I do not care much for your solution in that regard."

"No, I didn't suspect you would."

She fisted her fingers into his shirt. "Then you had best be successful. I am not inclined to have another man do to me what you did this night."

A wave of jealousy flamed his insides. He wrapped her in his arms and held her tightly against his chest.

You are mine!

But he held the words inside. If he failed, he would have no other choice but to let her go.

Chapter Nineteen

"Marcus!"

The sound of Lord Ellesmere's tone ricocheted down the hallway like a shot. Marcus stopped and turned to find the older man striding purposefully toward him. His walking stick assaulted the hardwood with a violence that sent a tremor of unease through him.

He dreaded the confrontation ahead. It had been late when he arrived home last night, the taste of Rebecca still on his tongue, the need for her still raging through his body. He hadn't wanted to wake Lord and Lady Ellesmere at such an hour to tell them he was leaving, but nor could he linger and wait. He'd arranged to have his belongings packed, with instructions to be loaded onto one of two hired carriages first thing in the morning. The second would convey Mr. Cosgrove and his daughter and both would carry on to Northill Hall. For himself, Hawksmoor had given him use of one of his carriages and drivers. If the weather held, he should be able to make the trip to Cornwall in four days, the return to Hampshire and Northill Hall in a little less.

At least a week before he could see her again. The separation pained him. He despised the idea of leaving her anywhere near the vicinity of Lord Walkerton, or Lord Selward, even with Nick there to keep her safe.

The sooner he made this trip, the sooner he could come home. To her. And hopefully with enough proof to be able to keep her in his life forever.

"I was just on my way to see you," he said as Lord Ellesmere drew closer.

"To inform me as to why your belongings are being loaded onto an awaiting carriage, no doubt?"

"Lord Ellesmere—" Marcus took a few steps forward, his steps were slow, reluctant. He had hoped to sit down with the marquess over breakfast and explain the situation to him—or as much of it as he could without compromising Rebecca's reputation.

"The footman indicated you were going to Cornwall. Is this true?" Agitation bit into the lines of the marquess's face.

"Yes."

"Because of this?" He thrust an opened letter at Marcus's chest. "It arrived with the morning post."

"What is it?" Marcus pulled the letter away from his chest and unfolded it, taking note of the fact it was addressed to Lord Ellesmere. As he read the words, acid burned in his gut.

"Would you care to tell me what this is about? What vileness brings this man's letter—his accusations—into my home? My family?"

Marcus refolded the letter and handed it back to Lord Ellesmere, but the other man refused to take it, backing away from the missive as if it were tainted. Finally Marcus let his hand, and the letter, fall to his side.

"It is nothing. I am dealing with the matter." He kept his voice steady though his insides quaked as if the earth shook and crumbled beneath him. In a sense, he supposed it did.

"Matter? Walkerton—" He spit the name out like poison.

"—has accused you of theft. From every indication he plans on taking the matter to the authorities. Lady Ellesmere has told me of your questions to her. Why do you refuse to heed her counsel and let this matter be?"

Marcus took a deep breath and forced his mind to remain clear despite the thoughts clamoring to get in.

"Because I need to know the truth. And I need Lord Walkerton to claim me as his son."

A vein near Lord Ellesmere's temple throbbed. "You need to let the matter be. The past is best left buried. Walkerton will never claim you and you are better off for it."

That Lord and Lady Ellesmere continued to keep their secrets about his parentage to themselves incensed him. His fists clenched at his sides until the letter crinkled and twisted in his grip.

"How dare you keep this from me," he whispered, an unfamiliar sensation growing in the center of his chest. It took him a moment to identify it. Betrayal. Both Lord and Lady Ellesmere had known all along Walkerton had fathered him. They could have told him, at any point in time they could have revealed the secrets of his past, but they hadn't.

They still wouldn't.

Had they made the same promises as Mary? Promises they would take to the grave as she had?

"It is better this way," Lord Ellesmere said.

"Better for whom?" The word shot out in anger.

Lord Ellesmere winced at the sharpness in Marcus's tone, but he made no effort to disguise it. What right did they have to keep the truth of his past a secret? To keep from him the history of whom he was? "I deserve to know!"

"You do not understand what is at stake."

"I understand all too well," Marcus said. His future, his love. "Everything is at stake."

"Marcus, please." Lord Ellesmere reached and gripped the wrist of the hand that held the letter. "I implore you."

But Marcus shook his head before the marquess could finish and his words fell away.

He took a deep breath. It had come to this. "I am indebted to you for everything you have done for me. You gave me a home, an education, a livelihood. You've changed my life. But I must do this. I must see it through to the end. I will go to Northill upon my return and keep you out of whatever happens with respect to Walkerton."

Lord Ellesmere's grip on his arm released and Marcus experienced the sense of being left adrift. He wanted to pull the older man back but he couldn't. If he rode toward ruin, he would take the trip alone.

"Please tell Lady Ellesmere good-bye for me. And tell her..." A lump lodged in his throat forcing him to push the words past it. "Give her my love and tell her I'm sorry for any pain and disappointment I have caused."

They stood facing each other. Lord Ellesmere's imposing presence filled the hallway, wrapped around him until every ounce of his being wished to be ten years old again so he could run to Lord Ellesmere for safety and solace. But he was not a child any longer.

"What you seek will bring you no comfort."

The fight left Lord Ellesmere's. Marcus had gone numb. Cold. In a matter of minutes he would leave this house—likely for the last time—and the life he'd known, the one he'd built for himself with careful thought and deliberation, would be gone.

He had spent years telling himself not to grow comfortable; that fate could change like the wind. Yet, he found himself wholly unprepared for the sense of loss that swept through him now that that day had come.

Despite the protests of Nicholas, Mother, Caelie, Abigail, Huntsleigh and, she was quite certain, little Lord Roxton, who had oddly taken to crying whenever the name Selward was mentioned—a fact Rebecca determined must be a coincidence as the baby had yet to meet the man—she had accepted Lord Selward's request to visit Sheridan Park when he arrived a few days prior to the annual summer party.

Thankfully, Mother had determined early on, when Rebecca had hoped to marry Lord Selward, that it would be inappropriate for them to stay under the same roof, and therefore Lord Selward and his parents were to stay with relatives a short distance away.

It wasn't that she entertained any thought of marrying the man—how could she after what she and Marcus had shared? Heavens, she had never known a body could reach such heights. That wickedness could be so delightful.

But with Marcus gone on his quest to find answers, she needed to do something. Something more constructive than twiddling her thumbs or, God forbid, doing needlepoint. Idleness did not suit her.

Protecting the man she loved, however, did.

She refused to stand by while Marcus threw himself into the current of his past to batter himself against its walls and demand the truth be revealed. She loathed the idea he had taken the trip to Cornwall alone, with no one to provide him with support and comfort should he need it. What if the news was bad? Or if there was no news to find? Marcus was not a man familiar with failure. Likely he would not take well to it.

But as she'd had no choice but to stay behind, she determined it best to remain in Lord Selward's good graces. Guilt pricked her conscience at the thought of leading him on with no intentions of seeing it through, but given he had done the same to her for the past two seasons, she did not let it bother her for long. Besides, if it meant she could exert some influence with respect to Lord Walkerton's decision to destroy Marcus, the ruse would be worth it.

Perhaps if she could establish whether Lord Selward was aware of the relationship between he and Marcus it would assist them in proving he was, indeed, Walkerton's eldest son.

"I hope your trip to Lady Dorman's went well," she said, as she and Lord Selward walked along the edge of the pond. Lily pads blanketed its surface until barely any water could be seen beneath. The bullfrogs hidden around the reeds croaked in the heat of the lazy summer afternoon. Once upon a time she had jumped into that pond and been dragged out by a pirate king.

How long ago that seemed today and yet it still put a smile on her face all these years later.

"Indeed, the trip was reasonably well made, thank you. Mother sends her best and Walkerton looks forward to meeting you."

"Does he? How kind of him to say." She wondered if such an event would come to pass. Nicholas and Marcus both gave her strict orders to stay away from Walkerton once the party got underway. Given his reputation, she would be wise to comply, but what if she could wheedle a confession from him? Would it not be worth the risk? Besides, the party would be filled with people. What could he possibly do to her? "I look forward to meeting him as well."

Lord Selward nodded, distracted. He stared off into the distance where several guests who had arrived a few days in advance of the party, rested on blankets and nibbled at the treats filling their picnic baskets. She had been too restless to sit and suggested she and Lord Selward take a walk. Though her companion had not held up his end of the conversation, not even to comment on the weather.

"My father was quite incensed at Mr. Bowen's sudden departure from London," he blurted out, surprising Rebecca.

"I beg your pardon?"

Instead of repeating his previous statement, he rushed on. "I have attempted to counsel him to use caution in his actions, but—" Lord Selward pursed his lips for a moment and a shadow crossed his face. It was strange to see him so upset. All she had known of him had been his even, somewhat bland, personality. But since his father's arrival, there had been a different side to him. Lord Walkerton's presence had left him troubled.

"But what?"

Lord Selward shook his head. "Caution and forethought are not things Walkerton excels at."

Fear bled through Rebecca like poison. "Do you think he will make good on his claim to contact the authorities?"

He nodded. "I have asked him to at least wait until the party has run its course. I do not wish to bring a pall over it. It would be the height of bad manners and likely not do us well when it comes time to sit down with Lord Blackbourne."

This was not the first reference he'd made to meeting with her brother at some point during the party, though he had yet to speak to her of any kind of a proposal. Just as well. She would have to tell him no and she did not want to turn him away just yet. Not until she had more information.

"Why does your father seem intent on ruining a man over something as silly as a watch? It is almost as if he holds ill feelings for Mr. Bowen that go far deeper than the issue at hand. Is there some aspect of their association I am missing, my lord?"

She held her breath. Waited.

Lord Selward stopped walking and turned to face the pond. In the silence, the croaking of the bullfrogs echoed. He glanced toward the other guests who were now a safe distance away.

"It is a family matter."

Her heart thrummed against her breast. "But Mr. Bowen is not family."

Silence.

Lord Selward bent to pick up a daisy near his boot and proceeded to pluck at its petals, disbursing them one by one, his movements a study in agitation. *He knows!*

"Lord Selward?"

He glanced down at her and turmoil turned his eyes stormy, the green aspects a turbulent sea; the blue darkened to thundering skies. "I do not wish to speak of it. It is a tiresome subject, is it not?" He forced a smile and blinked away the storm as if it was nothing more than a breeze. The mutilated flower dropped from his hand and fell to the ground.

"Not if it is one that bothers you," she said, pushing him, refusing to let go of the hope he could be an ally in their cause. He was a good man overall, nothing like his father. He stood to lose nothing in admitting Marcus was his brother. "Please. You can tell me. We are friends, are we not?"

"More than friends, I would hope. I have developed quite an affection for you, I am not ashamed to say. I had hoped—" He stopped. Smiled then dropped his gaze, and her heart went out to him. He was as much an innocent bystander in this madness as she, perhaps more so. To see him hurt bothered her more than she'd expected it would. "Should we return to the picnic?"

"Lord Selward, as you know, Mr. Bowen is a dear friend. It would grieve me to no end to see any malice inflicted upon him by your father." She took a deep breath, then added, "*His* father."

Lord Selward's head shot up. "What did you say?" She did not answer, did not have to. He had heard her perfectly well.

In the silence that grew between them a strange understanding drifted in to fill the space. He knew. She knew. And now he knew she knew.

"Your brother—"

He shook his head. "Don't call him that."

She took a calming breath. "Whether I refer to him as such or not does not change the truth." She reached out and touched one of Lord Selward's fisted hands. "Would you honestly stand by and let your father ruin him? It is such a petty matter, this watch."

"Walkerton has no interest in my opinions on the matter. He blames Mr. Bowen for the state of his life, such as it is."

"But why?"

Another shake of the head as he continued to avoid her gaze. "I cannot say. He does not take me into his confidence. I had no knowledge of an—association with Mr. Bowen until I sent word to my father informing him I planned on courting you with a view to making you my wife."

Her breath caught. She had never heard Lord Selward speak so plainly. So honestly. "And what did he say?"

"Due to your brother's friendship with Mr. Bowen, he counseled me to drop my suit. I sent a letter back—he was in Italy at the time—requesting an answer as to why that would matter. His response came while you were in mourning for your father. He stated Mr. Bowen was his by-blow and he didn't care for me to have an association with a family so closely connected to him."

Rebecca's skin tingled. "Do you still have this correspondence?"

"Perhaps. I do not know." He picked a small stone out of the grass and whipped it into the water. It skipped twice and sank.

"Is that why you turned your attentions to Lady Susan?"

Color tinged his cheeks and he nodded. "I did not want

her. Father insisted I look elsewhere for a bride, but I had settled my mind on you and as much as I tried to be the dutiful son, I could not forget you."

His explanation vindicated her and made it easier to forgive his fickle heart, not that it mattered any longer. In truth, she was thankful for his lackluster pursuit of her. Had he not turned his attentions elsewhere, she would not have had the opportunity to pursue her feelings for Marcus. Likely she and Lord Selward would have married and that would have been that. Her first kiss with Marcus may have never happened, the daydreams of her youth would have grown fallow and been put away.

What a sad state of affairs that would have been.

"My lord, I understand you feel a loyalty to your father, but in this regard he is wrong. Mr. Bowen is a good man, and I believe he will return the watch in good time. It would cause me no small amount of distress should anything happen to him in the meantime."

"Do you have feelings for him? It appeared over the past few weeks that he attempted to court you, though I could not ascertain your level of interest in the man."

"Mr. Bowen is like family." And soon, would be in truth, though she refrained from saying as much now. "Is there anything you can do to keep your father from taking action? It would mean the world to me."

"I will do what I can, my dear." Hope and expectation lit his eyes and self-reproach filled her heart as he took her hands in his. "I want nothing more than to see you happy, even if it means championing Mr. Bowen, against my father. I will do what I can."

"It would be greatly appreciated, my lord."

He nodded but did not look too hopeful. "I cannot make any promises into how successful an endeavor it will be. My father is not a kind man. It is not a pleasant thing to admit, but he has shown throughout my life a complete lack of compassion for the plight of anyone but himself."

Lord Selward's description of his father's character did not bode well, but she refused to give in to despair. "Whatever you can do would go a long way to casting you in a favorable light where my brother is concerned. Mr. Bowen is one of his dearest friends." And hers.

Shame wrapped its tangled roots around her and squeezed. She did not want to lead Lord Selward on or lift his expectations, but what choice did she have when Marcus's future—his very life—may depend upon it?

Marcus closed his eyes and rubbed his fingertips against his lids. It offered no respite. Lingering behind them, the image of Rebecca, her head thrown back in passion, refused to leave, tormenting his memories and his conscience. He could still taste her skin on the tip of his tongue. Still feel the slickness of her desire. Still smell her scent, an intoxicating blend of fire and earth. He groaned and let his head fall back against the cushioned seat of the carriage. He tried to divert his thoughts to no avail. She infiltrated every aspect of them until everything led back to her. To that moment in the study when she'd begged him to give her release.

Only the thinnest thread of restraint had kept him from taking her then and there, against the desk like some rutting animal. Disgust filled him. She deserved better than that.

Better than him.

Time and distance had made things clearer. He had no right to ruin her. No right to her at all. Honor dictated he let her go. Let her marry Selward and have the life she deserved.

Her passion for him would dissipate in time, surely, until he became little more than a memory.

A man she used to know.

The idea filled him with a heavy sadness as if he had stuffed his pockets with stone and now sunk into a deep river, its placid surface growing farther and farther away.

He glanced out the window hoping for a diversion from his thoughts.

The landscape had changed little from his memories, faded though they were. He had driven long days, changed horses often, and stopped only when darkness made travel dangerous and sleep a necessity. He did not want to waste time. The purgatory he'd been living in had worn him down. He needed to find answers. He needed to make things right with Rebecca. Worthy or not, she had set her heart on him and stolen his in the process. While good sense counseled he let her go, honor dictated he make things right. That he marry her.

The idea thrilled and frightened him in equal measure.

If he were to fall to ruin, so might she. He needed answers. He needed to know if the truth would prove their salvation, or their undoing.

He was a bastard, that much he knew. Walkerton was his father—that, too, had become irrefutable. A disconcerting idea having that man's blood coursing through his own veins, a man who tossed people away as if they held no value, ruining lives without rhyme or reason. Is that what he had done to Marcus's mother? Used her and cast her aside, leaving her to her fate the way he had Alma or Mr. Cosgrove?

Marcus shook his head. Hopefully his mother's blood would prove the stronger of the two.

And what of his mother? Lord and Lady Ellesmere refused to release her identity. Had she been a relative? Close family friend? Finding her identity would be key in unlocking the door to the truth and allowing he and Rebecca to be together.

It was this hope he clung to, the only bright light in the turmoil that roiled within him as he vacillated between right and wrong. Honor and good sense. Holding Rebecca tight or letting her go.

In the distance he could see the water, smell the salt in the air. When he closed his eyes, he could still picture the craggy edges of the cliffs and the foamy waves as they battered the jutting rocks and shores. The desolate beauty of the landscape suited his mood and claimed the wildness that warred inside of him. This place had framed his early years and had burrowed deep within him. Buried, but not forgotten. He breathed it in, needing its strength more now than ever.

"We're here, m' lord."

Marcus had already informed the man he was not a lord. Not by a long shot. But his driver did not seem to take to the idea and Marcus had grown weary of reminding him.

The stench—a mix of despair and poverty—hit him before the pathetic excuse for a house came into view. He remembered it well. Some memories refused to die. The fence that lined the rutted road had toppled in spots, rotted through in others. A single cow stood behind it munching at the sparse grass. The carriage came to a gradual stop in front of the cottage. It had not weathered the years well. The thatched roof was in disrepair and soot, dirt and salt air had discolored the exterior walls to a shade that he had no name for.

Save for the lone cow and a thin strand of smoke oozing from the chimney, the place appeared deserted.

He stepped down from the carriage and glanced over the rolling hills to his left. If he ran to the top of the highest one, he would see Braemore in the distance. How many times as a child had he done that? Escaped for a few moments to sit atop that hill and stare, wishing he could turn back time. Wishing he could go home.

It had never happened. He had not set foot in Braemore since the day after his mother's funeral. Lord Ellesmere preferred to handle the business for that particular estate himself. Over the years, Marcus had tried to talk the marquess into letting him take it over, but he'd steadfastly refused without indicating his reasons. Marcus had never understood his reticence.

Until now.

"Wait here," he said to the driver, as if the man had somewhere else to go.

Weeds had overtaken the cobbled stones that led from the road to the cottage until only the memory of them remained. He waded through until he reached the door, lifted his hand and knocked twice. No answer. He tried again. The place was not big enough that anyone inside of it wouldn't have heard. It contained only three rooms—the main room that had served as kitchen and sitting room and two small bedrooms where the family slept. He'd been relegated to sleeping in the barn, though on the coldest nights, he'd sneaked inside and found warmth near the kitchen stove. He'd usually received a beating if didn't escape before the family awoke, but it had been a small price to pay to keep from freezing to death.

When no answer came with his second knock, he pushed at the door. The hinges creaked as it swung inward. A fetid stench greeted him and he took a step back to gulp in fresher air before going inside. The interior remained unchanged. Dark. Dingy. Depressing. The echo of voices past stained the discolored walls. Sharp words, quarrelling, cries from the younger children. From himself when his aunt and uncle brought out the belt and thrust their frustrations onto his hide. The thin scars he bore from those beatings had faded over time, though the memory had not.

He'd spent most of his time outdoors working or inside the kitchen. He'd never been invited into the rest of the house. It had been made clear to him he was nothing more than a burden, an unpaid servant meant to earn his keep. He'd done his best, but it had never sufficed. He'd been beaten for his efforts, made to go without.

It had been a miserable existence that even now made him want to turn and run.

He held his ground.

"What you want? Ain't nuthin' here worth stealin'."

The voice startled him, drifting out of the shadows as it had. As his eyes adjusted to the dimness he sought it out and discovered a lump in a chair near the stove.

"Mrs. MacCumber?" He had never been invited to call her aunt. Had never wanted to. He took a couple of steps forward then stopped.

"What of it? Who are you?"

Her hoarse voice scraped against him. The years had not been kind. The dull brown of her hair had turned a mousy grey and frizzed around her head like a rat had nested there. Lines and dark spots made her face almost unrecognizable. She dressed herself in colorless grey rags that held no shape or form. A cane rested near the chair, nothing more than a piece of wood whittled down.

"It's Marcus Bowen."

She leaned forward and squinted and for a fleeting moment he thought she did not remember him. Then her expression altered. Her thin lips disappeared and her pale brown eyes hardened. "The bastard son," she snarled and sat back in her chair as if repulsed by him. Her words cut, but hoped poured through the wounds.

"What do you know of it?"

"Of wha'? And ain't you lookin' fancy." She gripped the thick knob of the cane with gnarled fingers.

He ignored her caustic comment and glanced about the room. "Where are the others?"

"Dead. Or gone."

"Mr. MacCumber?"

"Both."

No loss or regret washed over him at the news of his uncle's passing, only the disappointment that the information he searched for may have died with him. His mother and aunt had never been close. If there were secrets to be told, Mrs. MacCumber had likely not been privy to them. But he had come too far not to ask.

"What do you know of my mother?"

She said nothing and Marcus reached into his pocket and tossed a coin into her lap. She held it up, inspected it. Found it worthy of loosening her tongue.

"Mary Bowen was an uppity piece of baggage. Always thought she was better than me jus' cause she came back from London and married your da with 'is fancy position. She weren't no better than anyone. Couldn't even 'ave 'er own babes. Had to take someone else's cast offs."

He held his breath. "Tell me what you know about that."

Her squinty gaze looked him up and down and her mouth twisted to one side revealing gaps where teeth had once been. "You got 'em same uppity airs as her. Maybe that's jus' part o' your breedin', but I don't owe you nothin'. Took you in when I coulda cast you out. Shoulda too. You wasn't worth nothin' to me."

But he was now.

Marcus let out a long, slow breath and glanced around at the squalor in which she lived. Dented tin pots lay about on the planked floor and the disparate sound of drops plunked into them in a steady rhythm. The pile of wood next to the stove was dismally inadequate at warming the interior and chasing away the damp. The smell of rot and decay invaded every corner.

"Tell me what I want to know and I'll make it worth your while."

"Oh, you gonna sweep me away to a grand palace like what happened to you?" Her tone mocked him, as if he hadn't deserved saving any more than the rest of them had. Maybe she was right. Had Lady Ellesmere not shown up that day, what would have become of him? Would he still be here, living within these decaying walls?

Maybe. Though, in all likelihood, between the beatings and starvation, he would not have survived his childhood. He owed this woman nothing. If he walked away now and left her to rot, it was nothing more than what she deserved.

"No, I'm not," he stated flatly in answer to her question. "But I will see to it that this place is improved upon, made livable, and that you have food and supplies enough to get you through the winter." Beyond that, she was on her own.

She snorted, as if his offer insulted her. He remained silent. He was the best and only chance she had at finding ease over the coming winter. He would wait her out.

"Can't 'magine I know anythin' you want."

It was as much of an agreement as he would get. He took it. "We both know Mary Bowen wasn't the woman who gave birth to me. I want to know who did."

His aunt shrugged one hunched shoulder. "Not like she ev'r told me her secrets." But she knew something. He could tell by the way her gaze skirted about the floor like a rat hunting for crumbs. He waited and eventually it came. "Floyd sometimes did work at the property. Once said a fancy lady got 'erself in trouble and came out there t'stay."

His heartbeat accelerated but he remained still. "Who was she?"

"Can't say. Floyd didn't know either. Jus' that she was a

relation to Lady Ellesmere. They stashed 'er away up to the middle of nowhere 'cause God forbid anyone know 'bout it. Like their kind don' lift their skirts like the rest o' us." She snorted in derision.

Her words held the ring of truth and explained why the Kingsleys had taken him in after the Bowens had passed away. Why Lady Ellesmere had insisted he was family. Why they had been adamant he leave the matter alone. Lord and Lady Ellesmere abhorred scandal. To admit they had a bastard relative living in their home would be beyond the pale. So long as they could cover his existence under the guise of belonging to the Bowens, all was well, but the moment he had threatened that—

Pain cut through him. Had their reputation been more important to them than he was? Had he meant so little?

"Do you know the lady's name?"

She scoffed at him. "Ain't never seen her but once. Caught her out near the bluffs, belly stickin' out."

"What'd she look like?" Hunger for details riveted him to the spot.

"Small 'cept for the belly. Dark haired like you."

"Did she say anything?"

"I ain't never approached 'er. You think the high falutin' lords and ladies would deem to 'ave a conversation with me? I ain't their kind."

"What happened to the woman after I was born?"

Another shrug. "Can't say. She disappeared and suddenly Mary 'ad a new babe. Maybe your real ma 'ad to go meet with the King. La ti da." She waved a hand in the air.

Again Marcus waited but nothing more came. "Is that all you can tell me?"

The information was thin at best save to confirm his mother had been related to the Kingsleys, and a brief physical description. Small. Young. Dark-haired. Not much to go on.

His mind ran through the relatives he knew of. The only female relative on Lord Ellesmere's side had been a niece who, years ago, ran off with a man who claimed to be a member of the French aristocracy, but the timeframe didn't fit. His mother must have been from Lady Ellesmere side, but he could think of no one, as most of Lady Ellesmere's kin were now dead and gone, or moved to the colonies. Had his mother been exiled there after his birth?

It wasn't much to go on, but it was more than he'd had before he arrived and for that he was grateful.

"Thank you."

His aunt scowled at him.

Marcus took one last look around the dilapidated room that had briefly been his home, if one could call it such, and shook his head. How this place had formed him. It had taught him prudence in all things, to be unobtrusive, to not take chances that would get you noticed. He had carried these lessons with him into adulthood and in many respects they had served him well. But Rebecca had the right of it. Sometimes, a man had to throw caution to the wind where love and happiness were concerned.

Maybe the time had come for him to take her advice; to take a risk and make her his. If she loved him even half as much as he did her, surely it would see them through whatever fate threw their way. Was she not worth the risk?

Yes. A hundred times, yes.

"I will see to your comfort for the winter," he said, but made no more promises beyond. He turned and left the house that had haunted his nightmares. He did not look back.

He would not return.

Chapter Twenty

January 15th

The pains have started to come. It will be soon now. I have been ill for the past week. Mother says that is normal, but I can see the lie of it in her eyes. I fear never holding him, that I will be gone before I have the chance. Before I can tell him—I do not know why I believe it to be a boy, but I do—

I need him to know he is loved. That it is not his fault. That he should never feel less than worthy of my love. I need him to know I don't blame him, whatever happens, he was the perfect ending; the only one who could wash away the ugliness of what happened. I love him. I have not yet met him and still he is a part of my heart as if his beats in time with mine, making them as one. Whatever happens, I will see him protected. If I can give him nothing else, I can give him that.

Please God allow me the chance to do at least that.

The annual Sheridan house party spared no expense when it came to entertaining their guests for a fortnight. The official start of the party began with a ball, which Rebecca generally considered her second favorite. Her least favorite had always been the one held at the end of the two weeks because it signaled the party was over. Ah, but the middle one, that was her favorite. By then, all the guests had arrived, the mood was chipper and there was still a full week of festivities yet to come.

But this year, as the music ended and the guests finished the last steps of the quadrille, she left the dance floor, her usual joy nowhere in evidence. Nor would it be until she received word Marcus had returned from Cornwall. Relief mingled with excitement over what Lord Selward had admitted and she could not wait to share the news with Marcus. Now, he could return the watch to Walkerton, perhaps in exchange for his confirmation that he fathered Marcus, and they could start their lives together without the threat of scandal and ruin hanging over their heads.

She searched the crowd, hoping beyond hope he would appear amidst the sea of bodies dressed in all their finery. He would gift her with a smile that promised untold delights once they were alone and their finest lay on the floor about them in wild abandon. The wicked thought brought a rush of heat to her cheeks and a deep ache farther down. She had experienced that wildness, had been overcome by the power of it coiled within her, unleashed by the touch of his hands until she'd been left dazed and speechless. Unable to resist. Unwilling to, for she had asked for it. Practically begged him for it.

Wanted it still.

Wanted him.

"Your punch, my lady."

Lord Selward returned from the refreshments table with a

glass of sweet punch and she accepted it with a weak smile. She wished she could give him more, but her heart wasn't in it. Her heart had riveted its attention on someone else and refused to be diverted from its course. The steadfast determination she had once used to pursue Lord Selward had vanished. Had he noticed? Could he sense her interest had waned?

"Thank you." She took a sip and wished it contained something stronger. "Are you enjoying yourself?"

"Indeed, I am. And you?"

"Yes, of course," she lied. Despite the personal conversation they had shared two days earlier, he had reverted back to his usual banal topics of conversation, as if it had never happened. So far this evening, they had exhausted the topic of the weather, which of the dances was her favorite—she said the reel, though in truth it was the waltz, but she did not want to give him false hope where that was concerned. Now, it appeared, the topic of enjoyment of the festivities had run its course as well.

She sighed.

Would marriage to Lord Selward have been as dull as this conversation? He did not appear to have any interest in delving into deeper subjects. He behaved as if the confidences they had shared earlier had never happened. She had tried to broach it this evening, but he quickly steered her back to safer ground. Would this mean he would not back up his earlier claim that Marcus was his brother? And if he refused, what then?

She brushed the thought away. She would not dwell on the negative. This had to work out. It simply had to. She would entertain no other outcome. Happiness was within her grasp and she had every intention of grabbing hold. It would not slip through her fingers the way it had for her mother.

"Would you care to dance? I believe the next set is to be a

reel. Your favorite." Lord Selward asked, his even voice breaking through thoughts that had run wild.

"Oh." She let him take the cup of sugary liquid from her hands and set it on a nearby table. Then he held out his arm like the perfect gentleman but, as she took it, they were interrupted.

"Lady Rebecca."

She turned, Lord Selward instantly forgotten. Her heart lodged in her throat and relief swept through her. He was here. He had come home. It took every ounce of will not to throw herself into Marcus's arms. A smart move as he appeared most weary, still dressed in his travelling clothes. Regardless, he had never looked more handsome and she longed to touch him, to be sure he actually stood there and that she didn't imagine it.

"You came back."

He smiled at her, a private smile just for her, heedless of who might see it or decipher its meaning. "Of course. May I speak with you?"

She nodded.

Lord Selward stepped forward. "Forgive me, Mr. Bowen, but Lady Rebecca and I were just about to dance the reel."

Marcus said nothing, simply stood there and stared at Lord Selward, his gaze roving over the younger man's face. Rebecca's own bounced between the two of them, trying to find some resemblance, but came up empty despite the shared blood running through their veins.

"I'm afraid I must insist," Lord Selward said, though Marcus had made no move to take her away, or suggest she leave and forget her promised dance with him.

"I believe that is the lady's decision to make," Marcus indicated and something opened up within her. A realization. Marcus had always treated her with respect, given her opinions equal weight, as he would have Nicholas's or Lord Ellesmere.

Life with him would be a partnership in the truest sense of the word. He would listen to her views, discuss them with her, and debate them if he disagreed until they reached a compromise or understanding. She would be heard; talked to, valued for whom she was.

She turned to Lord Selward and placed a hand over his. "Forgive me, Lord Selward. But Mr. Bowen and I have an important matter to discuss. I would prefer not to put it off until later. Would you mind terribly if we postponed our dance?"

Lord Selward's jaw tightened and his eyes blazed, the most emotion she had seen from him save for when he told her about his father's admission. He inclined his head toward her and reluctantly let go of her hand.

"Certainly. I see Lady Susan has arrived. Perhaps I shall inquire if she would care to take your place."

The double meaning in his words were not lost on her, but she no longer cared beyond wishing better for him than to spend a lifetime with a harpy like Lady Susan. "You're a kind man, my lord." She hoped he understood how much she meant those words, that she wanted the best for him. He *was* a good man, just not the one she wanted.

"Lady Rebecca?" Marcus offered her his arm and she took it, letting him lead her through the crowd and out of the ballroom into the hallway beyond. He leaned down and whispered into her ear. "Where can we talk?"

"Upstairs," she answered and pulled him toward the back stairwell used by the servants where their departure would not be noticed. She by-passed the receiving room when Marcus slowed. She wanted to speak with him in private, to have him to herself without interruption. She directed him up another set of stairs, toward the third floor then down the hallway to her bedchamber.

"Rebecca." His voice held a warning, a promise that if

they continued on there might be no turning back. But she had no intention of turning back where he was concerned. A thrill rushed through her and she pushed open the door and led him inside, shutting it behind them. She turned, her back against the solid oak. A lamp, its wick turned low, filled the room with a subtle light that did battle with the shadows.

He stood beyond her reach, staring at her. She wanted to say something, to go to him, but something in his eyes kept her pinned in place, her knees too weak to hold her weight. His gaze burned into her, through her. It promised wicked delights, pleasures she had yet to discover, to understand.

"Marcus..." She whispered his name and it was all that was needed to remove the distance between. He pulled her into his arms, kissing her as if she were the very air he needed to breathe. She opened to him, allowing him to plunder her mouth, to taste and tease and torment until her body longed for the same attentions and she despised the layer of clothing keeping her from feeling him—all of him. She had no understanding of where this passion and desire came from, how long its embers had smoldered inside of her, nor did she care. They roared to life now at his touch and she did not want it to ever stop.

"I have missed you desperately," he said, the words scalding her skin as he kissed a trail along the curve of her neck. She threw her head back in reckless abandon, clawing at his clothing, wishing them gone.

"I feared you would not return."

"I could never stay away from you." He lifted his head, his passionate assault briefly halted as he touched her face, traced its lines as if committing them to memory. His eyes, so deeply brown, drew her in until she became lost and wished never to be found. He shook his head. "I did not discover much in the way of new information."

Her heart sank. She had held out such hope he would come back with the answers he needed. "What did you learn?"

"Only that my mother was a relative of Lady Ellesmere and that I resemble her to some degree, I suppose. I do not know what happened to her after my birth. Where she went, what became of her. I do not even know her name."

She tightened her arms where they wrapped around his waist, pressing her body into his in an effort to offer whatever comfort she could. "I have learned something that night bring you cheer."

He pulled away far enough to peer down at her, his eyebrows pulled together. "What have you learned?"

"I spoke to Lord Selward—" Marcus scowled but she pressed on. "He admitted to your relationship—that you are brothers. His father had told him to end our courtship because of our families' close association. Lord Walkerton admitted, in a letter to Lord Selward, that he was indeed your father."

"In a letter?"

"Yes. He was away at the time and so their conversation took place through correspondence."

Marcus released her and took a step back as if he needed distance to absorb the information. She missed his closeness, the warmth of his body against hers. "Does he still have this letter?"

Rebecca nodded. "I believe so. When I asked, he did not give me a direct yes or no, but indicated perhaps he had kept it. If we can get it from him—"

Marcus gave her a dubious look. "Why would he give it up? How would that serve his best interests?"

"How would it hurt him? He has nothing to lose by allowing you to be acknowledged. And he is a good man. I do not think he wishes you ill."

"Perhaps not yet, but what about when you refuse his

proposal? Do you think he will look so kindly toward me then?" Something passed over his features, something unsettled. "Unless you do not plan to refuse him. Have you changed your mind in that regard?"

"Would I be here with you now if that were the case?"

He smiled and her heart lifted. "No."

Marcus held out his hand and she stepped forward, letting hers slip into his but instead of clasping it tightly, his fingers slid up her forearm until they reached the end of her glove, catching its edge and peeling it downward. She assisted him, moving in the opposite direction until the silk encasement fell away. She reached for her other glove, impatient to have it gone, and pulled it off.

"If he has the letter," Marcus said, reaching for the buttons of his wool jacket and relieving them of their moorings one by one. "We may have what we need to keep you from losing everything."

"And then we can be together." Her breath hitched in her throat as he pulled off the coat then his waistcoat. Heat burned deep within her.

"Would you like that?" A soft smile played about his lips. Lips that had kissed her thoroughly. What else might they do to her? She longed to discover all the pleasures he could give, and what she could provide in return.

"Most desperately."

Marcus tossed his collar and cravat onto the floor. "How desperately?"

She wanted to answer, truly she did, but he had gone and pulled his shirttails from his trousers, undone his cufflinks at the wrist and yanked the garment over his head to reveal the glistening golden skin beneath and whatever words she had been about to deliver were lost.

Heaven above but he was a glorious specimen of man. Lean muscles rippled along his ribs and carved into the ridges of his belly. Broad shoulders and a strong chest made her think of the statues of Greek gods littered about the gardens beyond and yet that did not do him justice. For he was not carved of stone but made of sinew and bone. When he moved, as he did now, it came to life.

He approached her and kissed her with the same desperation he had asked her to define. His hands buried into her hair until pins clattered onto the floor around her feet and the gorgeous structure Nancy had painstakingly spent an hour creating, loosened and fell about her shoulders in thick waves.

He pulled away, his chest rising and falling against her. "God help me, but you are a glorious creature. I cannot control myself where you are concerned. You are my downfall."

"Is that such an awful thing?" She let her hands trace over his rib cage, reveling in the bare skin, warm and taut. What an amazing thing, to touch someone in this way. To touch him.

His breath caught and he rested his head against hers. "I thought so once."

"And now?"

He lifted his head and smiled and her toes curled within her slippers. Deep within her the ache he created, the ache only he could tend, pulled at her.

"Now I wonder if you might not be my salvation."

"Truly?"

He smiled and the gesture warmed her heart. "Indeed. I have tried every way I can think of to convince myself to let you be, to allow you a life left untouched by whatever the future brings me."

"And were you successful?"

"I'm standing half-naked in your bedchamber. What do you think?"

She laughed. "This is quite a departure for you. Are you certain you are prepared to throw caution to the wind?"

"Do I have a choice?"

She shook her head. "If you try to leave me, I shall dog you to the ends of the earth. I shall throw myself into pools of water and make you save me until you have no choice but to throw your hands up in surrender. And when you do, I shall be so kind as to save you in return."

She leaned forward and kissed his neck as he had done to her, finding the pulse where it beat beneath his skin. She touched it with the tip of her tongue and it jumped in response. His hands gripped her hips and pulled her against the hard ridge of him and the ache deepened still. Throbbed.

"I may require saving if I don't find a way to convince you out of this infernal gown you are wearing."

"Infernal?" She nibbled at the sharp line of his jaw, her hands roaming over his muscled shoulders. "I thought it rather pretty."

"It's quite lovely. I have no doubt every man in the ballroom was stunned into stupidity when you made your entrance." His head fell back, allowing her better access. "But I suspect what is underneath it is nothing short of magnificent and I wish to be the only man to discover that."

She stepped away from him. "Do you? Well, I suppose it would only be fair of me to give you the opportunity to prove yourself correct in that regard."

A roguish grin made gooseflesh rise on her skin.

"Turn around," he commanded.

She obeyed and his fingers worked the long line of buttons at her back, slowing as they reached the upper curve of her buttocks. There, he took his time, torturing her with his touch as it brushed lightly against her.

"Hurry," she urged, unable to stand it.

"Patience." He reached up to her shoulders and pulled the gown down to her elbows. When he released it, it rushed to the floor in a wicked whisper, leaving her exposed in a way she had never been before. She should have felt shame. She didn't. Instead, she relished the freedom, the promise of what was to come. She wanted him in a way that defied everything she had known up until this moment.

Inch by inch, her stays loosened until he pulled it away and dropped it on the floor. "When it comes time to re-dress you, I am not certain I will be up to the chore with all these contraptions you wear."

She turned to face him, wearing nothing but her linen shift, drawers and stockings. "Perhaps I will need to stay like this then."

He shook his head and took a step back, then another until he reached the bed and sat on its edge as if his legs would no longer hold him upright. With efficient movements, he tugged off his boots and when done, nodded at her shift. "Take it off for me."

A hint of embarrassment tinged her cheeks and liquid warmth pooled between her thighs where the ache had become almost unbearable. She reached for the hem of her shift and slowly lifted it, revealing her bare skin inch by inch. He disappeared from view as she pulled it over her head, but she heard his swift intake of breath as her breasts were exposed to his view.

When the shift fell from her grip she moved to cover herself.

"No." He held up a hand to stop her, then turned it and motioned for her. "Come to me."

Marcus held his breath as she honored his request, taking tentative steps until she reached him. He took her hands and held her arms aloft when she thought to cover herself from his gaze yet again. From the soft glow of lamplight, he could see the tinge of pink heat color her cheeks and cross the expanse of skin above her glorious breasts, full and soft and inviting his touch and taste.

He could not resist her.

He released her hands and placed his on the curve of her hips. His thumbs teased the bone and reached inward to the dark tuft of hair at the juncture of her thighs. He longed to kneel before her, worship the hidden folds, taste her essence. To give her the pleasure she craved and to join her in the blessed aftermath of release where possibilities were endless and no obstacle seemed insurmountable.

He closed his eyes and relished the thought, then pushed it aside. He must go slow.

His hands traveled across the silky skin over her rib cage, coming to rest against the soft undersides of her breasts, cupping them with a gentle touch.

She held onto his shoulders and his muscles shifted beneath her touch.

"You are more beautiful than I imagined."

"Did you imagine it often?"

"Every day. Shall I show you what else I imagined?"

Her fingers flexed against him. "Please."

He smiled and leaned forward, lifting her breast to his mouth, capturing the hardened bud and pulling it inward until she gasped and arched against him. He flicked his tongue over it and a low moan escaped her lips.

"Do you like that?"

"Oh, yes," she whispered.

"Shall I continue?"

She nodded, her mouth pursed into a thin line.

He pulled at the thin pink ribbon on her drawers and slid them downward, over the silk stockings until they pooled at her slippers. God help him. He had never seen a woman so beautiful and wondrous as her. She was a brilliant mixture of taut skin and soft curves, enticing secrets and an open heart.

He wanted nothing more in that moment than to bury himself inside of her, discover the secrets she kept at her core, hold them within him and never leave.

He pulled her to him and turned until she lay upon the bed, her legs bent at the knee to dangle over the edge. He brought her into a sitting position then placed her hand upon the buttons of his trousers. "Undo them."

She glanced up at him and dragged her bottom lip between her teeth. The tip of her tongue shot out then disappeared once again and he groaned inwardly, imagining what that tongue could do to him.

Her nimble fingers worked against the buttons and brushed his hardened cock until he feared he might finish before she did. Once done, she grew bold and yanked his trousers and underclothing downward, but her boldness disappeared in a gasp as his erection sprung free. She sat back quickly and stared, her silvery eyes wide and glowing in the faded light.

"Oh." And then, "It's rather large."

He laughed and kicked off his trousers until he stood before every inch of skin bared for her to see. "Thank you."

"That's good then?"

"It doesn't hurt." Although she may disagree on that account this first time. He promised himself he would take his time, be as gentle as possible to make this as good for her as it would be for him.

"Can I touch it?"

Sweet Jesus. Deliver him from curious females. She had no idea what she asked and he had no power to deny her request. "Yes."

Her fingertips touched him and she drew her hand back quickly as if scalded. His body shook with the effort of holding still, when all he truly wanted was to push her back against the downy mattress and sink deep inside of her, ridding himself of the painful need her touch created. Though if this could truly be considered pain, he had never been happier to be on the receiving end of it.

Her hand wrapped gently around his shaft. With a mischievous smile, she leaned forward and placed a kiss upon the tip. Nothing prepared him for the pleasure that tore through his body, singeing everything in its wake until nothing else remained save the exquisite torture of her mouth toying with him. His fingers threaded through her hair and held her there for a glorious moment as her tongue flicked over him. If he did not stop her this evening would end before it even started.

He moved with swift determination and gently pushed her back onto the mattress, hovering over her. "You, my sweet little minx, are a wonder. I am almost afraid to know how you knew to do that."

"Isn't that what you did to me?" Her hand lingered on her breast where he had kissed her. "Was that the wrong thing to do?"

He shook his head. "God no. But—" How did he explain it to her. "Do you recall how it felt, when we were in your brother's study and I touched you?" He slid his hand down over the tuft of hair.

The muscles in her throat moved as she swallowed. "Yes."

"Tell me." His hand slipped away and he knelt before her.

"It felt wonderful."

"It started off slow, did it not?" He pulled her closer to the edge of the mattress. "Open for me," he whispered.

She hesitated for only a brief second before spreading her legs to either side of him. "Yes. Then it built."

He leaned forward, his hands sliding up the front of her thighs. "And then what?" He lowered himself and put his mouth against the folds of her core, pressing into her. Her hand flew downward, not to stop him, but to hold him against her center, as if to contain the sensations his touch stirred within her.

"Then it grew stronger. You stroked me and it grew stronger. More."

"Like this?" His tongue lashed out and licked her. She tasted of honey and fire and he had to hold himself back.

She bucked against him. "Yes. Oh, yes." Then, "Do that again."

He did, slower, increasing the pressure as he went until he reached the nub at the top and pulled it gently into his mouth and teased it. She let out a cry and he continued until she writhed beneath him, her breath coming fast and hard. She grabbed at his hair to gain purchase and held him there while he kissed and suckled and licked and tasted. She rocked against him, the rhythm of her body quickening until another cry wrested from her and her body arched and stiffened and he felt her muscles contract and then blissfully release.

After a moment, once her breathing returned to normal, he stood and slipped his arms beneath her, lifting her farther onto the bed. He nestled between her thighs and wondered how a place so new could feel so much like home. How a *person* could feel so much like home. And yet she did.

"Did you like that?" He kissed her collarbone, neck, earlobe, temple. He could not get enough of her. Would never get enough of her. The idea rocked him so deeply he stopped for a moment, frozen in time as the truth of it swept over him and removed everything in its way.

After this moment, there could be no turning back. He could stop now, right now, and she could go on, recover from this and remain enough of an innocent to marry without questions being raised. She could marry a titled lord, one without the baggage or threats hanging over his head as Marcus did.

Guilt and honor continued to wage their battle while the

touch of her skin burned into his, branding him forever. He belonged to her. Now and always. But did he have the right to keep her as his own, to ruin any chance of a future she had free of scandal and ruin?

"Stop thinking."

Her voice startled him. Her words even more so. "I am not—"

"You are," she said. "I can see it in your face. Your brow is doing that thing."

He lifted his head to better look at her. "What thing?"

The light flickered over her ivory skin like a lover's caress and jealousy hit him. He wished to travel the same path so the last touch she knew would be his. Always his.

"The thing where the two lines appear right here." She reached a hand up and pressed her finger between his eyebrows. "And then you purse your mouth into a rather grim line." Her fingertip slipped down the line of his nose and landed against his mouth. He opened it slightly and nipped at her, making her giggle, which he decided was, next to her moan of pleasure, perhaps his favorite sound in the world. "If you were thinking to stop now—"

"I was," he admitted.

"Then you need to change your way of thinking."

"I should not ruin you."

She smiled at him. "I am already ruined." She touched his face and he turned into her hand. "Do you honestly believe I could ever do this with another man? Let someone else touch me as you did, knowing I wished him to be you? My heart is not so fickle that it will allow me to transfer my affections so easily."

"Perhaps you should try." It would be better for her in the long run, and in the end that is all he wanted—for her to be happy. Safe.

"No." She leaned up and kissed him, teasing him in much

the same way he had her, proving what a quick and eager student she was. Not to mention effective. She rocked against him and his protests melted away, his cock hardened. She was right. She was ruined. As was he.

There was no turning back.

"Marry me, then?"

"I thought you might never ask," she said, then kissed him once more, the feel of her smile against his sheer bliss. "Now, kind sir, will you perhaps finish what you started?"

He smiled and his heart filled. A lifetime of happiness with this woman stretched before him and filled him with wonder. No matter what happened, he would protect her. He would ensure her happiness no matter the cost.

"If my lady wishes."

"She does. She wishes it very much. But--what of my stockings?" She lifted one leg in the air and he glanced over his shoulder at the slim, shapely limb and the white silk tied securely above her knee by a dainty green and pink garter. Tiny pink rosebuds, embroidered into the silk traveled down her leg in a winding fashion along a vine of ivy that reached to her ankle.

"I think I should like you to leave them on."

"Why?"

He shook his head and turned back to her with a smile. "I cannot say. Other than to admit there is something sinfully sexy about having you while you're wearing nothing but soft skin and silk."

She let out a small laugh and wrapped both legs around his hips so the silk rubbed against him and he hardened even more. The tip of his erection pressed against her opening, already slick from where he'd kissed her and brought her to the point of ecstasy before letting her tumble over its edge. "Then I shall leave them on. For you."

Her kissed her once again then lifted himself onto his forearms and shifted his hips, entering her part way before stopping. "Does this hurt?"

She closed her eyes and let out a slow breath then shook her head.

He withdrew slightly, pushed in a little farther. The twin lines she had accused him of wearing creased between her eyebrows. Her hand gripped his upper arm.

"Rebecca?"

She opened her eyes, silver and magical. "It feels...odd."

He had no ready response to that as he waited for her to grow accustomed to him. His body begged for release, but he held back, resisting his own need. He did not want to rush her.

She arched her body and he sunk farther into her. She winced. "Oh!"

Shit! He moved to withdraw but her legs tightened against him and refused his retreat. The torture of it was almost more than he could bear.

"I'm fine," she said and arched her hips once more. He slid fully inside her, enveloped by her warmth. Her breath caught and he froze, but surprise became a smile. "Do that again."

He withdrew half way then slowly repeated the movement.

Her smile grew. "That feels quite—" He did it again. "Oh, yes. I like that." The words came on a breath and her body lifted to meet his thrusts. "Please, don't stop."

"I don't want to hurt you."

She shook her head. "I have that ache again."

She moved her body as if searching for the release they both craved. Her hands gripped his shoulders, anchoring her as she moved against him, taking over, seeking her own pleasure and leaving him no choice but to move with her to find his. He wrapped his arms around her, holding her against him and filled her again and again, listening to her breath, knowing when she grew close to climax and trying desperately to hold on as her body trembled then shuddered. Finally his control snapped and he joined her in the void where only their hearts and bodies existed and everything else remained at bay.

In that moment, Marcus understood the meaning of forever. Understood he would do whatever it took to keep it. To honor it.

To honor her.

Chapter Twenty-One

Rebecca stretched and a thrill shot through her as her bare skin moved against Marcus's. Her silk stockings had eventually been removed and any hope she had of recovering the brilliant hairstyle Nancy had managed, forever gone. She'd be lucky if she could find half the hairpins where they had scattered about the floor and who knew where else. She hoped they didn't end up rolling over onto one.

"Do you think anyone has missed us?"

She and Marcus had been gone nearly two hours, but likely the party had another hour of life left in it before the revelers returned to their beds. She, for one, had no wish to leave hers. She found the more times she and Marcus shared their bodies, the more she liked it. The pain that had initially shocked her at his invasion had faded from memory, painted over by the pleasure to be found in his embrace.

Was it any wonder Abigail and Caelie wore such secret smiles since their own weddings?

Marcus kissed her temple, his eyes still closed since their last coupling where he had placed her on top of him and allowed her to set the pace. The heady sense of power had made her pleasure all the more potent and she was eager to try it again.

"I'm sure if your brother suspected what we were about he'd be banging at your door and demanding my head."

"Which one?"

He opened his eyes and squinted at her until she could not help but laugh. Warmth spread through her when he joined her with a smile of his own. "Minx."

"Perhaps, but I am your minx."

"Indeed you are." Marcus pushed himself up on his elbow. "I will speak to your brother first thing in the morning and see about procuring a special license. I do not want to take the chance of waiting in the event we have created a babe this evening."

His hand traveled to her belly and she covered it with her own. "Do you think we did?" The idea filled her with a sense of wonder, to think of Marcus's child already growing in her womb.

"I cannot say, but we cannot chance it. I won't have our child being born a—" He stopped short, but his meaning fell between them as reality intruded into the warm cocoon their lovemaking had created.

She touched his face with a gentle hand. "I would love him no less and protect him just as fiercely, as I'm sure your mother did you."

"Do you think she did?"

"Do you not?"

"I do not know. I have not read the last entry."

Rebecca lifted herself up on her elbow. "Why ever not?"

He avoided her gaze, but she could see it in his eyes nonetheless. The uncertainty. The fear.

"You do not want to know how her story ended."

He shook his head in answer then gave her a wan smile. "Cowardly, isn't it?"

"No." She reached up and pressed her lips against his mouth, infusing all the love in her heart for this wonderful man into that one touch so he would know, whatever the end, good or bad, it would not change her feelings for him. "I think it quite normal."

He chuckled and kissed her back and for a moment she hoped they could push the world away a little longer, but as quickly as the kiss began, it ended and he looked at her with regret.

"I cannot stay." He hesitated. "The sheets will have—"

She nodded, cutting him off. The telltale signs of her loss of innocence would be readily visible. "I will have Nancy take care of it."

Marcus's hand trailed down her face and neck, his lingering touch testament to his reluctance to leave her. Soon, he would not have to. She longed for that day, to tarry in bed for as long as they wished and let the day go on without them while they stayed beneath the covers exploring each other, talking, laughing. He smiled at her as if understanding her unspoken thoughts.

"There is a hunt on the morrow. I will try to speak to your brother beforehand."

"What of Walkerton's threats with respect to the watch? I do not know how much longer we have before he makes good on them."

Marcus pulled her into his arms and she tucked her head beneath his chin. "I will return the watch to him tomorrow." She heard the smile in his voice when he spoke next. "I cannot have my bride marry me from a barred cell."

The idea of him being in such a predicament frightened her far more than any scandal, but she did her best to maintain a lighter air so he did not know. "It would make the wedding night most difficult to enjoy."

"Then that seals it. I cannot risk disappointing my wife on the first night of our marriage."

She pulled away and gave him a kiss. Bride. Wife. His. How she loved the language that bound them together and drew a future she could invest her heart and soul in. "You could never disappointment me." She pushed lightly at his chest. "Now go. It is much easier to sneak away while the shadows are still long and the hallway dark."

He stole another kiss, quick and passionate. "How tawdry you make it sound."

"Enjoy it while it lasts." She laughed. "For soon we shall be an old married couple and your days of sneaking and tawdriness will be well behind us."

"Perhaps the sneaking," Marcus said as he threw back the covers and rose from the bed, giving her a full view of his magnificent backside. "But I do hope the tawdriness lasts well into old age." He glanced over his shoulder and frowned. "Were you just looking at my backside?"

She smiled. "I was simply doing my part to maintain the tawdriness."

And suddenly he was beside her once again, and sneaking into the hallway's shadows was put off for one last tumble in the bed they had shared.

"Ah, and this must be the beautiful Lady Rebecca."

Rebecca stopped short, her path through the library blocked by a man she had not met before. He was of medium height with plain brown hair, though grey had threaded through his temples and streaked it throughout. She did not recognize him but trepidation crawled up her spine and the hair at the base of her neck stood on end.

"Lord Walkerton?"

He bowed slightly. "At your service."

"We have not been properly introduced," she said, hoping to put him off, to slip away. She wanted nothing to do with the man threatening to ruin Marcus and destroy their future, though the second part he had no knowledge of. Their engagement would not be announced until after Marcus spoke with Nicholas and she had the opportunity to break the news to Lord Selward. She did not want him to learn of their plans publically. He deserved better than that and she needed to maintain a good relationship with him. In the event Lord Walkerton refused to acknowledge Marcus, Lord Selward may be the only one who could back up Marcus's claim.

"Indeed, we have not. An oversight on my son's part given your close relationship."

She did not care for the connotation in his tone. "We have an acquaintance, my lord. I consider Lord Selward a friend."

"Ah. Friend is it? Well." He smiled at her and she searched for some hint of Marcus in him, some sense that they shared blood and that, despite everything she had learned about the man, she might find something redemptive. She could not. For all his slick politeness, Lord Walkerton remained difficult to read, his expression closed off beneath a veneer of politeness that lacked any hint of sincerity.

"If you will excuse me, my lord. I am on my way to see my mother about this evening's entertainments."

"Then I would be only too happy to provide you escort. It has been quite some time since I have seen the lovely Lady Blackbourne. You favor her in some regard. Not surprising my son would be so taken with you."

The man offered Rebecca his arm and despite the warnings that clamored in the back of her head, she took it. Perhaps if she could ingratiate herself to Lord Walkerton, she could make him see the sense in acknowledging Marcus as his son. The chances were slim she could convince him so easily, but she was not one to pass up an opportunity when it presented itself. Besides, after last night, the need to be Marcus's wife had increased tenfold. She did not care to be separated from him for another night, and while she recognized that their marriage was unlikely to happen so quickly, the sooner the better. Her hand traveled to her abdomen then, realizing what she had done, she let it drop away as Lord Walkerton led her out the French doors and onto the stone terrace.

"She is awaiting me in the greenhouse, on the other side of the gardens."

"To the gardens it is then." He smiled and, despite the early hour, she detected the hint of brandy on his breath.

Again, instinct warred with her to make her excuses and leave the man behind, but she hushed it. This was necessary, and besides, it was broad daylight. What could the man possibly do to her? Enough guests milled, some preparing for the hunt and others for an excursion into town. She would only need shout to bring a handful of them running to her aid.

The Sheridan gardens were a splendid affair. A labyrinth of bushes and flowers and statues made it almost maze-like. Many of the hedges were well over six feet high in several sections and zigzagged their way across the vast property leading to a beautiful grotto or opening up to a lovely pond filled with lily pads and croaking frogs. It was a place made for days such as this where the summer sun spread its rays over the stunning landscape and brought with it a warm breeze and the promise of things to come.

"My son informs me we are to be family soon, my lady. I find that a most enticing prospect."

"Is that so? I was under the impression you were not overly enamored of the association."

Lord Walkerton brushed her words off with a wave of his hand. "Forgive my son's reticence at not making it official well before now. He is all about propriety and properness. Dull as wood, I say. A shame I've a wife of my own, or I would snatch you away for myself."

He laughed at his own jest, but his words made her stomach squirm. "I'm certain I would have some say in that matter."

He made no comment as if she had said nothing at all of import; his dismissive silence a clear indication her wishes were of no concern to him. She glanced back over her shoulder toward the library. Should she return?

He walked on, bringing her with him. "I have decided my son has tarried long enough on the matter and therefore I have taken it upon myself to meet with your brother later this day on the matter."

Rebecca stopped when they were halfway down the sweeping stone steps that led from the terrace to the gardens. "I beg your pardon, Lord Walkerton, but Lord Selward and I have not broached the subject of marriage as yet and no proposal has been made. You get ahead of yourself."

"A minor detail." Lord Walkerton tugged on her arm and she had no choice but to continue along or risk slipping off the smooth stone.

Rebecca changed topics. She did not care to dwell on Lord Walkerton's expectations. They mattered not. "My lord, I wondered if I might speak with you about Mr. Bowen. I understand he is in possession of an item that—"

"My watch. Yes. I'm afraid it is true." He leaned in closer to her and the strong scent of brandy swamped her. The hair tingled at the base of her spine as they reached the bottom of the stairs. She stopped for a moment, ill at ease at the prospect of heading into the high hedges with him.

"He did not steal your watch, my lord. His mother gifted him the watch and because of this, it holds a strong sentimental value to him, hence his reluctance to let it go."

The sun glinted off Lord Walkerton's bloodshot eyes and his cheeks held a florid cast to them, as if had just come in from the cold, despite the warmth of the day. The man looked as if overindulgence and avarice were gaining the upper hand on him.

"Is that so?" His glance slid down her face and dropped to the bodice of her rose-colored morning dress. It lingered there long enough to make her skin crawl before he lifted his gaze slowly back to her face.

He'd leered at her! She bit down and swallowed the revulsion that climbed up her throat. She needed to stay focused. If she could convince him not to pursue charges against Marcus and acknowledge him as his son, it would be worth a few more moments in his despicable company.

"Yes, it is," she said. "I believe Mr. Bowen wishes to discover how his mother came into possession of the watch—"

"I know full well how she came into possession of the watch. She took it from me during our…assignation," Lord Walkerton said, dragging out the last word, caressing it with his tongue. "Your Mr. Bowen is my by blow."

Rebecca tried to catch her breath. Had it really been that easy? "Then you acknowledge this?"

Walkerton pulled on her arm and her feet stumbled over the uneven stone sunk into the path where it skirted the edge of the garden. Rebecca dug in her heels.

"That he is my bastard? Yes." Walkerton looked at her with the same expression his son gave her when discussing the weather. As if it were of little import, nothing more than a way to fill the silence. As if he fathered children without the benefit of marriage on a regular basis.

His easy admission left her stunned and when he tugged her arm she stumbled along, onto the path that led to the maze. Was this all the proof they needed? Or would he have to claim it publically? State such on a more official document that would satisfy the dictates of Father's will?

"Lord Walkerton!"

A lady's voice cut through the miasma of questions rushing through Rebecca's mind. Lord Walkerton stopped and they both turned. Standing at the top of the stone stairwell was Lady Franklyn, resplendent in her riding habit of deep plum. Rebecca had not been pleased when Mother had insisted on inviting Lord and Lady Franklyn, and their acid-tongued daughter, Lady Susan, but at that moment, she was quite thankful Mother had not listened to her. The interruption allowed her head to clear enough to see the folly of going into a maze, arm in arm, with a man who made her skin crawl and put her instincts on edge.

"My, my," Lord Walkerton said, his voice slithering out of him in equal parts charming and deadly. "Lady Franklyn. I had not realized you were in attendance. Were you hoping to make a last ditch effort to barter your daughter off to my son?"

"I would not sell you my worst enemy, Walkerton."

Rebecca had never cared much for Lady Franklyn. Though beautiful in her cold, imperious way, she had always proven herself to be very selfish, caring little for who her actions harmed or what scandal she left in her wake. It had been such behavior that had put her on the dock the day brigands set upon her. Marcus had stepped in, nearly losing his own life in the process. Still, during her entire acquaintance with Lady Franklyn, she had never seen such anger and—was that fear?—pulled tight across her lovely features.

"Sometimes a man doesn't need to purchase such things, my lady. Sometimes they are offered to him and sometimes he simply takes them."

Something about his words, the way they were said, made Rebecca's stomach roil. Lady Franklyn looked as if Lord Walkerton had marched up the steps and slapped her across the face. There was something more at play here, something she had no knowledge of, yet stood in the middle of.

"Lady Rebecca." The duchess held out a hand. "Come with me. Your mother is asking after you."

Rebecca held no illusion that Lady Franklyn lied through her teeth. Mother awaited her at the greenhouse where she busied herself with choosing the arrangements for this evening's dinner. If Mother sought her out, Lady Franklyn would be the last one she sent, though she did not see the need to point this fact out. She wanted away from Lord Walkerton. She had what she needed. He'd admitted to fathering Marcus and being well aware of the fact.

She released his arm as if it had caught on fire and lifted her skirts, hurrying over the pathway and back up the steps. Lady Franklyn continued to extend her hand and when she took it, the duchess's gloved fingers tightened around hers and pulled Rebecca tightly to her side.

Lord Walkerton smiled at them both, his cold eyes fixed on Lady Franklyn. "I bid you good day then, ladies. Lady Franklyn, I expect we shall meet again at the hunt. I look forward to it, as always." He made a courtly bow then turned and disappeared into the hedges.

Rebecca let out a long breath she had not realized she'd held.

Lady Franklyn let go of her hand and rounded on her. "What were you thinking of, going with that man?"

"I—I—" She stumbled over an explanation, unable to give the truth and not able to come up with anything else. What business was it of hers?

"What your mother was thinking inviting that beast is beyond me!"

"He is Lord Selward's father—" *And Marcus's.*

"He is a monster with deviant desires." Lady Franklyn grabbed Rebecca's shoulders and gave her a small shake. "Stay away from him. Do you hear me? If he walks in your direction, you turn around and leave. Do not allow yourself to be alone with him. Promise me!"

Rebecca nodded, afraid of the desperation in Lady Franklyn's tone, and the fear that ravaged her eyes.

She was more than happy to stay away from Walkerton now that she had the information she needed.

She must find Marcus and tell him their worries were over.

Chapter Twenty-Two

January 18th

My sweet boy with your dark hair and sweet smile. Marcus William Wallace. They let me hold you in my arms and suckle at my breast, though I have already failed you in that respect as my milk will not come. Mary promises me I shouldn't worry as sometimes this happens. Still, it pained me to give you to another woman to do what I, as your mother, should be able to do, but my body is battered from your birth and my strength has not returned. A fever burns in my blood and I can barely hold my pen. Forgive the messiness of my writing, but I wanted to put the words down for you before it takes hold. I need to tell you that I loved you beyond all measure. I had never known such a love existed and now—now—I understand Mother. How I resented her trying to save me, to keep me from harm and hurt. But it is no less than what I will do for you. What I must do. I will not have you face a life where you are looked down upon. Where you must pay for my mistakes, for what I was unable to stop.

I could not protect myself, but I will not fail you in this regard my sweet, sweet boy. I love you beyond all measure. Never doubt that.

Marcus closed the journal and let his head fall against the high-backed chair, his heart bursting with wonder and confusion and...love. Yes, love. For a woman he had never met, never had the chance to know. And yet, reading her words, digesting them bit-by-bit, he knew her well. Understood her in a way most of those around her had not. Her words allowed him a glimpse into her private world, into her mind and heart. He'd absorbed her fears and her hopes and her determination.

And her love.

She had loved him. Without question, without reserve.

She had not abandoned him as if he were an embarrassment or a shameful reminder of her fall from grace. Her words, which had started out as a curse, tearing away everything he had believed, in the end became a gift. One handed down to him by the woman who had given him life, through the woman who had raised him and loved him as her own. Both women deserved the term Mother.

He had never seen her face, had no name to pin to her, but he recognized her heart. Forgave. Understood.

He breathed in the fresh air that wafted through the breakfast room of Northill Hall. Something fell into place and brought with it a sense of peace that settled deep inside of him.

He lifted his head and looked around him, seeing Northill in a different light. Not just a structure with walls and furniture, but a home. His home.

Mr. Cosgrove had done an impressive job in the week he had been here getting the neglected grounds shipshape and culling out the staff who had grown lazy in their duties. His daughter, Miss Cosgrove, had done her part as well. The housekeeper had moved on well over six months ago and the maid who had taken over lacked the skill to command the remaining staff on their duties. Miss Cosgrove took them all in hand and by the time Marcus arrived, the main rooms had been cleaned and cleared, fresh flowers set about and windows thrown wide to air the place out.

Despite his initial reticence at accepting Northill Hall, it had been the right thing to do. A sense of ownership and permanence rooted him, a feeling he had not had since his early childhood at Braemore. As Marcus glanced around, he imagined the manor house overrun with children, little dark-haired miniatures of their mother with ink black hair and silvery eyes and he smiled. The image warmed his heart, much as memories of the night before heated his blood.

He should not have taken such liberties with Rebecca, but for the life of him he could not regret what they had shared. Even now, hours after he had left her bed, he could still smell her scent on his skin, hear her breath in his ear urging him on, begging for more. She was a wonder.

And she was his.

He'd meant to speak to Nicholas early that morning, but Rebecca's brother had been gone on estate business and would not return until shortly before the hunt. It mattered little. The outcome would be the same. Honor dictated he do the right thing and his heart demanded it. Looked forward to it.

"You are full of smiles this morning, my lord."

Marcus glanced up at the sound of Miss Cosgrove's gentle voice as she entered the room bearing a tray. "Indeed, I suppose I am. Tell me, have you had much success in interviewing candidates for the position of housekeeper?"

Miss Cosgrove had proven well suited to running his household, unfortunately, having a beautiful young lady sharing his home in such a capacity would not do. People had a tendency to talk and he did not care to have her reputation sullied. Her father had high hopes that with a new position secured, his daughter would be able to have the life he'd envisioned for her—a husband, children, a home of her own.

"Not as yet, my lord, but I have only just begun. Surely there are many capable women who will be thrilled to take such a position. Until then, I am perfectly happy filling in." She set the tray down and handed him a letter. "This came for you with instructions to deliver immediately."

Marcus accepted the envelope and flipped it over. It bore the Franklyn seal. Curious. Lord Franklyn had been feeling under the weather and had not come to the party, though his wife and daughter had. Did one of them send the missive?

"Will you require anything else, Mr. Bowen?"

He glanced up at Miss Cosgrove and shook his head. "No, thank you. That will be all."

He returned his attention to the letter and broke the seal. The feminine scrawl filled the page in loops and flourishes but the words painted a far less pretty picture. Anger and bile churned inside of him.

"Bastard!" He crumpled the letter in his hand and vaulted from his chair, taking off at a run, his earlier happiness gone.

He needed to find Walkerton.

Even with the fastest horse from his stable, the ride from Northill to Sheridan Park lasted interminably long. Marcus left his horse in front of the house, having torn up the circled drive and shouted instructions to the footman as he burst into the manor house, caring little of etiquette or propriety.

"Rebecca!"

His shout echoed through the hallways, reverberated off the marble floors and tastefully decorated walls. Somewhere behind him, Charleston, the butler, followed behind calling his name, but he paid him no heed. This was not the time for manners or being announced or whatever else Charleston had in his head that he thought needed doing.

"Marcus, whatever is it?"

He stopped short and looked straight up where the stairs to the floor above opened and fanned outward on either side. Rebecca hung over the railing calling down to him. He didn't answer but bounded up the stairs two at a time until he reached her and pulled her into his arms, caring little if anyone saw them.

Somewhere he heard Charleston gasp.

"Did he hurt you?"

Rebecca muffled an answer against his chest and he reluctantly loosened his hold. She glanced up at him. "Who?"

"Walkerton!" He held her at arm's length and looked her up and down. Nothing appeared amiss, but appearances could be deceiving.

"Of course not."

He lifted an eyebrow. "Rebecca..."

She let out a small huff. "I am fine, Marcus. Truly. Although, you must obviously favor your mother, as I can find no redeeming qualities in the man who makes claims to have fathered you. He tried to lure me into the gardens, but thankfully Lady Franklyn had her wits about her and stopped him."

"And where were your wits? You know he is not a man to be trifled with."

"My wits were busy extracting his confession that he did, indeed, father you. A confession he gave rather easily, I might add." She smiled at him, the gesture illuminating her face with a radiance that glowed from the inside out. If anything had happened to her—

He pushed the thought aside. "He admitted to it?"

Rebecca grabbed the lapels of his jacket and pulled him closer until her soft breasts pushed against his chest, diffusing his anger for the moment while his attentions changed course and focused on the sensations of having her lithe little body pressed into his created. God help him, there was nothing he wanted more than to march her back up to her bedchambers and crawl beneath the covers. There, he could keep her safe. There, he could shut the rest of the world out so only they existed.

"Yes, he did." Her smile grew. "I am certain between Lord Selward's admission and Lord Walkerton's, we have all we need. Don't you agree?"

"Perhaps." It hardly mattered at the moment. He wanted her safe. He didn't want her risking herself on his behalf. He could not live with himself if anything—or anyone—harmed her. "I want you to stay away from him. The man is not to be trusted."

"You sound like Lady Franklyn." Her brows snapped together as her nimble brain put two and two together. "Was it she who told you I met with him? She is the only one who saw us together."

Marcus nodded. "She sent me a note indicating you were not safe with him around."

Her nose wrinkled and he could not stop himself from running the tip of his forefinger down its short length to smooth it out. "Why did she send it to you and not to Mother or Nicholas?"

He shook his head. He did not care why Lady Franklyn had sent him the note, only that she had and when he arrived, he found Rebecca no worse for wear. This time. But what of the next time? If she continued to insert herself in these matters, she ran the risk of being injured, ruined, or worse.

"Promise me you will stay away from Walkerton."

"I only want to help. This is my future too, after all."

He wrapped his arms around her and rested his chin atop her head, her soft hair tickling his skin. The idea that she looked forward to their future made his heart swell, but first he must ensure they had one, and he could not do this if anything happened to her.

"You have helped more than you know in ways you can't imagine." She had given him purpose. Strength. The ability to look past the present and see a much different future than he thought possible. And she had removed the restlessness that dogged him since his run in with the pointy end of a brigand's knife. She had allowed him to dream, something he had forgotten how to do.

"Promise me," he repeated, whispering the words against her hair. Her body relaxed into his and her arms slid around his waist and squeezed.

"I promise. But I do not want to give Walkerton a chance to ruin you. I know the watch holds a sense of attachment for you, but I truly think it best if you return it as planned. For all our sakes."

Marcus pulled away. The absence of her warmth bled through him and he longed to have it back, but not now. Not yet. He reached into his pocket and pulled out the watch.

"I will catch up with him on the hunt and return it as promised. I have all I need." The journal contained the essence of his mother, who she had been, what she had felt for him. The watch was nothing more than a means to an end. Something she had kept to perhaps lead him in the direction he needed to go without having to say the words or commit them to paper for anyone to see. She had considered her downfall a private matter, to be shared with only him and while it made identifying her near impossible, he had not given up hope yet. "When I come back, we will speak with Nicholas and procure a special license."

Her hands reached up and grabbed his where they held the watch, her smile luminous. His heart swelled. She wished the marriage as much as he and embraced their future despite all the things he could not give her. She looked beyond what society expected from her, what she had been borne to assume as her due and had the courage to follow her heart. To see him for who he was at the core.

He could not wish for more.

"Then I shall let you go and wish you luck." She lifted his hand and pressed her lips against his fingers where they curled around the watch. "I love you, Marcus."

The words, plainly spoken, shot through him. How easily she accepted him, how warmly she gave to him. She was a wonder. His wonder. He would do whatever he must to ensure she had everything she deserved.

"No more than I love you." Though he'd uttered the words to her over and over in his mind for years now, he'd never spoken them out loud. They held a magical quality and seeing her expression light up with joy went beyond anything he could have imagined.

He leaned down and captured her mouth in his, putting into his kiss everything in his heart until they were both breathless and Charleston, who lingered nearby, cleared his throat, on the verge of an apoplectic fit at such a bold display of impropriety.

Marcus broke the kiss and peered down into her face, memorizing its angles and the way the light played against her ivory skin. He loved her. Heart and soul. It seemed such a simple thing. Such a perfect thing.

It was everything.

"I must go and catch up with the hunt." He kissed her fingertips and slipped the watch back into his pocket for safekeeping.

"Go. I am off to meet with Mother. Be safe, Marcus. Do not take any unnecessary chances with Lord Walkerton. As you said, the man is unpredictable."

He nodded, but made no promises in that regard. He had every intention of warning the man away from Rebecca by whatever means it took to prevent a repeat of this morning's incident. He would thank Lady Franklyn for her interference and call their accounts square.

With reluctance, he left Rebecca behind and went to catch up with the hunt.

And with the bastard who had fathered him.

Finding Walkerton proved an easy task. He had lagged behind the others and Marcus came upon him suddenly in a clearing. Walkerton's unmanned horse stood grazing in the tall grass as Walkerton ambled out from behind a copse of trees, fumbling with the fall of his trousers having just relieved himself.

"Walkerton!"

Marcus drew his horse up and dismounted, noting the man's hunting rifle remained secured in its holster against his saddle. The earl stopped his approach when he spotted Marcus and pulled a flask from coat pocket.

"What do you want?"

"To speak with you." He moved closer but stayed out of arm's reach. Walkerton had exposed his volatile temper at the Devil's Lair and he had no wish to get pulled into it if such could be avoided. Though doing the man violence after his attempt to lure Rebecca into the garden maze was no less than what he deserved.

"I've nothing to say to the likes of you."

So much for fatherly love. "What were your intentions this morning with Lady Rebecca?"

Walkerton grinned, but the expression held no mirth, only a sickening insinuation. "Pretty little thing, isn't she? Hardly surprising my son practically salivates at the mention of her name." Marcus's body tensed and his fists clenched. Walkerton snickered. "Guess you and Selward have inherited your father's appreciation for beauty, though neither of you seems to have two blessed clues what to do about it. I thought at least you would have, given what you are."

He delivered the last bit with a sneer of derision, as if his offspring had disappointed him greatly. What had his mother seen in this man? What did anyone?

"And what am I?"

Walkerton took a step toward him, taking another swig from the flask. "A bastard, my boy. Or didn't the lofty Lord Ellesmere inform you of such? Likely not, I suppose, given the stodgy old man's aversion to anything that holds the stink of scandal about it." He whispered the last part and Marcus itched to wrap his fingers around the man's neck and squeeze but he held himself in check.

Not yet.

"I'm surprised he agreed to take you in, given what people must have assumed," Walkerton continued. He leaned back on his heels but the motion off-centered him and he had to put a leg back to stop from toppling onto his arse.

"Lord Ellesmere is a good man, not something I believe you've ever endorsed with your own behavior."

"My, my. Such lofty judgments from the high and mighty Mr. Bowen. Are you still calling yourself Bowen? Born to aristocrats and raised by servants. Such is the lot of a bastard, is it not? No one really wants the burden. I imagine Ellesmere cursed God and everyone else when he discovered the Bowens had up and died on him. Though, I don't know why he didn't just leave you to rot in Cornwall. Guess the old man had a bit of a soft spot for his kin in the end. Such as it were."

Marcus stilled, the words reverberating through him. "What do you know of it?"

Walkerton snorted. Another swig. The damn flask had to be near empty by now at the rate he sucked on it. "I might have had a few drinks at the time, but I still remember which doxy I stuck my prick in."

Marcus's brain worked furiously, pulling the cryptic words offered by Walkerton and marrying them against the clues already in his possession. His heartbeat increased and banged out the seconds.

"I do like the young ones," Walkerton continued. "They like to put up a fight, don't they? Pretend they don't like it, don't want it. Makes the taking more exciting that way, with a bit of a tussle. Hardens the cock better than the most skilled whore, I always say." He grabbed the member in question as he said the words. The motion disgusted Marcus. The truth splayed before him in unforgiving hues.

His mother had not given up her innocence. It had been taken.

I could not protect myself, but I will not fail you...

Walkerton had raped her.

Calm. Breathe.

He struggled to hold back. To not kill the man where he stood. Would the same fate have befallen Rebecca had Lady Franklyn not intervened?

"Who was she?"

Walkerton leaned forward close enough for Marcus to smell the stench of brandy on his foul breath. "Who?"

Breathe. Just breathe. He did, but it offered little help. He still wanted to strangle the life out of the man and leave him in the woods to rot. "My mother."

Walkerton threw his head back and laughed then looked at him with amusement. Marcus clenched his fist with such force the bones of his fingers ached.

"You mean to tell me Ellesmere didn't tell you? Well, that is rich, isn't it?" The idea appeared to delight him and Walkerton stumbled out something akin to a two-step, giggling like a child as he did so. He stopped mid-dance and fixed his gaze on Marcus. "It was Ellesmere's precious little girl, of course. Oh, and let me tell you, she was a prize. Tight and tasty and feisty as—"

Marcus didn't recall swinging. He barely registered the impact of his fist against the hard bone of Walkerton's jaw. The man hadn't even hit the ground before Marcus jumped onto his chest and pummeled his face with a fury he could not contain, had never experienced before. Before the secrets were revealed. Before the ugly truth stared him in the face.

Walkerton had raped Lady Lilith Kingsley. His mother.

She had died years before his arrival to London, at the age of sixteen. Just a girl. Everyone believed she had fallen ill while she and Lady Ellesmere toured the continent and passed away before their return. She hadn't even been presented to society for her first Season and yet somehow, Walkerton had gotten his hands on her, robbed her of her innocence and left her to her fate as if it was just another day to him.

Time lost all meaning. Marcus could not say if he'd been beating the man for a minute, an hour, or the better part of the day. His hands had gone numb beneath his leather gloves, the only feeling left in him cold, hard rage.

In the distance, someone shouted his name. He ignored it.

This man, whose seed had fathered him in such a violent manner, had to pay for what he'd done. Be prevented from ever doing it again. Was that his intent when he attempted to lead Rebecca into the gardens? Would she have met the same fate as his mother? And how many others had there been?

Someone shouted and something solid and unyielding slammed against him, throwing him off Walkerton. He landed flat on his back, the weight of whatever hit him landing across his chest, trapping him against the hard ground. The breath whooshed from his lungs, paralyzing him for a brief moment. He blinked and looked up.

Glenmor.

"Let me up," he rasped.

"I'll not. You've done your damage. Leave it be." Glenmor had him well pinned, his arms at his side allowing him no range of movement to toss him off.

"Shit!" Nick snarled from nearby. "Is he dead?"

"Sadly, no." Spence.

"I'm not done," Marcus shouted and tried to buck Glenmor off.

He held fast and called over his shoulder for reinforcements. "A little help here!"

Spence landed on his legs. "Sweet Judas, man. What were you trying to do? Kill him?"

"He deserves nothing less."

Nick joined them and loomed over Marcus and the blanket of bodies that held him down. "What the hell is going on?"

Marcus remained silent. He did not know what to tell them, the truth still too raw and ugly to repeat. Lady Lilith Kingsley was his mother. Lord and Lady Ellesmere, his grandparents. He glanced up at Spence. *His cousin*. How long had he wished for family, only to learn it had been there all the while without his ever knowing?

How many times had he passed Lady Lilith's portrait in the hallways of Ellesmere House and Lakefield Abbey, without realizing the import of her life and death? Her loss had left a deep hole in the hearts of both Lord and Lady Ellesmere, so much so that her name was seldom spoken. Her stories rarely told.

The truth, so far from anything he had ever imagined, twisted inside of him seeking a place to land. He closed his eyes and allowed the pain and anger of being denied the truth for so long seep deep into his bones until it replaced the blood in his veins, the breath in his lungs. The beat of his heart.

With Walkerton dragged from his sight, Glenmor and

Spence released him and the three men formed a wall between him and the earl. Slowly, reason resurrected itself.

He stood and brushed the grass and dirt from his jacket then strode to his horse, offering no explanation. He needed time to come to terms with what he had learned. He mounted and kicked his heels against the horse's sides, urging it forward, demanding it outrun the voices calling him back. There was no going back.

Eventually he slowed and turned the horse in the direction of Northill. In the distance a shot rang out, but he paid it little heed. A hunt was going on. He pitied the poor fox, cornered and scared. Is that how his mother had felt when Walkerton preyed upon her innocence?

He reached into his pocket for the watch. In all that had happened, he had not returned it. Had his mother grabbed it as she tried to fight off Walkerton's advances? Had she hung onto it as proof of what he had done, something to use if necessary?

He would never know. Anger surged anew and the watch burned against his palm. He had promised Rebecca he would return it to Walkerton to prevent him from trying to ruin them. Beating him senseless had not been part of the plan. In all likelihood, it would only make him more inclined to take action. Assault and thievery.

Marcus pulled up on the reins. He'd lost his head and made things worse.

He'd been ill prepared.

Despite the warnings he'd received about digging up the past, he hadn't prepared himself for the truth when it finally came. His birth had killed his mother, as if she had not suffered enough at his conception. Meanwhile, Walkerton roamed free, likely perpetrating the same violence against other women as he had Lilith.

He wanted nothing more to do with Walkerton, save to

stop him from destroying any more lives. The sight of the watch made him ill. He wanted nothing more than to return it as promised; to shove the tainted gold timepiece down Walkerton's throat until he choked on it.

Marcus turned his horse around and returned to where he had left the earl prone on the ground, unsure of what his friends had done with him, or what lies Walkerton may have told them about the altercation. Likely he had painted Marcus in the worst possible light. It hardly mattered. His friends would discern the truth.

But as Marcus approached the spot where he had left Walkerton moaning on the ground, the man was not to be found, though his horse remained off in the distance standing in tall grass making a meal out of it. Nick, Spence and Glenmor were gone. Had they taken Walkerton with them to see to his injuries and left his horse behind? It seemed unlikely they would leave a prime piece of horseflesh roaming about the woods.

Foreboding slithered up Marcus's spine. He nudged his mount forward, pulling the reins up short. Twenty paces away, Walkerton laid on the ground, sightless eyes staring up at the cloudless sky. Next to him rested his rifle.

A hole had ruined the front of the earl's expensive buff riding jacket. Blood spread dark and crimson across the breadth of his chest, discoloring the wool. A chest that no longer rose and fell.

Behind Marcus, the pounding of hoof beats drew closer.

Chapter Twenty-Three

Rebecca's slippers barely touched the steps as she flew downstairs to the main floor, skidding to a stop at the scene that greeted her when she reached the receiving room. She had been out for a walk with Caelie and Abigail when the men had returned and wasn't aware of what had happened until after Nancy reached her room, breathless from running up two flights of stairs to deliver the news.

Lord Walkerton was dead—murdered!—and the local constable now questioned Marcus upon the suggestion of Lord Selward!

Nicholas approached her as she entered, holding his arms out as if to shield her from what took place behind him. She noted Huntsleigh and Lord Ellesmere, and several men she did not recognize by name though their uniforms would indicate they had come with the constable.

"Rebecca, you shouldn't be here. Wait for me upstairs and I will come as soon as I can."

"Do not shoo me away. What has happened? Why are they questioning Marcus?"

Nicholas used his body to force her backward into the hallway, his form too large to see around. "It is still being sorted out."

"Nancy said Lord Walkerton was murdered. How can that be? And why would they suspect Marcus?" None of this made sense. He had promised to return the watch to Walkerton and let the matter drop. Hardly a meeting that should have resulted in the kind of violence that left a man dead.

"They are merely questioning him, for all the good it is doing them. He hasn't said more than ten words since they began their infernal inquisition."

The tone in Nicholas's voice did nothing to soothe her nerves. "Do they truly believe he did it? Why? And do not order me to go upstairs and wait patiently. I am not going anywhere until you tell me!"

Nicholas's shoulders slumped. "Very well. But I doubt you will like what I have to tell you. Come." He led her to a small bench farther down the hallway and waited until she sat down before he joined her.

She braced herself. "What happened?"

He took her hand. Not a good indication of things to come. She wanted to snatch it away, as if by doing so she could change the news from bad to good.

"We came upon Marcus and Walkerton during the hunt. Walkerton had lagged behind, too drunk to find his way, we assumed, though no one seemed too concerned. But we had also lost sight of Lady Franklyn and a few others from her party. We thought perhaps they had become lost where the pathway divides near the stream, so Spence, Ben and I doubled back. When we reached the open field near the old cabin, we came upon Marcus and Walkerton. Marcus was on top of him, beating the man senseless."

Rebecca opened her mouth to say something but nothing

came out but a strangled sound she didn't recognize as her own voice.

Nicholas let out a long breath. "We put a stop to it, though it took some doing. Marcus was in a rage. When we asked him what it was about, he refused to answer, then he mounted up and left. We thought it best to let him go and calm himself and we still had Walkerton to contend with. We offered to escort him back to the house to see to his injuries, but he refused so we left. We still needed to find Lady Franklyn and the others. Shortly after our departure, we heard a shot and doubled back. When we arrived, Marcus stood over Walkerton's body."

Fear, swift and rampant, swept through Rebecca until she shook from head to toe. "Did he say what happened?"

Nicholas shook his head. "No. He still hasn't, other than to indicate they had fought earlier over a personal matter of which he would not divulge and then he left. The latter of which Spence, Ben and I confirmed."

Had this been her fault? Had Lord Walkerton's attempts of earlier that morning set Marcus on a course of violence that caused the earl his life? She did not doubt for a moment Marcus would protect her, but to kill a man after the fact, in cold blood? It didn't sit right. The Marcus she knew would not do such a thing.

"I need to see him."

"You cannot right now. The constable—"

"Hang the constable!" The words shot out of her in a fury and she squeezed her brother's hands where they held hers. "Please, Nicholas. I must speak with him immediately. I will force myself into the room and carry on with high hysterics if that is what it takes."

"When did I become inundated with a household of strong-willed women?" He muttered. He looked up, addressing the ceiling before returning his gaze to her. "Let me see what I can do."

Several long moments later, Marcus appeared in the doorway of the receiving room and looked down the hall to where she sat. She stood, her hands clasped against her belly to stop them from shaking. He hesitated a moment then slowly made his way toward her, stopping just out of reach. A haunted expression cut into the angles and shadows of his face. That, above all else, scared her the most.

She rushed forward and threw her arms around his neck and kissed him, the need to touch him overwhelming, but his lips were cold and unmoving, refusing the solace she tried to offer. She touched his face, wishing there was some way she could erase the trouble weighing heavy on his brow. "I was so worried when I heard the news. Are you hurt? What happened?"

He pulled her hands away and took a step back, releasing her.

"Walkerton is dead," he said, his voice flat, unemotional.

"I know." She shook her head, confused. He pulled away, not just physically, but emotionally. He had crawled into that place inside of him she had seen him retreat to from time to time when he wished to be alone. She wanted to grab hold of him and pull him back, but it was too late. He'd already left her.

She glanced down and blinked away the tears that sparked in her eyes. His knuckles were split and swollen, the telltale signs of his altercation with Walkerton in clear view.

"They think I did it."

She nodded but refrained from asking if it was true. It couldn't be. Could it? She took a step forward, needing him to erase any hint of doubt weaseling its way into her heart, but Marcus took a step back and refused her outstretched hand with a hard shake of his head. "No."

"Marcus, I—"

He held up a hand, interrupting her. Just as well. What could she possibly say to make this situation better? What witness could she bear to make the constable believe Marcus would never commit such a crime?

"You should go," he said and the words had a disturbing finality to them, as if he were telling her to go away for good, and not just for now.

"Will you come to me later?"

He looked at her a long time and the truth of his expression, its remoteness, the distance he kept between them, the deadness of his voice, sunk in with cold certainty. He would not come.

Before she could say anything else, the constable appeared in the doorway. "Mr. Bowen? We still have more questions, sir, if you please."

Marcus nodded though did not glance in the other man's direction, his gaze riveted on her. "I will not have you involved in this. Go."

And with that, he turned and strode back to the receiving room. The constable gave her a questioning look before following and shutting the doors behind him, leaving Rebecca alone.

The sound of her heartbeat echoed up and down the empty hallway. After a time, she forced her feet to move and returned upstairs to find Mother and the others. Surely, something could be done.

Marcus's head pounded. Nicholas had cut short the constable's litany of questions, insisting he had reached the point of repetitive madness searching for answers none of them had to give. Once the man left,

Marcus retired alone to the library, hoping the quiet calm of the room would quell his unease that any luck he'd possessed had just run out.

He had not killed Walkerton and therefore, logic dictated, he could not be held responsible for his death. But logic did not always factor into such matters and he could not deny the events preceding Walkerton's death made him look remarkably guilty. He had beaten the earl senseless and moments later he'd been shot dead with his own rifle. With no one to provide witness or state otherwise, his innocence proved a bit of a moot point. The constable was hungry to prove his worth by finding a perpetrator for the crime.

He clenched and released his hand, the cuts that riddled his knuckles pulled and cracked from the effort. His gloves had proven inadequate protection from the blows he'd visited upon Walkerton. He stared at them and marveled at the fact that only this morning these same hands had touched the woman he loved, caressed her soft skin, sunk deep into her glorious mane of thick midnight hair, traced the line of her lips before kissing her deeply until every cell in his body rejoiced.

This morning he had imagined a future bright and clear. Tonight, he watched as that future crumbled to rubble at his feet.

Walking away from Rebecca had killed him. When she'd thrown her arms around him, he'd wanted nothing else but to lose himself in her embrace, give in to her kiss, but he couldn't. He refused to make any more promises he couldn't keep. Things were bound to get uglier before they got better. *If* they got better. The constable was a most ambitious man. To have a peer of the realm murdered on his watch would not go unanswered. And what a boon to have a commoner at hand to take the fall.

That an innocent man might hang for a crime he had not committed hardly mattered. Marcus suspected that was the real reason Nicholas gave the man the boot. He saw it too and while he could not prevent the inevitability, he could delay it as long as possible.

But not forever.

Regardless, Marcus would not drag Rebecca down with him. She did not deserve this. He did not have the protection of the House of Lords behind him. He was but a common man in the eyes of the law. If found guilty, he would hang.

He took a sip of brandy, his third. The liquid burned his throat but failed to reach beyond that, nor did the fire he'd kindled in the hearth. He'd gone numb. Against the truth of who he was; against what had happened to his mother. Against the loss of Rebecca and the future they'd dreamed of.

He downed what remained in the glass and set it aside, letting his head fall into his hands.

In life, Walkerton had destroyed his mother's life. In death, it seemed, he meant to destroy Marcus's as well.

"You look like hell."

He started, lost in thought, and glanced up to find Spence had entered the room. "Thank you."

"My pleasure."

"Did you come here to tell me that?"

"No, I came here to say it's been nice knowing you and that I shall remember our years together fondly."

Marcus pulled his head out of his hands and stared at his friend. No. His *cousin*. He shook his head then regretted the action as brandy swam around his brain.

"You think he won't kill you?"

"The constable?"

"No, Nick." Spence lifted his eyebrows and his pale blue eyes registered both worry and amusement. He picked up the empty brandy snifter. "Sweet Judas, man. How much have you had to drink?"

"Too much." *And not enough.* Walkerton was dead. Lady Lilith Kingsley was his mother. He was not only a bastard, but also the result of a heinous violence enacted against an innocent. To top things off, the future he had envisioned with the woman he loved was no longer a possibility. Likely there wasn't enough brandy in the world to rectify any of that.

"Well, Rebecca told Nick you and she—that you—" Spence made a face and stared at the row of books on the shelf nearby as if one of them contained the word he searched for.

Marcus's heart stuttered in his chest. "That we what?" He waited for Spence to answer.

Spence cleared his throat and rolled his hand in the air. "You know."

"No, I don't."

"You're going to make me say it? That you and she…made love." He whispered the last part and under different circumstance the idea that a reformed rake such as Spence would whisper such a thing would have proven most comical. But this wasn't under different circumstances. This was under the worst circumstances possible.

"Shit!"

What had she been thinking? He wanted her removed from this. He'd given her up to keep her out of it. She had no right to dive in headfirst as if this was just another pond he could rescue her from. He couldn't. He couldn't even rescue himself.

"If it helps, she claimed the, uh, coupling was completely mutual." Spence took the seat across from him. "I'm not sure that helped your cause with our dear friend, however."

Marcus's stomach lurched and the brandy he'd imbibed threatened to make a return appearance. Spence quickly tucked his boots safely under the chair.

"Where is she?"

"Likely Nick has locked her in her room, which I'm certain she will find a way out of. What were you thinking seducing Rebecca like that?"

"I didn't seduce her!" He winced and held his head as the shout reverberated the inside of his skull making it ache anew. "And that's a little pot calling the kettle black, isn't it?"

Spence had the decency to appear at least a little chagrined. He had, after all, pretended to be Caelie's husband while traveling to London without the benefit of a proper chaperone. He was hardly in any position to cast stones.

But it wasn't Spence he needed to worry about. It was Nick. And Rebecca's future.

"Perhaps you can claim temporary insanity."

"Based on what?"

"Based on being insane enough to think you could get away with such a thing. If Nick has his way, the constable will never get a chance to prove a case against you, which I'm sure will disappoint him greatly given the fervor with which he questioned you today."

"I was not trying to get away with anything. I planned to marry her. I was going to speak to Nick today."

"And now?"

Marcus shook his head. He had no idea what he would do now, only that he would keep her safe.

"I will fix this."

"You're damn right you will." Nick's voice burst into the room, his tall stature and ominous claim filling it. Marcus had a strange sense of déjà vu, only the last time this scenario played out, it was Spence sitting in his place and Marcus suggesting calm minds prevail.

He did no such thing now. He deserved Nick's anger and whatever came with it. He'd jumped the gun, made assumptions and promises that fate made it impossible to keep. Now they would both pay the price for his folly.

"Spence, leave us," Marcus said, but his friend—*cousin*—shook his head.

"Afraid not. I may be the only thing standing between you and certain death. For once, I will have to be the voice of reason."

"I'm doomed," Marcus muttered. He closed his eyes and mustered his strength, then stood to face Nick.

"This has nothing to do with you. It is between Rebecca and me."

Nick advanced on Marcus until he was within striking distance. Fury burned in his eyes. "As her protector, this has everything to do with me!"

"If it makes any difference," Spence offered. "He loves her."

Nick turned to Spence then back to Marcus. "What?"

"He loves her. Good God, Nick. We covered this already. Marcus loves her. Has loved her. Will love her until the end of time. And your sister obviously shares these feelings as you well know if you've been paying any kind of attention at all. You really shouldn't be so hard on him. He has enough on his plate right now what with Constable Curly—"

"Hurly," Nick corrected.

Spence waved his hand. "Whatever. It's just a matter of time before the man finds enough reason to put a noose around our friend's neck if we don't find a way out of this."

"A walk in the park compared to what I'd like to do to him." Nick turned back to Marcus. "Bloody hell, Bowen! You are supposed to be the sensible one of us! I trusted you to behave as a gentleman!"

Trust. What a funny word. He'd trusted the Bowens were his parents. He'd trusted Lord and Lady Ellesmere to be truthful. He'd trusted that his life was exactly what it seemed. He trusted it would continue to be so. And yet, as it turned out, none of that had been true.

"When has love ever been sensible?" Spence asked Nick. "Was it sensible when Abigail tried to ruin you? Was it sensible when you nearly married a woman you could barely stand to share air with? Was it sensible when you tried to destroy yourself with guilt? Was it sensible when I fell in love with Caelie and married despite every conviction I had that the institution was better avoided at all costs?"

Nick stared and Marcus both stared at Spence.

"There is no sense to love, Nick." He threw his arms wide. "I thought by now you would have figured that one out. It didn't make sense for you, it didn't make sense for me—and now it doesn't make sense for Bowen. That's just the way of it. I'm certain he has every intention of marrying her—"

"I don't."

Spence and Nick turned slowly toward him.

"I beg your pardon?" Anger and disbelief honed Nick's words until they were dagger-sharp.

"I can't marry her. It will ruin her in society. I'm a bastard, all but accused of murdering the man who fathered me. If charged and found guilty, I will hang. Is that what you want for her?"

Nick stood silent a moment, then, "No."

As much as he had expected Nick's answer, his agreement cut deep—a reinforcement that Marcus's instinct to leave her was the right one, no matter how much he wished otherwise. He took a deep breath and then his words sealed his future without her.

"I thought we might enlist Glenmor. He's in need of a bride—the wealthier, the better. He's a good man and he'll be good to her. Perhaps if you approached him about brokering a marriage deal between the two." The words cut like razors against his throat as he spoke them, the idea of her with another man—even one as good as Benedict Laytham—was akin to sinking a blade deep into his heart.

Nick shook his head. "She will never agree to it. She loves you. Her whole purpose in telling me what transpired was to ensure you married her. She will not be put off so easily."

"She will have to be. I will not marry her. I will not drag her into this mess and force upon her the consequences that come with it. Better she turns away now and for good."

"Gentlemen, might we have a word with Marcus, please? Alone."

Marcus looked past Spence and Nick to Lord and Lady Ellesmere who stood in the doorway. Though phrased as a request, it had been anything but. Spence pulled at Nick's sleeve to get him to acquiesce, despite the fact his sister's future had yet to be settled. As the two filed out of the door, Lord Ellesmere closed it behind them and turned the key, locking them in—or others out. Marcus couldn't determine which.

Lord Ellesmere motioned toward the sofa and chairs near the windows. The curtains had been pulled closed and no noise from evening entertainments broke through the walls. A pall had been cast over the festivities for the time being and most guests had taken to their rooms as night fell and they realized no more new tidbits of information would be forthcoming.

Marcus followed and waited for them to be seated on the sofa before he took the chair next to them.

"It appears you have found yourself in quite the predicament." Despite the understatement of his claim, the gravity of Lord Ellesmere's voice told a different story.

"You need not worry over it," he said. "I will handle this on my own. It will not cast a stain upon you. You and I have severed ties, if you'll recall."

Lady Ellesmere gasped as if his words were delivered as an

unexpected slight. Perhaps they were. His emotions concerning the elderly couple were twisted and snarled until he could make no sense of what they were. He had never admired a man more than Lord Ellesmere and yet he had kept Marcus's past from him, willingly. Lady Ellesmere had showered him with love and warmth, rescuing him from a horrid situation but she kept her reasons for doing so locked away from him.

Had they known the struggle their daughter had endured as she wrestled with the decisions she had to make? Did they understand the courage she'd displayed, the love she'd shown him even before his birth when he still grew inside of her? Had they known all of this and held their silence on it?

Lord Ellesmere studied his hands, slightly gnarled around the knuckles where age had taken its toll. "Our ties can never be severed, son."

Marcus remained silent, unsure if the statement was based on fact or simply feeling. The Kingsleys had always treated him as family. It had been he who had refused to take part, keeping himself separate; afraid it would all be taken away.

"What was it you and Walkerton fought over? The watch?"

"No." Marcus straightened in his chair. How much of what had happened to her had Lady Lilith revealed to them? Some, all, none? Her journal gave no indication.

He stood and walked to the window, pulling the curtain away to stare up at the midnight sky. The day had started so differently. It had been hours since he'd held Rebecca pressed against him, surrounded in the security of her love, yet it felt more likes years, as if this morning had been nothing more than a lovely dream.

"If not the watch, then what?"

"We fought about my mother," he said.

"Mary?" Lady Ellesmere asked and he heard the rustle of

her skirts as she turned to look at him. She sounded surprised, which surprised him. Did they not know it was Walkerton who'd fathered him? Doubt crept in.

He shook his head and pressed a palm against the cool glass. "Not Mary."

Silence reigned and somewhere to his left the crackle and pop of the fire filled the void. He stared at his reflection, watched as it wavered in the lamplight. Paintings of his mother hung on the walls of the Ellesmere estates. He had seen them his entire life, but now he knew, when he gazed upon them next, it would be with different eyes.

"He speaks of Lilith." Lady Ellesmere whispered the name of her daughter with a reverence filled in equal amounts with pain and love. "It was him, then?" The question hitched in her throat.

His hand dropped away from the window and he clasped them both behind his back. "Yes. You didn't know?"

"Not for certain. We suspected, but—"

"Then you are my grandparents." He turned to face them. "And you kept it from me."

His accusation cut through the air with a harshness born of anger and betrayal. He'd had a right to know. They should have told him.

"You don't understand." Lord Ellesmere shook his head but said no more.

"You're right," he conceded. "I don't. I don't understand how you could have kept such a thing from me. Bastard or not, I had a right to know who my true parents were."

Lord Ellesmere nodded and lifted his gaze to stare at some far point on the other side of the library. "Likely you are right. But until we learned of the watch and whom it belonged to, we only had half of the story. Less than that, I suspect, as Lilith would not reveal the details to us no matter how much we begged her to do so. I suspect she was too ashamed that she had given him her innocence, been seduced by a man as despicable as Walkerton—"

Lord Ellesmere stopped and looked away, but his words filtered through Marcus's anger, the truth of them landing with an unsettling sound.

They thought she had done this willingly. That it had been nothing more than a lapse in judgment. Given his own reaction to what Walkerton had done to her, could she have expected anything different from her own father? Lord Ellesmere revered his family, protected them with a fierceness of will that kept them all safe and secure. Had he known the truth, he would have killed Walkerton with his bare hands, then revived the man long enough to kill him a second time. Nothing less than what he deserved. But someone had already beaten him to it.

"She was not seduced," Marcus said. No matter the hurt it caused them, he would not let them think she had been the one to fall from grace.

"I beg your pardon?"

"The watch had been entrusted to Mary Bowen by your daughter—my mother, along with a journal she kept during the time of her confinement."

"No!" Lady Ellesmere stood then sat just as quickly as if the shock took her legs out from under her. "I would have known had she kept a journal. I was with her every day."

"But not every minute of every day."

Lord Ellesmere reached a hand out to take his wife's. "What did it say?"

The marquess tensed as if bracing against what, deep inside, he had suspected all along.

"Walkerton didn't seduce her. He raped her. She said as much in her journal and Walkerton admitted it to me today. That is why we fought."

Lord Ellesmere stood and strode to the desk on the other

side of the hearth. He bent over and gripped the edge with such force Marcus could see the whites of his knuckles even from the distance that separated them. Lady Ellesmere pursed her lips, her shock less pronounced. Had she suspected? The two had shared a closeness evident in Lilith's tone whenever she wrote of her mother. While Lady Ellesmere may not have known the details of the secrets her daughter kept, she had known they existed nonetheless.

"Why did she not tell us?" Anguish strangled Lord Ellesmere's and robbed Marcus of his anger. Seeing their pain changed things. They were no longer the people who had kept from him his past, but instead two parents who had done whatever was necessary to protect their daughter, and when they failed to do so in life, they had ensured they did in death, keeping her secrets buried, their suspicions silenced, and her reputation intact.

Could he blame them for that? Had his mother not done the same for him? Would he not do the same thing for his own child?

"She did not want to cause either of you further distress. She considered it her pain to bear, not yours."

"But I would have—I could have—if I had known—" Agony tore Lord Ellesmere's voice to shreds and Marcus fisted his hands at his side feeling the same conviction as his mother to protect the two people who had shown nothing but love and good intentions toward her. Toward him. They had risked greatly bringing him into their home as ward. Had anyone put enough of the story together, even suggested the idea of it, their daughter's reputation would have been ruined beyond redemption. They had risked that to keep him safe, to afford him the life they believed he deserved. To surround him with the love and security only family could give.

"She tried to save us as much as we wanted to save her," Lady Ellesmere said, letting her own tears flow freely. "My sweet, brave girl." She turned to him and smiled through her tears. "You are so much like her, you know. You have her goodness. Her heart."

The only words sweeter than the ones Lady Ellesmere spoke had been the declaration of love from Rebecca's lips the night before. Perhaps that would be enough to sustain him through this. It would have to be.

"We will not hide the truth any longer," Lord Ellesmere said, releasing the table and straightening to his full height, shoulders back, ready for battle. "If Lilith can reach beyond death to tell the truth of who you are, we will not deny her choice to claim you." He crossed the room and placed a firm hand on Marcus's shoulder. "You are our grandson, every bit as much as Spencer and I am proud to say it."

But Marcus shook his head before his grandfather finished speaking. "No. Do not. Not publically. It will only bring hardship. That I know is enough." And it was.

He had never sought public acknowledgement. Never needed it. He had only wanted the truth. Wanted to use it to build a future with Rebecca. Now he had the truth, and the other, well that was not to be. There was little point in having others suffer because of it. "The Bowens raised me for eight years; they instilled in me good values and treated me as their own. They earned the right to be remembered as my parents and I know Lilith felt much ease in knowing Mary would take her place where she could not."

For a moment, he thought Lord Ellesmere would argue, but in the end he only nodded. "We will leave the decision with you, but know if you change your mind, we will stand by you proudly and without question."

"Thank you." Marcus let out a long breath as weariness descended. The toll of the day pushed against him. "I shall turn in now, I think. I expect tomorrow Constable Hurly will have more questions for me."

His grandmother stood and took his hands, pulling him down to kiss both his cheeks. "Goodnight, sweet boy. Things will look better on the morrow."

He wished he believed her, but he suspected things were going to get much darker by dawn. Fate was not done with him yet.

Chapter Twenty-Four

Rebecca paced her room, her mind working furiously, reviewing the events of the past twenty-four hours over and over again. Instinct insisted she had missed a piece of the puzzle. Something vital. If only she could find it, their problems would be solved and everything wrong would become right.

She refused to consider another possibility, because to do so meant accepting defeat. It meant a life without Marcus, and that she simply wouldn't have.

But no matter how many times she traversed the expanse of her bedchamber, the missing piece remained elusive. At this rate, she'd wear a pathway straight through to the hardwood beneath the carpet and be no further ahead than when she started.

She stopped and let out a long breath. Her head hurt, her heart ached and her body longed to have Marcus next to her where he belonged. Their limbs entwined, their breath mingled, their bodies joined. But he had turned her away.

Foolish man. Did he honestly believe she was better off without him? That she could marry another? For heavens' sake, not an hour ago, Nicholas had actually come to her room and floated the possibility that she consider Lord Glenmor as a husband instead! Not that there was anything wrong with Benedict Laytham. Truly, he was as handsome as they came and really quite charming. She enjoyed his company immensely, but she did not love him. Not as she did Marcus. And she would marry no other but Marcus.

There *had* to be a way out of this for them. There simply had to be! But how was she to discover it if no one would talk to her? She'd asked both Nicholas and Huntsleigh what questions the constable had asked of Marcus, but they'd patted her on her head and sent her on her way. As if she didn't have a right to know. As if it wasn't her future at stake.

Which left only one other to give her the answers she needed.

She opened the door to her room and peered out into the hall. A few lights still burned. Nicholas had threatened to lock her in her room earlier when she confessed she and Marcus had made love, but Mother refused him such an option, insisting Rebecca was no longer a child and should therefore not be treated as such. Thankfully, Nicholas didn't argue with Mother. She could prove quite obstinate on certain matters when she put her mind to it.

Rebecca tiptoed on bare feet down the length of the hallway and around to the other side where Nancy indicated Marcus had taken a room. She put her hand on the cool brass handle and took a fortifying breath. He would not be happy to see her. In all likelihood, he would deny her requests for answers in a misguided attempt to protect her. As if she was the one in danger.

It mattered little. She had no intentions of leaving once she stepped foot inside his room. He would have to toss her over his shoulder and march her back to her own bedchamber if he wished to be rid of her and even then, she would simply march right back. Like Mother, she too could be quite obstinate when need be.

She turned the handle and opened the door a crack. Pitch black greeted her. No fire burned in the hearth, no candles lit the room. For a fleeting second she feared he may have returned to Northill and all her stealth had been for naught. But the feeling left almost as soon as it arrived. He was here. She could feel him, somewhere deep in her bones.

She slipped through the opening and closed the door quietly behind her, turning the key in the lock to prevent any further unwelcomed visitors. If Nicholas decided to check on her through the night and found her gone, this would be his first stop. She did not need him barging in where he didn't belong in some misplaced attempt at salvaging her virtue. There were far more important things at stake.

She stepped farther into the room, stumbling slightly as her toes tangled into something lying on the floor. She threw her arms wide to keep her balance then knelt down to feel about for the offending item. Her hand hit wool. His jacket? She swept an arm wider for any other obstacles and discovered a boot, then a second boot. His trousers were next to them.

Good heavens, every stitch of clothing he had worn riddled the floor between the door and his bed! She smiled at the image of such disorder coming from the very neat and orderly Mr. Bowen, but the smile quickly faded. He'd had a trying day by even the most stringent standards. He must have shucked his clothing and collapsed into bed.

Rebecca stood and untied the sash of her robe and let it fall to the floor amongst Marcus's things. Her nightdress followed and the cool night air raised gooseflesh on her bare skin.

She stepped carefully until the edge of the bed brushed her thighs then she reached for the blankets and pulled them back. With slow, deliberate movements, she slid beneath the covers and sidled over toward the middle where she found the warmth and solidity of Marcus's sleeping form. She molded herself to his back, curving her body against his. A thrill went through her when she realized he had not bothered donning a nightshirt for sleeping.

Did he always sleep like this? She smiled. If not, she would heartily suggest it going forward. The sensation of skin on skin proved a most intoxicating mix.

He moved and his breathing changed, though it was another moment after that before wakefulness took hold and pulled him from his exhausted slumber. His body stiffened then relaxed.

"It's me." She pressed her lips against his shoulder.

"I know." He turned over to face her. "You can't be here."

She smiled into the darkness and rested a hand against his chest. His heart beat steady beneath her palm and she splayed her fingers to touch as much of him as possible. "And yet here I am."

"Your brother is ready to kill me. Do you really want to hasten my death by adding fuel to the fire?"

"My brother loves you and, despite all his blustering, is thrilled we are to marry. He will not harm a hair on your head."

"I cannot marry you. I have told Nick as much and he does not disagree."

"You *can* marry me and my brother does not have a say in the matter. You told me you would marry me and I am holding you to that promise."

"Rebecca—"

She moved her hand to find his lips and stop whatever nonsensical reason he thought to give her as to why they could not marry. "You're trying to protect me, I know and I love you for it, but it is unnecessary."

He spoke through her fingers. "You will be ruined if—"

She pressed harder against his mouth. "I will not. And even if I am, what do I care? I could go the rest of my life never stepping foot in society again and be quite happy, but only if I could do so at your side."

Marcus reached up and pulled her hand away. "Have you always been this stubborn?"

She raised her eyebrows then remembered he could not see her. "Yes. And my stubbornness will continue for as long as your foolishness."

"Protecting you is not a foolish endeavor. A difficult one, yes, but not foolish."

She wiggled closer and wrapped her arm around his middle. The muscles in his back shifted and moved wherever she touched, coiled strength that hid beneath his calm exterior. Such wonderful things he hid beneath the surface. She could not wait to discover and explore each and every one of them.

"I love you for protecting me, but you are giving up on us before you even start the fight."

His hand lifted and buried itself in her hair and he brought his forehead to rest against hers. "A fight I do not want you to be a part of."

"There is no helping that. This is my fight as much as it is yours and I will not be set aside as if I have no say in the matter. I can help. Did I not get Lord Selward to admit he received in writing Lord Walkerton's admission you were his son? And did I also not get Lord Walkerton himself to admit the same?"

"At your peril."

"I was in no peril. Lady Franklyn—"

"The man raped my mother!"

She stilled, Marcus's harsh admission shocking her silent for a moment. "He did what?" And then, "Have you discovered your mother's identity?"

He pulled away. A sharp snap sounded and a match flared

to life. A few seconds later dim light from the bedside lamp chased shadows across the bed.

When Marcus returned, he slid a hand beneath his pillow and left the other lying in the space between them. He did not touch her, his sudden absence like a cold wind. She longed to reach for him, but sensed it best she not. Not yet. Her heart pounded.

"My mother is—was—Lady Lilith Kingsley."

Rebecca shook her head, denying his declaration. It made no sense. "But Lady Lilith died decades ago while traveling. She was but sixteen. Only a young girl."

"She had not been traveling. Lady Ellesmere took her to Braemore for her confinement. They said they were traveling abroad before her first Season to avoid any hint of scandal."

"But..." She shook her head. "But then Lord Walkerton—?"

"Raped her."

The admission hit her like a slap. She had met with the man this morning, so intent on getting the answers they needed that she had refused to listen to instinct that demanded she retreat. What would have happened had Lady Franklyn not stopped them and demanded she stay away from him? Would she have met a similar fate as Lady Lilith?

A chill settled over her. Marcus reached out and drew her close against him. She buried herself in his arms and embraced the security found there.

"Is that why you fought with him?"

He nodded.

"Lady Franklyn said he was a vile and deviant man, but I had no idea his depravity went so deep. Poor Lady Lilith." Her heart went out to the long dead girl; the woman who had given birth to the man Rebecca loved.

Her head snapped up and knocked Marcus's chin causing him to grunt.

"That means you are a Kingsley. Lord and Lady Ellesmere's grandson. Just like Huntsleigh!"

Marcus rubbed the underside of his chin. "No, not like Huntsleigh. I am still borne on the wrong side of the blanket under rather horrid circumstances. I cannot make public the truth. To do so would be to ruin the reputation of a woman who does not deserve it after everything she endured. Everything she did for me. And I will not have Lord and Lady Ellesmere relive the truth of what happened to their daughter every time someone thinks to whisper and gossip about it, as if it was nothing but grist for the mill. I will not cause them such pain."

Rebecca nodded and her love for Marcus grew, that he would turn his back on the truth he had so valiantly sought so as not to cause pain to others, regardless the cost to him.

"Did you tell the constable any of this?"

He shook his head. "To what end? It will not change his opinions. If anything, it would only make me appear guiltier in his eyes. He believes I went back and finished what I started."

"But you didn't." She didn't need to ask. Even though Walkerton deserved nothing less in her estimation, she stood firm in her resolve that Marcus was not the type of many to kill in cold blood.

"No. But the other lords are pressuring him to find the person responsible and if that person is someone other than one of their ilk, all the better. I doubt they'll look beyond me for the real culprit."

Fear turned her insides to ice and she held him tighter. She had foolishly assumed that since Marcus hadn't committed the murder that would be the end of it. How naïve. The situation had become much more dire. What was to stop Constable Hurly from charging Marcus with a heinous crime he had no part in? Unless they could prove otherwise, he could hang. Panic shook her core.

"We must do something then! Prove your innocence." Desperation clawed at her and her mind worked furiously. "We cannot allow this to happen. We can't—"

He kissed her, trapping her unspoken words and stealing them away. His lips were soft and the pressure of them light and teasing. "Hush."

"No!" They had to save him. This wasn't fair. They were too close to happiness to have it torn away.

"Yes," he whispered, his mouth at her ear, then the curve of her neck. His hand slid down her side to the dip of her waist then over the rise of her hip. His touch seared a path until desire burned hot within her and the need to be with him, fully and completely, overwhelmed her.

"Marcus." She moved against him, feeling his hardness press into her, knowing he wanted her with equal fervor. She explored him, the muscle and sinew that stretched over bone and created the planes and angles of his body. A body that brought such untold pleasures. Pleasures she had only begun to divine. Pleasures she wasn't ready to give up.

"We can't risk it," he told her, staying her hand as it traveled down the ridges of his stomach. "I will not leave you with child."

"I will not allow you to leave me at all!" How could he even entertain such a thing? "Why are you so willing to give up?"

His fingertips touched her face, her brow and nose and lips sending rivulets of pleasure to war with the fear and desperation building inside of her. "I am not giving up. But I am not risking your future either."

Tears choked her and she grabbed his wrist, holding on to him to keep from spiraling into the dark abyss. "I will not leave you. Do not ask me to."

Marcus said nothing but after a moment his body relaxed. A small victory. He turned and extinguished the light, plunging them into darkness. "Turn around," he said, settling next to her.

She did as he bade and he pulled her back, fitting her back against his front as if they were two spoons resting in a drawer. His warmth suffused her and the strength of his arms helped settle some of the fear that had invaded her heart and turned the blood in her veins to ice. She rested her hand over his and relished the closeness.

"I love you," she whispered into the darkness.

He hugged her tight. "I love you more."

"I do not think such a thing is possible."

"Nevertheless."

She heard the smile in his voice and let it wrap around her. "That is poor as far as arguments go."

He chuckled and the sensation reverberated against her back. "Go to sleep. I will wake you in time to find your way back to your room without being detected."

She snuggled against him. She had no intentions of going anywhere. When the sun rose, it would find her here, and she would remain at his side until she found a solution to retrieve them from this mess. But for now, her tired mind needed rest. Come morning, it would be refreshed and she would set it to work once again.

Darkness still prevailed when Rebecca jolted awake; the image of Lord Walkerton dragging her into the gardens invaded her dreams and refused to fade upon waking. Someone had called his name, stopped him, the voice sharp, desperate...afraid. She squinted at the memory, searched through the darkness to find its source. Reaching out as if she could touch it. Touch them. And then the mist in her mind cleared.

A swift intake of breath sent a shot of pain through her chest.

Could it be?

She turned slightly to look at Marcus's sleeping form; thankful exhaustion had taken him deep and still held him in its clutches. The first hint of sunrise crept through a crack in the curtains. She eased out of his arms. He shifted and she held her breath waiting until he resettled before she moved again.

She dressed in a rush then quietly quit the room, stealing one last look at the man she loved before quietly shutting the door. She would not fail him.

She would save him.

Save them.

Chapter Twenty-Five

"Rebecca, dear, what are you doing at this ungodly hour?"

"It cannot be that ungodly, Mother. You are awake after all," Rebecca stated, though she was surprised to see her mother, still in her dressing gown, her new grandson swaddled in her arms while Abigail looked on from the overstuffed chair Nicholas had moved into the nursery for her.

Her sister-in-law gave a light laugh. "I'm afraid that is my fault. Little Roddy has quite a set of lungs. His wailing could wake the dead. I took pity on Nicholas and came to the nursery where your mother found me. I happily handed him over."

Rebecca leaned over her mother's shoulder to peer down at the babe. He had lost the wrinkled appearance of a new infant and fattened up until he resembled a cherub with his pink cheeks and blue eyes. Mother claimed both she and Nicholas had both been born with blue eyes as well, so it remained to be seen if he too would inherit the silver of his father and aunt. Either way, he was a handsome boy with his shock of dark hair and an easy smile. When he wasn't wailing up a storm that was. And best of all, his parents had finally settled on a name—Roderick Henry Alexander Sheridan.

"What has you up this early?" Mother asked, tickling Roddy's chin until the baby gurgled with pleasure.

Rebecca sat on the ottoman in front of Mother's rocking chair and glanced over at Abigail who shook her head. "Have no worries, your brother has filled me in on what has been going on. Have you come up with a solution to save dear Marcus? I for one would much prefer to plan a wedding than a trial."

"I hope so, but first, Mother I need you to answer some questions and I need you to be honest, even if you think it is something I need not know."

Mother glanced up from Roddy, wariness in her gaze. "What is it you need to know?"

"I need you to tell me about Lady Lilith Kingsley, Lady Franklyn and Lord Walkerton," Rebecca said, ticking the names off on her fingers.

"Lady Franklyn? Why ever are you asking about her?" The forced levity in her mother's voice did not match the tight smile she gave.

"Please, Mother. Marcus's life may depend upon it. Did Lady Franklyn know what happened to Lady Lilith?" Rebecca did not care to reveal Lady Lilith's secrets, or cause Lord and Lady Ellesmere any undue pain, but she must save Marcus. Surely, if Lady Lilith could speak to her, she would beg her to do whatever necessary, even if it meant giving up long-held secrets.

Her mother's eyes grew wide and her voice dropped to a whisper. "How do you know of that?"

"Know of what?" Abigail came out of her chair and settled on the corner of the ottoman. Rebecca sidled over to make room.

"Mother?"

Roddy fussed as tension wound around the women surrounding him. Her mother stood and passed the baby to Abigail who took him willingly. Her mother paced to the window where the morning sun filtered through and lit her face with its soft golden rays.

"It was a long time ago. Lilith was younger than both Lady Franklyn and myself. We were both quite fond of her. She had a sweet, gentle nature that endeared. We had taken her under our wing, treating her as we would a little sister. Much as I had done with Lady Franklyn upon her debut the year before. Lilith's first Season approached. I remember how excited and eager she was. Lady Ellesmere had allowed her to attend a few parties, smaller affairs deemed acceptable. Lady Franklyn and I watched over her, kept the gentlemen at arm's length. She was a remarkable beauty, even at sixteen you could see the promise of who she would become."

Mother's voice caught. She pressed a hand against her lips and turned her head away. Rebecca did not move, nor did Abigail or Roddy for that matter. Rebecca wanted to fly across the room and embrace her mother, take on the pain her memories brought, but she remained still, waiting for the rest of the story.

Abigail shook her head. "Do you mean to say you and Lady Franklyn were friends once upon a time? But I thought...doesn't she claim to be much younger?"

Mother turned back to them, a wry smile playing on her lips. "A myth she likes to perpetrate to lure in younger lovers. And she has maintained her beauty well enough that none of her lovers bother with the math." Mother's expression turned wistful. "But once upon a time she was a different person. Kinder, less angry and bitter."

"What changed her?" Abigail asked.

But Rebecca already knew. "It wasn't what changed her. It was *who*—Lord Walkerton."

Mother nodded. "He is—was—an awful man, though many of us didn't see it then. A charming manner and handsome face can cover any number of sins. He would befriend you; make you feel as if you were the most engaging and remarkable creature to ever walk the earth even though he had recently married another. If anything, he used that to appear less threatening. Why would he try anything untoward when he supposedly loved another?" But the deep scowl on her mother's face told a different story.

"Did you fall for it?" Abigail asked.

"My heart was otherwise engaged by a man who embodied all the traits Lord Walkerton pretended at. I'm afraid he didn't stand a chance with me. But, even then, Lady Franklyn craved attention."

"And Lord Walkerton lavished it upon her."

Mother shook her head. "He had set his sights on Lady Lilith. Lady Franklyn could barely stand it. She was the jewel of the ton that year and to be usurped from anyone's attentions set her back. But it also opened her eyes, for what kind of gentleman—married or otherwise, put his attentions on an innocent young girl not yet presented?"

"How did Lady Lilith react to the attention?" Marcus had revealed some of what he knew of his mother, painting a picture of a young woman faced with the worst kind of circumstance. Somehow, she had found the strength and courage to rise above, to overcome.

"Until then, Lilith had led a fairly sheltered life. Lord and Lady Ellesmere kept a strict eye on her and the men in her life treated her with kindness and respect, but it led her to believe all men shared the same character. This trust made it easier for Lord Walkerton to get close. Closer than was proper." Her voice dropped and guilt laced through it. "Closer than we should have allowed had we not been so wrapped up in our own lives."

Rebecca stood and walked over to her mother, taking her cold hands. Long buried memories had robbed them of warmth. "What he did was not your fault."

Abigail rose from the ottoman and joined them. "What did he do?"

"He forced himself upon her," Rebecca said.

Tears glittered in her mother's pale grey eyes and she pursed her lips. "He must have. She had no interest in him beyond friendship. He was years older than she. She would never have gone with him willingly. She was young, but she possessed an uncanny intelligence and a sensible nature."

The description sounded eerily familiar.

Abigail pressed Roddy closer to her. "How awful. Oh, how awful. Is that why Lady Lilith left to travel the continent?"

"She did not go to the continent," Rebecca said. "She went to Cornwall. To Braemore."

Abigail pulled back. "That is where Marcus lived..." The words trailed away as realization dawned in the same way it had with Rebecca. Slowly. Strangely, as if light shifted and the colors around you had suddenly taken on a different hue. Her sister-in-law took in a deep breath and looked from one of them to the other. "Did you know?"

Rebecca's mother shook her head. "No. But I thought her sudden departure odd. She said nothing about going on such a trip and I am sure she would have. While away, she never wrote, which I found odd and quite unlike her. It made me wonder, but then she passed suddenly and..." Mother stopped and a tear slid from the corner of her eye. She brushed it away and took a deep breath. "Years after, when Lady Ellesmere returned with Marcus, I couldn't help but speculate. He was born in January; Lilith left London in late June and she had passed away in January. That, coupled with his age, made me suspect. But it was as I watched him grow and become the man he is, that I grew more certain. I could see his mother in him so clearly. His steadiness, his quiet warmth. He smiles and it is her smile I see. It breaks my heart and fills it all at the same time."

Abigail jostled Roddy in her arms. "But why was Walkerton not punished? Why did someone not ensure he—"

"I suspect she never told her parents what transpired. She loved them dearly and would have done anything to protect them from further pain. You'll remember, Spencer's father and uncles had caused no end of scandal for Lord Ellesmere to deal with at the time. Lilith possessed a gentle soul, but a strong spirit. She would not have added to their burden by telling them the worst. While she'd have had no choice but to reveal her pregnancy to them, she would have carried the weight of how it occurred on her own."

"Good heavens. I can't imagine. But—" Abigail turned to Rebecca. "How does Lady Franklyn factor into this?"

"I think she knew," Rebecca answered and looked at her mother. "Did she?"

Her mother sighed. "I cannot say. Shortly after Lilith left London, Lord Walkerton turned his attentions to Lady Franklyn, but she spurned him. A fact he did not take with any grace."

"Do you think—" Abigail didn't say it, but the question hung in the air around them.

"He did to her what he did to Lilith? Perhaps. Though at the time, I had my own troubles and did not pay close attention. Maybe I should have." Mother bowed her head as she spoke of the man in her past. The man who had captured her mother's heart and held it still, though it had been thirty years since she'd seen or heard from him.

Rebecca did not know how her mother endured. Was this what awaited her if she could not save Marcus from the fate Constable Hurly seemed determined to deliver?

"It was around that time when Lady Franklyn began to change," Mother continued, turning back to the window, leaning her hip against the frame and staring at the gardens that stretched out to meet the horizon. "She became bitter and pushed everyone away; those of us who used to be friends somehow became enemies. Perhaps she thought if we got too close we would see what he had done to her. I do not know."

"What happened to Lord Walkerton?" Abigail asked. "Did he simply walk away untouched?"

Mother took a deep breath. "If you mean was he ever held accountable, then no. No woman ever came forward and made accusations. It would have meant ruining themselves to do so. But..." A look crossed her face as if seeing the events of thirty years ago with new eyes. "It was around that time Lord Franklyn showed an interest in Lady Franklyn. There was a significant age difference between them, but for the daughter of a viscount, garnering a duke's attention was quite a boon."

"Do you think Lord Franklyn knows what happened to her?" Abigail asked.

Mother tilted her head to one side and lifted a hand to twist a wayward blonde curl around her finger. "It is difficult to say, though Lord Walkerton's presence in London ended abruptly after the wedding of Lord and Lady Franklyn. Since then, Lord Walkerton has spent a limited amount of time in London and when he returns, he rarely shows his face in polite society, as if he had been banished and was afraid of being seen."

"Only a man with the power and clout Lord Franklyn wields could manage such a feat," Rebecca suggested. "Do you think that was his way of protecting his new wife?"

"I wonder," Mother said. "Lord Franklyn is a good man, and he has been good to Lady Franklyn, though she seems intent on destroying any decency that once lived within her." She gave Rebecca a sad, telling smile. "I lost many of those dear to me that Season. Had it not been for Nicholas to care for, I do not know how I would have made my way through it."

"I, for one, am most glad you did." Abigail reached out and gave her mother-in-law a hug, a gesture that made Roddy giggle as he became sandwiched between two women who understood the travesties of life and its rewards.

"As am I," Rebecca said.

Mother smiled. "Have I given you what you needed?"

Rebecca kissed her mother's cheek; damp from the few tears she'd allowed to fall. "I believe so. Thank you."

Her mother touched her face with a gentle, knowing hand. "And now you will try and save Marcus, will you not?"

"Yes."

Her mother nodded. "Good. Be careful, my dear. And if you need me, I am always here for you. Please know that. I could not help his mother, but I hope I can at least help Marcus now."

"Thank you, Mother."

"And I will do my best to keep Nicholas from playing the part of the great protector," Abigail offered.

Rebecca looked at the two women. Both had stood in her shoes and understood the stakes of saving someone they loved beyond all measure, no matter the cost.

The same stakes she now faced and vowed to overcome.

Marcus did not care for waking up alone. In fact, he liked it even less than sitting in Nicholas's study being interrogated by the bloated Constable Hurly, who had puffed himself up even further with an overfed sense of self-importance, oblivious to the enemies he had made in a certain marquess, future marquess, and very irate earl, especially when they were dismissed from the room, leaving the two men alone.

"Procedure," the constable had claimed. Though Nick had voiced another name for it. Regardless, Marcus had sent them off. If they stayed, they would have continued to interrupt the constable incessantly and this damnable inquisition would drag on for the better part of the day. Marcus wanted it over. He needed to find Rebecca and get answers of his own, such as why had she sneaked out of his bed in the wee hours without so much as a by your leave? He suspected it had little to do with preserving her reputation and everything to do with saving his.

A fact that worried him to no end. There was no telling what trouble she would immerse herself in on his behalf. Keeping that woman safe proved a full time endeavor.

"And after you left Walkerton, who was still lying prone on the ground following your altercation, correct?" The constable paced in front of the desk Marcus sat behind, holding his hand in the air, index finger erect.

"Correct."

"You were on your way to where?"

"Northill Hall."

"The property formerly owned by Lord Franklyn, gifted to you upon saving his wife, if I understand correctly."

"You do."

"And yet you did not reach your destination. Why is that?"

Marcus leaned forward on the desk and rested his head against his fisted hand, flicking Constable Hurly a bored look. "I believe we covered this yesterday, or do you not recall our conversation?"

The constable stopped pacing and turned to glare at Marcus, his jowls swinging slightly, reminiscent of a basset hound. "I recall you provided a cockamamie story about wishing to return a watch to Lord Walkerton, which I find questionable given the circumstances. I do not often find men who pummel another into unconsciousness only to then gift them with a gold watch."

Marcus did not care for the unspoken accusation. "Lord Walkerton was not unconscious when I left him and I did not intend to gift him a watch. It belonged to him."

"If the watch belonged to Lord Walkerton, why was it in your possession? Do we need to add thievery to your list of charges, Mr. Bowen?"

"I was not aware I had been charged with anything as yet, Constable Hurly. Has this changed? If so, I believe this conversation shall be terminated immediately." A delightful thought, as the more he listened to the pompous windbag, the more he longed for the sweet tones of Rebecca's voice—her laughter, her whispers. The fact that she presented a far prettier sight to behold than Constable Hurly only increased his need to wrap this questioning up in short order.

"I am merely trying to get to the truth of the matter, Mr. Bowen."

"I sincerely doubt that. If you had any interest in the truth, you would be looking for the individual responsible for Walkerton's murder. And when you find them, I hope you will let me know as I would like to shake their hand."

Hurly turned on his heel and faced Marcus who had leaned back in his chair and stretched his legs out beneath the desk. "I find your smart tongue exceedingly offensive!"

"No more offensive than I find you in general, Constable, I assure you." He stood and rolled the tension from his shoulders. "Now, if you have nothing new to ask me, I see no need to prolong this interview." His need to find Rebecca grew with each passing moment. He needed to find her and ensure she did not do anything foolish. Or dangerous.

"I am not finished with you, Mr. Bowen."

"A shame," he said. "As I am quite finished with you, Constable Hurly."

He ignored the man's sputtering as he made his way to the door and opened it quickly, only to jump out of the way as Nick and Spence stumbled forward from the other side.

"Right," Spence said, straightening and pulling at his cuffs. "Yes. You are quite correct, Nick. The pattern in this wood grain is, in fact, completely different than the one next door. I stand corrected."

Nick cleared his throat and nodded. "Perhaps in future you will not think to question my superior knowledge on wood grains and such."

"Superior knowledge? I don't recall saying anything about that," Spence snorted, apparently forgetting they had not been discussing anything of the sort. Likely they'd been standing on the other side of the door, their ears pressed against it.

"Gentlemen." Marcus lifted his eyebrows at the pair of them and glanced at his grandfather who remained standing in the hallway beyond. "Might I be of some assistance?"

"Oh, Bowen," Nick said, as if he had not noticed him standing there. The man's acting skills left much to be desired. "I did not see you there."

"Too busy discussing wood grains, as it was," Spence said, motioning toward the now open door. He inclined his head toward the other man. "Constable Curly."

"It is Hurly, my lord," the constable said, straightening, which made his protruding belly stick out even farther.

Lord Ellesmere stepped into the room, his commanding presence deflating the constable. "Can I assume this infernal questioning of Mr. Bowen is at an end? Have you finally satisfied yourself that he had nothing to do with Lord Walkerton's death?"

"I—I am afraid not, your lordship. Despite Mr. Bowen's

claims that his return was of an innocent nature, I can find no evidence to prove this."

"Nor can you find any evidence to prove it was anything but," Lord Ellesmere stated.

"N-not necessarily. Lord Blackbourne stated when they returned, Mr. Bowen stood over Lord Walkerton's body."

"The man was already dead," Spence said, throwing his arms wide. "You can't kill a man twice!"

"More's the pity," Lord Ellesmere muttered, his jaw tense and anger stamped into every line of his face. Marcus did not blame the man. Walkerton had raped his daughter. Likely if he could resurrect the dead man, he'd do so for nothing more than the pleasure of releasing a torrent of pain on him in recompense for what he had done.

"I am not accusing Mr. Bowen of murdering the man twice, my lord. I am certain he only did the deed once."

"Then I am certain you are a bona fide idiot." Nick stepped toward the man and lorded his superior height and breadth over the much shorter and stubbier constable.

"I beg your pardon, my lord, but I am entrusted with the job of ascertaining who is responsible and every circumstance points to Mr. Bowen. They fought and shortly thereafter the man was found dead. What other conclusion can one draw?"

Spence shook his head. "That someone else did the deed?"

"I am afraid not, Lord Huntsleigh."

"Then you would be quite wrong, sir."

Heads swiveled in the direction of the open door where Rebecca stood, her hand wrapped around the wrist of another. A good thing, as her companion appeared ready to flee back down the hallway should she decide to let go.

Chapter Twenty-Six

"Rebecca." Marcus said her name as a warning, but she ignored him and inserted herself into the middle of the men, dragging a reluctant Lady Franklyn with her.

She had never looked lovelier, though he did not think he had ever seen her dressed more plainly in an unadorned morning dress of white and blue, her hair tossed into a messy concoction at the base of her neck. She stood like a warrior princess of old, chin held high and shoulders back, ready to do battle. His Athena.

"If you gentlemen would be so kind," Rebecca said, "Lady Franklyn and I would like to have a word with the constable."

Marcus didn't think Lady Franklyn wanted to have a word with anyone if the firm set of her jaw proved any indication. Nor could he ascertain what the duchess had to do with any of this. "Rebecca, what is this about?"

"This is about saving our future, Marcus."

From the corner of his eye he watched Lord Ellesmere's eyebrows lift, his gaze moving from Rebecca to land on Marcus. During the confessions of last night, he had not had the opportunity to bring up his plans to his grandfather where Rebecca was concerned. He had not thought it pertinent, given he was no longer certain those plans would come to fruition.

"Now, gentlemen, if you please?" She glanced at Nick and Spence then gifted with Lord Ellesmere a gentler smile than the firm one given the other two.

"Lord Ellesmere should stay," Lady Franklyn said, speaking for the first time. Her voice shook and she avoided meeting the gaze of anyone present. "As should Mr. Bowen."

"I think we should stay as well," Nick said. "I do not know what is going on here, but I am not leaving my sister—"

"Your sister is in good hands." Spence prodded Nick in the direction of the door despite his protests. Marcus suspected his cousin had little interest in being in close proximity to the duchess given their past history if such could be avoided. Nick finally acquiesced and the doors shut behind them.

It was Lord Ellesmere who spoke first. "What is the meaning of this?"

"Perhaps we should sit?" Rebecca suggested, motioning toward the sitting area on the other side of the room.

Rebecca and Lady Franklyn sat on the sofa, while the men took the chairs around them. Marcus rested his forearms against his legs and leaned forward, his hands clasped in front of him.

Rebecca turned to the constable. Gone was the impish girl, or the sweet young woman he had fallen in love with, and in her place sat a woman every inch the lady she had been raised to be.

"Constable Hurly, I understand you are attempting to get to the bottom of how Lord Walkerton met his rather abrupt and deserving end."

"Indeed, my lady. But you need not fear. I believe I have reached my conclusions and—"

"I have heard your conclusions and they are wrong."

The constable sputtered at her plain speaking. If the man disliked being told he was wrong by a man, being called out by a woman appeared even less to his liking. "I beg your pardon, my lady, but this is a matter for men. A fine lady such as yourself—"

"Do not deem to condescend to me, Constable Hurly," Rebecca said, her voice firm and uncompromising. Where had that come from? Marcus watched her in wonder. "I can assure you my astuteness and education far outweigh your own and I will not be treated as if my knowledge is of no value simply because you have determined in your own small mind that my intelligence is based on my gender."

The constable's eyes widened and Lord Ellesmere gave a rare smile beneath his trim beard. "I suggest," the marquess said. "That you allow the lady to say her piece."

"In truth, Lord Ellesmere, it is not my piece that requires a voice. It is Lady Franklyn's." She nudged the duchess and gave her a nod of encouragement, a strange sight given the strained relations between Rebecca and Lady Susan.

Lady Franklyn sat straighter and took a deep breath. Her gaze skimmed past the others and came to rest on Marcus. "I did not thank you for saving my life at your own peril, Mr. Bowen. An oversight on my part, not because I did not feel your actions worthy of praise, but because I did not believe my life worth saving." The last few words hit Marcus hard, pushing him back into his chair.

Lady Franklyn cleared her throat and a sheen of moisture glistened in her eyes. Though her admissions caused her obvious pain, Marcus could not fathom what they had to do with the matter at hand. He did not require her thanks. Pulling Rebecca away from Lord Walkerton's grasp and warning her away from the earl made their accounts paid and cleared.

Unless...

His gaze shot to Rebecca whose triumphant expression told him all he needed to know.

"Stop." He held out a hand as Lady Franklyn made to continue, cutting her off. "Don't." She would be ruined. Not even Lord Franklyn could help her come back from this one. He could not allow her to do this.

She shook her head. "No. You saved my life at great cost. The least I can do is return the favor." She turned to the constable. "I killed Lord Walkerton."

The constable sucked in a breath and held it until his cheeks turned an unhealthy red.

She returned her attention to Marcus. "I have wrestled with this all night. I tried to tell myself you would be safe. You were innocent and therefore would not be convicted, but Lady Rebecca came to me this morning and suggested otherwise. She convinced me I could not allow that to happen. She was right. I am not an honorable woman. I know that." Her voice cracked and she dropped her gaze for a moment to collect herself. "I have done much wrong in my life. Hurt people." She looked up and this time turned her attention to Lord Ellesmere. "I allowed others to be hurt when I should have known better and tried to stop it."

Lord Ellesmere tensed, her reference taken, absorbed and, as his muscles visibly relaxed, forgiven.

"This is preposterous!" Constable Hurly pushed out of his chair. "I will not allow you to vilify yourself for the sake of this individual. You are a duchess, my lady. You would not inflict harm on anyone, of that I am certain. It is despicable that you should allow her to try and take the guilt on your behalf, Mr. Bowen. Shame on you!"

"Sit down, you fool." Lady Franklyn's voice whipped out, sharp and direct. Surprised, the constable dropped like a stone back into his chair as if her words had taken him out at the knees.

Rebecca reached over and patted the other woman's hands. "Continue."

"I had become separated from the hunting party," Lady Franklyn said. "As I tried to find my way back to the group, I came upon Lord Walkerton. He was attempting to mount his horse with little success. I approached him to ask him to point me in the right direction to rejoin the others." She hesitated and her expression changed, turned unreadable. "When I noted the state he was in, I dismounted and offered him whatever assistance I could."

Marcus detected the lie in her tone. Given her vehement warning to Rebecca to stay away from him, he doubted she would have offered Walkerton a bucket of water if he'd been set on fire. But he did not stop her, nor call her on it.

"Instead of accepting my help, he—" Her breath caught and dropped her gaze back to her lap. "He..." She pressed a hand to her lips and while the affectation rang false, the fear in her eyes did not. The truth became clear. Lady Franklyn had been a victim of Walkerton's violence, though not on this day.

"That's enough," he said.

"No!" Lady Franklyn shook her head with force. "It is not enough. People should know what a bastard he was." She turned to the constable, her eyes filled with a fire that squelched the fear. "He accosted me. He accosted me and I was forced to grab the rifle from his horse and protect myself. Afterward, I panicked. I felt shame and...and..." The fear returned and she dropped her gaze to where her hands rested in her lap.

Lord Ellesmere stood and addressed the constable. "Do you have what you need to settle this matter, or do you wish to cause the duchess further distress by reliving this horrible ordeal?"

Marcus rose and joined him. A united front against the enemy. "I believe the duchess has been put through enough. It took great courage for her to come forward with the truth under such deplorable circumstances. A truth I am certain will go no farther than this room."

Constable Hurly's mouth opened and closed like a fish gasping for air. "People will want to know the outcome."

"The only ones who need know the outcome are Lord Walkerton's family. And I am certain when they hear it, they will wish the matter to remain private. As will the Duke of Franklyn," Rebecca suggested.

"But I—that is—" The constable continued to bluster but no one appeared to be listening as Rebecca's smile of triumph beamed at Marcus.

Lord Ellesmere stepped away to offer his arm to Lady Franklyn. "My lady, may I escort you back to your room?"

"If it pleases everyone, I wish a private word with Mr. Bowen," Lady Franklyn said.

"Perhaps you could escort Constable Hurly out, Lord Ellesmere," Rebecca suggested. "I shall come with you."

Marcus stared at Rebecca's back as she and his grandfather book-ended the near apoplectic constable. As she reached the door, she glanced back and smiled at him, her expression filled with such love it robbed him of breath. She had done it. She had saved him.

He shook his head still trying to understand how she had put all the pieces together. Pieces that had eluded him until Lady Franklyn confessed.

"I did kill him," Lady Franklyn said, once they were alone. "And I don't regret it. He deserved nothing less after all he has done. Would continue to do."

"But it was not yesterday that he attacked you, was it?"

She didn't answer him and in that silence he heard the truth. When she spoke again, her voice softened and he saw a much different woman than the one he had come to know. How different she might have been had Walkerton not entered her life. He took the seat next to her on the sofa and she reached out and touched his arm.

"Your mother was like a little sister to me and I failed her. Nor did I take heed when she warned me about him."

"She warned you?"

Lady Franklyn nodded. "She sent me a letter. It arrived two days after her departure from London. She knew I had an interest in Lord Walkerton. I believe she wished to warn me away, to bring me to my senses. At first, I did not believe her. I could not comprehend something so vile had happened to her right beneath our noses. I could not let it stand. I sought out Lord Walkerton and confronted him with her accusations. He admitted to what he had done, and suggested she left because she was with child. He acted as if it meant nothing. I was horrified. I threatened to turn him into the authorities. He grabbed the letter from me and then..." Her jaw tensed.

"You do not need to continue."

She shook her head. "No. I have kept my silence long enough. He did to me what he had done to your mother and left me there in my shame and humiliation. He took with him the only piece of evidence I had against him." She looked at Marcus and in her expression he saw a sense of relief, vindication. "If I spend an eternity burning in the depths of hell, I will never regret meting out justice on that man. I failed to protect your mother from him and it is a shame that will haunt me for the rest of my life. But I will not fail her now. I will not stand by and allow her son to accept the consequences of my actions."

"You could face severe consequences."

Lady Franklyn laughed, showing the determined and carefree woman she'd once been, but in a flash it disappeared and the Duchess of Franklyn returned. "I am the wife of the Duke of Franklyn, Mr. Bowen. He will not allow anything to happen to me. Besides, as far as the constable knows, I was in peril, fighting for my life and virtue. What else could I have done?" She shrugged and stood and Marcus joined her. "I will be just fine, have no concerns on that account."

"Either way, your debt to me is paid in full." She smiled and patted his arm then crossed the room to leave. Before she reached the door, however, another thought entered his mind. "Was gifting me Northill your idea?"

She turned and smiled. "Every gentleman needs a home of his own and sufficient property to maintain him." Her expression softened. "Be happy, Mr. Bowen. You are nothing like the man who fathered you and every bit your mother's son. Never forget that. She would be so proud of the man you've become."

Chapter Twenty-Seven

"How is marriage treating you thus far, my lady?"

Rebecca stretched and smiled as Marcus whispered his question against her belly as he made his way down the length of her body. She shivered at his touch. It was mid-afternoon and though both had duties to attend to with respect to the running of Northill, he had convinced her that he could simply not concentrate on his work until he attended to his wife first. Given that she felt the need to be attended to, the decision to join him in their bedchamber came with little argument on her part.

"Well, sir, it has been but three months, however I do believe I can make the claim that I find it most...satisfying."

"Is that so? In what way?" His mouth had stalled on her belly and she squirmed, wishing he would continue with his travels and do that thing he did with his tongue that reduced her to a writhing mess of sensation and pleasure and many other things she had no words for. "Why have you stopped?"

"I'm listening." He turned his head and pressed an ear to her abdomen.

"For what?" Tendrils of his dark hair tickled her skin.

"A heart beat. Do you think there's one in there?"

She laughed and threaded her fingers through his hair. "I am certain there will be in time." Especially if their frequent afternoon sojourns to the bedchamber continued. Though, excited as she was to fill their home with miniature replicas of her husband, she selfishly wanted him all to herself for just a little while longer.

He lifted his head and stretched out next to her, tossing his arm and leg over her to pull her close. "Fair enough. Though Spence is quite put out that given we are related he cannot marry any of his offspring to ours."

Rebecca laughed, lightened by all the changes that had occurred in her family bringing them happiness beyond measure after much trepidation and hardship. "Poor man. How will he ever survive?"

Marcus kissed her neck and she forgot her question until he lifted his head and smiled down at her. "He suggested we gift him with Westmorough Manor as compensation."

"Good heavens! He is after my inheritance. The cad!"

"He claims the evidence he gave the courts to prove you were marrying the eldest son of a titled peer required recompense."

She kissed her husband's smile and let happiness fill her. His smiles came much more frequently than they once had and his stoic manner, while still evident, possessed an ease that had not existed before. A change brought about not just by their marriage, but by the closeness and understanding now shared between himself and his grandparents.

"If that were to be the case, then I should be gifting Westmorough to Lord Selward. It was the letter from his father he gave the court that convinced them."

"Hm. I do not think I will go out of my way to thank your former suitor."

"Your brother."

He scowled. Her husband had yet to come to terms with their relationship despite Lord Selward's fledgling attempts to make things right between them. When the circumstances of his father's death and character were revealed, Lord Selward had made amends, providing the court proof of Marcus's connection to Lord Walkerton. His mother's identity, however, remained unrevealed, as it was unnecessary to satisfy the constraints of her father's will.

"Let us not talk about family connections and property. I find I am much more interested in another particular landscape," Marcus said, moving over her. She bent her legs and wrapped them around his hips, pulling him closer.

"And what landscape might that be?"

"The one that starts here." He shifted and kissed the tip of her breast. "And ends somewhere a little farther south. Shall I show you the exact location?"

She smiled. "Oh yes, please. Geography has always been one of my most favorite subjects."

"Well then," Marcus said, kissing her rib cage. "Prepare yourself, my lady, for I am about to provide you with a thorough education."

She laughed with joy and then lost herself in her husband's tutelage, applying the knowledge she had accumulated thus far to ensure she was not the only one learning lessons that day.

Though the most important lesson she had learned had been the one her mother had tried diligently to teach. *Follow your heart.*

She had not had to follow it very far and when she did, Marcus had been waiting.

She sighed as his mouth and hands and heart gifted her everything she desired. As it turned out, very good things came to those who waited.

And even better things came to those who followed their hearts.

A Sneak Peek

THE LADY'S SINFUL SECRET ~ BOOK 4

The sweeping landscape, filled with rolling hills and hardy wildflowers, stretched out to meet the early October sky. Gloria shivered against the unexpected chill of the morning as it infiltrated the wool of her plum riding habit. Shifting in her saddle, she took in the beauty displayed along the outer edges of Sheridan Park where an invisible line separated Blackbourne land from that belonging to the Sutherlands.

All around her, the tips of the leaves had started to change their colors, turning from a lush green to the promised bounty of rich reds, oranges and yellows. The beauty was a sight to behold and the fresh air and invigorating ride a welcome diversion from the commotion in her home as her children busied themselves with preparations for a party celebrating her upcoming birthday.

Not that she didn't appreciate their desire to throw a party in her honor, but try as she might, she could not seem to muster the same level of enthusiasm for the upcoming event. What was there to celebrate after all? Getting older? Being alone? Lacking purpose? Her husband was dead and buried, bringing an end to a rather insufferable marriage and now, as she stood on the precipice of turning nine and forty, she realized her work as a wife and parent was...done.

Over.

"Perhaps you should take a lover to distract yourself."

Her dear friend, Lorena, had made the bold suggestion. Imagine such a thing! The very idea left her scandalized. The Dowager Countess of Blackbourne did not take lovers. She...she...

Gloria let out a sharp breath. In truth, she didn't know what a dowager countess did once her children were grown and married, but likely riding about in the early morning until your cheeks flushed and your nose turned red was a much safer bet than taking a lover. Her family had suffered enough scandal over the years without her adding more to it.

Besides, she'd had a lover once, a long time ago, and the results had been disastrous. Not the type of distraction she cared to repeat.

Also by Kelly Boyce

THE SINS & SCANDALS SERIES

Book 1: An Invitation to Scandal

Book 2: A Scandalous Passion

Book 3: A Sinful Temptation

Book 4: The Lady's Sinful Secret

Book 5: Surrender to Scandal

Book 6: A Sinner No More

Book 7: The Sweetest Sin

Book 8: A Most Scandalous Christmas

Book 9: A Hint of Scandal

THE BRIDES OF FATAL BLUFF

Book 1: The Outlaw Bride

SALVATION FALLS

Book 1: Salvation in the Rancher's Arms

Dear Reader

Thank you so much for reading *A SINFUL TEMPTATION* – I hope you enjoyed Marcus and Rebecca's story. This is the third book in the SINS & SCANDALS SERIES and by far the most challenging as I tried to pull all the pieces together. I loved telling their story, though, even if they did take me on a bit of a wild ride!

For those of you who are new to the series – find out where it all began with AN INVITATION TO SCANDAL (Nicholas & Abigail) and A SCANDALOUS PASSION (Spencer & Caelie).

Following A SINFUL TEMPTATION, I'm taking a brief break with the full-length novels to write a novella where we finally discover the true identity and story behind Lady Blackbourne's lover. This is a story I've been wanting to tell since completing AN INVITATION TO SCANDAL, so I hope you will enjoy it!

To keep up to date on what's new, upcoming releases, sneak peeks on cover reveals, and be entered into contests, please visit my website at www.kellyboyce.com and sign up for my newsletter.

If you enjoyed this book, please consider leaving an honest review at your favorite retailer. It is always appreciated!

All the best!
Kelly

Acknowledgments

Once again, my awesome husband gets the biggest nod here. Between working full-time at the day job and writing during a large portion of the time in between, I'm surprised he remembers what I look like. Yet when I do manage to come up for air, he feeds me and convinces me I can keep going. Babe – you're the best! I couldn't write a hero as awesome as you.

A big thanks to my sister and cheerleader, Alyson. There's a special language sisters speak. Thanks for the giggles. Moth.

To my family—you guys are rock solid and your own special brand of crazy. I wouldn't have it any other way.

It's amazing the people you meet on this journey and I've been blessed with an amazing crew of great friends who I can't imagine not having in my life. Pamela Callow, Julianne MacLean, Cathryn Fox – keep the wine & dinners coming! Anne MacFarlane and Annette Gallant – commiseration and a kick in the pants are always appreciated.

To my great editor, Nancy Cassidy – I still owe you a bottle of wine (or two) for this one!

To coffee crew at The Second Cup on Portland and Starbucks at Scotia Square. If not for the steady supply of lattes, this process would have been a whole lot tougher.

And last, but definitely not least, to my readers for coming along for the ride! Thanks for being there!

About the Author

Kelly Boyce started writing stories in Grade 2 when her favorite teacher, Mrs. Matheson, showed up with a box filled with plot ideas and she was immediately hooked. But it wasn't until she read Lisa Gregory's *Bitterleaf* that she fell in love with historical romance. Once she discovered Romance Writers of Atlantic Canada and learned how to turn those stories into books, it was full steam ahead.

A life-long Nova Scotian, Kelly lives near the Atlantic Ocean with her amazing husband and a clownish golden retriever with a stubborn streak a mile wide. She loves writing stories about relationships and creating a sense of community around the hero and heroine filled with secondary characters who take on a life of their own.

Along with ***The Sins & Scandals Series***, she has also released several western historical romances with Harlequin. The first two, **The Outlaw Bride** and **Salvation in the Rancher's Arms** will soon be re-released under her own banner, while the remaining, **Salvation in the Sheriff's Arms**, and two Christmas novellas: **The Cowboy of Christmas Past** and **Christmas in Salvation Falls** are still available through Harlequin.

Currently, she is hard at work developing a new three book series on the Lindwell Family, who were introduced in ***The Sins & Scandals Series***.

Copyright © 2014 Kelly Boyce
This book is licensed for your personal enjoyment only. All rights reserved, including the right to reproduce this book, or a portion thereof, in any form. This book may not be resold or uploaded for distribution to others.

This is a work of fiction. Any references to historical events, real people, or real locales are used fictitiously. Other names, characters, places and incidents are the product of the author's imagination, and any resemblance to actual events, locales or persons, living or dead, is entirely coincidental.

ISBN: 978-1-7782864-8-3

Cover design: Kim Killion
Editor: Nancy Cassidy

CPSIA information can be obtained
at www.ICGtesting.com
Printed in the USA
BVHW051809071022
648927BV00009B/874